AN ISOLATED INCIDENT

SONIAH KAMAL

FiNGERPRINT!

Published by

FiNGERPRINT!

An imprint of Prakash Books India Pvt. Ltd.

113/A, Darya Ganj, New Delhi-110 002,
Tel: (011) 2324 7062 – 65, Fax: (011) 2324 6975
Email: info@prakashbooks.com/sales@prakashbooks.com

facebook www.facebook.com/fingerprintpublishing
twitter www.twitter.com/FingerprintP, www.fingerprintpublishing.com
For manuscript submissions, e-mail: fingerprintsubmissions@gmail.com

ISBN: 978 81 7234 532 7

Processed & printed in India by HT Media Ltd., Noida

Praise for the Book

'Soniah Kamal has written a riveting and deeply engaging novel about the longstanding turmoil in Kashmir and the multi-generational impact of the conflict on one ordinary family. With remarkable poise and elegant, precise prose, Kamal explores identity and exile, hope and disillusionment, and the myriad fault lines in the lives of the people living in the shadow of war. A wonderful novel'

-Khaled Hosseini, author of the novels
The Kite Runner and *And the Mountains Echoed*

'In a captivating debut novel, Soniah Kamal peels back the headlines of the global now with nuance and beauty to explore the enduring human issues of love, war, migrations, faith, and fortitude. *An Isolated Incident* is a lyrical and powerful novel written with razor-sharp intelligence and tenderness. It will linger with you long after you are done'

-Ayesha Mattu, editor and author of
Love Inshallah: The Secret Lives of American Muslim Women and
Salaam, Love: American Muslim Men on Life, Sex, and Intimacy

'I loved *An Isolated Incident*. Soniah Kamal is a flawlessly intuitive writer whose unpretentious yet shimmering prose sneaks up on you like remembering a simple proverb you're suddenly old enough to understand. A magically familiar other world filled with true note characters, I did not want this story to end, but the reward is that I will carry it inside me forever. If you're bound by family yet compelled by your dreams and desires, you will find this lucid and powerfully addictive novel worth every penny'

-Kola Boof, author of the novel
Sexy Part of the Bible and the memoir *Diary of a Lost Girl*

'*An Isolated Incident* is a gripping, heartbreaking tale of the reverberating effects of trauma, and of finding peace in the most unlikely of places. Kamal masterfully weaves this complex story of loss, love, and war, and skilfully explores the effects of PTSD, and of losing and finding oneself'

-Christal Presley, author of
Thirty Days with My Father: Finding Peace from Wartime PTSD

'*An Isolated Incident* is a searing exploration of identity, belonging, and the many meanings of home in our global world. A bittersweet love story that traverses continents and cultures, it grips the reader in its myriad shades of loss, longing, and redemption. With deep, psychological insight and prose that wraps around you softly like a pashmina shawl, Soniah Kamal has written a hauntingly beautiful novel that stays etched in one's mind and heart'

-Shikha Malaviya, author of the
poetry collection *Geography of Tongues*

'Soniah Kamal's *An Isolated Incident* dazzles. This novel is a lovely read; warm, involving, and well crafted. As Zari and Billal and their families struggle to make sense of their fractured world, we recognise the hope and promise of love. I felt for Zari and Billy—for all of them'

-Jessica Handler, author of *Invisible Sisters: A Memoir* and
Braving the Fire: A Guide to Writing about Grief and Loss

'A delicate novel about global conflicts and inner torments, Soniah Kamal's *An Isolated Incident* illuminates not just the history of Kashmir, but also the dislocation of its children. This novel is a welcome and linguistically rich reminder about the varieties of love and the myriad ways we yearn for belonging'

-Ali Eteraz, author of the memoir
Children of Dust: A Portrait of a Muslim as a Young Man

For

Abaji and Moji
my beloved grandparents
also known as
Kahwaja Mehraj ud din Pandit and Rabea Begum

&

Shazia
the cousin I didn't know in life but whose
death is my first memory

'He only says, 'Good fences make good neighbors.'
Spring is the mischief in me, and I wonder
If I could put a notion in his head:
'Why do they make good neighbors?''

Mending Wall
Robert Frost

PART 1

THE SON
1997 - 1998

1

Srinagar, Kashmir, 1997

The cleaning woman glances at her wristwatch, a gift from the Zoons, and hurries towards their residence, huddling in her thin shawl against the crisp morning air. She sneezes. A stray dog, peeing outside the boundary wall of one of the bungalows alongside the road, bares its teeth at her and growls. She quickens her pace and, turning the corner, is surprised to find the Zoons' main gate half open. She pauses for a second before walking up the gravel driveway towards the house. Surely Mrs Zoon will be standing at the doorway waiting to admonish her for tardiness. But there is no Mrs Zoon. And the front door, always kept locked, is wide open. From deep within the house, she can hear the Zoons' pet ducks quacking.

She enters the house with timid steps. She crosses the drawing room first, then the family room, past the staircase that leads to the bedrooms upstairs, and out the back door into the pergola leading to the kitchen. In the kitchen, white gilt-edged crockery lies smashed on the floor. Ants march in military lines over spilled food. She screams as something whizzes past her. Just a duck, she assures herself as she grabs a rolling pin and presses towards the back garden.

She smells it first, an acrid, iron odour, like rust on garden tools. When she comes upon the small pond bristling beneath the sunshine at the far end of the property, she slaps her chest.

"Hathay vay," she moans, "Yi kya goam? What has happened?"

They are lying at odd angles. Clothes spattered with congealed blood. Still. Lifeless. Dead. She sinks into the grass, slapping her chest in disbelief, her wails fracturing the air. She sees the movement suddenly: a body rocking to and fro, cradling a little boy. She inhales, stutters through a prayer of protection. It takes her a long moment to realise that it is not a spirit she sees, but a living soul and, rising on shaky legs, she goes over to the girl and touches the girl's bloody shoulder. The girl flinches. The girl is alive. The cleaning woman runs back to the house to call for help.

The girl rocks back and forth, her tall frame halved as she curls around the little boy like a tight shell. She clutches his paint-stained fingertips and won't let go, can't let go . . . not even when the police arrive and putter around her like pigeons in a field of crumbs, their pencils scratching against their lined notepads:

Bodies.

The sun shone down the mountains and into the valley, nuzzling warmth into the autumn air and brightening the shabby billboards—Kashmir Emporium, Pamposh Pashminas, Kingfisher Handicrafts—looming over the Boulevard, the main thoroughfare of the city of Srinagar. Three girls and a fidgety little boy made their way through the afternoon crowd towards the maize-seller standing on the sidewalk overlooking Dal Lake.

Zari ordered a cone of roasted kernels and dug her fists into the pockets of her pale peach cardigan as she searched for loose change. Her mouth watered as the vendor tossed the orange kernels in hot salted sand, the lake breeze scattering the smoke from the brazier into beautiful filigrees which, nevertheless, stung her eyes. A few steps away, Baz, her four-year-old nephew, hung over the cement railing looking out at the lake. His mother, Zari's sister Kiran, clutched him by the neck of his jacket, even as she and Sonea, Zari's best friend, prattled on about the latest fashion trends.

"Zari Khala," Baz called out and Zari turned to him as he pointed to a carnival of birds flying overhead, their lean bodies and tapering necks casting spear shadows over the rippling water. "Zari Khala, can I draw the birds with the new paint set you got me?"

Zari nodded, joy filling her at the prospect of the simple pleasure of painting birds with her beloved nephew. She smiled at no one in particular as she stood waiting, the crowd bustling all around her. Since the strict curfew, on account of a shootout between the police and some militants the week before, had been finally lifted this morning, everyone was out and about for the sheer thrill of being able to leave the confines of their homes.

The girls' trip to the Boulevard, however, had purpose. Kiran, here on her annual holiday from Dubai where she had moved to after marriage, had come to purchase presents from a particular gift shop. She was a loyal customer, Kiran always asserted, though Zari and Sonea joked that she always patronised the shop on account of the discount her 'loyalty' guaranteed.

Taking the cone from the vendor, Zari savoured the warmth seeping into her hands. She picked out a handful of soft kernels for Baz and fed him, kernel by kernel, as they followed Kiran and Sonea crossing the road through the tangle of vehicles. Rickshaws, cars, bicycles, bullock carts, scooters, all had come to a fume-ridden halt at the traffic light impotently alternating between red and green. No one honked, for word had travelled fast that up ahead a car of teenagers had been stopped mid-road for a routine frisking.

Once on the other side of the Boulevard, the girls strolled past souvenir shops where display windows advertised steep discounts; past handicraft shops where dejected shopkeepers called out to lure them in; past restaurants where waiters stood listlessly amongst empty chairs and tables. Zari knew these waiters were lucky for still being employed, that these establishments were lucky for still being open where so many were out of business, their rusting 'Closed' and 'For Sale' signs hanging like dogs tags on bodies no one knew what to do with.

Baz took hold of Zari's hand as they passed a man in genie pants engrossed in photographing a plastic bag floating at the edge of the lake. Or was it the canoe with a soldier on patrol, his upright rifle an incongruous companion to the rower's oar with its heart-shaped paddle? Zari couldn't tell which scene the man's lens was focused on, but she was pleased that hippies were alive and well in Kashmir despite the warnings of the tourism department, and she felt as great an affection for their apparent permanence in the Valley as she did for the Dal, no matter how polluted it was becoming.

"Can you believe how many people are here today!" Zari said to Kiran and Sonea. "It's just like in the old days. Except for," she added bitterly, "the soldiers."

Before the troubles began, the Boulevard had been a tourist haven, and Zari and her friends used to spend long hours playing a game of guessing a tourist's country. Now, they guessed which region in India a soldier came from, a deduction, at times, simply a matter of puzzling together headwear, complexion, and facial hair. Before the troubles had begun, Kashmir had been the film industry's prime destination for shooting romantic songs, and Zari and Kiran would spend as much time as they could hanging around film sets to catch a glimpse of film stars. Now, the only shooting occurring was from behind guns. When they had been Baz's age, Zari and her friends used to play police versus robbers. Now, Baz and other children played freedom fighters versus army.

"Did you know," Sonea whispered to Zari, "Kiran wants to organise an independence rally?"

"I know." Zari rolled her eyes. "Then *she'll* return to Dubai and *we'll* be stuck here to deal with the aftermath."

The girls became quiet as they neared a soldier leaning against a crumbling wall, daunting in green fatigues, his semi-automatic rifle hanging ready from his shoulder. In Hollywood films, soldiers paraded up and down streets abuzz with flags and preening local girls who dreamt of being whisked away to romantic lives by these young men in their smart uniforms; not so here, Zari thought. Almost automatically, she began to walk a little faster, not that speed equalled safety. Death was around every corner. A guerrilla could lob a grenade and she could die in the attack. Or, in the ensuing mayhem of flesh and blood, the military could begin shooting indiscriminately and she could fall victim to that. Or, after some order was restored, she could be rounded up, arrested, and then questioned—since she was Kashmiri, she must know something. "In any case," disgruntled personnel would mutter, "someone has to pay."

Zari fingered the mandatory identification papers in her

bag as they hurried past the soldier, avoiding even a glance at the tips of his black boots. Men were routinely arrested for the pettiest of reasons and neither girl wanted to tempt fate. Once past the soldier, Sonea leaned into Zari. Now that the curfew was lifted, she said, when did Zari suppose school would reopen? Of course, it was only a matter of time before they shut down again. And had Zari heard? Yet another teacher had resigned! Apparently, a student with a failing grade had threatened to report the teacher as a militant unless the grade was fixed.

Zari wished that for once, just for once, Sonea— everyone—would stop thinking, talking, eating, sleeping Occupation and Independence. She wished that she herself could stop thinking about how Occupation constricted her life, her concerns, her dreams. Zari shook her head at her pettiness. This war had ruined people, and all she could think of was its effect on her. And yet . . .

Zari glanced at the Dal's rippling surface flowered with shikaras, the wooden punts half-covered with awnings of either colourful tarp or rippled silver tin or plain old wood, and wished she could climb into a shikara and fall asleep, trusting the willow-lined waters to take her to a land where Occupation was non-existent and Independence a throbbing, thriving reality.

"Balloon-vaul!" Baz cried out as he saw a balloon-seller setting up his makeshift shop next to a sand bunker at the intersection ahead. He began pulling Zari towards the man. "Zari Khala, balloon-vaul. Please! Please!"

"I'm going to get him a balloon," Zari said even as Kiran made a face. "Let me spoil him." She tousled Baz's hair. "I see him too seldom to do otherwise."

Kiran smiled. "After you're done indulging his every wish, meet us in the handicraft shop."

Baz wanted a yellow balloon. As they waited for the balloon-man to blow it up, a soldier strolled up and stood beside them. He sucked noisily on his cigarette as he eyed Zari and blew smoke in her direction. Zari swallowed. She told the balloon-man to please hurry up, and clasped Baz's hand. He was a brave child who'd grown up hearing of bomb blasts and baton charges and whispers of girls ruined and men tortured, things Zari knew Baz didn't understand because of the questions he was always asking her. But Zari believed that children deserved to be protected, as long as possible, from answers which would only escalate their fears: Why was she purchasing the balloon as fast as she could? Why was the soldier sidling up to them and whistling in that way? Why had he ordered the balloon-vaul to return Zari Khala's money? Why had the soldier's words turned the balloon-vaul red, and Zari Khala white?

Zari's breath quickened as the soldier chucked his burning cigarette at her feet and, lunging forward, stroked her hair. Baz grabbed his balloon, Zari grabbed his hand, and they ran, the soldier's cackles fading behind them. By the time they caught up with Sonea and Kiran, Zari had managed to wind her hair into a tight bun, not a single strand loose.

"Mama, Mama!" Baz waved the balloon in Kiran's face. "A soldier made the balloon-vaul give it to us for free."

"You two could have waited for us," Zari said, half in tears as she related the incident to Kiran and Sonea.

"Thrat pyas! May lightning gouge him!" Sonea muttered

when Zari was done recounting what had transpired. "Badmash kolae! Lout!"

"Uniformed louts." Kiran looked back, flushed and angry. "Which one is he?"

"We've left him far behind, thank God." Zari slapped her forehead in frustration. "I just wish I could report him to the police, but, knowing them, they'll just take our address and sell it to the very same soldier."

"Let's try the freedom fighters." Sonea squeezed Zari's hand. "Maybe for once they can help."

"No doubt they are *dying* to help," Zari said. The pro-independence freedom fighters were impotent thanks to the pro-Pakistan separatists. And the pro-Pakistan separatists would lecture *them* on the hazards of women leaving their houses unaccompanied by a male guardian. No doubt, they'd tell her she'd invited trouble by leaving her hair loose. There was no one to turn to, and the entire valley knew it.

"I swear," Zari drew Baz close to her, "had he touched Baz, I would have kicked him in his you-know-whats."

It was false bravado, Zari knew, merely bottled up fury. And what was bottled up fury but a recipe for a poisoned soul? The whole valley was bottled with poisoned souls and there was no antidote in sight. Souls helpless before the full power of the Indian armed forces in Kashmir: the police, the army, the paramilitary, the Border Security Force, the Central Reserve Police Force, the Special Operations Group, that special title given to the freedom fighters who had turned themselves in to the Indian government who, in turn, designated them spies. All these armed forces totalled over half a million. Half a million men whose job it was to capture no more than a few thousand insurgents. Zari's fiancé, Imran, claimed that this disproportionate ratio of armed forces to insurgents was really in order to keep the civilians in check.

Zari turned to Kiran and Sonea. "Listen, I'll tell Imran about the soldier when the time is right, okay?"

Kiran nodded and put her arm around Zari. "Do you want to go back home?"

Zari looked down at the cracks in the weathered sidewalk. If she allowed these people to scare her, she could just as well give up trying to live life as normally as possible. "You came to shop and that's what we're going to do."

Linking hands, with Baz between them, his yellow balloon floating above, the girls marched to Kiran's handicraft shop and walked into its cramped interior with its warm bright lights and soothing scent of damp willow bark. The shopkeeper recognised Kiran and sent his assistant to get complimentary soft drinks for them. As they settled on the squeaking sofa, the eager shopkeeper began laying out his wares: silver samovars, crewel-work covered bedspreads, papier-mâché egg cups, mirror-work cushions. As artefact after artefact was paraded before them, and Kiran haggled away, and they sipped their fizzy drinks, Zari distanced herself from the menacing world outside and allowed herself, instead, to daydream about Imran and how, one day, they would decorate their own house.

The auto-rickshaw bringing them home hiccupped through quiet suburban roads before delivering them at their gate in a great belch of puttering smoke. They proceeded to the back garden where Zari's parents were relaxing by the duck pond, snug under their pashmina shawls. Behind them a maple tree sparkled golden red, its leaves fluttering in the breeze like a net of butterflies. Baz leapt into his grandmother's open arms, waving the balloon in her face, and, despite the girls' instructions, excitedly told his grandparent's about the soldier and the free balloon.

"What happened?" Mr and Mrs Zoon shrieked.

Since the incident could get them banned from going on further shopping trips, even going out at all, the girls downplayed it enough that the Zoons turned their attention back to the parcels tumbling from their arms. Zari exchanged a relieved look with Kiran. Their parents had been successfully distracted, and they themselves were home, and home, even in these troubled times, was synonymous with safety. Zari unwound her hair and shook it to rid it of the soldier's touch.

"How are all these samovars, hookahs, and paintings going to fit into your suitcases, Kiran?" Mrs Zoon asked as she picked up one thing and then another.

"I think I will need an extra suitcase," Kiran replied a little sheepishly.

"I'm telling you to stay within bounds," Mrs Zoon said, "stay within bounds. But no! You have to take gifts for people you hardly know."

"Don't worry, Kiran," Zari said as she gave her mother a quick hug, "behind your back, Mummy praises your generosity."

The kitchen boy, Ahadu, interrupted them with steaming teacups of golden kahwa, plump cardamoms and cinnamon bark floating on the surface of the sweet tea, and a plate of naan-khatai. Baz crammed two of the sweet biscuits in his mouth, the falling crumbs attracting the ducks.

"Tea?" Mrs Zoon asked Mr Zoon over the quacking.

"Odih cup, half cup," he said as Zari, standing behind him, peered over his shoulder to see what he was reading in *Times Asia*—the winter Olympics committee was embedded in some scandal. Nothing new, always some scandal somewhere. Her gaze fell on the badminton rackets lying in one corner of the garden under the sagging net.

"Badminton?" she challenged Sonea and lunged towards the better racket without waiting for a response.

"Cheater!" Sonea shot back and grabbed the frayed racket.

"Best of three!" Zari shouted across the net before throwing the shuttlecock up in the air and smacking it over the net. It hurtled over Sonea's head and landed in the shrubs behind her.

"No fair!" Sonea grumbled as she retrieved it. "You're too tall for me."

Zari grinned and volleyed another impossible shot Sonea's way.

"You just wait," Sonea said, huffing back to the shrubs.

"Zari," Mrs Zoon called out, "Imran might drop by any moment, mind you don't get too dishevelled."

"I'm sure *he* won't mind," Zari mumbled. Once her father—in spite of her mother's cries of 'what will people say?'—agreed with Kiran that there *was* some good in allowing Imran and Zari to get acquainted with each other while engaged, Zari lived for Imran's visits even though they were always chaperoned. It satisfied her to see Imran hold his own in debates with her father, and it was pure delight to see him entertain Baz, and sheer pleasure to see him strum his guitar, a passionate hobby, the muscles and bones in his hands playing a melody of their own under his skin.

"I don't care whether Imran minds or not," Mrs Zoon admonished her. "*You* should not give him the opportunity to mind."

Zari blew air out of her cheeks and tossed her racket down.

"You won because of my mother," she said to Sonea who was high-fiving Baz.

"Fair and square, Ms Champion," said Sonea, mimicking a snooty classmate. "Fair and square."

They laughed, doubling over with mirth.

"Stop laughing like that!" Mrs Zoon said. "You'll invite the evil eye."

The girls tried, but catching each other's eye, they doubled up all over again.

"Please," Mrs Zoon turned to Mr Zoon, "please tell them to stop."

"Stop," Mr Zoon said.

"Mummy," Zari said, sobering up, "nothing bad will happen just because we're laughing."

"How about we cry to keep away the evil eye?" Kiran winked at Zari.

"Look," Mrs Zoon said to Mr Zoon. "Look how these sisters gang up on me."

"Girls," Mr Zoon did not look up from his magazine, "don't gang up on your mother."

"You are just the same as your daughters," Mrs Zoon said, shaking her head. "All of you against me."

"We're not against you, Mummy." Zari planted a kiss of apology on her mother's cheek and sitting on the grass, she began to organise the day's scattered purchases into piles. She looked up as Azra, the cleaning woman, approached them and squatted next to her to help.

"Go home," Zari admonished her affectionately. "Your work is done for the day."

She returned Azra's small smile. The poor woman had aged so much since her son, Rafeeq, had disappeared, her face perpetually wan and frazzled, her once hefty body shrunk as if deflated from inside. As kids, Zari and Rafeeq had played together, and she did not want to imagine where her tubby playmate with a love for bubblegum had disappeared. Even her father had made inquiries, quite persistently, but to no avail. Someone said they'd seen him being hauled off to one of the torture prisons that weren't officially supposed to exist, but the police refused to confirm any rumours. Instead, they taunted Azra and told her that her son had probably run away to Bombay to become a hero.

Azra, however, swore that a neighbour with a petty grudge had falsely accused her son on charges of terrorism, but the police didn't care. They had neither the time nor the inclination to affirm or reject her hypothesis. Their promotions depended on quotas which had to be filled, and so that was that. However, as they began to be better acquainted with Azra, a few of them began to replace their taunts with gently discouraging shrugs. Azra swore this was worse for she didn't want to like the policemen or to feel sorry for hounding them.

Azra glanced at her wristwatch, and sighing, she rose. Mrs Zoon opened her purse for some cash.

"For today's bus fare," she said, holding out some money.

"Oh no," Azra protested, "no need, no need."

"Take it, take it," Mr Zoon said. "But keep in mind that when, God willing, Rafeeq returns home, he will have to repay every penny."

Azra took the cash with a sad smile. "All I pray for now is to be able to bury him in the Martyr's Graveyard with all the other innocents."

Zari couldn't bear to look at Azra as she left, and they were all helplessly silent until the main gate clanged shut behind her.

"Poor woman," Mr Zoon said, picking up his tea.

Zari fingered the filigreed spout of a silver samovar, the beautiful etchings rough to touch. She could hardly imagine how Azra bore her grief.

"Poor, poor woman." Mrs Zoon shook her head even as she muttered a prayer to save her family from misfortune and to bless Azra with closure. Then she called out to Ahadu to bring more tea.

ᗯᔕᗯ

By the time Sonea left, dusk had fallen. The Zoons went inside for a simple dinner of white rice with chicken stewed in yogurt and ginger. Afterwards, Mrs and Mr Zoon watched

TV with their daughters until, finally succumbing to their yawns, the elderly couple retired to their bedroom upstairs, Baz fast asleep in his grandfather's arms. Zari and Kiran sprawled over the sofa as they settled down to watch *Golden Melodies*, this particular episode a special tribute to the fifties. As the gorgeous Nargis, daughter of a Muslim mother and Hindu father, lit the screen, Kiran began to lament how such a marriage, even today, was only really feasible in the film world and Zari, looking at her sister, wondered if Kiran's passion for social issues was a result of their growing up in an environment which itself qualified as a social issue.

Thak-thak-thak.

It took the girls a second to realise that someone was knocking on the front door. They sat up. Kiran turned to Zari, a finger on her lips. More raps. More insistent. Kiran clutched Zari's hand. They tiptoed to the front door.

Voices.

Male.

Militant?

Military?

Just last month the military had raided a house a few doors down and taken away the son—an adolescent obsessed with philately—for questioning. When the boy returned, he had acquired a collection of bruises and burns as assorted as any body of stamps, but he'd returned, alive, and so the neighbourhood called him Lucky Boy and his parents thanked God.

The doorknob rattled violently.

Zari and Kiran tiptoed hurriedly to their parents'

bedroom upstairs. When the sisters woke up their parents and whispered about the knocks, Mrs and Mr Zoon bolted out from under the warmth of their rosebud comforter even as they took care not to wake Baz who had been sleeping between them. Mr Zoon picked up his spectacles from the bedside table and rattled off names while Mrs Zoon waited with phone in hand, but they knew there was nothing anyone could do in the event of such a visit. Calling the police might only make it worse.

Just as it occurred to Zari to lock the bedroom door, the door slammed open and three young men entered the room. All of them carried guns. They were wild-haired and reeked of sweat and urine. Ahadu stood quaking and blubbering between the two stocky ones. Baz woke up to the commotion and began to cry. The gangly one looked at Baz and barked, "Quiet!" Zari looked him in his eyes before she leapt to Baz and buried his face into her shoulder. A hard, sick knot planted itself in her stomach. She knew she would get into trouble with her parents later for challenging the man, but she welcomed all the reprimands in the world as long as there would be a later. The gangly one disabled the phone next to her mother's side of the bed. The stockiest— his eyes pink and watery—snickered at Zari and Kiran's pyjamas. Mrs Zoon sidled in front of the girls and Zari broke into a defiant sweat, scared for her mother, but also proud. The gangly one turned to Mr Zoon.

"We want something to eat, somewhere to bathe, and somewhere to sleep for the night. And also, mosquito coils, match boxes, and band-aids."

Mr Zoon rose as fast as his arthritic knees allowed. Refusing these men anything would be an unnecessary risk and so, with the music of the end credits of *Golden Melodies* wafting through the house, he left with two of the men to fulfil their demands.

Ahadu rose to a timid stance between the women and the pink-eyed man left behind. The man laughed outright. Loyal are you? He looked the petite Ahadu up and down. We need loyalty like yours. Why haven't you joined us yet? Ahadu stared at the floor. Why hasn't he joined us? the man snarled at the women. Have you stopped him? He glared at Mrs Zoon. We are bringing freedom and you have failed to send this able-bodied fellow to join us in our noble cause? Mrs Zoon swallowed. Why you have failed? The man rubbed his eyes. Tell me. He wiggled his fingers at Ahadu. Have they forbidden you? He prodded Ahadu's leg with the gun. Answer! Ahadu jumped and began swearing to God that no one had forbidden him. He just hadn't gotten around to it. The man bared large rotting teeth. You want to join us now, right now?

Before Ahadu could answer, Mr Zoon returned to the bedroom. The gangly intruder warned them not to cause any trouble and locked them all inside the bedroom. Ahadu cowered in a corner, whimpering that he didn't want to join these men, he knew the things that could happen to militants, and they were not to let them take him.

"No one will let them take you," Zari said as she rocked Baz. Kiran sat beside them and put her arms around her sister and son. Mrs Zoon prostrated on the prayer mat, clutching her wooden rosary, her voice a litany of 'Ya Allah, ya Mohammed, see us through this night.' Mr Zoon sat beside his daughters, his head cradled in his hands, and spoke of holidays they would take once this ordeal was over.

Zari nodded intermittently at her father. Each bargained with God: take my life if it comes to that, but keep everyone else safe.

No one slept that night. In the early morning as the sun began its climb into the sky, the doors flung open.

"Breakfast," the gangly one said and, before he could settle on Zari or Kiran, Mrs Zoon and Ahadu sprang up.

∞∞

Zari was a little girl when the freedom struggle had first begun. She remembered her father's bedtime stories giving way to Kiran's questions. Kiran would sit up, her elbows digging into the pillow in her lap, her mouth wide open as if to devour their father's answers, and Zari, even as she clutched Kiran's nightie, would try to imitate her elder sister's enthusiasm.

Over the centuries, their father would begin, the valley of Kashmir had been ruled by Buddhist, Hindu, Muslim, Afghan, and Sikh dynasties, with individual rulers leaving behind legacies of tyranny, neglect or grand benevolence. In 1846—Zari would try to imagine 1846—the British empire defeated the Sikh dynasty with the help of a Hindu feudal lord to whom they then sold—their father would swipe his forearm across the expansive, crackling map to smooth out the wrinkles—the following lands: the Muslim dominated Kashmir valley, the Hindu dominated Jammu plains, the Buddhist dominated Ladakh mountains, and the smaller surrounding tribal territories of Baltistan and Gilgit. These different territories, their father said, were made one by a treaty and named the State of Jammu and Kashmir—Zari imagined a patchwork quilt, where pieces neither mixed nor matched, but were sewn together with a thick thread—with the Hindus and Buddhists and Muslims learning to live together with their faiths overlapping harmoniously. And this harmony, Zari imagined as thick threads of different colours creating myriad patterns on the quilt.

As time passed, the state became a principality ruled by a Hindu dynasty even though the population was predominantly Muslim. In 1947, their father continued, the subcontinent was partitioned into the sovereign nations of India and Pakistan. Principalities such as the state of Jammu and Kashmir were given the choice of either joining India or Pakistan or becoming an independent country. Their father recalled his parents praying for the dithering Hindu prince to declare Jammu and Kashmir independent, but, before the prince could reach a decision, tribal men from Pakistan invaded Kashmir in order to take it by force just as India had taken over by force the principalities of Junagadh and Hyderabad.

The prince turned to India for military help. India made help contingent on the prince's acceding to India. The prince did. And, since then, India and Pakistan have been at war, one way or the other, over whom the state of Jammu and Kashmir belongs to, with China also laying claim to territory. In the 1980s, Kashmiri Muslims began to clamour for independence, and the pro-Pakistan separatists also joined the ring. Their father always sighed here and rubbed his eyes so hard Zari imagined he was trying to flush something out. India was not pleased at this development and so, their father said, you girls see soldiers patrolling the streets and trying to extinguish the insurgency.

Their father would finish by asking Kiran if he'd

answered all her questions. She would say yes. But there was one question their father was unable to answer, then and now: When would it end?

When the independence struggle had begun, Zari remembered everyone saying it would be over within a matter of days, months, a year. Just a matter of time now, everyone believed, before the freedom fighters unshackled Kashmir from the claims of India and Pakistan. But now, nine years later, everyone feared they would never see the end. Zari even went so far as to fear the end would never come.

She watched through the window as the intruders, having stuffed themselves with breakfast, and packed the leftovers, walked out the driveway and disappeared into the morning mist as if they were college boys stooped with books and thoughts and not weapons and a cause. Militants. Guerrillas. Insurgents. Freedom fighters. Zari didn't even know what to call them anymore. She remembered a time when they'd invoked safety, not terror. A time when they'd genuinely belonged to Kashmir, when they had been indigenous fighters and not men overtaken by foreign forces with agendas of their own. Now their knocks—whether in a remote village or in her upper-middle-class neighbourhood—were met with curses and their forced recruitments with suicides. No one knew which group was knocking, native or outsiders, asli or naqli, real or imposter. Which group would shoot you for sheer practice, sheer sport, sheer rage at someone or some other situation that the laws of transference had delivered to your door.

These fighters, once rising to fix what was broken in the land, now a part of the shards themselves, breaking apart as they were into different groups fighting for supremacy amongst themselves: some pro-independence, some pro-Pakistan, some under the Indian government's counter insurgency payroll, and some neither for nor against, just that it felt good to be powerful, thanks to the gun in their hands, the gun that enabled them to bleed each other for different goals although the end results were identical: injecting misery into the lives of ordinary Kashmiri citizens.

∞∞

At breakfast, the Zoons sat in the courtyard under the fig arbour, their noona chai untouched and growing cold in their mugs. Squirrels dashed around, oblivious and uncaring of why they were getting more than their usual share of the flaky bakirkhani pastry. Only Baz ate with abandon, dipping his pastry in the pink tea, seemingly recovered from the night's ordeal despite his long list of questions: Who were the men? Why did they stink so much? Why had they come? Were they going to come again?

"No," Zari assured him. "They will not come again."

Mrs Zoon bristled. "Why won't they come again? Listen," she turned to Mr Zoon, "we have to leave before something else happens. We have got to leave."

A steely look came into Mr Zoon's eyes. "The worst is over," he replied slowly, "and everyone knows that militants seldom return to the same house."

"Zari," Mrs Zoon said, "ask your father—"

"Mummy, Papa, please!" Zari wished her parents would not sink into a cold war at a time like this.

Mrs Zoon stared Zari down. "Ask him what faction

he thinks they were with. Pakistani separatists or Kashmiri freedom fighters?"

"Papa—"

"I heard your mother and God only knows." Mr Zoon pinched the bridge of his nose beneath his spectacles. "It could even have been the army testing our allegiances. I only know that an indigenous freedom fighter would never terrorise fellow Kashmiris."

"Girls, please inform your most knowledgeable father that these days they are all the same, and that everything is justified in the name of their causes."

"Don't be ridiculous," Mr Zoon said. "Kashmiri freedom fighters are honourable—"

"How do you know?" Mrs Zoon said. "All I know is that whoever those men were, they have frightened us to death."

"Roosevelt said, 'There is nothing to fear but fear itself.'"

"Good for Roosevelt and good for you." Mrs Zoon turned to her daughters. "Did we say anything unusual in front of Azra yesterday?"

"Now Azra is suspect?" Zari looked at her mother. "She loves us."

"She loves her son more," Mrs Zoon retorted. "If I was in her position, I would be more than willing to accuse someone falsely if it meant some information about the whereabouts of my child."

"No you wouldn't." Zari stared at her mother.

"Desperation can make us all act in unforgiveable ways."

"Well it shouldn't." Zari crossed her arms.

"Behave yourself, Zari," Mrs Zoon said, "and don't answer me back."

"Mummy," Zari said softly, "none of us said anything to Azra and, even if we did, I refuse to believe that she would ever report it to anybody, no matter how desperate she got."

"Mummy," Kiran said, "I agree with Zari."

"You!" Mrs Zoon gave Mr Zoon a withering look. "You have put me in this position where I suspect everyone. Anyone with any sense has long left the Valley or is preparing to leave it. Allah only knows why you refuse."

"You know perfectly well why I refuse." Mr Zoon pushed his spectacles up his nose. There are two types of men who continue living in unsafe locales: the poverty stricken and the loyalty stricken. Mr Zoon fell into the loyalty stricken category, a trait he shared with Sonea's father.

"We are not opportunists or nomads," he continued. "How can you even consider abandoning your child just because it has become crippled?"

Zari had always considered Kashmir her motherland, but wasn't it the mother, she wondered, who was supposed to protect her children? The bakirkhani in her mouth turned to sludge.

"But what if they'd killed us? Huh? Or worse?" Mrs Zoon's gaze flickered over her daughters. "Then what?"

"Mummy, please!" Kiran hushed her mother, gesturing towards Baz who, at the mention of the word 'killed', had stopped chewing his food, his eyes large with fright.

"Kya goi? What happened?" Zari pulled him into her lap and proceeded to tickle him while her parents, forced into silence, glared at each other but remained sullenly quiet until lunch.

At lunch, the haaq sank untouched on the mounds of white rice in their plates. Mr Zoon listlessly fingered the glistening mustard greens as Zari fed Baz, and Kiran and Mrs Zoon just stared at their plates. Mr Zoon spoke up, breaking the silence that had shrouded everyone.

"Kiran and Baz must return to Dubai on the first flight out and," he beamed feebly at Mrs Zoon and Zari, "why don't you and Zari go visit your sister?" Mrs Zoon's sister was married to a Kashmiri settled in Pakistan. "I can surely arrange for visas."

"What use will that be if we have to return here sooner or later?" Mrs Zoon grabbed hold of Mr Zoon's knees in supplication. "Please, I beg of you, please, let us all visit her, or, better yet, let us *all* move to Delhi. I refuse to leave without you."

"And I refuse to run away." Mr Zoon's mouth was set obstinately. "This is my home."

"This place is no longer worthy of being anyone's home!"

"This is my decision," Mr Zoon said, "Kiran and Baz off to Dubai, and you and Zari off to your sister's or to Delhi until things settle down here—"

"Which they never will—"

"—and I will visit when I can, but I won't leave. I can't. Please try to understand."

"And please try to understand," Mrs Zoon said amidst furious tears, "that I can't leave without you."

"That is your decision," Mr Zoon said. "But this is where I was born. And this is where I will die."

Zari and Kiran glanced at each other as their parents bickered. While Zari admired her father's stance, she wished he could see that his loyalty to Kashmir endangered them all. Then again, why couldn't her mother take a stance and leave without him? Surely he would follow? Why couldn't her mother see that while she accused her father of irrational loyalty, she too was at fault for irrational loyalty?

Zari's head ached. What sort of a horrible daughter was she, so ready to judge her parent's loyalties, so ready to leave behind her father and her motherland? If her parents so much as guessed at her thoughts, they would be ashamed of her. Angry and disappointed with herself, Zari did the only thing she had any control over and, mashing an extra big bite of rice and greens, she scooped it into Baz's waiting mouth.

That evening they gathered, without any appetite, for the routine of teatime. They watched the local news as the news anchor reported an increase in tensions along the Line of Control between India and Pakistan with firing from both sides of the ceasefire line. A car bomb had exploded in Jammu, killing one Special Task Force officer and two civilians. A politician veering away from the official account of matters had been arrested for questioning. There was no news though, of what they had suffered. There was no real news of real people like them.

"But what if they do come again?" Mrs Zoon said

fearfully as the news anchor shifted to the weather forecast.

"Impossible," Mr Zoon said. "Everyone knows lightning does not strike in the same place twice. Whatever it was, it is over."

"There is no guarantee." Tears dripped down Mrs Zoon's cheeks. "There is no guarantee."

"Mummy," Kiran said, "Please don't cry, please. Papa tell her to stop crying."

The knot in Zari's stomach tightened as she kneeled before her mother with a box of tissues.

"Why is Naan crying?" Baz asked in a small voice.

"Naan is not crying." Kiran smiled at him as brightly as she could.

"Yes she *is*!" Baz folded his arms and gave his mother the best four-year-old glare he could muster.

"Where's the balloon I got you yesterday?" Zari asked him, drawing him towards her and kissing and tickling him.

"I was playing with the ducks and the balloon caught on a bush and thorns popped it."

"Let's open the new paints I got you then, and I'll show you how to make fingerprint birds."

The minute Baz zoomed out of the room to get his box of paints, Mr Zoon slammed his palms in supplication at Mrs Zoon. "For God's sake, stop terrifying everyone with your weeping!" He pointed in the direction of the kitchen. "You want Ahadu to hear you and become hysterical again? As it is I've had to promise him a small fortune in return for keeping quiet about last night. And koorie, my little girl," he turned to Zari, "perhaps better to not utter a word to Sonea either."

"Now Sonea is suspect!" Zari was distraught.

"Don't be foolish!" Kiran put an arm around Zari. "It's for her good. The less she knows the better she's protected."

∞⟀∞

For the sake of normalcy, it was decided that they would go ahead with the original plan of having Imran and Sonea over for dinner. Sonea arrived early, as usual, so that she and Zari could get ready together. They sat in the latticed balcony attached to Zari's bedroom, applying Sonea's favourite fuchsia nail polish to each other's toenails. It was a mild evening, the calm breeze shot through with the scent of fried onions from the kitchen. Zari told Sonea what had occurred, feeling guilty all the while that her need to share had taken precedence over the desire to protect. Sonea squeezed her hands and told her not to worry. She'd have done the same. Besides, it was all over and they were all safe: everyone knew lightning didn't strike twice in the same place.

Imran arrived with a basket of fruits for the family and a yoyo for Baz. Within moments, however, his twinkling eyes grew serious and he lost his trademark smile as Mr Zoon informed him of the events of the previous night. After a while, Imran forwarded an idea. It was true that Zari had only just turned eighteen and that she should complete high school and college before marriage, but what with curfews and schools and colleges shutting down indefinitely with scarcely a notice, and the resultant postponement of exams, and the general tumult that students underwent in these times, could they not wed before he departed for Australia to finish his MBA? Zari could study there just as well. In fact, until things settled in Kashmir, they might very well remain there.

Zari's rush of excitement was tempered by the looks on her mother and Sonea's faces even as her father agreed it was indeed a plan to consider and Kiran agreed even though her input had not been sought. Celebration was an expert at survival, rearing its head, if only for an instant, in the direst of circumstances and soon all the women warmed to the idea and began to discuss wedding preparations.

Zari caught Imran looking at her yet again, the green flecks in his brown eyes radiant in the firelight. He was handsome and she was lucky—she was going to be married sooner rather than later. And then, as her mother constantly told her, she could do whatever she liked—get a suntan, get a boy-cut, a tattoo, pierce her nose! Anything! Everything! As long as her husband approved. Zari was sure that Imran was not the sort to control or forbid her desires and so she couldn't wait to get married. She would miss her family, yes, her friends and home too, in fact she abhorred the thought of her parents living in Kashmir all alone, but she could not wait for her married life to begin.

Zari wanted to jump and clap and dance. But, as would befit a bride-to-be, she suppressed her excitement and, instead, splayed her palms over the bonfire and imagined the flames turning into the delicate vines of orange-red henna which would decorate her fingertips, her palms, her wrists, burning, searing into her being the fierce sweetness that was the promise of marriage, companionship, children, love.

She would remember that it was a cold night. That the bonfire crackled and spit. That Ahadu had just served another round of Lipton tea. She would remember that Baz was scrambling after a duck. His scream. She would never forget his scream. His scream, the final lucid memory she would be able to conjure up between the moment of reality and the moment of speculation, before the lumps emerging from the dark, darkened into shadows, and the shadows lengthened into bodies . . .

∞∞

Bodies.

The police scratched the word into their notepads.

Bodies.

The nephew. The mother. The father. The sister. The best friend. The fiancé. The kitchen boy. All dead.

Bodies.

Height. Weight. Identification marks.

All duly jotted down in their notepads.

They were drinking tea, in the garden, sitting by the pond, under the night sky, the bonfire blazing and then— Zari shook her head—then it was all blank, like sound turned off in a film, like an unfocused camera lens. She could see and hear everything, yet nothing was truly audible or visible. The passage of the night. The flittering of ducks in the dark. The ugly red of sunrise. The morning mist condensing into slimy dew. The smell of wet, fallen leaves. And blood. Then Azra. Azra touching her shoulder, calling her name, bringing her back into focus.

It was finally Azra who would release Baz's fingers from Zari's grip. Azra who would scour the paint from under

Zari's fingernails. Azra who would scrub Zari's toenails clean of the fuchsia nail polish. Azra who would validate memory, and yet wash her clean of it.

"Does she suspect foul play?" the police asked, nodding in Zari's direction.

Zari heard the *hsh-hsh-hsh* of official markings on paper, the *krich-krich-krich* of starch stiff uniforms, the *fut-fut-fut* of polished boots in the bloodied mud. Foul play? The knot in her stomach stiffened. She managed to shake her head. Even in her daze, she knew *this* could very well have been police sanctioned. And if it hadn't been, she still dare not tell them about the militants' unwelcome visit the night before for fear that they'd conclude her family were sympathisers, in which case, *this* would be perceived as deserved.

Zari clung to Azra. Azra who would cover the Bodies with floral bed sheets. Her mother liked floral patterns. Her father's spectacles were on the ground next to a broken teacup, rosebuds on one jagged half, golden leaves on the other. A policeman peered at soggy papers lying on the grass, at the seemingly abstract patterns of large thumbprints surrounded with little fingerprints. He turned to no one in particular: "What is this?"

Let's open the new paints I got you and I'll show you how to make fingerprint birds.

Zari's stomach constricted. Her teeth clattered. She clawed at her bloodied shoulder, realising, suddenly, that the bullet which had merely wounded her was supposed to have killed her. Along with everyone else. She started to scream.

She was whisked to the hospital where nurses, their eyes choked with sympathy, wordlessly fussed over her wound with gauze, scissors, tape. Once her wound was concealed under a thick layer of bandages, she was sent for an internal exam. As she suffered through the examination, Zari stared at the water stains eating the mildewed wall. She wondered if there was something wrong with her. A normal person would have died from the shock and the horror. Why was she still alive?

For the next few nights, Zari was parcelled amongst various relatives. No one left her alone for a second, always someone by her side, someone holding her limp hands day and night, someone forcing her to sip tea, drink broth, down tranquilisers. There was a small demonstration downtown by a women's rights group. There was an editorial. People kept coming to console. Offer sympathy. Tch tch tch. Only eighteen years old . . . better the poor girl had died . . . or killed herself . . . her life will be a nightmare . . . no one will marry her and without marriage, husband, children, simply a future—what life?

Schoolmates kept away from Zari for fear her bad luck would contaminate them. To the couple of classmates who telephoned, Zari shook her head. They would talk about Sonea. How could she tell them of the obscenity that was Sonea's fuchsia toenails splattered with blood? The disbelief as Sonea's body burned on the funeral pyre? The enormity and finality of a dead body?

Zari had nothing to relate to anyone—her distraught brother-in-law from Dubai, Imran's shocked family in Australia, Sonea's hysterical parents who finally decided to leave the Kashmir valley for the Jammu plains: no one. A few days later, Ahadu's family would give his name to the baby born to their clan. A few weeks after that, Azra would find employment elsewhere, knowing that whatever the salary, whatever the cost, she'd adjust. Her brother-in-law, too, would leave within a month. He patted Zari on the head and wished her well. She looked into his grief-swollen eyes and saw her turmoil mirrored, but without Kiran and Baz, her brother-in-law seemed more and more a stranger, a man with whom she could never live, no matter their shared pain, because he was not a blood relative. And, as gossipmongers began to insist, he was now, for all purposes, a single man, an eligible man, a man who could, if he wanted Zari to reside with him, make it happen only by marrying her. Impossible, she said. He agreed, thankfully, and left.

Everyone agreed that Zari too, must go.

Zari must leave Kashmir.

Who knew if forever, but at least for now.

Zari didn't want to go but there was nothing to stay for, nothing left to protect and yet, there it was, an iron padlock clasping shut the front door of her house and blushing shamefully under her accusatory gaze. Soon, trees her parents had planted would be pregnant with fruits for picking, fruits which would go from ripe to rotten and fall and bruise the overgrown grass. Soon overgrowth would swamp the stone walls, take over the brick flower borders, weasel onto garden furniture and ensnare the delicate pattern of the wrought iron grille. A few seasons and the dwelling would fall to wild, a haunt daring children to touch its gates and survive. The home Zari's parents had tended, the grounds they'd preserved, the gardens they'd nourished, all gathered in their cheeks a dirge of a farewell that followed Zari long after she departed, leaving behind the sum that had been her life.

2

Zari woke up, flinching. Above her, the seat belt sign was turned on and the smoking sign turned off. The elderly lady sitting beside her was jostling her shoulder at the very spot where the bullet wound was still a crusty lesion. We're descending, the lady mouthed. Zari rubbed her sore arm and glanced out of the window at the land below, a crisscross of roads, matchstick cars, and snow. So many tasty meals you missed, the lady said as she pinned her dupatta in place over her henna-dyed hair. Sixteen hours you have slept like the dead! Lucky Girl!

Zari tried to imagine the horror on the lady's face if she told her just how many sleeping pills she'd taken in order to face this flight. Would Lucky Girl be all right by herself? Was there family coming to meet her? Yes, Zari assured the lady, family was coming to meet her.

This was technically true because the Nabis—her host family in America—were distant relatives. The Man, an orthopaedic surgeon, was originally from Kashmir, the Woman, a paediatrician, was originally from Pakistan, and their three children had been born and brought up in America: a twenty-two-year-old unmarried Daughter, a college-going nineteen-year-old Son, and a younger Daughter, four-and-a-half years old—a little older than Baz and enough of a reason for Zari to have declined accepting their offer of staying with them in America had it not been for her Khala's threat to otherwise marry her off.

As the plane landed and taxied to a stop, Zari waited for the rush in the aisle to subside before retrieving her own and the lady's carry-ons from the overhead bins and then helping the lady to the air bridge. After the lady settled herself in the awaiting wheelchair, she patted Zari's head and blessed her with a long life and the prayer that God would grant a girl so helpful and respectful a stellar husband. As Zari walked on, she blamed her tears on the cold air leaking in through the fine gap between the plane and the ramp.

Entering the airport, she was engulfed by the hubbub of fellow travellers. There were white people everywhere, reminding her of the tourists in the Kashmir of her childhood, the men's necks flushed and the women's freckled shoulders sunburned. She remembered how, no matter where they were from—Britain, Europe, Australia, Far East, America—they would wave at the child she'd been then, a chirpy child with a sunny wave of her own. Like Baz.

Zari kept her gaze averted from the children around her as she made her way to the customs area. She kept her head bowed as she tried to block their merriness from twisting her guts. She had not looked anyone in the eye these past two months. She hated people looking her in the eye.

"Look up please." The officer at the customs desk commanded as she held Zari's passport to the light. Zari looked at her. She had blue eyes, as blue as the jacket Baz had been wearing the day they'd gone shopping on the Boulevard. Zari looked away.

44

"What is the purpose of your visit?"

"To look at colleges."

This is what she'd been told to say, for it was better to lie than subject people to the inconvenient, horrible truth.

"What do you plan to study?"

"Environmental Engineering."

It was Sonea who'd dreamt of studying Environmental Engineering.

"Welcome to the United States of America. Enjoy your stay."

ᣟᣟ

She'd left Kashmir with her suitcase, the modern man's shadow, for her Uncle's house in Delhi. Uncle was her father's younger brother, and his uncanny resemblance to her father disturbed her. We should have our own faces, Zari thought, we should be able to stand alone. In those early days, all she could do from sunrise to sunset was pace, a manic pacing that dampened the tumult inside of her, while at night, the sensation of lifeless eyes following her was at its strongest. She could smell their deafening accusation: *How are you still alive?*

Uncle's wife, Lili, an English Literature teacher, tried to help by dispensing Shakespeare. "Come what may, time and hour run through the roughest day," she said, hugging Zari at the airport. And over a cup of hot milky tea the next morning, she whispered encouragingly, "Adversity's sweet milk, philosophy." After one week, she tried to coax Zari outside, saying, "All things ready, if our minds be so." And by the end of a month, sighing over Zari's unpacked suitcase lying in one corner of the room they'd given her, Lili spoke wistfully, "What wound did ever heal but by degrees?"

Zari bore Lili's wisdom as best as she could, but it barely helped at all in the beginning and as weeks passed, it only irritated her. Then, one night, she overheard Lili talking to Uncle in the kitchen, blaming the whole tragedy on her father's unwillingness to leave Kashmir.

"Don't say such a thing," Zari said, bursting into the kitchen. "Don't you know the dead are supposed to be revered no matter what?"

"But my dear," Lili replied, flustered at being overheard, "no matter what, neither should the dead be romanticised."

Zari crouched on the floor, cradling her head between her knees, rocking back and forth, keening: "I don't want to stay here. I want to go home. I want my family back. I want my life back. I don't want to stay here. I want to go home. I want my family back. I want my life back."

The following day, when neither Uncle nor Lili were able to calm her, Lili suggested she visit her Khala in Pakistan. In fact, Lili added magnanimously, Zari could leave her suitcase—still unpacked—here.

Zari took her suitcase with her. She left nothing behind. Her mother's sister, Khala, had not been granted a visa in time to attend the funerals, but since the incident, she'd telephoned Zari daily to sob and lament. When Zari arrived in Pakistan, Khala pressed Zari to herself at the airport, kissing her, patting her, stroking her hair as if she couldn't believe that Zari had survived. And Zari, crushed against Khala's elephantine bosom, inhaled sharply. She wanted to stay in Khala's arms even as she wanted to push her away, for Khala's embrace was as tender as her mother's and smelled the same, a mix of sweet perspiration and fried cumin and lavender body spray.

"Look, look at my niece," Khala said to her husband, Khaloo, who stood a respectful distance away, his hands clasped behind his back, his bowl belly puffing out his kurta, his gaze averted modestly from Zari. "Look at what has become of my beautiful niece." Khala shuddered. "Zari, my love, now you are here with your Khala, and what is a Khala but another mother?"

"I don't want to replace my mother." Zari broke away from Khala's hold. "I want everything the way it was."

"Allah, Allah, the world is no longer the way it was," and Khala lumbered into the back seat of the taxi Khaloo had arranged and wept unabashedly without a care for the taxi driver who was eyeing her, Zari could see, with pity and curiosity. Khaloo turned around from the front passenger seat, handed Khala his handkerchief, then rolled down the window, and proceeded to have a smoke. Khala kept repeating how she was a mother to Zari now, how she had begged Zari's mother to leave Kashmir, how that snooty Lili's connections had at least enabled a quick visa for Zari.

Zari tuned out Khala as best as she could and gazed out of the taxi window at the broad, manicured Islamabad roads giving way to the narrow, traffic-clogged streets of its older twin city, Rawalpindi. Her mother had always talked about taking her and Kiran to visit Khala in Pakistan, about going to see the Faisal Mosque, picnicking in the Margalla Hills, watching the riveting Pakistani TV dramas while feasting on Khala's famous goat-feet curry—and now here she was, alone.

Khala was still sniffling when the taxi entered a lane crammed with squat houses squashed between a long row of tiny shops—a vegetable vendor, a ladies tailor, a shop selling cigarettes and paan, a cloth dyeing establishment, the black cauldrons bubbling with liquid colours transforming all classes of cloth—and parked before a tin gate. While Khaloo haggled with the taxi driver over the fare, Khala unlocked the gate and propelled Zari past a cubicle-sized garden, straight through a cramped house, and into a bedroom with a single bed and an embroidered picture of the Kaaba, sent by her daughter who had married and settled in Saudi Arabia, tacked onto a wall.

Khala, vowing to never leave Zari alone with her nightmares, moved in with her that very day, but, as days turned into weeks, no matter the consolations she offered, she could quell neither Zari's panic attacks, nor her nocturnal wanderings, nor the need for the lights to remain lit throughout the night. Even Khaloo, seeing Zari's state, stopped muttering about the growing electricity bill. Each morning, Khala clambered downstairs after the muezzin's call to dawn prayers to find Zari pacing the kitchen and the living room, her wooden bead rosary clenched in her hands, her eyes wild, her frame grown more gaunt. Khala would hold Zari close and try to find words to begin a healing until, finally giving up for the moment, she would switch the TV on to religious dirges because human words, as far as she was concerned, could never rival the words of the Quran.

Khala urged Zari to find comfort in God's words, even though Zari was adamant that it was meaning and purpose she sought. Khala would shush her and remind her that God knew best the purpose and meaning behind lives and deaths. But, when she'd unravel Zari's bandage in order to change it, she could not stop her own tears from falling even as she urged faith in God.

"Eat, you have to eat," Khala would insist each morning as she placed a breakfast of tea, boiled eggs, and buttered toast and jam before Zari. "Eat, my love, or people will say I'm starving you. And when are you going to unpack your suitcase?"

Zari would sit at the dining table, staring at the grey-blue yolk protruding through the taut skin of the eggs, at the singed toasts, at the rim of the plate, reflecting, in the shiny plastic tablecloth, the outline of a faraway face.

"Of course you don't want to talk," Khala would sigh as she settled next to Zari with a tray of either potatoes to skin, okras to behead, or bitter gourd knuckles to scrape off. "But I do, otherwise I will go mad."

Zari would grab the knife and take the tray out of Khala's hands and begin to chop the vegetables mechanically as she tried to distract herself as Khala kindled memory after memory, for Khala was the medium of memory, a living repository of happier times, bringing to life ghosts who had more to say then simply: *why did you live and not us?*

"There are no ghosts," Khala would assure Zari. "But, my love, even if there were, why would they torment you?"

Each night, as they lay in bed, Khala would try to convince Zari that her late fiancé, Allah bless his soul, would want her to get married, and each night Zari would swear that she never wanted to marry.

"But your mother's soul will not rest in peace until she sees you married and settled!"

"Please don't say that," Zari would reply in a brittle voice. "I never want to have so much to lose again."

Khala would wring her hands and fret and fret and wring her hands, the damp of the encroaching winter worsening her arthritis until the local masseuse was summoned for treatment and the house was steeped in the pungent palliative scents of ginger roots and neem leaves simmered in mustard oil. One morning, as Zari sat in the bedroom, wearily eyeing the suitcase—it was daring her to unpack, daring her to find space outside for the things within—Khala's session ended and she beseeched Zari to get a massage too. Surely it would be good for her, Khala said, in any case, it could hardly harm her.

"Zari Baji," the masseuse said, flexing her oily hands, "let me give you a special head massage guaranteed to drain away all your worries."

"Go, my love, for my sake." Khala cupped Zari's face in her hands and looked into her eyes. "Be a good girl. Go outside and get some fresh air."

Zari and the masseuse moved to a patch of the garden, the desiccated grass sliced by the shadow of the clothes line. A sparrow sitting on the garden spigot, flustered at their approach, flew to the bare poplar outside the gate. The masseuse squatted in the weak sunshine, Zari sitting cross-legged before her, and dug her fingertips deep into Zari's thick hair, kneading her way up from nape to crown.

"Baji," the masseuse spoke after a couple of minutes, "if you don't mind, I have advice."

Zari shifted uncomfortably in her woollen coat. Another well-wisher advising devotion to the Quran, to Allah, indeed piety would cleanse, if not her body, then at least her soul. Before she could decline the offer, the masseuse's lips closed upon her small ear.

"Baji, I know a doctor who can fix all. You give me five thousand rupees and I will give you doctor's name."

Zari rose as anger and consternation battled within her and she began to shriek at the masseuse to leave her alone. Khala rushed out. The masseuse repeated her advice. Khala took off her shoe and began to beat her.

"You filthy" —she struck her arm— "ignorant" —she struck her back— "woman" —she struck her shoulder— "how dare you!"

Zari's stomach knotted as the masseuse cowered and yelled and she jumped in between the two women, only to have the masseuse shove her away, screaming, "Don't touch me, you manhoos, accursed girl."

A newly-wed, sunning herself in the next garden, peered over the crumbling wall. Neighbours began gathering on the rooftops like crows.

"Kya hua?" a mother of five called out. "What happened?"

Zari fled into the house. Khala found her in the kitchen, wielding a fruit knife and vowing to fix all those responsible for her situation. Khala said the whole world was responsible. How many could she fix? She was to leave revenge and vengeance up to God. She was to concentrate on fixing herself alone.

A few days later, Khala informed her that the Nabis, faraway relatives in America, had accepted her request to host Zari for a while in order to help her heal.

∞∞

Despite the strict instruction to remain by the luggage carousel, Zari trudged towards the automatic doors that led outside to get away from the family reunions taking place all around her, reunions which left her all too aware that she was homesick even though she was homeless. Outside, Zari hunched in her woollen coat against the winter chill. Dirty snow sparkled under the beams of cars lining the road, the long stream of white headlights and red tail lights glimmering like candles at a vigil. A couple, holding hands, came out to smoke and, once done, they stubbed their cigarettes in a concrete pillar ashtray and began to kiss.

It was the sort of long, lingering kiss Zari had only witnessed in English films, and that too secretly because she and Kiran were supposed to fast forward the racy bits, except that, Kiran had explained to Zari, it was important for them to see all this so that their wedding nights would not take them by complete surprise. Zari could see the sixteen-year-old Kiran standing in front of the muted TV, the remote control clutched in her hand and ready to be used at the slightest hint of movement from the corridor. This will not do, Zari counselled herself as she fished for a tissue in her pockets, only to be assaulted with more tears as her fingers brushed against her mother's wooden rosary and she took out her hand and held, instead, the suitcase handle for support.

"Excuse me, are you Zari Zoon?"

Zari's fingers tightened around the handle as a petite girl with a blue streak in her short black hair peered up at her. She wore skintight exercise pants with a matching top and, despite the cold, her midriff was bare. A silver wire looped around her belly button like a mercury tongue. Wath chus rawromus, Zari's mother would have said, she has lost her way. Her father would have concurred. Kiran would have said live and let live.

Zari's throat constricted yet again.

"Are you Zari Zoon?" the girl repeated.

Zari nodded.

"I'm Salsabil Nabi." The Girl held her hand out. Not knowing what else to do, Zari took it.

"We've been looking all over for you." She flipped open a cell phone and dialled a number. "Dad, I found her," she gave Zari a nod. "She's outside."

The two girls stood side by side, looking everywhere but at each other. The Girl cleared her throat after a moment. "How was your flight?"

Zari nodded an okay. Behind them, a pair of automatic doors whined open. Zari turned just in time to catch a pair of roly-poly legs in polka-dot tights darting towards them followed by a Man and a Woman.

"Miraage!" the Woman called out, "Slow down, there are cars on the road."

But the Little Girl came to a standstill only when she reached Zari, and gazing at her shyly, thrust a paper into her hands. Snowflake stickers surrounded a turquoise WELCOME.

"I drawed it," the Little Girl said. "Do you like it?"

Zari nodded, not trusting herself to speak. She had gone through her house in Kashmir and gathered as many of Baz's drawings as she could find, stuffing them all into her suitcase before she'd left.

"I'm four years old." The Little Girl held up three fingers. She was prancing around, close to the curb, too close, and Zari's hand shot out reflexively to draw her back. Baz's sweet face gazed at her, grinning, then crumpling up, accusing her. Zari returned the drawing to the girl and crossed her arms.

"Miraage, are you trying to get yourself killed!" The Woman finally reached them. "Asalaam-ai-laikum," she said, giving Zari an obligatory hug before standing back to appraise her, her small dark eyes boring into Zari. Though she was half Zari's height, she looked daunting, her sleek brows and mouth twists of kohl and crimson in a face pulled taut by a severe ponytail.

"Welcome! Welcome!" the Man said, panting as he came to a halt behind the Woman. His wide smile crinkled up his forehead and his large sea-green eyes. "Welcome to America. Welcome to our home. Bussah, ahk suitcasah, only one suitcase?"

The Man's Kashmiri was a blow that bruised Zari with loss and longing. She found herself saying softly in English, "Please, if you don't mind, please don't speak to me in Kashmiri."

It began to rain as they left the airport, the heavy drumming on the roof of the Mercedes drowning Baz's accusations still reverberating in Zari's ears. She and the Elder Daughter were in the back seat with the Little Girl between them. They stopped at a kiosk where the Man handed a parking ticket to a uniformed attendant. Sonea would have admired the attendant's purple nail polish. The Woman turned around. Her eyes flicked over Zari.

"Please wear your seat belt," she said with a quick smile. "It's the law in this country."

Zari reddened and fumbled with the belt. The Elder Daughter leaned over the Little Girl and helped her.

"You must be tired and hungry," the Woman said.

"We'll be home soon," the Man said. In English.

Home! Zari bit the insides of her cheek to keep from crying.

"Very long flight," the Man was saying. "It can get very tiring. Depending on who is sitting next to you, heh?" His eyes met Zari's in the rear-view mirror. She attempted a smile at the Man's joke. The Elder Daughter groaned while the Woman playfully swatted the Man on his arm. Zari had never seen a woman smacking a man before, let alone a wife her husband. She sat up, her hand accidentally brushing against the Little Girl's, who immediately took hold of her hand as if it was her right. Zari extracted her hand and folded her arms.

Once they were on the highway, the Woman turned back. "Music?" she asked.

The voice of Munni Begum, one of her father's favourite

singers, wafted through the car. Breathe, just breathe, Zari instructed herself even as she felt the seat belt constrict her. She tried loosening the seat belt, but didn't know how to do it and didn't want to ask. She turned to the window, placing her hot forehead on the cold glass. The snow-stricken land rushed by in rain smeared shadows. There was no chaos on the road. No tension. No honking. No aggressive, angry gestures or curses. There were no sandbag bunkers, no soldiers, no army jeeps with mounted machine guns patrolling the roads. Nothing but a strange, calm, patient silence. It might as well have been curfew time except that, here, there were no curfews. She remembered when Kiran had first gone to Dubai. There are no tanks on the streets, Kiran had kept repeating. No crackdowns, no cordons, no curfews, no ID searches. I have to keep reminding myself, she had said, that *this* is normal.

When they turned off the highway and onto double-lane roads without any medians, Zari was astonished to see no one running the red lights or zigzagging across the lanes in order to get ahead. There were no jaywalkers, no cows obstructing the traffic, no stray dogs and cats rooting through litter. No one was using walls or hedges as public toilets. There was no graffiti, no litter, no beggars. In fact, there were no pedestrians on the snow-cleared sidewalks, not a single soul on the long grey monotonous road which branched off, ever so often, into residential communities.

Zari read the names—Seven Oaks, Thorn Hill, The Summit—and she wondered, with guilt-ridden ungraciousness, if other American families were hosting people like her, damaged goods from other damaged nations. As they passed neat little neighbourhoods sitting upon carefully manicured lawns, it occurred to Zari that there were no boundary walls or fences or gates around the houses—here, houses sat in the open, like open invitations, unlike back home where houses sat within the confines of fat boundary walls. And there was no telling, either, who lived in these houses. Back home, metal plaques—Zoon Residence—flanked either side of the gate, lest someone miss the owner's name the first time round.

The Man turned into a neighbourhood called Three Meadows, and drove into the driveway of a red brick house with an A-line roof the colour of wet oak leaves. One of the triple garage doors opened. The second the car was parked and the engine turned off, the Elder Daughter sprang out and, within moments, Zari was being ushered in through a stained glass front door and into a dark maple-wood floored foyer where a large mirror in a delicate silver and gold filigree frame was affixed between two sleek black chairs.

Somewhere inside, a phone rang. The Elder Daughter hurried in, leaving Zari alone with the Little Girl who tugged Zari's coat. Did she want to see her playroom? Did she want to see her favourite dinosaur set? Did she want to play tea party? Zari shook her head. The Elder Daughter returned and handed Zari the phone—it was Khala—and led Zari, presumably for privacy, to a dining room with a twelve-seater table under a chandelier that looked like a cloud of suspended raindrops.

"You did not call," Khala cried. "I have been so worried."

Zari imagined Khala slapping her chest in consternation.

"We only just returned from the airport, Khala."

"How was the flight?"

"Fine." Zari studied her distorted reflection in the

bevelled glass door of the crockery cabinet. She looked dishevelled, destroyed like the paper boat she'd once left out in a storm.

"Thank God. And your wound? Bleeding? Pus?"

"No."

"Thank God. And the Nabis?" Khala's voice lowered, as if she feared she might be overheard.

"Fine, Khala, they seem fine."

"God willing, they will find some cure for you. Help them help you, my love, help them help you."

Zari blinked back tears.

"And my love, in the meantime, I am searching for a good husband—"

"You said if I came here you would not mention marriage."

"Now that you are there, you will begin to feel like new, and soon marriage will appeal to you—you will see. Only one dream your mother had for you—"

"I don't want to get married."

"We will discuss later. Now, give the phone to Mrs Nabi."

Zari handed the phone to the Woman who had been hovering outside the dining room and heard her assure Khala that all was well and that they would fatten Zari up in no time and Khala was not to worry. There was no mention of why Zari was here in the Nabis' house, under their roof, and Zari couldn't tell if this omission made her feel better or worse.

The Woman was hanging up the phone when the Elder

Daughter beckoned Zari to follow her into the kitchen. Zari had never seen a kitchen so grand and yet it was so antiseptic, with its stark white walls and white marble countertops and glass backsplash and fixtures of stainless steel. Zari focused on a dish on the island. The dish was brimming with cherry tomatoes, green chillies, and knots of ginger and garlic.

—Ahadu squatting on the kitchen floor, the soft belly of a tomato yielding to his paring knife. Her mother at the gas stove, adding handfuls of fresh coriander to a pot of simmering stew. Her father popping his head into the kitchen to breathe in deeply the promise of a delicious meal—

Zari blinked. The memory shimmered, shattered. The kitchen reeked of scorched samosas despite the blaring industrial strength exhaust fan. Off the kitchen, on a spilt level, was a bay-windowed alcove with a round table where the family probably ate their meals. At the moment, the table was laid out with platters holding a cheese cake, hummus and pita chips, and the scorched cocktail samosas.

"Hope you're hungry." The Elder Daughter smiled as she filled a kettle and set it on the burner. Zari was not, but she nodded anyway.

"Can I get you anything before the tea is ready?" The Elder Daughter's deep smile brought out the dimples in her small face.

"A glass of water, please."

The girl stood on tiptoes to open a cabinet, and taking out a glass from amongst a variety on the lower shelf, filled it directly from a dispenser on the outside of the fridge. Zari had never seen water flowing directly from a fridge. It was like something out of the future, except in this country it was already here—she could not wait to tell her family. Zari put the glass of water on the counter and steadied herself. She had forgotten, for a moment. How could she have forgotten at all?

A tugging at her sleeve. The Little Girl. Again. This time, carrying a doll tray laid out with miniature cups and saucers decorated with dinosaur stickers. Zari's throat tightened. She had not packed any of Baz's toys—his miniature sports cars and dump trucks and railway engines. How could she have forgotten his toys?

"Tea?" the Little Girl asked, her eyes dancing.

Before Zari could answer, the Man and the Woman entered the kitchen, dragging her suitcase between them. Back home, this task would have fallen on Ahadu.

"Miraage," the Woman admonished the Little Girl, "that's it. Go play by yourself."

The Little Girl pouted and shook her head, her curls slapping against her cheeks.

"Maju," the Man knelt before her, "Zari needs to leave some space for our tea. Come, Daddy will drink tea with you."

He was doing this for her sake, Zari was sure, and yet, as the Man scooped up his younger daughter and proceeded to tickle her, she realised she would have preferred being pestered by her. Zari stared at them. Maybe her Khala was right. *They* hadn't succeeded in killing her, but maybe, they had succeeded in driving her mad.

"Zari," the Woman said a little sharply, "let me show you your room. Why don't you freshen up before tea?"

It was less a request and more an order and Zari followed the Woman up a winding staircase into a spacious landing and past a den with leather seating and a computer on a desk, through a hallway plastered with photographs, until they came to a bedroom with an attached bath.

Zari stood in the bedroom, listening for the Woman's footsteps to recede before allowing herself to take a deep breath. She looked at the room she'd been given. It was the largest room yet, but it was not to her liking. She would not have put a floor lamp in any corner, looming, as it did, tall and foreboding like the muzzle of a rifle. She would have never wallpapered any room of hers in so bleak a navy blue, or laid a denim quilt over the white-wicker framed bed or hung nautical sketches over it, or decorated the white-wicker chest of drawers with a conch shell vase, a mermaid candle, and a stack of *Reader's Digest* the colour of old tea.

Her bedroom back home was all light wood and patchwork cushions. The attached balcony, shaded by an apple tree whose tart offerings she'd grown to love, was her favourite place to sit and daydream. Her second favourite place was her bed with its plump mattress and thick patchwork quilt and the tape player within easy reach on the bedside table and the tarnished full-length mirror reflecting the wall space she'd decorated with a medley of Baz's drawings, ribbons she'd won for sports and academic achievements, and photographs of her family and friends.

Zari's gaze fell on a photograph of the Nabi family in a seashell frame on a small table by the door. The Man's arm was slung around the Elder Daughter's slouching shoulders while the Woman cradled the Little Girl, an infant then, and the Son sat beside her. Zari slammed the photograph face down and it lay there, toppled, resigned, and that upset her even more. She turned away, determined to ignore it, and strode to the wicker armchair with its big denim cushion seat next to the window overlooking the cul-de-sac.

Lowering herself into the chair, Zari grimaced at the stiffness surrounding her bullet wound. Opening her purse, she searched for the ointment Khala had prepared for her and came upon her passport and ID papers. Back in India and then in Pakistan, she'd handed her papers to her guardians for safekeeping, but here, here she alone was responsible for her belongings. And her own self. Returning her papers to her purse, Zari pushed aside the sheer curtains and looked out into the evening as far down as the cul-de-sac permitted. Fantasies of revenge and vengeance seemed alien here. Evening was descending and the downpour had turned into a drizzle. Water trickled off trees and bushes and metal mailboxes at the ends of driveways. She saw a cat slipping under an evergreen hedge separating this house from the next. Zari jumped as a car roared down the street and into the Nabis' driveway. A young guy loped out of the car. The Son, she presumed.

Letting the curtains fall back into place, Zari slid off her sneakers and flexed her toes. She released her hair from the yellow butterfly clasp, stroking out the tangles all the way down to her waist, and sinking back into the chair, she closed her eyes and savoured the quiet.

A knock on the door. The Son, come to deliver her suitcase, his smile so big Zari was afraid his face might break. His pine needle scented cologne enveloped Zari. He smelt like a summer day back home, rich with the promise of picnics and games of badminton and cricket matches. He was lanky but muscular, his wavy hair worn a little longer than her mother would have deemed respectable, his ebony-eyed gaze gentle; Sonea would have declared the Son cute.

Before he could enter the room, Zari walked up and dragged in her suitcase.

"Hi." He held out his hand. "I'm Billy."

"Thank you," she said politely. And shut the door. And turned the lock. Her breath caught. There was no lock on the door. The lock had been disabled. *Anyone* could walk in on her *anytime*.

Zari calculated the direction of Mecca as her mother had taught her to, and unzipping the outer pocket of her suitcase, took out her prayer rug and unfurled it upon the cream-coloured carpet. Sitting cross-legged on the rug, she cupped her hands in entreaty and looked towards the ceiling. Faces glared down at her—bulbous eyes and halos of streaming hair.

Zari screamed. She jumped and scrambled through her purse for her pink razor. Only when the skin of her forearm broke and tiny beads of blood emerged was she able to calm down enough to peek at the ceiling. They were still there, except now she saw that what had seemed like eyes and hair were simply sun medallion patterns in the crown moulding and not ghosts peering through plaster. It was not her family.

But they were here. Their presence was as palpable as the beating of her heart. They had accompanied her across the oceans. They had followed her. Had they boarded onto planes of their own? Or slipped through portals from place to place? Held onto her coat-tails? Or burrowed into the folds of her heart? That she carried them in her heart comforted her even as it terrified her.

One day, after an assault of memories at her Uncle's place, Zari had found herself dry heaving in the bathroom. She'd picked up a razor from the ledge atop the sink, a delicate pocket knife of a razor with a pink handle and serrated silver teeth. She'd run the teeth over her forearm in long parallel cuts, and as blood beaded up, she'd expected to feel pain but had felt only relief.

Slicing relief into her flesh was turning out to be the best—the only—solace in India, in Pakistan, and here in America. In a moment, she would feel better, and, in another moment she would be better enough to join the family for the tea and snacks she had no appetite for, to present herself sanely when she felt anything but, and to appear grateful for this sanctuary when she had not asked for it.

As she headed downstairs, Zari slipped on her woollen coat, making sure the fresh welts on her arm were covered.

3

Billy dashed across the campus towards the parking lot just in time to catch his adviser about to drive off in his dented Pontiac. He knocked on the glass, touched his watch, and indicated he'd lost track of time. His adviser shrugged, rolled down the window, and told him to reschedule, yet again. As he watched his adviser drive away, Billy berated himself for oversleeping, yet again, and began to trudge back to the campus. The week had unleashed yet another freezing Friday afternoon, and friends and foes had emerged on the Commons, the ends of their cigarettes burning warm holes into the otherwise grey day. Billy turned towards the campus newspaper office, avoiding, as best as he could, the slush on the cobbled walkways as he lectured himself to get his priorities on track and his major decided. He'd idled long enough.

In the beginning of his freshman year, he'd been certain he wanted to major in journalism. Then he'd decided anthropology was his calling. Sophomore year, political science had called out instead, followed by philosophy and, midway through it, the import of being a foreign correspondent had gripped him and he'd reverted back to journalism. But now, with the declarations of majors due, he was teetering again.

Of late, he had been wondering if he would have even

considered journalism at all if his beloved Dada, his paternal grandfather, had not been a journalist. But then, even as a child, his parents always reminded him, he'd manically jumped from choice to choice: astronaut, firefighter, mailman, candy store owner, trash collector, policeman, ice-cream store owner, zoo keeper, vet, dolphin trainer, marine biologist, video game maker, social worker, psychologist, journalist—all remnants of childhood fantasies.

Entering the newspaper office in the basement of the Media Studies building, Billy settled into his swivel chair. The heat of freshly printed papers, the air charged with looming deadlines, Mack the Knife playing on the CD player on a loop—all so thrilling in the beginning, were now so routine. He looked at his notes for his next column, *World Matters*, and wondered, yet again, how much the written word really mattered. Tomes had been written on the troubles in Kashmir, and yet, here was Zari, her plight mocking the promise and power of the written word to bring change.

She'd been with them for two weeks now. He had been nervous about meeting her, but he'd also been eager to help her in whichever way possible. They were all eager to help, even his mother, although she had been against Zari's coming. In fact, Billy was pleasantly surprised to find his mother trying to religiously follow the instructions given to them by the psychiatrist they'd conferred with before Zari's arrival:

-Force her to participate in daily activities like choosing a movie to watch or deciding what to have for dinner.

-Be Sensitive. A joke that's simple and harmless for you might hold negative association for her.

-Do not mention her family unless she does. And, if she does, do not avoid eye contact.

-If she cries, let her.

Before Zari's arrival, his mother had had them convinced that Zari would, no doubt, be a younger version of her own mother, an army widow who, after her husband was killed in the 1965 war between India and Pakistan, had wailed and wept her life away. But Zari was a dry-eyed fortress of pleases and thank-yous and the fact that she did not want to speak or be spoken to in Kashmiri was proof enough for Billy that she was a dry-eyed wreck. As it was, she seldom spoke and she never really looked at them, not even at Miraage who was adamant that Zari was her new best friend and would, therefore, barge into the guest room whenever she pleased. Billy had suggested reinstalling the guest room lock so that Zari could have some privacy, but his mother had disagreed—it gave her comfort to know that she could supervise Zari at will.

Zari emerged from the guest room only at meal times, and then too, she would silently peck at the Pakistani food his mother, otherwise averse to cooking, would have painstakingly prepared, speaking only when spoken to, all the while waiting, it seemed, to escape back to the sanctuary of the guest room. That she took religion as seriously as his mother, if not more, seemed clear to Billy, for whenever the guest room door had been ajar, he'd glimpsed Zari either praying on a beautiful red and green prayer rug, or pacing with a rosary in hand, or reading from the Quran.

Soon after she'd arrived, the holy month of Ramzan had begun, and Zari and his mother were diligently keeping fasts day after day. Billy had decided to show his solidarity by fasting on the days he planned to visit home—an hour's drive from his college—such as today, when he would much rather have welcomed the steaming cocoa everyone else in the newsroom was enjoying.

Billy glanced at his notes:

Why Oklahoma City bombing is terrorism and the nuking of Nagasaki is not? After Hiroshima, what need for Nagasaki?

Why demonstrators rallying for freedom are disrupting peace, yet authorities cracking down with batons and guns and tear gas are deemed peacekeepers?

Were the atrocities in My Lai, Vietnam, easier to perpetrate because the victims did not look like the perpetrators?

But, in the demonstration in Kashmir, the fact that the police were beating people who looked just like them had certainly not garnered compassion.

Billy wondered if Zari had ever been caught in a demonstration like he had. He laughed at himself. A political demonstration was paltry compared to her experience. He longed to ask her what exactly had happened. But, ever since she'd shut the door on his face the first day they'd met, they'd had no interaction, and he was hardly in a position to ask her about anything. The fact was that no one in his family knew how to *help* Zari, let alone know what to say to her, though they all had questions. All he knew was that there had been two break-ins and that Zari had lost her family in the second one. But were the break-ins connected? Who were the perpetrators? What had the police concluded? Who had found Zari? But none of them had the guts to probe Zari for details, not even his mother.

Billy looked up from his notes just in time to see a

familiar pair of black boots with neon red laces stamp by the basement window. The newspaper's star reporter. After dating him for a brief spell, she'd dumped him because, she said, he wasn't ambitious enough, and had then promptly taken up with the editor-in-chief, a rooster of a guy born convinced that he was going to win the Pulitzer. Billy checked his watch. Time to leave anyway if he wanted to get home in time for iftari to break the Ramzan fast.

∞∞

Two weeks in this country and Zari had nothing stain-free left to wear. She stood at the porcelain sink in the bathroom, trying to scrub the sleeves of her blouses free of blood stains. Cursing her preference for pastels, she held up a sleeve against the light and grimaced at the still discernible rows of rust-coloured spots. She'd escaped detection at her Uncle's and Khala's homes by constantly wearing her dark woollen coat, but here she'd look demented if she wore her coat indoors when the family kept the central heating on a suffocating high. The Elder Daughter actually wore tank tops indoors. In fact, the whole family dressed as if it was summer indoors. *They* were mad.

Zari laid the blouse's wet sleeves before the space heater in the room and prayed that at least this one shirt would be wearable in time for iftari. She needed an iron is what she needed and her eyes filled up with furious tears at her helplessness. How could her Khala have sent her here? Amongst all these people she didn't know and all these things she didn't understand? These past two weeks she'd been terribly lost. Simple things had confounded her. She would look for drinking glasses on the right side of the kitchen cabinet, only to remember that it was so at Khala's

69

house. She would grope for the light switch to the bathroom on the outside wall, only to remember that that was at her Uncle's house. Too many mornings, she would still wake up thinking she was back home, only to remember that that world was gone.

Memory was insidious: there was intense longing for the past, but also a savage mourning for the lack of a future. As for the present, the present frightened her. She could swear she heard ducks quacking. She imagined raps on the front door. Imagined doorknobs being rattled. It did not matter that there was a security system installed in this house, for if locks on doors and padlocks on iron gates back home could fail, then why not America's plastic security systems? No one was breaking in, Zari would tell herself sharply. She was safe, she would counsel herself, safe albeit lost.

One morning, after everyone had left, she'd braved the laundry room, only to stare at the washing machine and the dryer in absolute confusion, and when she'd finally found the instructions printed on the undersides of the lids, she'd been unable to decipher the instructions and was too scared to guess in case she accidentally broke the machines or flooded the house.

She had started talking to the ghosts, softly at first, but now more stridently. She whispered her fears of completely falling apart to her mother, complained to her father about having no spending money, discussed with Sonea how to ration toiletries, confided in Kiran that she was terrified at the prospect of running out of sanitary napkins, that she kept seeing the fully-stocked supply cabinet back home. Would those supplies rot while she, Zari wondered, rotted here, dependent on the kindness of strangers, having to be polite, having to show up for meals when all she wanted to do was curl up and turn to stone?

The Nabis were kind: the Woman constantly inquiring if there was anything special she wanted to eat, the Elder Daughter, a personal trainer, offering free yoga classes daily, and the Man diligently advising her to spend at least some small part of the day outside for fresh air. And the Little Girl—why didn't the Parents simply demand she leave her alone? Having discovered that the guest room had no lock, the Little Girl would barge in whenever she pleased and insist that Zari play tea party, or dinosaur hunter, or read her a story. And Zari would indulge her as best as she could until she could no longer bear it or until the Woman herself barged in to hustle the Little Girl away.

Zari touched the sleeves of her blouse. A little dry, but the stains were still evident. She would have to brave her suitcase, an ordeal that always left her exhausted, for some sort of cover-up. She gently laid the suitcase flat on the floor and rested her cheek on its warm leather exterior. This suitcase was the sole thing on earth she could any longer call a home. This soft giant of a mothball-reeking suitcase into whose frayed innards she'd crammed all the belongings of her family that she possibly could. This suitcase so old its once sparkling buckles were now dull and its once alert pull handle prone to getting stuck. This sad looking suitcase, once upon a time a new purchase full of promise, converted, with the passage of time, to just an ordinary vessel her mother had not the heart to throw out because it harboured fond memories, and now nothing but a receptacle bearing the burden of being Zari's only semblance of family.

Zari sat up and slowly tugged the suitcase zipper along

the teeth, the slow groan echoing in the room like the reluctant invocation of an ancient spell. Flipping back the top flap, she took a deep breath and sank her hands beyond the top layer of her clothing to her family's belongings. The items bled memories into her skin—the Ludo game board her mother and Baz played, Baz's paint box and drawings, her mother's dupattas, her father's pillbox fur winter hat, Sonea's barrettes left behind during sleepovers, the photo album of her engagement to Imran, Kiran's black shawl, the border a trim of silver paisleys chasing one another.

Zari drew out the shawl and burrowed her face in its softness. The silver paisleys pressed against her mouth; she inhaled the faint glory of all the perfumes her sister had ever worn—would ever wear. She saw her sister in the shawl, a ghost reaching out to her, touching her, entering and breaking into her, injecting her with a million memories. She could not breathe. She *had* to breathe. She could not wear the shawl. She *had* to wear it. She had no choice.

Zari heard her mother's voice, her sister's whisper, both urging her to brace herself, to *understand*. They were with her. They were by her side. They were here in all the ways and in all the forms she needed them to be. Zari rose and the shawl opened itself up and she stepped into the shawl and it wrapped itself around her and it hugged her and held her close and made sure it concealed her stained sleeve and it was all guidance and good intentions; yet, Zari shivered as she headed down to break her fast.

The weather had taken a turn for the worse with a sharp wind whipping between houses and causing everything in its path to shudder and wheeze. Shehla was glad to be indoors, in the cosy house, even if she was hungry and thirsty. In fact, the turbulent weather outside enhanced her appreciation for the order brought about by the holy month of fasting—a month long paean to abstinence, from dawn to dusk, from eating, drinking, sex, lying, gossiping, everything that could lead humans towards the turbulences of a sinful soul and physical gluttony.

Shehla sat at the head of the dinner table, gazing longingly at the iftari spread she'd prepared: pakoras, fruit chaat, cholay, cheese crackers, dahi barhey, and vegetable noodles. She didn't know why she'd bothered. Zari was not going to eat anything and she and the kids would have been just as satisfied with dates and orange juice leading straight into keema-rice or pizza or pasta. Did Amman have any idea how much of her time was spent looking after his 'good deed'? Even today he was conveniently on call at the hospital while she was here, catering to Zari.

Shehla peered at Miraage seated next to her at the table, studiously colouring a T-Rex in her colouring book, her chubby fist wrapped around a slender crayon. Try as she might, Shehla could not detect any hint of Zari's presence having done any damage to her little girl's spirits. Not yet. Kissing Miraage, Shehla vowed to redouble her efforts at healing Zari because the quicker she healed, the quicker they could send her back to her Khala's and the lesser the chances of any damage being done to any of her children.

Shehla looked up and smiled perfunctorily as Zari entered the kitchen with a handsome black and silver shawl draped around her shoulders. Were these normal times, she would have asked Zari where she'd purchased it and for how much, instead, Shehla merely motioned for her to come and take a seat.

"Look!" Miraage held up the T-Rex for Zari's inspection.

"Good colouring." Zari gave a weak smile and pulled out a chair far from Miraage.

"Sit here!" Miraage squealed, patting the chair beside her, and after a moment's hesitation, Zari slipped into it. Miraage handed Zari the T-Rex drawing.

"I made it for you. I'm going to colour a Maiasaura for you as well. Do you want blue or green?"

"Green," Zari finally managed. "Green is fine."

Miraage beamed with such joy that Shehla looked kindly at Zari. Poor creature! What a terrible kismet! Shehla muttered a quick prayer to protect her family from envy and the evil eye.

Salsabil flew down the stairs two at a time and entering the kitchen, reached for a handful of dates from the platter on the table.

"Beta," Shehla checked her, pushing the platter out of Salsabil's reach, "why aren't you fasting?"

"Period. Sorry." Salsabil peeked at Zari who, as usual, seemed to be in a world of her own.

Shehla shook her head. Salsabil's menses conveniently kept her company during most of Ramzan since a menstruating woman was not permitted to fast. It was Amman's fault, really, that the children were so lackadaisical about religion. Amman was a cultural Muslim, the sort who made a big deal of things like Islamic heritage and Chaand Raats and Eids, but was lax about the rest. She would never forget the way he'd merely chuckled when a young Billal had innocently informed his Quran teacher that the first man and prophet on earth was Charles Darwin. Shehla had expected names to guide character and had therefore named Billal for the first man to sound the call to prayer, Salsabil for a fountain in heaven, and Miraage for the Night Journey that the Prophet Muhammed had taken to the Heavens where he'd met God and the other Prophets—but it had all been to no avail. The children were as laid-back as their father, if not more so, and Shehla had grown to comfort herself by reasoning that while it was her duty to educate the children about the essentials, it was God's duty to make worshippers out of them.

The front door opened and then banged shut. Billy rushed in, bringing with him a gust of cold air from outside.

"Billaloo!"

"Mom, don't call me that!" Billy glanced at Zari, embarrassed.

"What a wonderful surprise!" Pleasure sweetened Shehla's face. "Home again, two weekends in a row."

"Can't resist your cooking, Mom," Billy said as he tossed his hat and muffler onto the counter.

"Can't resist her doing your laundry either!" Salsabil snorted as Shehla handed Billy a plate as if he couldn't get one himself.

"It's not my fault Mom gets to it before I can." Billy slid into the chair opposite Zari. Zari's gaze was fixed, he noted, on the lone scrawny date on her plate. He looked down at the wealth of obese dates his mother had piled onto his plate and realised he could not possibly eat heartily in the presence of Zari's grief.

On TV, worshippers circumambulated the Kaaba in Mecca, and once the clock in the corner had counted down the seconds to breaking the fast and they'd recited the breaking fast prayer, they bit into their dates and began passing the food around.

"Mom," Miraage piped up, "can I have macaroni and cheese?"

"No," Shehla said, shaking her head as she squirted ketchup over Miraage's noodles. She turned to Salsabil. "And why should my son do his laundry as long as I'm alive?"

"Because," Salsabil said, "he's going to end up expecting his wife to wait on him hand and foot the way you do."

"Which," Shehla said sweetly, "reminds me—"

"Mom!" Salsabil groaned. "Here we go again. Why are you always after me to get married? Why don't you pester Billy to declare a major?"

"Hey," Billy protested, "don't turn this on me." He looked at Zari, but she appeared deaf to their bickering, which was perhaps a blessing, because although during the first few days she'd been here they'd all been on their best behaviour, it now seemed to Billy that his family was fast reverting to normal.

"There is no harm in hearing me out," Shehla said to Salsabil even as she glanced at Billy. While Shehla admired her son's empathetic nature, she desperately wished he would be more attracted to lucrative pursuits instead of raising banners, shouting slogans, and walking for this cause and running for that one. How she wished she hadn't allowed Amman to convince her to let the kids choose their own career paths to happiness. How she wished she'd stressed

Doctor-Engineer-Lawyer-Entrepreneur as the kids were growing up. Now Billy was a hippie-wannabe while Salsabil taught people to execute Jumping Jacks, not that it really mattered in Salsabil's case because, eventually, it was her husband's job to provide for her, and so it was Billy, her darling do-gooder son, whose future worried Shehla.

"I'll hear you out, Mom," Salsabil was saying, "if you let me move out."

Shehla turned her attention back to her daughter. "Your father and I have told you that the only way you are 'moving out on your own' is after marriage and that is that."

Salsabil crossed her arms. "Who is it this time?"

"Doctor."

"So not into doctors."

"God only knows what types you are 'into.'"

"Piercings." Salsabil smiled sweetly. "Tattoos. And it wouldn't hurt if he was really hot too."

"Where am I supposed to find a Pakistani self-mutilating Rock Hudson look-alike?"

"Rock Hudson was gay," Billy informed his mother, grinning mischievously.

"Behave yourself," Shehla said, frowning.

"Zari," Salsabil asked, "what sorts of guys do you like?"

Zari looked up from her plate and around the table as if she'd just realised she was not alone. Finally she said, "I like my fiancé."

There was complete silence as the Nabis snuck glances

at each other. Billy wondered if anyone else had noticed that she'd used the present tense while referring to her fiancé. Should they ask about her fiancé? All they knew was that he too had perished.

"I-I-I need help with operating the washing machine."

∞⌘∞

Zari stood in the doorway as the Son explained the controls on the washer and the dryer and then pointed to the line of containers of detergent, fabric softener, bleach, dryer sheets, and stain removers. Zari looked from one container to the other, and tried to hold herself together at the memory of her mother's intense pride in her efficiency and skill in all aspects of housekeeping, from airing out the bedding, to grocery shopping on a budget, to paying the servants' salaries, and to keeping track of the laundry. And now, here she was, her mother's daughter, defeated by laundry.

When the Son completed his instructions, Zari entered the laundry room with her basket of stained clothes. She wished he would leave so that she could use the stain remover even as she tried to ignore the fact that she was alone with him. She loaded the clothes into the washer, shut the round glass door easily enough, poured the detergent into the measuring cup and then, staring at the receptacles, was lost all over again. He was by her side in a second, pointing to the receptacle at the top and turning the control knobs even as he reassured her that the first time was always the most confusing. The washing machine began to rumble and throb.

"Thank you," Zari managed. But it exhausted her. Asking for help with her dirty laundry had finally, completely, orphaned her, and the next moment, she fled past the Son, the ends of her black shawl whipping him.

∞∞

Billy frowned as Zari rushed out. Had he inadvertently upset her? Should he follow her? The laundry whirled in the washing machine, soap suds clouding the window. He tried to imagine his family murdered while he sought refuge at home after home only to end up in a place where the simple act of washing clothes confounded him. He couldn't.

"Hey!" Salsabil strode into the laundry room. "Where is she?"

"Don't know. And are you mad? Why did you ask her what type of guys she likes?"

Salsabil flushed. "Mom was pestering me about marriage just the way her Khala constantly pesters her over the phone about her getting married, and I thought she would . . . you know . . . relate. I feel terrible."

Billy nodded. "Wasn't it weird, the way she spoke about her fiancé?"

Salsabil shrugged. "Maybe it's a good thing that she brought him up."

"Maybe."

They looked at each other.

"By the way," Salsabil said as she turned to go, "glad to see your lazy butt doing some laundry, even if it's not your own. When you're done with Zari's, you're welcome to mine."

"You wish," Billy called out as Salsabil left.

When the laundry was washed and dried, Billy began to fold the clothes—long-sleeved blouses and kurtas, jeans and cotton pants. A bra—white with tiny flowers in pale yellow. He stared at the bra in his hand, and then promptly dropped it back into the laundry basket and dishevelled all the clothes.

Making his way upstairs, Billy found the guest room door ajar and Zari on the prayer rug. Knocking, he entered and placed the basket on the bed.

"I dried the clothes for you." He stood before her, not knowing where to look. He wished he could ask her how she was able to pray to God, day after day, after what God had put her through.

"Thank you," Zari mumbled, glancing at the basket on the bed. Why had he transferred the clothes from the washer to the dryer without asking her? Were there any blood stains on the blouse sleeves? If so, had he noticed them? Why was he standing here? Why wasn't he leaving?

"Listen," Billy said, "anytime you need any help with anything, please feel free to let me know. I'm serious, day or night." He flushed. "I mean . . . just . . . anytime." His gaze fell on the silver photo frame lying face down on the small table next to the door. It was a family picture, he knew, and he kicked himself for not having the forethought to have removed it from the guest room.

"I need this," he said, and picking it up, he left.

Zari's expression was blank as Billy shut the door behind him gently. Later, she would have liked to share with someone that most of the stains had come out and that the ones that were left were hardly perceptible at all. But there was no one to share such information with. Except for the spirits, there was no one with whom she could share her life.

Billy returned to his room and banged the door shut. He tossed the frame onto his desk and wondered what other mistakes they were all unintentionally making. After a while, he turned on the TV. The History Channel. Black and white footage of the Berlin Olympics, wild clapping, gaunt children. What—who—was on the other side of the camera clicking away? Whoever it was, Billy envied the necessary detachment of the photographer that allowed for taking such photographs. On TV, Miep Gies was talking about having hidden the Frank family. Billy turned up the volume. The interviewer was asking her if she had been scared of the Nazis.

But it was the right thing to do, she said.

Hours later, Billy heard the cry right outside his door as if someone had eaten a hot chilli. He scowled. Salsabil trying to smuggle her boyfriend into her room. Was she planning to wake everyone up and get herself into trouble?

Opening his door, Billy was about to tell his sister to keep it down when he caught the tail end of Zari's shawl, the silver border whisking round the corner of the hallway. He shut his door. Put his ear to it. This time he heard sobs. Should he try to comfort her?

I'm sorry. When my cousin died, the ghost memories really hurt . . . all the things that could have been. So I know what you're going through, I do. And who knows if it will ever get better.

He had to say something, anything, and opening the door, he walked out into the hallway, stopping under a collage of family photographs that plastered the wall, unsure of what to do next. Zari came around the bend, saw him, halted.

"I'm . . ." he began, "I'm so sorry—"

Zari's cry was the strangest yet. She looked at him with fear, but also disdain, as if she was challenging him to say something, anything that would make any difference.

Billy searched for appropriate words of consolation, of hope.

"I . . ." He faltered.

She turned and ran.

Billy slunk into his room wishing he could just go to Kashmir and somehow restore her life. For the first time since the demonstration in Kashmir he'd been caught up in as a kid, Billy felt his life directly affected by politics. And even now, just like then, he was helpless.

4

Srinagar, Kashmir, 1987

Billy banged the steel tumbler onto the lacquered cedar chest and jumped back as warm milk leapt for freedom. He sheepishly watched Mauj jee use the ends of her chiffon dupatta to mop up the milk until there was no trace of the accident ever having happened. Once done, she pinched his cheeks playfully and then took out a fresh dupatta from her armoire and arranged it over her hair, tucking the ends behind her large ears. Mauj jee *was* old, Billy concluded, as old as the candy cane he'd once found in the refrigerator back home, so brittle that just nipping at the wrapper had made it crumble.

As Mauj jee slowly pocketed the dull gold armoire key, Billy promised himself he would take care of her even after they left Kashmir and went back home. After all, she was his Dada's sister, and Mauj jee had assured him that being a grand-aunt was as good as being a grandmother, especially since his own grandmother was long gone to heaven.

"What is it, my little one?" Mauj jee settled cross-legged on the shaggy namdah laid out on the hardwood bedroom floor. "Why are you frowning?"

"I want eggshells in my milk, just like Dada." Billy scrunched his forehead harder.

Mauj jee stroked Billy's unruly bronze-black curls off his face and ran her doughy finger down his forehead to smooth the furrows.

"Eggshells! Eggshells!" Billy knew he was acting like a baby, but he was enjoying Mauj jee spoiling him. At least that is what his mother had whispered to his father the night before in the guest bedroom the four of them were sharing, he and Salsabil on the sun-aired mattress on the floor, and their parents in the elaborately carved bed which looked like a hairy mammoth: *She's spoiling him Amman, and then, when we go back, we'll have a rebellion on our hands.*

Billy had asked Mauj jee what a 'rebellion' was and she told him a rebellion was doing what one liked, for a good reason, without caring about what anyone else said. Well, he was doing *rebellion* now.

"Eggshells!" Billy pounded the cedar chest.

"Shh," Mauj jee said. "You'll wake everyone up from their afternoon naps."

Billal stopped. If his mother woke up, she'd tell him to stop disturbing Mauj jee and make him go play with Salsabil and their cousins, all girls. He wouldn't have minded playing cricket with Shafi, Mauj jee's teenage chore boy, or watch him whittle wood into thumb-sized animal figures, but he always had to wait until Shafi was done with his duties.

"I wouldn't tell Mom about the eggshells, I promise," Billy pleaded. "It will be our secret."

"You mischievous little monkey!" Mauj jee sucked on

her hookah, a tall, golden creature, the pipe trimmed in blue velvet. "Raw eggs can make you ill. As it is you children from abroad have no immunity."

"Why did we get the shots then?" Billy asked as he rolled back his tee shirt sleeve to show Mauj jee the faint needle prick marks.

"You poor child!" Mauj jee kissed the marks. "Undergoing such discomfort in order to visit your own homeland. Now," she grinned wickedly, "if you ask again in perfect Kashmiri, I will reconsider."

Billy stared at her. His and Salsabil's spoken Kashmiri was dismal, although Mauj jee had remarked that they were much more proficient in Urdu, their mother's native tongue.

"Umm," Billy stammered, "meh choo . . . umm . . . tah-hools . . . eggs . . ."

Mauj jee chuckled gleefully at Billy's mangled efforts. "That was good for my heart," she said, kissing him. "How about this—I promise you raw eggs if you are fluent in Kashmiri by your next visit."

"But Mom told Dad this is our one and only trip. We only came because you're ill. Are you very ill?"

Mauj jee's eyes narrowed. "You listen to me; you are not some tourist to visit this land only once. Kashmir is your home. You come whenever you want. One and only trip! Pah!"

Billy nodded solemnly. A heartbeat later, "Could Dada swallow fire like circus people?"

"He was brave, not mad." Mauj jee brought her knees up to her chest, her voluminous floral tunic ballooning over her frail calves. "But he could have if he wanted to. Your Dada sacrificed three of his fingers in a battle and not one ouch did I ever hear from him."

Billy splayed his hands. "Which fingers?"

Mauj jee held up her middle three fingers and Billy gazed at them with awe. Why had his father never told him Dada had been in battles, let alone sacrificed his fingers? His father never told him anything. It was only under Mauj jee's tutelage these past few days that his paternal grandfather had leapt to life in the form of a seven foot burly hero who ate raw eggs, drank from the teats of antelopes, vanquished foes with a single stroke of his sword, wrestled lions with his hands tied behind his back, and outsmarted djinns and made them bow to him.

"Your Dada didn't even flinch when he saw your father's scars." Mauj jee peered down at him. "Have you seen the scars that spread across your father's back like a hand-held fan?"

Billy nodded. The scars looked like a rope course he'd done at a summer camp once.

"Do you know how he got them?"

"In college, when his motorcycle was hit by a car and he fell on broken glass."

"Who told you that?"

"Dad did."

Mauj jee cupped Billy's chin. "You ask your father since when shattered glass leaves long welts as scars. Do you know how your Dada died?"

Billy shook his head.

"He was murdered."

Billy flung himself into Mauj jee's lap.

"Hathay beikul! Silly boy!" Mauj jee hugged him. "There is nothing to be scared about now." She kissed him. "Your Dada was murdered a long time ago."

"How?" Billy whispered.

"He was shot."

"With a gun?" Billy's eyes widened as Mauj jee nodded. "Did they catch who did it?"

"No."

Billy pressed himself into her harder.

"But here is the good thing," Mauj jee tilted his face upwards, "your Dada was shot for his ideals. For his noble ideals and you should be proud! Your Dada, Abdullah Nabi, was a great man, a man of men, your Dada was a freedom fighter. "

"Dad said he was a journalist."

"He was that also towards the end," Mauj jee shrugged, "but first and foremost he was," she raised her head with pride, "a freedom fighter."

Billy loosened his grip around Mauj jee's waist. "What's that?"

"A very brave person who sacrifices himself for the good of his country." Mauj jee puffed on her hookah so fast the water in it gurgled like a goblin jumping in fury. "It's a sign," she muttered between puffs, "that the Day of Judgment is upon us when the young do not know the history of their elders."

"I want to know the history."

"How would you like to see history—something of your Dada's?"

When Billy nodded, Mauj jee unlocked her armoire and extracted a tightly knotted cloth bundle. The knots kept slipping from her gnarled fingers until, finally, she allowed Billy to take over, his young nimble fingers putting to use the badge he'd earned for the Boy Scouts. Inside the bundle was a hat shaped like a canoe with tall sides. Billy ran his fingers over the coarse black-white-grey whorls.

"Goat wool," Mauj jee said as she set it on his head like a crown.

The hat slipped down Billy's face. He sniffed the yellow silk lining. It smelt of lion and eggs, of bloody fingers and epic battles fought on magical mountains under twisted skies.

"Dada had a big head." Billy cradled the hat against his chest.

"Yours will grow too," Mauj jee said. "A big head carries an intelligent brain. You are Abdullah Nabi's grandson! Make your Dada proud. My God," Mauj jee looked deep into his eyes, "I swear you are his spitting image."

Billy ran alongside the rampart overlooking the Dal, slapping each lamp post he passed. This was his first night out on the Boulevard, Srinagar's main road. He glanced back at his family strolling along the lake shore promenade amongst a hive of other tourists as the evening set in pinks and coppers. He could see them getting closer, his mother hurrying a little to catch up with him even as she said something to his father. Billy skipped a little faster. He'd told his parents that afternoon that Mauj jee had said he was Dada's spitting image and they both told him she needed spectacles. Then, when he'd asked how shattered glass could leave long welts, his mother had snapped, "since your father told you it does." But, when he'd said, "Mauj jee said Dada was murdered. Is it true?" the dismayed glance his parents exchanged said it all—they were hiding something from him.

The garlands of naked bulbs that lit the street up like a long row of Christmas trees distracted Billy and he slowed down a little. 'Full! Full! Full!' signs decorated hotels. Souvenir shops, their doors propped open, blared the same Indian movie music his parents played back home. The scent of sugar twirled into pink and blue cotton candy clouds sweetened the air and each time Billy passed a restaurant, his mouth watered at the entrees listed in broken English on the sidewalk menus.

"Stop!"

Billy braked at his mother's voice. He turned back and she pointed to the concrete steps in front of him, leading to the lake's edge where shikara rowers—balancing on the prows of the shikaras, canoe-like boats with colourful awnings and with names Billy found funny: *Robot, Mickey Mouse, Paradise Perfume*—called out the fares to the many destinations on the lake.

Billy skipped up and down the steps while his parents bargained with the shikara rowers until they finally settled under the red-white-blue awning of a shikara. *The Vite House*, the plaque on its bow declared.

The Vite House sliced through the lily pads towards houseboats docked along the far shore of the lake. To Billy, they looked like hulking battleships and he imagined his Dada leaping from houseboat to houseboat in hot pursuit of lions and djinns. The wind rose, the shikara swayed sideways, and Billy allowed his mother to hold him close until they arrived at the foot of the wooden stairs of a houseboat named *Titanic Deluxe*.

"Titanic? Really?" Salsabil grimaced.

Their parents hushed her as they climbed out of the shikara and into a gregarious welcome. Billy watched as men surrounded his father, laughing, slapping him on the back, embracing him. Look at you, they said, we've all gone bald and you look like a walking-talking shampoo advertisement! Billy stared at his father who looked as if he'd discovered treasure.

"Thank you for inviting us," his mother said to the hosts, Uncle and Mrs Uncle. "The houseboat is lovely and Amman tells me that the Wazwan is a real treat."

"No mention, no mention," Mrs Uncle said. "You cannot come to Kashmir and not eat the traditional feast of kings."

Mrs Uncle bade all of them to follow her off the *Titanic* and on to the willow-lined bank temporarily transformed into a cooking ground with myriad cooks preparing the Wazwan, a traditional thirty-six course dinner. The head-cook, perspiration marbling his forehead, welcomed them without missing a beat as he directed his culinary orchestra of peeling, measuring, chopping, mixing, stirring, searing, braising, frying. A young cook, his sleeves rolled up his elbows, an elastic headband over his hairline, pummelled steaks flat on a stone tablet and waved at the children. Fully aware their mother had one eye on them, Billy and Salsabil raced from cauldron to cauldron, peering into the large mouths and generally getting in the way of all the cooks who, nevertheless, graciously allowed the 'English-Foreign' children to hold the hockey stick sized stirring spoons and pose as Amman took photos of them at every dish: the glossy braids of seekh kebabs, rogan-josh in a crimson sauce, translucent opal of yakhni, the goshtaba, a huge silken meatball simmering in yoghurt with mint, ginger, and aniseed, all to be served over white rice in communal platters.

There were other children there as well and they all started playing tag. Billy, clutching Salsabil's hand, galloped back into the *Titanic*, racing through the dining room with its long ornate table for fourteen, through the drawing room with its carved walnut wood furniture, through the three bedrooms with their damask draperies, their footsteps shaking the cedar board flooring, stopping only when one of them crashed into a silver stool.

Mrs Uncle gave all the children a stern warning and herded them into the master bedroom where a group of teenagers was playing carom. She left all the children there, ordering them to stay still and be quiet. As soon as she left, Salsabil and the older children gathered around the carom board, peering over the players' shoulders and generally making a nuisance of themselves. Two children Billy's age took out their electronic games and Billy stood behind them wishing he hadn't listened to his mother and had brought his game too. Wait for your turn, they said. Still waiting half an hour later, he went to complain to his mother.

Billy marched onto the *Titanic's* deck which was divided into segregated sitting areas. On both sides Mrs Uncle had arranged for tea and refreshments—platters heaped with nuts and dried fruits and baby apples with finger long knives piercing their rosy flesh. On the men's side, ashtrays cropped up between the outdoor lamps and mosquito coils lining the trellised railing. On the woman's side, a floating market of shikara vendors had gathered by the hull and Billy found his mother intently watching a shawl vendor pull a mouse-coloured shawl through a ring finger ring, claiming this was proof that the material was pure shahtoosh made only from the hair of baby goats.

"Mom," Billy jiggled her arm. "Mom! Listen! You said I couldn't bring my game, but the other kids brought theirs. Mom!"

His mother flashed him a warning and Billy, glaring, strode to the men's side and stood behind his father's chair next to the railing. The men were deep in conversation and smoking cigarettes, one after the other, and Billy's gaze followed the bubbles of creamy smoke gliding over the water, at the waves lapping against the boat, the silver spangles smashing into each other. A plastic bag floated by and got caught against a reed along the bank. Far up the banks, he could make out an adult and a child carrying bundles of sticks on their heads, making their way, perhaps, to one of the lights twinkling through the chinar trees that carpeted the mountains. And above them all, the full moon's reflection in the lake below, bathing a lone shikara in all its silver-gold glory.

"—freedom fighters."

Billy whipped around.

"Kashmir cannot be turned into a Beirut!"

"It will be if our sovereignty continues to be disrespected like this. We were promised a vote by the United Nations in 1948. Now it is 1987!"

"Our politicians are Indian puppets and India will never permit a jewel like Kashmir to be voted into independence, or worse, handed over to Pakistan."

"Then bloodbath it will have to be."

"Bloodbath! Huh! We Kashmiris are nothing but complaining cowards."

"You mistake our pacifist nature for cowardice. I assure you, if our leaders continue to dance to the Indian government's tune, there will be a bloodbath."

"By God, you are looking forward to turning Kashmir into Beirut!"

"I would rather sacrifice my sons to fight for freedom than continue living in chains. Let there be a bloodbath!"

"Excuse me," Billy piped up, "what is 'bloodbath'?"

"Billal!" His father's face clouded over. "Why aren't you playing with the other kids?"

There was a general round of coughing and Mr Uncle called out to Mrs Uncle—hathsa, hey, when will dinner be served?

❧❧

Billy sat in Mauj jee's lap, recounting the injustice done to him. During their sightseeing trip to the Shalimar Gardens this morning, instead of his mother apologising to him for not letting him bring his game to the party on the houseboat last night, his parents had lectured him on eavesdropping.

They'd even forbidden him from asking Mauj jee about the word bloodbath.

Mauj jee kissed him. She was about to speak when Shafi came in with her daily dose of medicine—sundried bitter gourd—for her diabetes, a local remedy recommended for controlling blood sugar. Billy scrambled off her lap as Mauj jee spooned the powdered gourd into her mouth, and, bracing herself, downed it with water. Billy had tasted it once and could well believe its medicinal properties because it tasted like the worst possible opposite of sweet. It tasted, he imagined, like the hide of a horny toad.

When Shafi left for the kitchen, Billy asked if he could see Dada's hat again. Mauj jee handed him the key to the armoire—she was safekeeping the hat for him along with other mementos—and Billy took the hat out and balanced it on his head. If only he could somehow live in Kashmir and America at the same time. Once he returned, he would miss Mauj jee and Shafi and everything else. And yet, if his prayers came true and they moved here, then he would miss his friends and his school and everything there. Billy jabbed at his tears.

"Kya goi aaz? What has happened to you today?" Mauj jee asked. "Come here!"

Billy slipped into her arms and breathed in her jasmine talcum powder.

"I'm going to miss you when we leave," he said in a small voice.

"You silly boy, I will always be with you."

"How?"

"In here." Mauj jee tapped his chest. "In your heart, just as you reside in mine. Now, do you want ice-cream?" And so saying, Mauj jee called Shafi, handed him some money, told him to fly to the bazaar, and to take Billy along. "Now, no more tears," Mauj jee said as Billy broke into an excited smile. "And I'll tell your parents *I* gave you permission to go, and when you return, I will tell you what is bloodbath."

Billy and Shafi ambled along a wide alley bustling with locals and tourists alike. Radio programmes burbled out of small establishments, their cramped interiors reminding Billy of magic shops in fairy tales. He wanted to buy everything—the remote control cars on display outside a toy store, the wristwatches gleaming in glass cabinets, the houseboat and shikara-shaped key chains a hawker waved under his nose. Billy couldn't stand still for the excitement of endless possibilities the market presented. At the ice-cream kiosk—a machine dispensing vanilla and chocolate twirls into cones—they lingered on the stoop instead of hurrying home. Opposite them, a bicycle repair shop and a bakery were doing brisk business and Billy licked his lips as scents of sweet and savoury pastries spilled out from the bakery's open door. The music shop next door was changing songs every few minutes and Shafi sang along to each one, bowing and clapping whenever Billy said he should become a professional singer.

At first, Billy mistook the chanting for a funeral procession—he'd once seen mourners in a movie, clad all in white, carrying a bier—but then he saw the mob, marching, fists thrust in the air, shouting: Azaadi, Freedom, Azaadi. Shopkeepers waved customers off stoops, turned off the music, and drew down shutters. Some bystanders joined the chanting while others clutched at one another as police jeeps screeched to a halt around the square and policemen leapt out, their batons striking flesh.

Billy shrank against Shafi. Shafi grabbed his hand in the erupting pandemonium and turned homeward, forcing Billy to run harder and faster than he'd ever run before. They circled a burning tire, the smouldering flames undulating copulating snakes. Smoke bruised the sky and the stench of melting rubber ate the air and devoured the delicious bakery scents as screams and shouts replaced the songs Shafi had sung along to. Billy gagged, his eyes stinging—it was tear gas, he would learn later. The crowd dispersed every which way, running as fast and as hard as they could. A few stood rooted, brave, foolhardy, continuing to protest even as their eyes burned red. Someone picked up a rock and aimed it at the police.

They ran, harder, faster, Shafi sure-footed in his rubber sandals, cursing as Billy, despite his sneakers, kept skidding on the dirt roads. It took them a while to get through lanes cramped with fleeing people, but they finally arrived home safe, only coughing, spluttering, and out of breath. News of the impromptu demonstration against rigged elections spiralling out of control had already reached Mauj jee's house. And, when Billy saw his family standing at the gate, his fright turned to exhilaration. He was home, all was well, and he flew towards his father.

"I saw the freedom thing! I saw the freedom thing!"

His father slapped him and then hugged him, all the time apologising for having brought them here, for insisting that they had to see where he'd grown up. There was no need to see anything, his father said. The past was past.

"It's okay, Dad," Billy said even as his cheek smarted. "I'm glad we came."

He was sorry to see his father on edge and his mother's migraine in full swing. Even Salsabil was subdued. Mauj jee's hands, Billy saw, were quivering like frantic birds as she kept repeating to herself "my fault, my fault." Billy ran to her and flung his arms around her and squeezed her with all the love in his heart.

When his father booked their return flight for that very night, Billy begged him to cancel it, hating himself because their sudden departure was, no matter what his parents said, all his fault. He didn't want to leave Mauj jee. Or Kashmir. Not like this. Not without having time to say a proper goodbye to each and every thing. Shafi gave Billy a squirrel he'd carved from walnut bark. He'd meant to teach Billy how to whittle one, but there was no time to do that now. There was time for nothing now but to cling to Mauj jee with all his might. He might never see her again. He couldn't bear that. They had to wrench him out of Mauj jee's arms. *Remember*, Mauj jee told him, tapping his chest, *remember*. Then she kissed him one last time and let go.

On the plane, even Salsabil was crying. Billy refused to speak to his parents, but when he did, it was only to ask them that if Kashmir was unsafe for them, then how come Mauj jee and Shafi and everyone else remained? Why wasn't his father telling him how he really got his scars? Why hadn't he told him Dada was a freedom fighter? That he'd sacrificed his fingers during a great battle?

"Enough," his mother reprimanded him, her voice

sharper than ever. "Your Mauj jee is senile. There are no lions, no djinns, no—"

Billy put his hands over his ears. Back home, he envied his friends' their grandparents who took them out for movies and concerts and sleepovers. His mother's mother was the only grandparent he'd ever really known. She'd lived in Pakistan and they'd visited her annually each summer until her death three years ago, but those visits had been boring—except for playing in the sweltering garden, there had been nothing to do and there had never been anything good playing on TV.

But Kashmir had been different. Billy's warm feelings had begun at the Srinagar airport where three carloads of relatives had arrived to welcome them. Fireworks erupted in his tummy each time he'd understood a Kashmiri word; the first, much to his delight, a curse word uttered by a grumpy porter at the airport.

Mauj jee had been waiting for them at the house. He'd seen her as the taxi had turned in from the gate, a fat but frail figure, dressed in a pale pink pheran, pacing the verandah. When he had clambered out of the car, she had embraced him as if she would never let him go.

"I have finally set eyes on Amman's children," she kept declaring, "now I can go to my maker in peace."

She'd taken Salsabil's hands in her own, kissing them, stroking them, but Salsabil, uncomfortable with being touched, had slid her hands away. Billy thought that was rude of her and when Mauj jee clasped his fingers, he held on despite her bone-crushing grip.

Their very first day, family, friends, and acquaintances

had visited well into the night. Back home, their days were structured and perfectly scheduled, and uninvited guests unheard of. Here, guests dropped by at whim and hosts accommodated them with genuine smiles. Billy had gawked at the impromptu party spilling from Mauj jee's living room into the courtyard. He'd sat under Mauj jee's wing of an arm, his bottom on a plush carpet, his back against a sausage pillow, feasting on the pistachios and figs before him. Mauj jee kept kissing him and saying "shush wandey, zue wanday, krehnamaaz wandey," endearments Billy had only heard before from his father.

Amidst noisy, rowdy talk, where everyone interrupted each other and nobody seemed to mind, relatives regaled them with anecdotes about their father when he was no taller than them. Scallop-edged photographs were hauled out of walnut wood chests and passed around, hand to hand, each eye taking them in with wistful smiles and bursts of laughter. Proof that his parents were once children, always made Billy feel weird. He wondered if he would have liked to play with them. His mother must have been one of those bullies that adults said had leadership qualities, and his father he couldn't quite imagine. But here was his father, a toddler, next to a towering, falcon-nosed young man.

"Who's that?" Billy asked.

"Tch, tch, tch! You don't recognise your Dada?" Mauj jee had slid the photograph out of the album and tucked it in his hand, the first of the many mementos she would give to him during his visit.

Now Billy stared out of the plane window, stunted with disbelief that places and people could be left so quickly and with such little ceremony. Staring into the long, dark night, he realised with a sinking heart that he had forgotten to take the mementos Mauj jee had been keeping safe for him, including his Dada's hat with its scent of lions and eggs, of bloody fingers and epic battles fought on magical mountains under twisted skies.

5

Billy glanced out of the basement window of the newsroom and watched snow boots squelch past in the icy sludge outside. True the window, a sliver of cheap glass overlooking a cracked sidewalk, was jammed shut and his view was limited, but it was, nevertheless, a view. Sometimes Billy would find the clack of his fingers on the keyboard in rhythm with the footsteps outside and the accidental harmony would delight him with its hint that there was some rhyme and reason to this ridiculous world.

He took a sip of his scalding coffee, savouring the warmth. He'd been home and fasting the entire weekend and had driven back to campus only this morning. He knew he risked missing his column's deadline, but, each time he tried to write something, he was assaulted by the memory of Zari's face in the hallway.

"Hey Bill-o!"

Billy looked up as his friend Ameer, cultural critic at large and reviewer of movies du jour, stepped in. Billy held up a finger.

Achilles chose a short life with guaranteed fame, Billy typed as fast as he could, *instead of a long but unremarkable existence. We too have a similar choice to make: to live with our eyes focused on our backyards or to turn around and engage with the world at large, no matter how much we pretend that if we ignore the world, it will ignore us.*

He hit send.

"Done." Billy stretched his arms.

Ameer handed Billy the feedback that had come for his column. "You missed a great party this weekend."

Billy shrugged and flicked through the letters. Three thumbs-up. One downer. Apparently, he should stop reporting on current events and switch to covering dog shows. He wondered how his Dada, journalist par excellence, had dealt with the downers. Had he even gotten any? Billy wondered if he should ask Zari about his Dada. Not that, he was sure, she would have heard of his grandfather. No one seemed to have.

"Dan and I are planning to play basketball," Ameer glanced at the wall clock, "right about now. You coming, bro?"

Billy shook his head. "Paper due."

"And I'll bet you need to be home to do it. How *is* your house guest treating you?"

"Don't be absurd." Billy shook his head as Ameer winked and left. Ever since he'd mentioned helping Zari with the laundry, Ameer and Dan had been teasing him about her. But fact was, since that night, Zari seemed to be going out of her way to avoid him. Also, lately, his nightmares about his trip to Kashmir had returned with renewed ferocity.

Billy took out his wallet and extracted his most prized possession: the lone letter from Mauj jee. The scratchy pale blue paper, the border of thick red and navy stripes, the stamp with Gandhi's spectacled face, the scrawl of the address—*To: Master Billal Nabi*.

For months after their return from Kashmir, Mauj jee had called him regularly and he, in turn, had written to her regularly about school work, soccer games, and assurances that he was practising his Kashmiri. Billy could still recall his thrill when after months of waiting, he'd finally received that one letter from Mauj jee. His parents had not been home when the mail had been delivered and he'd spent agonising hours wondering how to open the aerogramme without damaging its contents until he had realised that he had no choice but to seek help from his parents. The minute their car had entered the driveway in the evening, he'd been out like a shot, badgering his parents, not relenting until his father, still standing in the driveway, had slit the envelope open with the nib of the fountain pen in his pocket so that the edges came away looking like shredded lace. When his father handed him the letter, Billy caught his breath. Velvety black ink sprawled over the blue page like unruly ocean waves at night time. The letter was written in Kashmiri and the very fact that it read from right to left had excited the little boy that he'd been.

Billy had his father read the letter out to him over and over again until he'd memorised the translation.

My Dear, Darling, Beloved Billal,

I trust you are well, my one and only. Ever since you left, I give thanks daily to God that you were not injured in the demonstration that unfortunate day, that you all departed in a timely fashion, for matters here are disintegrating day-by-day.

Thanks be to God that you all visited when you did and I saw all of you—I can now die in peace. Billal, remember to study hard.

Make your parents proud, make me proud, but most of all make your Dada proud. How proud he would be of you, you are not capable of imagining.

My love, my darling, take care of yourself, and if Allah wills, we will meet once again.

My love to your bright sister and salaam to you parents

Your beloved Mauj jee.

In his last phone conversation with Mauj jee, she had sworn that she'd written him other letters as well, but he had never received any of them. Eventually, Billy had concluded that they must have all either gotten lost in the mail or had never been allowed out of Kashmir in the first place. He had not permitted himself, not once, to suspect that his parents could be right, that Mauj jee might be a delusional old woman.

Two years after their truncated trip to Kashmir, Mauj jee had passed away and Billy's grief pooled onto that lone letter. Even now, he sometimes woke up in a cold sweat, convinced that he needed to revisit Kashmir to gain closure. He'd wanted to go there after high school, but was deterred by the rising tensions in the region and by his mother's superstitions. It was a miracle that he'd survived the demonstration once, she had said, and she was not going to allow him to tempt fate again. Appealing to his father would have been useless since he always seconded his mother's irrational fears. His parents, Billy knew, had hoped that with Mauj jee's death, his fascination with Kashmir and his hero worship of his Dada would come to a natural end. Instead, it had surged. 'The One Person In History I Would Most Like To Meet' was always Dada no matter who the class placed on a pedestal that year. 'My Best Summer Vacation Ever' was always Kashmir no matter where else the Nabis vacationed. 'What I Would Like To Do When I Grow Up' was always 'Make My Dada Proud.'

While other kids played with video games, Billy enacted his Dada's battles with the djinns and lions with nothing more than a GI Joe and a plastic zoo. As he grew older, he snooped through his parents' paraphernalia for family history—snippets, snatches, scraps, whatever he could find—the way other boys prowled for porn. And the way his parents looked at him when he asked questions—How did Dad get his scars? And Dada's murderer? Was he ever caught?—he might as well have been asking for porn. His queries were uniformly met with "We really don't know." Together, his parents formed a formidable wall. One he was determined to breach.

In the coming years, Billy took to devouring all the material he could find on Kashmir and India and Pakistan—books, journals, newspapers—desperate for some mention of one Abdullah Nabi. There was none. After stumbling upon his father's address book one afternoon, a despairing fifteen-year-old Billy wrote to relatives scattered across the world, people he'd never met. The few who wrote back reiterated what he already knew: lions, djinns, journalist, fought for an independent Kashmir, died for it too, actually, was murdered, but why did Billal wish to probe something so terrible? He was young, he should forget the past and enjoy the life his parents were providing for him, Allah bless them; he should study hard, move ahead. How were his studies going, for that matter? What were his hobbies? Did he like Science? Would he become a doctor like his parents? His parents ignored the back and forth of the correspondence as if they knew, all along, the bland responses he'd receive. But the more they insisted that the past had nothing to do with his present and the future, the more they tried to sever the frail thread Billy was clinging on to, the more convinced Billy became of the opposite. Without concrete knowledge of his past, he did not know how to pave a future.

"It seems," Billy often complained to Dan, his best friend since elementary school, "that my entire clan is deliberately suffering from a collective amnesia regarding Dada, and they want me to follow suit."

"Lucky you," Dan always answered. Dan's father's family went all the way back to the seventeenth century—his mother still had close family in Ireland—and Dan was subjected to family lore ad nauseam. Dan thought Billy insane for wanting to wilfully chain himself to the past when he could just as well dive into the future, a story-less blank.

"I don't want to be chained," Billy had said. "I want to be anchored."

But there was no anchor; there was barely enough to be moored to, a fact Zari's presence had only further reinforced.

Billy quickly gulped down the last of his coffee and rose to wrap things up and head home. Eid was all but upon them, and every time he thought about the festival, he wondered what Eid celebrations had been like at Zari's house. He tried to imagine her at the Moon Sighting funfair where his sisters bought bangles and had henna applied to their palms, tried to imagine her at the Eid lunch party frequently hosted by his parents, tried very hard to imagine her thoughts during all the festivities this year, but he could not. As Billy hung his coffee cup to dry and picked up his car keys, he wondered how Dada would have eased Zari's first Eid after the tragedy. And that too in a foreign land?

Zari peered out of the window as the Jolly Maids van backed out of the driveway and disappeared down the end of the road. Each time the Nabis' cleaners came and left with nothing but a brief, courteous nod in her direction, she couldn't help but think about Ahadu, their kitchen boy, Azra, their cleaning woman, and her mother, and the instantaneous exchanges of familiarities between them all. Alone in the unbearable quiet left in the cleaners' wake, Zari walked out of her room to the landing and inhaled the lemony scent of wood polish. On the spur of the moment, she opened the Nabis' bedroom door. Lingering traces of the Woman's perfume, a scarf thrown carelessly over the foot of the bed, flowers, chintz curtains, dark wood furniture, all with gold knobs and robin blue accents.

It occurred to her that she could bang the door shut, slam it, and kick it—there was no one to bear witness to her transgressions, but she shut it gently instead, and padded through the carpeted hallway towards the Little Girl's room. It was a confection, all white frills and pink tulle. The Elder Daughter's room was a mix of tartan and cane. The Son's room, despite vacuum lines on the floor, was a mess and Zari wondered if the cleaners were instructed to leave his clutter and chaos alone. Her throat tightened at a postcard tacked onto his wall: houseboats on the Dal at night time. Zari shut his door behind her with a bang, but there memory was, burrowing up unbidden: lily pads on the Dal suckling on the summer sun, and in the winter, the Dal a vast blue ice-skating rink, and in autumn a golden blush of leaves changing colours.

The ghosts followed Zari as she hurried downstairs. The TV would distract her; the TV was invented for distraction. In the family room, she manually switched on the giant screen, but was then confounded by the myriad buttons on the remote controls. A bird twittered outside. A dog howled back. She could go for a walk, she decided, even though a walk risked bumping into neighbours or one of the many children whom she could see from the bedroom window every day, jump-roping, skate-boarding, biking. Their merriment made her ill.

The garage door roared open and Zari dropped the remote control into the wicker holder—there was no time to flee upstairs—and rushed to the kitchen—she would say she was getting a glass of water—just as the Woman walked in, her arms laden with grocery bags. A flustered Zari asked if she could help put the items away. The Woman beamed and handed over the paper bags and then stood watching her put away milk, butter, strawberry jam, and freshly ground almond butter, still warm in its plastic container.

"A little more than a week of Ramzan to go," the Woman said as she nudged off her clip-on earrings and rubbed her earlobes, "then Happy Eid!"

Zari concentrated on dumping the apricots into the fruit bowl. She had heard the Woman describe Eid as the Muslim Christmas to God knows whom over the phone and how equally festive a celebration it was with its bangles and henna application and new clothes and feasts. Zari had managed to survive Ramzan—the various abstinences deepening her belief that fasting was God's way of teaching tolerance for greater losses—but the thought of Eid was intolerable.

The phone rang just then. It was Khala.

Handing the girl the phone, Shehla went upstairs to her bedroom to change out of her slacks and blouse and into a comfortable pair of jeans and a kurti. She looked forward to informing the psychiatrist they were consulting that not only had Zari put the groceries away, but that she'd offered to do so of her own accord. Shehla was under no illusion that anything was going to *heal* Zari, for she was well aware how some people became too fragmented and how difficult it was for them to then recover all their parts, let alone fit them back together seamlessly, but she was upset and angry over Zari's seeming lack of interest at availing opportunities available to her.

Zari had previously vetoed home therapy, drawing therapy, music therapy, therapy in general, until the psychiatrist had aggressively renewed her first recommendation that Zari at least keep a journal, and so Shehla had purchased a journal and had been looking for a good time to insist Zari use it. This sudden turn in Zari's attitude, Shehla prayed, was a sign that the girl had come around and she extracted from her dresser the bag with the journal.

When Shehla returned to the kitchen, Zari was still on the phone. From the distress on her face, she knew Khala was recommending marriage again. While Shehla agreed with Khala that Zari could not spend the rest of her life unmarried, she also thought it was a little too soon to thrust the girl into a union. And it would also be hardly fair on any man to be lumped with Zari, no matter how good-looking she was. Damaged goods were, after all, damaged goods.

Poor Khala! Shehla thought as she took the home-delivered chapattis and potato curry out of the freezer and put them into the microwave to thaw. Khala was only trying to help Zari as best as she could, as they all were, and she would be thrilled to hear of Zari's progress. As soon as Zari hung up the phone, Shehla, determined to continue with the conquest, took the bag and led Zari to the back deck and seated her on the sofa-swing overlooking the back garden.

"Beta," Shehla handed her the bag, "I will honour the fact that you don't want to see the psychiatrist, if you honour a request of mine."

Shehla knew she'd made an error in judgment as soon as Zari extracted the lace-covered journal with the heart-shaped lock and key. It was a journal perfect for a young girl desirous of penning her first romance, not for a girl like Zari.

"Look," Shehla said, trying to ignore her faux pas, "the goal is to simply record your thoughts. Also, I've bought Miraage a journal of her own, so please keep yours out of sight. My little Maju is still struggling with the concept of yours-versus-mine. Oh, look, it's Erin!" And Shehla waved in relief as her neighbour strolled into the garden with a shih-tzu at her heels.

Zari nodded as the Woman went down the deck steps, her ponytail swinging behind her. Did her Khala, the Man, and this Woman now walking across the garden, did they have any idea the toll their prescription of 'fresh air' took on her? Looking out at the garden, all Zari could see was the badminton net stretched taut between two poplar trees, the rackets walloping the air, the whoosh of the shuttlecock, the laughing faces as they argued over who should retrieve the shuttlecock from where it had landed.

Zari glanced at the Woman and the Neighbour standing at the borderless boundaries of their respective gardens. She could hear snippets of their conversation: How chilly this winter is turning out to be! But before you know it, spring will be upon us! True! The shih-tzu crossed over into the Woman's garden and proceeded to relieve itself. The Neighbour rushed over with a plastic bag.

"Hi there, Zari."

Zari gave a tiny wave back. She did not correct the Neighbour's pronunciation. Not Zaa-ree as in starry. But Zur-ee as in hurry. She looked down at the journal the Woman had placed next to her on the swing. She and Sonea had kept a joint diary once, filling the pages with bad poetry and giddy dreams. She couldn't imagine writing about her cutting herself or about her nocturnal pacing or her panic at the mere thought of the fast encroaching Eid. How ugly the words would look on paper. This year, relatives would visit the graves, graves she was incapable of visiting, but graves she thought about all the time. Back home, there would only be mourning during Eid this time, while here the Nabis would celebrate, and try as she might, she could not reconcile herself to the indisputable fact of life: the world did not stop just because someone's world came to an end.

For the first time since her arrival, Zari couldn't wait for the Little Girl to burst into the guest room, as she did every afternoon after coming home from school, and pester her. Ten minutes later, there was the Little Girl with a drawing she'd made for Zari at school, her chatter about dinosaurs and tea parties turning into a squeal of disbelief and pleasure when Zari handed her the journal and told her to keep it.

Later that evening, after the fast was broken and dinner eaten, Zari returned to the guest room only to hear the Family quarrelling in the upper lounge. She could hear the Little Girl scream in between sobs: I did not *take* the journal. I did not! I did not!

Zari huddled in her armchair with her hands over her ears until, suddenly, she heard a small voice whimpering inside her, and she pressed her ears harder and harder until she could no longer ignore the whimpering inside and the cries outside as both the living and the dead assaulted her together. Finally, she rose, and on unsteady legs, made her way to the den where the Family was gathered with Miraage in their midst.

"I gave it to her." Zari dug her nails into her palms in order to steady herself. "She didn't take it. I gave it to her."

Five pairs of eyes pierced her. The Little Girl flung herself around her waist.

"I told them you gave it to me. I told them you were my friend."

"Why?" The Woman's voice was cold. "When I told you to keep it out of her reach, why would you purposefully try to get her into trouble?"

"Not . . . purposefully. I—" Zari stopped. She had not meant to get the Little Girl into trouble, and yet, she had.

"It was evidently a misunderstanding," the Son offered.

"Of course," the Man said, smiling uneasily. "A misunderstanding."

The Woman turned to him with a baleful gaze before turning back to Zari. "I would appreciate it," she said to

Zari, "if, in the future, such misunderstandings did not arise. Come here, Miraage," she opened her arms wide, "don't you like the rainbow journal?"

The Little Girl clung to Zari. "I want the lock and key one."

"Miraage—" the Woman said.

"Shehla—" the Man began, but the Woman cut him off with a flick of her hand.

"You want to exchange journals, Miraage?" Zari broke in.

The Little Girl nodded and gazed at Zari with adoration.

Later, when the house was asleep and the voices in her heart had hushed, Zari paced up and down in the guest room. Her new journal lay on the armchair, a journal fit for a child drawing happy stick figure families under sunny blue skies. She picked up the journal, flipping through its blank pages, a cornucopia of colours, a manufactured rainbow. It reminded her of all those evenings when she and Sonea had lain on their tummies, their bare feet prancing in the air, scribbling in their joint diary with different coloured felt-tip pens until their musings had inadvertently created a rainbow. She did not know what had happened to that diary, in whose house it had ultimately found a home even if it lay discarded and forgotten in some dust battered corner, or if it had been tossed in the trash, and, as panic over yet another unknown began to overwhelm her, she opened the journal and began to write frenetically, her pen stabbing the pristine page with wounds of ink:

I won't be able to survive Eid.

Breathe. Just breathe.

∞∞

Eid fell on a wet, windy, intermittently sunny day. The road leading to the Islamic Centre was clogged with cars, a metallic snake slinking forward despite itself, thanks to the policeman directing traffic. There had been a time when the local mosque had been a rented office space squashed between a used-books' store on one side and a Mediterranean grocery store on the other. Since then, it had migrated to bigger and better venues, until, finally, land was purchased, an architect was hired, and a proper mosque with a traditional dome and a minaret was constructed. The new mosque now boasted of a segregated prayer area and expansive grounds that enclosed a garden, a community hall, a kitchen, a meeting hall, and a classroom for children; it was no longer just a mosque, it was an Islamic Centre, and this Eid morning it bustled with adults exchanging pleasantries and excited children running about.

After Billy managed to find them a parking spot, he and Amman strolled towards the automatic doors of the main building. The entire length of the walkway was lined with enterprising young people handing out brochures—Urdu Elocution, Arabic Lessons, Quran Exposition, Henna Application, and a flier with a low-resolution picture of a child, dishevelled and crying, holding the burnt remains of a teddy bear. *Trouble Spots*, read the top line, and underneath the picture: *Palestine, Chechnya, Bosnia, Kashmir, More*. Billy recognised the guy with the fliers—he'd seen him at political meetings—and tried to dash past, but the guy spotted him.

"Hey! Billal, right?" the guy beamed. "You here to help?"

"No." Billal cringed as Amman took a flier. "Just here for Eid prayers."

As they walked away, Amman steered Billy off the concrete and towards the lawn where there was little risk of being overheard.

"What is this?" Amman tapped on the flier. "What have you involved yourself in now?"

"I'm not involved in anything, Dad, whatever 'involved' means. And anyway, if you're not going to tell me about Dada, then I have to find out about him through other means."

"What is it that you are hoping to find out? You know everything there is to know about him!"

"That's not true."

"Is that so?" Amman tore the flier up and thrust the pieces into his coat pocket. "Listen to me, Billal. Enough is enough. I want you to drop this obsession and stop trying to find out 'these things' you imagine your mother and I are keeping from you, or even pester me about matters which serve no purpose except inducing depression. Why can you not respect my wishes?"

"I want to know about my history." Billy hated the desperation in his own voice. "I *need* to know my history."

"Your mother and I have provided you with everything you need to know in order to have a safe and successful future."

"For Christ's sake—"

"Billal!"

"I don't even know how you got the scars on your back, and until I do, I cannot move on. *I cannot.* Why don't you get it?"

"Be happy that you have parents who want you to live your own life instead of burdening you with theirs."

"Burden me. Please. Burden me."

"Be quiet."

"And as for 'live my own life', that's a joke, Dad. You and Mom wouldn't even let me go to Kashmir after high school."

"We said you could go to Europe."

Billy scowled. "This Europe craze, it started with white kids searching for their roots, just like me, a brown kid wanting to find his!"

"Again this brown nonsense! How many times do your mother and I have to tell you that you are just American?"

"In case you haven't noticed, being an American does not mean I'm colourless or that everyone else is colour-blind."

"Of course it does."

"What world are you living in, Dad!" Billy grit his teeth. *You are just American.* He had grown up hearing this. But the world outside demanded precision and exactitude and thus the birth of hyphens—his father was Kashmiri-American, his mother was Pakistani-American, and he, he was an uber-chimera: Kashmiri-Pakistani-American. "In case you missed the memo, Dad, may I remind you, yet again, that this is a land of immigrants?"

"No immigrants." Amman waved a hand. "Only American."

"I'm not some island, Dad," Billy said, shaking his head. "I'm a part of you. And where you come from is a part of me. It's not fair that you won't tell me my history."

"Nothing to tell that can do you any good to hear."

"Shouldn't I be the judge of that?"

"I am your father and I know what is best."

Amman stormed off to the prayer area. A little later, father and son stood side by side in the prayer line. All around them, rows upon rows of men were going through the same motions and invoking the same prayers as if they were a single entity. Communal prayer had always sent shivers up Billy's spine for the unparalleled equality it conferred upon disparate people, but now, as his forehead touched the prayer mat, he wondered what his father was thinking. Was he praying that he lose interest in his past even as Billy himself prayed that his father would gain a desire to share it? Whose prayer would God deign to fulfil and why? Billy ended his prayers annoyed by his cynicism.

After the prayers, Billy and Amman embraced friends and strangers—Eid Mubarak, Eid Mubarak—before heading home. They did not exchange a word on the drive back.

Zari barely slept the night before Eid. In the early hours of the morning, she opened her door to the Woman groggily handing her the phone. Khala was only the first in the long line of phone calls that would last all day. Uncle and Aunty Lili called from Delhi. Then her brother-in-law from Dubai, sounding so broken that for a moment, Zari put aside her own pain as she found in his pain an identical longing for

Kiran and Baz. A constant stream of relatives followed, one after the other, crying, commiserating, consoling. By the time Sonea's parents called, Zari could do no more than press the phone to her ear, nodding her head to their kind words, seeing Sonea in all her beauty, from the tip of her upturned nose to the fuchsia nail polish she'd loved on her feet.

The deluge of memories that came with the words, the accents, and the inflections bridged gaps in time, space, minds, and hearts. It made the past palpable. Never mind that sanity said it was gone. She could shut her eyes and taste what had once been home. But, instead of comforting her, the memories increased her guilt at having stayed alive.

Zari was curled up in the armchair by the window when the Elder Daughter knocked on the guest room door and entered with a mug of steaming tea in her hand. She set the mug on the windowsill and handed Zari a bag. Zari looked inside. Sanitary napkins. Her thank you, a moment later, came out as a croak.

"I just thought . . ." the Elder Daughter paused. "Listen, if there's anything you need, you just have to ask me or Mom."

"Soap," Zari managed to say. "Soap and toothpaste."

Salsabil nodded and turned to leave.

"Wait." Zari licked her lips. "Salsabil." The Elder Daughter's name fell from her lips with an unaccustomed softness. "Salsabil, I cannot thank you enough for this." Zari tipped her head at the bag.

"Please." Salsabil put her hands up. "There is nothing to thank us for."

But there was, Zari thought, as Salsabil left. She had been preparing to barricade her heart against the pain she knew the celebration and gaiety of Eid would bring, but, instead, the Woman, Shehla, had told her right after Khala's call, that the Son, Billal, had called a family meeting and suggested that they celebrate this Eid as would befit a family in mourning. The family had agreed unanimously, Shehla said, the only concession being bangles for Miraage, and the Man, Amman, and Billal attending the mosque for Eid prayers.

Consequently, their first lunch after a month of fasting was a sober affair. Just the family sharing a simple fare of mutton pulao, cucumber raita, and sivyaan for dessert. Zari managed to force down a few bites of the food as talk flowed around the table and everyone else heartily tucked into the fragrant goat meat cooked in basmati rice and spices topped with seasoned yoghurt. Amman and Shehla discussed who'd been at the mosque that morning. Miraage counted her glittery glass bangles with Salsabil, laughing every time they tinkled against each other. Only Billal was quiet. As the Nabis lingered over their dessert of vermicelli stewed in sweet milk, Zari, for the first time since her arrival at their house, felt compelled to remain seated until everyone was done with their meal. But the next instant, she rose suddenly.

"I wanted to say . . ." she swallowed, faltering. "I wanted to say thank you, to all of you. Thank you for not . . . I will never be able to repay—"

"Beta!" Amman smiled kindly. "What repayment! You are family!"

"It was Billy's idea," Salsabil broke in. Her brother's thoughtfulness had inspired her own impulsive act of goodwill towards Zari and thus the supplies in the bag.

"An excellent idea!" Amman slapped Billy on the back and so, tacitly let go of the unpleasantness they'd had at the mosque. "Unlike his other ideas, his mother and I approved of this idea wholeheartedly."

"It wasn't for your approval." Billy looked up from his ramekin, at Zari, and caught her looking at him; she held his gaze for a moment longer than necessary.

"You know what," Billy crossed his arms, "I think we should cancel Miraage's big birthday party this year."

"I've already delivered the invitations." Shehla's voice was pinched.

Miraage's brows furrowed. "Will I still get birthday presents?"

Billy flicked her nose playfully. "You'll get cake!"

"No." Zari shook her head. "I cannot allow this. I cannot disrupt your lives any further."

"It's not a disruption," Billy said.

"Yes it is," Zari said resolutely. "But more importantly, it's not fair on Miraage. Or on anyone."

"That's settled then!" Shehla squinted at Billy, warning him to not push things any further. "Now," she said, getting up, "who wants tea?"

As Zari stood to help clear the dishes, Miraage tugged at her shirt, clamouring to be taken to the deck. The cushioned swing was cold despite the afternoon sunshine, and when Miraage snuggled onto Zari's lap, Zari pressed the sunny little girl to her chest.

"Will you come to my birthday party?" Miraage looked up at Zari. "Will you? Will you?"

"We'll see," Zari said to appease her.

The *kwee-kwee-kwee* of the swing going back and forth lulled Miraage to sleep and Zari rested her chin on the little girl's shoulder and shut her eyes. The child's voice inside began in a whimper but grew shrill by the second in its struggle to find the correct words:

Are they replacing us? Who is this? Have you forgotten me?

Zari gathered Miraage into her arms and handing the sleeping child to Shehla in the kitchen, she ran up to the bathroom in her room, vaguely registering the value pack of soap and toothpaste next to the sink. Only when she drew the razor blade through her skin, and blood surfaced on her forearm, and relief flooded her, did she calm down. But it was a hollow relief, for Baz's voice lingered in her ears like the echo of an echo. Help me God, Zari prayed as tears joined the blood. How am I supposed to balance a life torn between those who are here and those who are forever gone?

6

Music and laughter from the basement wafted up to the guest room. Zari, sitting in the armchair, her knees bobbing, got up, went to lie on the bed, turned this way and that, got up again, paced to and fro, sat back on the bed. Miraage's birthday party. To go or not to go—as Aunty Lili would put it, Zari thought wryly—that was the question. She rose again, perched at the edge of the armchair, looked out of the window in time to catch a magician's truck parking in the Nabis' driveway and a tall man in a purple and gold cloak emerge with a golden bag. A moment later, the doorbell rang and then minutes later the wild shrieks of excited children.

Zari twisted the ends of her chiffon dupatta as the whispering gathered in her heart: *Will the magician pull rabbits out of a hat? Doves out of thin air? Coins from behind ears? Can I go? Can I see? Will you take me?* And then, tiny, ethereal fingers pulling her towards the music and the laughter, walking her down the stairs and into the basement, giddy at the bounty of balloons and streamers and party hats. She saw Billal first, his back towards her, kneeling before the stereo system, adjusting the music. She stood at the door, watching the children running amok, watching the adults trying to maintain some order. She did not dare enter, not yet, still hesitant, guilty. She was still there at the door when

Miraage saw her, and ran to her and hugged her and pulled her across the room, pointing out the candyfloss kiosk, the balloon animal kiosk, the turreted jumping castle, and all the while the tiny, ethereal fingers clutched Zari's fingers harder, holding on, propping her up, the child's voice reverberating along her every nerve: *show me, show me, show me.*

Miraage came to a stop in front of the magician's table, and hands on hips, her tulle and diamanté dress flaring around her chubby calves, she introduced Zari to her friends, as 'my bestest new cousin.' The chattering children quieted for a moment as they gazed up at Zari with their missing-tooth smiles, and the grip on her hand grew tighter still.

The grip relaxed only when the magic show began, as coins appeared from nowhere, as a rabbit peeked out of a top hat, as silk handkerchiefs blossomed into pretty white doves, until, as the magician took his final bow, the tiny fingers lifted hers in applause, then, suddenly, disappeared, were gone, and she stood there, empty-handed, but at peace because, for the first time, the ghosts, instead of crying, had had cause to laugh.

After the show, Shehla collected Zari from the magician's table and delivered her to a large group of muffin-like men and shining ladies dressed in elegant blends of Western and Eastern styles. The Nabis' friends were eager to meet Amman's niece from Kashmir, who, Amman had informed them earlier, was here to look at colleges. They barraged her with well-meaning questions: Which colleges? Where? What did she plan to study? Was she missing home? How many siblings did she have? What did her father do? Zari could have answered these questions in a million different ways but she simply said: Still scouting. Not sure. Environmental Engineering. Missing. One sister. Forest Department.

When they drifted back to their conversations about cricket scores and discount buys, Shehla patted the small of Zari's back. "Good girl," she whispered with pride. "Very good behaviour. I can now honestly inform your Khala that you are getting better." Zari gave a fleeting smile and sidled away to the cake table. When she had been a little girl, Kiran had taught her to make paper dolls, and Zari, in turn, had taught Baz. She had guided the heavy scissor in his small fingers, and, together, they'd cut along the traced outlines of the paper dolls without so much as a second thought to the discarded silhouettes. But those silhouettes had been dolls in their own right, outlines of their former selves, shadow dolls that did not protest or resist at being trashed and so, as such, they behaved.

As she was behaving at the birthday party because Baz was again holding her hand and guiding the outline of the person she'd once been, his memory imbibing her with strength, his little heart beating inside hers, his voice alive with joy as she sang Happy Birthday, his hands quivering as she clapped when Miraage cut the cake and blew out the candles. Zari grabbed the cake knife before one of the caterers could and began slicing and handing out pieces of the two-tier cake.

"I asked for chocolate."

A guy stood before her in tan cargo pants and a white shirt stretching over swarthy shoulders, his crew cut thick and bristly.

"Hi." He grinned. Fine wrinkles gathered around his

close-set eyes and abounded at the corners of his full mouth. "I'm Fahad."

Zari gave him a quick, small look and replaced his slice of vanilla cake with chocolate.

"I hear you're scouting colleges. I could show you around if you like . . ."

Mumbling incoherently, Zari turned to the next person in line.

∞∞

Fahad kicked a balloon out of the way and strode over to Billy who was fiddling around with the stereo.

"She's cute." He nodded in Zari's direction.

Billy looked up from the CD in his hand. Zari was leaning over Miraage's birthday cake, slicing away so diligently that she might as well have been etching a fine line in a work of art. Her lilac kurta was long-sleeved and loosely fitted, and when she moved, the fabric waltzed around her. The chiffon dupatta around her neck slipped up and down her clavicle, playing hide-and-seek with a small brown mole just below it. Her cheeks were flushed, and her thick braid pulsed, and she seemed lit up from inside. It was the first time he'd seen her involved in the world; warmth washed over him.

"She's engaged," Billy curtly told Fahad and turning his back to him, returned to the CDs, looking up, every now and then, to take in Zari.

∞∞

Later, after all her presents had been unwrapped and she had changed into her new triceratops pyjamas set, Miraage came to say good night to Zari. She wrapped her arms around Zari and told her it had been the best birthday party ever because Zari had been there, and then, after a small moment of hesitation, said that if Zari took her to the park then life would be perfect!

Zari's stomach clenched. Baz was whirling inside her, cartwheels of excitement, begging her to go to the park, just to see it, just once, and Zari nodded, yes, she'd go to the park, but once, just once.

∞∞

The trips to the park became a daily ritual for Zari and Miraage once the little girl returned from school. While Miraage played in the dinosaur skeleton sandbox, swung from monkey bars, and careened face down on candy-coloured slides, Zari sat on benches, under towering elms, and observed the world in front of her. It was a world without army tanks and guns, without nervous harried expressions and pinched faces, without curfews and nocturnal raids. Instead, dogs chased Frisbees, skateboarders whizzed by, and joggers greeted her with nods. How serene it all was, how peaceful—how unfair. Twice she'd teared up in broad daylight and both times she'd been left alone, people looking at her, then looking away. She was relieved by this indifference, this avoidance, that this was a country where a public crying did not mean a public spectacle. The lack of spectators had made her feel anonymous, safe, better even.

∞∞

Billy jogged in the park whenever he was home from college. He stumbled the first time he saw Zari seated on the bench under the elm trees, her long legs crossed at the ankles. Zari, push! Miraage screamed from the swings. When Zari rose, Billy quickly jogged on. The next day, he saw her gingerly petting a Doberman. And the day after that, she was bouncing on a see-saw with Miraage. She was not all smiles, but neither was she the girl who roamed the corridors at night.

A few days later, Billy saw Zari squatting by the pond, one hand held out to the ducks, while Miraage played in the sand box just a little way off. She looked fragile, a wisp of a girl. Did she just wave? He took a deep breath. Yes. She'd waved. She'd waved at him.

∞∞

Zari stretched her hand out to the ducks, then, overcome, she looked away, her hand flailing through her hair. Billal. On the jogging track. Their eyes met. He strode towards her.

"Hi," he said, standing before her, his hands on his knees, sweat glistening on his forehead. Later, Zari wondered if it was his caring expression, or the concern in his voice, or even his hypnotic breathing that was her undoing, that made her mention the ducks. Or perhaps she was just exhausted of being scared of men, of knowing that even if she was the taller, the wider, the louder, they would still be able to metamorphose into vessels of limitless strength, like tsunamis and earthquakes and tornadoes and infernos. Or perhaps she spoke to him because he was, after all, simply Miraage's older brother.

She said, "I'd like to feed the ducks some day."

"Wait right here," Billy said and he ran to his house, grabbed slices of white bread, and ran back to the park. She was still there. By the edge of the pond. "Hi again," he said, palming his eyes from the sun, "you wanted to feed the ducks?"

☙❧

After that day, Billy tried to orchestrate his visits home to coincide with Zari's afternoons at the park. As a result, he and Zari began to regularly feed the ducks together. They would sit on the embankment, enough space between them to seat a sumo wrestler, and throw crumbs to the chubby quacking ducks gathering by the edge of the pond. In the beginning, they talked about Miraage.

"She knows what she wants," Zari would say.

"She's annoying!" Billy would laugh.

"She is diligent," Zari would persist.

"Another word for being stubborn," Billy would grin.

One afternoon, as the ducks dove for crumbs in the water by the purple hyacinths, Billy told Zari about losing his cousin. How they had all been vacationing at the beach, how the three-year-old Baber had run after the seagull, how they had sprinted after him, and how he had run even faster, laughing, straight into the busy main road.

"My aunt and uncle never had children after that." Billy cleared his throat. "I still dream about Baber."

"Do you believe in spirits?" Zari trailed a finger through the grass. "In ghosts?"

"I guess . . . I mean a few years back, I found a ghost, of sorts."

Zari looked up at Billy.

"I'd been rummaging through some storage boxes in the basement and came upon a storybook with an inbuilt recorder. Baber's voice was trapped in that machine, repeating one phrase for the rest of time '*Baber Billy. Baber Billy. Baber Billy.*'"

"My ghosts are like that," Zari spoke slowly, as if she had to circumvent a knot in her throat. "They're like voices trapped inside of me."

A plane tore through the sky, dragging an advertisement for an insurance company in its wake. Together they gazed at it until it dissolved out of sight.

"I wanted to take revenge." She spoke softly. Billy leaned towards her. "If I were a man, I'd have joined the freedom fighters. There is a group of women I could have joined, but their contribution to the freedom struggle is to crack down on jeans and lipstick." Zari pulled out a blade of grass, twirling it between her fingers. "My sister thought they were insane. My sister was like your sister. She believed she could do anything and everything. She was brave."

"*You* are brave."

Zari gave a bitter laugh.

"I mean it," Billy insisted. "Look at the way you continue to pray." He stopped at the look on her face. "I mean, nothing God does makes any sense half the time."

"I have to believe that whatever happened did so for a reason, and only God can provide a reason great enough. Otherwise, it is all nonsense and I refuse to accept that."

"I repeat, you're very brave."

"I have faith," Zari said simply.

Billy looked at her intently. "I talk to God constantly, but I don't know if I really believe anymore."

"My father used to say God goes on even if one cowers in a corner."

"My Mauj jee would have said something like that." Billy told her then about Mauj jee and the Kashmir trip. "There are moments," he said, fiddling with the zipper on his red windbreaker, "when I don't quite know how to process the," he paused, "the finality of not being able to see someone ever again."

Something inside of Zari cracked open and she found herself divulging her tale to him, to this boy who had helped her with the laundry and had rescued her from a painful Eid. In fits and starts, in bits and pieces, her voice faltering at first, out of practice, as if she were putting together a mosaic from badly cut tiles, she told Billy about the two sets of intruders, the first taking only supplies, and the second taking her entire life. She told him about Azra, the cleaning woman, finding her, about the intruders leaving the ducks alive, about how she sometimes feared she'd go insane with the need to know why they had spared the animals.

"Sometimes, it hurts so much I can't breathe." Zari touched her throat. "Why would they leave the ducks alive?"

"I don't know," Billy said gently. "But I am extremely sorry."

"Sometimes, I think sorry is the stupidest, most impotent word in any language."

Billy didn't speak for a long moment. "But it's better than silence. Anything is better than silence, isn't it?"

7

Shehla's oldest friend in the US was Farah, Fahad's mother. Their friendship, facilitated in the beginning by their living within an agreeable driving distance from each other, had maintained itself over the years. Billy and Fahad had, as a result of the friendship between their mothers, practically grown up together. One summer, the two families ended up vacationing in Lahore at the same time. Billy and Fahad went berserk under the dust-shot sunshine, pretending they were brave explorers and the manicured gardens dangerous jungles. They lay chin down in the lush green grass, their noses tickling the crumbly earth, their antenna eyes slinking after millipedes and beetles. They targeted lizards with air guns and high-fived each other when the lizards turbo-charged into skinny cracks. They caught toads under guava trees, pulsing hearts in their cupped hands, and, once the toads calmed down, let them loose into Salsabil's shirt.

"I hate both of you!" she said, stomping inside.

"Boo hoo hoo!" Fahad and Billy shouted, laughing hysterically and running off to suckle mangoes cooled in buckets of ice on the patio. In between the sticky fingers and thick, sweet juice running down their chins, the five years younger Billy, informed Fahad that Fahad was his best friend no matter what. More than Dan? Fahad asked. More than

Dan, Billy said. They sealed their friendship in a trial by fire, swiping their fingers through the tall flame of a candle they managed to procure from the kitchen.

"My Dada showed me this trick to keep it in longer." Fahad licked his finger before thrusting it into the flame.

"I bet," Billy boasted, "my Dada could have kept his finger there for hours."

"My Dada told me flaming a finger for that long is a physical impossibility."

"But I'm sure my Dada could have done it."

"You never even met your Dada."

"He could still do it!" Billy spoke through gritted teeth. "He could do everything. He was a freedom fighter. And they can do anything in the world."

"I told my Dada about your Dada and all the lions and the djinns and my Dada said if your Dada was *all that*, then he would be in all the history books, and everyone would know his name. But he's not, because he's just a *big lie*."

Billy pushed Fahad to the ground and wrestled him until Fahad broke loose and punched Billy. Their friendship was never the same after that, and to even call it a friendship was a stretch.

∞⬩∞

The day after Miraage's birthday party, Shehla answered the incessant ringing of the doorbell to find Fahad standing on the welcome mat.

"Salaam-ai-laikum Aunty Shehla," Fahad greeted her,

tipping his head respectfully. "I see Billy's car in the driveway, is he in?"

Billy was none too pleased to see Fahad and was even more displeased when Fahad, after five minutes of small talk, informed him that he had misinformed him: according to reliable sources, that pretty girl cutting the cake yesterday was definitely not engaged. Was she home?

After Shehla let Fahad into the house and left him with Billy, she went to check the mailbox at the end of the driveway. Bills, coupons, and a large manila envelope for Zari from her Khala. Shehla went into the kitchen and called Zari to come down. A couple of minutes later, Zari tore open the envelope to find a photograph of a neck-less man with shrubs of salt and pepper sideburns, seated between three young girls of varying ages. Khala's accompanying letter stated that the good man was fifty-two years old and a manager at a clothing store, that his wife had died of cancer, and that, though he had his pick of divorcees and widows, he was interested in someone who resembled his late wife, for his daughters' sakes, so that they could take to their new mother easily. Zari resembled his late wife. She was to think of her mother, Khala signed off, she was to marry him for her mother's sake, if not her own.

"Who's that?" Miraage asked, climbing onto the stool next to Zari.

"Yes, who is that?" Shehla asked, curiosity getting the better of her. Salsabil, just back from work, peered at the photograph, and when Zari told them that he was a prospective groom, Salsabil was aghast.

"You can't marry him. He looks like a frog, a hoary frog. You cannot marry a frog."

"Salsabil," Shehla spoke sharply. "I think Zari's Khala knows better than you what's in Zari's best interest."

Salsabil folded her arms, ready to battle her mother, but Zari broke in.

"Can I . . ." her voice shook. "Can I call Khala?"

∞◦∞

Zari took the phone into the drawing room.

"Please," Khala wept into the phone, "I beg you to say yes. Did not Prophet Muhammad, peace be upon him, wed a woman much older than him? Say yes, Zari, shush wanday, zooh wanday, my breath, my soul. His daughters will treat you more like a big sister than a mother. And, when you have your own children, they will help you take care of them."

She did not want children. She did not want to be a big sister. Or a mother. She did not want marriage.

"You are young right now," Khala yelled, "but you won't be young forever, and you cannot be single for the rest of your life . . . anyone is better than no one. And what do you mean he looks like a frog? *You* are the damaged goods. *You* need your *own* home! I will not hang up, Zari, until you promise to consider the proposal."

"All right, I will consider it," Zari promised. Khala hung up. Zari fumed. But she knew Khala was right. She could not spend the rest of her life shunting from house to house. Sooner or later, she would become that unwanted relative, the one tossed around, tolerated, considered the good deed for the year. She should be thanking God a proposal had come her way, frog or no frog. Pretty girls were dime a dozen, and they neither slashed their arms, nor were they terrorised by nightmares, and they most certainly were not damaged goods.

Zari slipped the photograph back into the envelope and trudged into the kitchen to return the cordless phone to its base. She stopped short in the doorway when she saw Billal and the guy from the birthday party, the guy who'd wanted chocolate cake and not vanilla.

Fahad beamed when he saw Zari. "Hello! How are you? How's it going?"

"Fine, thank you," she mumbled, ignoring Shehla and Salsabil's curious glances.

"What colleges have you looked at so far?"

Colleges? Zari squinted. Of course! This guy was under the impression that she was in the US to look at colleges.

"George Mason," Billy spoke up. "And George Washington. And John Hopkins."

Zari looked at Billal, grateful.

"Excellent," Fahad said. "And what are you planning to study?"

"Environmental engineering," Zari replied automatically.

Salsabil whistled even as Fahad said, "Impressive."

"Very impressive," Billy said, wishing Fahad would stop looking at Zari like that and just go home.

"Fahad, beta," Shehla broke in with a large smile, "Would you like to stay for dinner?"

Over the following weeks, whenever Billy came home from college, Fahad was there too, a regular at the dinner table now, helping to lay the table, carrying the dishes to and from the kitchen, and inviting himself to the chair opposite Zari. And, as if that were not enough, his mother and Miraage, and even Zari, gazed at Fahad as if he was a saint. In fact, Zari looked a little more radiant each time Billy saw her in Fahad's presence, her hair gleaming, her face a little fuller, her plate a little less empty. And he looked at her now, at the dinner table, as she served herself another helping of spaghetti.

Zari took another bite of the Pakistani styled spaghetti on her plate and stole a quick look at Fahad. Lately, she'd been having a recurring dream where Imran was opening the gates to a green pasture, and her mother's soothing voice was whispering in her ears: *When one door shuts, Allah opens another.* Lately, when she caught her reflection in the mirror, she knew she increasingly looked like someone attending a party and not a funeral. Fahad was always complimenting her. Fahad was full of compliments. And he spoke with great confidence, as if he could never be wrong. True, Zari did not like the way he spoke to Billal, but then Billal was equally rude to Fahad. Salsabil had told her that once upon a time they'd been best friends, but that their friendship had not been able to live happily ever after. Despite Salsabil's proclivity towards sarcasm, Zari realised that she was beginning to like the girl, her streak of blue hair, her belly ring, and all.

Across the table, Zari caught Fahad's eye. He smiled at her; she flushed. It was a smile that expected a smile in return. After dinner, as had become usual, Fahad lingered on to ask her if she'd like to go for a movie, or for coffee, or ice-cream, or just a drive? And, as always, she said no, no thank you.

One evening, after a Thai dinner ordered from one of Shehla's favourite restaurants, when they were sitting in the family room, drinking milky tea flavoured with cardamom, Fahad asked Miraage if she wanted to attend the Cherry Blossom Festival in Washington DC? Miraage nodded like a kitten on catnip.

"Then go convince Zari," Fahad said, "because we can't go without her."

"Please," Miraage turned to Zari. "Please please please."

When one door shuts, Allah opens another.

Zari glanced at Shehla, hoping she would withhold sanction, but, when Shehla nodded her blessing, Zari's insides plummeted before ricocheting back up.

Don't you think even your fiancé, God bless his soul, wanted this for you?

"All right, Miraage," she said, her gaze fixed on the calligraphy Allah hanging over the fireplace. "All right, we can go see the blossoms."

⌘

The next morning, an immaculately scrubbed Fahad arrived at the Nabis' house in his gleaming Porsche. He held the passenger door open for Zari even though she would have preferred to sit at the back with Miraage, where Billy, the self-appointed chaperone, sat scowling, his knees pressed up against his chest.

"Zari, you comfortable?" Fahad started the engine. "Because your seat can back up even more."

"Hey!" Billy protested even as Fahad grinned and winked at Zari.

Zari blushed and turned to the window, to the world rushing by outside, to the kaleidoscope of sparkling happiness outside—the azure sky, the emerald trees, the splashes of wild flowers, the silver sheen of the highway stretching out before them like a continuous mirage.

"May I?" Fahad's voice brought Zari back to the inside of the car. He leaned over to take a CD out of the dashboard. Zari pressed up against her seat. She saw a pocket Quran lying inside the dashboard. It was a sign—she was sure of it—a sign from God, a good omen. Fahad closed the dashboard and inserted the CD into the player. Nusrat Fateh Ali's qawwali filled the car.

"This is a Kashmiri dress, isn't it?" Fahad pointed to Zari's outfit.

Zari nodded. She was wearing a pheran, a voluminous tunic reaching down to her calves clad in a shalwar. Delicate embroidery spread in a long inverted triangle down the pheran's front, its sleeves, and down the two wide, slanted side pockets. It was the last outfit her mother had purchased for her, and as Zari had ironed it the night before, she'd felt her mother's hand guiding each stroke of the iron, imparting her blessings.

"It's gorgeous," Fahad said.

Zari blushed at the look he gave her. It seemed a marvel to her that she was even sitting here, alive, contemplating a future. *Future.* The patchiest of words in the whole world.

"You know," Fahad pointed to Zari's collar bone, "my Dadi says that women with moles on their collar bones are very lucky."

"And mine?" Miraage held up an elbow and pointed to a polka dot of a mole.

"Yours," Fahad said solemnly, "means that you are destined for a lifetime's supply of candy!"

"What's des-tinned?" Miraage said.

"It's when," —Fahad glanced at Zari— "you know you've met your soul mate."

Zari's heart somersaulted.

In the back seat, Billy's stomach turned. He wanted to punch himself. Why hadn't he said something like this to Zari instead of asking her stupid questions about God and faith?

"You know, Zari," Fahad continued, "my father told my mother once that although she was the most beautiful woman, there was no beauty like that of the women of Kashmir. I'd say he was a hundred percent right."

Billy scowled, and he was still scowling when Fahad parked the Porsche close to the Tidal Basin. The entire area was packed with people busy photographing the three thousand pink and white cherry blossom trees in full bloom—gifts from Japan in 1912 to foster friendship between the two peoples, Billy read out from the guide book he'd bought along. Billy's mood, however, did not improve as the day progressed. He scowled when Fahad and Zari walked ahead, leaving him to follow with Miraage; when Fahad insisted Zari eat an extra large slice of the cheese pizza they had ordered, although he was pleased when she polished it off; and again when, despite it being his idea, Fahad raced to purchase balloons twisted into floral bracelets for Zari and Miraage.

A little while later, they sat on the steps of the Jefferson Memorial, eating sugar-dusted funnel cakes. Fahad had seated himself one step below Zari and was plying her with the dessert while keeping up a continuous stream of flattering conversation.

"Zari," Fahad said, adjusting his sunglasses, "don't you think Bill-o here looks about ready to have a sunstroke?"

Billy gave Fahad a murderous look.

"Water?" Zari asked, shyly offering Billy her bottle of water.

"No thank you," Billy said, smiling at her unexpected offer.

Zari took a sip of the water herself and was capping the bottle when Fahad held his hand out.

"May I?"

Without a word, Zari handed the bottle to him. Fahad took a giant swig, not taking his eyes off her even once. Anger and frustration bulleted through Billy as Fahad drained the bottle and then promised Zari a lifetime's supply of water. Zari flushed and turned her head in the direction of the memorial and the giant statue behind white pillars.

"Is this the man who said 'by the people, for the people'?"

"Yup," Fahad said, brushing sugar dust off his pants.

"Nope." Billy bristled. "Abraham Lincoln said that.

Zari, this one's Thomas Jefferson, the Declaration of Independence guy. He's the one who wrote, 'We hold these truths to be self-evident, that all men are created equal, that they are endowed by their Creator with certain inalienable rights, among these are Life, Liberty, and the pursuit of Happiness.'"

Fahad hooted derisively. "But let's not forget that he owned slaves, and that the Native Americans were deprived of their rights, their lives, liberties, and happiness."

"Do you think," Billy said even as he nodded permission to Miraage to join a group of kids playing handball right in front of them, "that it's possible for someone as perfect as yourself to forgive the mistakes made by those who lived a century ago?"

"Some mistakes," Fahad shrugged, "are unpardonable."

"Do you really believe that?" Zari's voice was quiet.

"Yes," Fahad said. "Absolutely."

"Billal?" Zari said.

"I don't know," Billy said. He stretched his legs before him and put his hands behind his head. "I want to believe that everyone can be forgiven, but then there are people like Hitler . . ."

"You just proved my point," Fahad said. "Unpardonable."

"But there has to be a middle ground," Zari said softly, "between something being completely pardonable and something being unpardonable."

"Bill-o here hopes to solve all such philosophical problems that plague the world. But before that," Fahad grinned, "he needs to decide on a major." He held up his hands as Billy glared at him. "What! Your mom was regaling mine with tales about your indecisiveness. May I suggest computers or information technology? Goldmine fields these days."

"Not all of us obsess about the pursuit of money," Billy said. "Some of us want to change the world."

"All of us want to change the world, except that some of us don't mind making money in order to afford our philanthropy. What do you think Zari, what makes more of a difference, funded or unfunded good intentions?

"Please stop it," Zari said in a voice she hadn't used in ages. "Both of you."

She sat up, the sun gleaming behind her like her very own halo, her loose hair gathered over one shoulder, her eyes bright, her voice resolute as she repeated her injunction: Stop it.

Fahad jumped up. "I'm so sorry, Zari." He playfully punched Billy's shoulder. "Really, Billaloo and I are like brothers, aren't we Billaloo?"

Billy nodded for if he disagreed, he'd look like a jerk, and he kicked himself for not being the one to call a truce if only to placate Zari.

On the trip back home, Fahad asked Zari if she would meet his family. Was she free for dinner this weekend? Zari stared at the balloon bracelet on her wrist, and, finally, she nodded, yes, yes she would meet them.

In the back seat, Billy drew in a sharp breath and adjusted Miraage's dozing head on his shoulder. At this rate, by next week, he'd be attending their wedding.

8

Billy hovered around the den. He could see Zari glancing at the phone even as she helped Miraage assemble a jigsaw puzzle. Two days had passed since the trip to DC, and Fahad, let alone visiting Zari or following up on his dinner invitation, had not even called her once. Billy ruffled Miraage's pompom ponytail as he skulked past yet again. Zari's dismay enveloped her like a second skin. Billy couldn't believe she was the same girl who'd been so alive during the trip. She'd been glowing that day and she had waltzed back into the house a different person.

When the phone rang a little later, Zari brightened, but it was for Shehla, and Zari's disappointment was palpable. She told Miraage that she'd be right back and then disappeared into the guest room. Minutes later, Billy knocked on her door and, at a faint yes, entered. She was on the prayer mat, her palms cupped upwards in prayer, tears cutting her cheeks.

"Nothing is wrong," she said when he asked her.

"Zari—"

"Nothing is wrong, Billal." Her voice was sharp. "What could possibly be wrong?"

Billy returned to his room and slammed the door shut.

Zari's reticence was Fahad's fault. Kicking a pile of clothes out of his way, he punched a pillow on his bed before flopping down on it. It was late in the night when Billy dialled Fahad's number.

"Hello?"

"Fahad, its Billy."

"Billal?" Fahad's sleepy voice wavered. "How . . . how's Zari?"

"Why haven't you come over?"

"I meant to . . . I can't face her . . . feel wretched . . . for God's sake, I wanted to marry her."

"What the hell happened?"

"You don't know?"

"Don't know what?"

"Go ask your Mom."

"Spit. It. Out."

❧❧

When Billy got off the phone, he staggered to Salsabil's room and woke her up. Together they decided to confront their parents who had fallen asleep to *America's Funniest Home Videos,* the flickering TV light casting shadows on their sleeping faces and their bedroom walls. Billy turned off the TV and switched on his mother's bedside lamp, patting her shoulder even as Salsabil squatted beside their snoring father.

"Mom, Dad," Billy said. "Wake up."

"What's wrong?" Amman squinted in the lamp light.

Shehla shot up. "Miraage? Is Miraage—"

"She's fine, Mom," Salsabil said. "She's fine."

"Then what is wrong with you two?" Shehla's voice snapped with relief. "What time is it?" She glanced at the digital clock on her bedside table proclaiming 2:00 a.m. "Scaring us like this!"

"Is it true?" Billy asked. "What happened to Zari?"

Shehla and Amman glanced at each other.

"Was she raped?" Salsabil asked. "Was Zari gang-raped?"

"Salsabil! Your father is in the room!" Shehla looked at Amman, his tongue pressed between his teeth in distress. "Show some respect! I knew I should never have let your father convince me to let her come here. Talking about such a subject in front of your father!"

"How is saying *rape* being disrespectful?"

Mother and daughter stared each other down. Billy winced. Memory blistered his mind like water sizzling on a scorching pan. He remembered Zari in the hallway the night he'd heard her crying, the night he'd thought to inform her that life goes on. He remembered the way she'd jumped when she saw him, as if he was a wild animal.

"Why did we have to find out from Fahad?!" Billy's voice shook. He was standing with his arms crossed over his chest because otherwise, he feared his heart would bulldoze its way out. "Dad, you should have told us."

"I told you we should tell them, Shehla," Amman said. "I told you they would find out."

Shehla glared at Amman before turning to Billy. "You

kids do not need to be burdened with such information."

"We're not *kids*." Billy's voice cracked. He wished his mother would stop acting as if he and his sisters were made of crystal, forever a mere moment away from shattering.

"How can Fahad just dump her like this?" Salsabil put her hands on her hips. "It's not fair."

"Because," Shehla said, "his mother doesn't want him to be saddled with a girl who is emotionally crippled. Is that such a crime?"

Salsabil snorted. "Why'd he listen to her?"

"Because the Malik children respect their parents, unlike you two."

"It's because she's not a virgin, isn't it?" Salsabil said.

"Don't be ridiculous," Shehla said. "That's not her fault." She looked Salsabil up and down. "She's not some girl with loose morals."

"Dad!" Salsabil turned to Amman. "Fahad was going to marry her! Does no one get it? What if they were married? Would Fahad have divorced Zari? He didn't even have the decency to talk to her himself!"

"Talk?" Shehla's nostrils flared. "In our culture, it is not considered good to talk about such things."

"We're in the US," Billy said.

"And that means what?" Shehla said. "That we should become besharam and behaya, shameless and immodest?"

Billy's hands balled into tight fists. He was a fool. A mere change of geography could not change people. At least not people like his mother. No matter how many skirts she wore or apple pies she baked, she wouldn't change.

"I'll bet its people like you and Fahad," Salsabil said, "who drive girls to suicide."

Shehla's eyes glinted with anger. "This is neither a film, Salsabil, nor are we backward folk. No one is telling anyone to kill themselves! Fahad's parents want what is best for him, and what is best for him is to not be burdened with a girl like Zari. Again I ask you two, is it a crime to want the best for your kids?"

"No," Billy said, "but it's a crime to ignore what your kids want."

"Doesn't our experience count for anything?" Shehla said. "We are telling you—"

"Only," Billy said, "what you want to tell us."

Shehla blew air out of her cheeks. "We didn't tell you about Zari because she holds dear the same values that you so readily dismiss. It is that simple."

"Don't, Mom." Salsabil shook her head. "Don't even try to turn this around and make it sound like you didn't tell us about Zari because you wanted to protect her. There's a difference between privacy and deliberate concealment of facts. What if I was raped, huh? Would you tell me to shut up? Would you hide me away? Pretend that nothing has happened? Would you want me to kill myself because it would make life easier for you?"

There was a second, a split second so minute, so miniscule, so microscopic that even time found it hard to squeeze through and yet, it seemed to Billy that it was too long of a second before his parents shook their heads, but, by that time, Salsabil had already left the bedroom even though they were both calling out her name. They turned to him then.

"If your father and I," Shehla was saying, "really thought there was something wrong with . . . with being . . . would we have allowed Zari in our home?"

They looked lost and Billy felt orphaned by their silent need for him to parent them. He wanted to put his arms around them, console them, tell them they were not bad people or part of the problem, but he couldn't, so he left, even as they called out for him.

Salsabil was in her bedroom, pacing, a pillow clutched to her chest.

"They didn't mean it, Salsa." Billy sank into her loveseat. "They're just upset."

"You're taking their side!" Salsabil tossed the pillow onto the bed and glared at him.

"Why does everything have to come down to sides with you?"

"Because in *real* life, sides are all that matter!"

"Come on," Billy rose. "Let's go tell Zari that Fahad has abandoned her."

"Do Fahad's dirty work for him, you mean."

"Someone has to. Come on, let's go."

Midway to Zari's room, Billy turned to Salsabil, his mouth grim. "Look, do you think Mom has a point? Might Zari feel awkward knowing I know? I mean," Billy shook his head, "I feel awkward now that I know."

"You, Fahad, Mom, Dad, you're all the same!"

"Whoa—"

"All of you just worry about yourselves. How can you men even do such things to women?"

"*Us* men?" Billy's mouth fell open. "That's a bit harsh, isn't it? Calm down."

"Don't tell me to calm down! You want to change the world, Billy? How? By calming down? By floating through it? Hold on," Salsabil began to clap. "You have changed the world. You read about Kashmir obsessively only so you can come across some mention of our grandfather, your hero. You weep over Hitler's Henchmen. You read to the legally blind. You spent one Thanksgiving at a soup kitchen. You donated blood not once, but twice and," she gave him a thumbs-up, "every time you see one of those sponsor-a-kid advertisements, you swear one day you're going to do exactly that. What a fool you are, couch saviour."

Billy backed his car out of the garage and screeched down the road, headlights eating into the dark of night. His hands trembled as he swerved onto the freeway towards the college campus. He was sick of Salsabil's taunts when all he did was try his best to make a difference. What the hell did she expect him to say to Zari? The only rape victims he knew—if listening to strangers' personal stories meant knowing them—were the girls who spoke out during demonstrations in college. He wouldn't have known what to say to those girls willing to share their stories with strangers, so what in the world could he possibly say to Zari? I'm sorry your family was killed and I'm sorry that you were raped and

I'm even sorrier that Fahad turned out to be a jerk. *I'm sorry.* Even Fahad had said he was sorry. Sorry. Zari was right. Perhaps it was better to remain silent because the stupidest, most impotent word in any language was sorry.

9

They pushed, pulled, stripped, slapped, climbed, dripped, pointed,

watched flesh shy   away   from their fingers,

watched it   crawl back

shame-faced   into itself

laughing

at

hands knees hair

flailing to life

just to cover

punctured

BODYparts

Zari bolted up in bed. She hadn't had this dream for a long time. Not since Fahad's interest in her had ended abruptly. She had suspected something was wrong the very first evening when Fahad did not show up after the cherry blossom trip; the second evening, she was convinced. She'd gone to her room to pray, to demand of God an explanation for giving her false hope, but, when Billal knocked and asked what was wrong, his whole being pulsing with gentle concern, pity even, the full extent of her foolish dreams broke over her: it was this country, these people, who had lured her into forgetting herself—her Khala was right, she was *damaged goods*.

Late in the night—she'd found some relief in cutting herself, but sleep had eluded her—she'd heard an engine start up and she saw, from the window, Billal's car screeching out of the driveway. This morning, Salsabil had knocked on her door. They had not known, Salsabil told her. They had all been in the dark. She, Billy, Fahad. No one had told them about her rape.

The word, spoken out loud, assaulted Zari like a physical blow. It had not occurred to her that they did not know, but, with this face-to-face confirmation that they now did, Zari's insides ached. She'd stared at the glossy fashion magazine Salsabil had handed to her, pointing to a headline between *Dieting Tips* and *Trendy Spring Outfits—Date Rape Survivor Stories*. She had urged her to read the article because, Salsabil had insisted before leaving, *it* is not *your* fault.

Zari had put the magazine down. But, during the day, she kept glancing at the headline, right beside the model's elbow, as if even she was protecting herself from the story. All day Zari avoided looking the Nabis in the eyes, ashamed of the fact that they *knew*. It wasn't until that night, when she'd sunk into the armchair, cradling the magazine in her lap, that she finally opened it. She flipped past advertisements for perfumes, hair dye, collagen creams, fat-loss aids, teeth whiteners, anti-ageing potions, advice on how to drive *him* wild in bed until she finally came upon the article.

Four survivors. All but one now married. Their husbands were also photographed, as if *it* was nothing. Zari stared at the photographs. She tried hard to find herself in the robust smiles of these women from a seemingly different planet. And the men who'd married them, they were aliens too. But instead of solace and hope, the stories convinced Zari that Fahad had taken the culturally-appropriate action and that, although *it* was not her fault, she *was* to blame for dreaming the impossible. For hoping.

Zari went into the bathroom. She rolled up her sleeve and put razor to skin, waiting for relief and wishing, for the hundredth time, that she'd died with her family or that she was strong enough to ignore Islam's injunction against suicide. Afterwards, she left the room to pace through the silent house. Tiny lights, some blinking, some still, traced her movements like the eyes of accusatory predators—the red power button on the computer monitor, the amber on the handset of the cordless phone, the green digital numbers on the microwave, the blue oval on the refrigerator. Zari curled up on the kitchen floor, trying to battle the echoes, the shadows, the soundless weeping, or was it laughing, of the spirits.

Shehla backed out of the driveway as fast as she could. She had found Zari in the morning on the kitchen floor, rocking to and fro, and, as soon as Zari had requested to see the psychiatrist, Shehla had rushed to bundle her into the car. They were headed towards the clinic now, Shehla driving as fast as she could manage, and Zari sitting next to her, listless, hunched into herself, eyes shut. Shehla thought it was best to just let her be. The poor girl wanted help, and despite the circumstances, that was hope.

In the psychiatrist's waiting room, Zari hesitated over the forms she'd been given to fill. Did she have a *history*? Migraine? Depression? Schizophrenia? Dementia? No. No. No. No. When she was done, the receptionist whipped the forms away and slid shut the glass panel, but not before she gave—Zari was sure she did—*a look*. Zari broke into a sweat, and even though there was an empty seat across the room, she found herself sitting on the couch next to Shehla, who looked up and smiled at her with encouragement. Shehla's face held an expectation that flooded Zari with dread. A door leading into a hallway opened. A heavy-set woman with gentle ebony eyes stood on crutches, a calf bulging out of a cast.

"Zari Zoon?"

Zari rose.

"I'm Dr Wasti. Please call me Sarah." Sarah bade Zari to follow her down the hallway, and in a friendly voice mentioned the cast was on account of a skiing accident. Zari stepped into Sarah's coffee-scented office and sank into a wing-backed armchair opposite Sarah's and prayed that this psychiatrist could make sense of the events—heal her once and for all. She looked at the certificates hanging on a wall, the cabinet crammed with books, a small cactus in a planter, on the desk a glass bowl full of mints and a photo of two little girls on a beach, kneeling before a sandcastle, their dark chocolate complexions gleaming against the yellow straps of their bathing suits.

Zari turned as Sarah settled into the opposite armchair and elevated her cast onto a footstool. Five fuchsia toenails glared at Zari from the cast.

Zari's heart swelled with pain as Sonea's toenails flashed before her eyes, the colour of flames. She told herself the world delivered reminders of loss everywhere and that she had to learn to absorb them without letting them absorb her. She told herself she could cope. She had to cope. Sarah's toes twitched.

"Zari?"

Zari blanched.

"Are you all right?"

She was not, and she leapt up and ran out of the room, down the hall, and into the waiting area. The receptionist shrank behind the glass panel. Shehla sprang up. Zari opened her mouth but no sound came out. Sarah hobbled behind her. The two women silently walked her to the car, Zari trying not to stare at Sarah's toes.

They drove back in a silence thick with failure, and though Zari shut her eyes the entire ride, she was not blind to Shehla's censure and pity. Shehla had barely pulled into the garage, when Zari, terrified of entering the house where she was sure the ghosts were waiting to laugh at her, bolted out of the car and ran down the road.

Billy was walking to his anthropology class when his cell phone rang. Salsabil, but she was talking too fast, and the only two words he heard were Zari and missing. Billy turned towards the campus parking lot, got into his car, and drove straight to the park where he and Zari had made a routine of feeding the ducks at the lake. But she was not anywhere to be seen, not by the banks of the lake, not by the slides or the swings, not on any of the benches. He ran along the jogging trail but she was not there either. Not at the skateboard ramps, or the basketball court, or by the dog park. He jammed his hands into his pockets, deciding to head home and get the details of what exactly had happened. He was trudging back to his car, when, on an impulse, he turned once more to the pond, and by pure chance, caught a glimpse of Zari through a crack in the wall of conifers by the water's edge.

He was by her side within minutes and when she saw him, she buried her face in her hands.

"Look at me, Zari," Billy pleaded, wishing he could take her in his arms and just hold her. "Please look at me. I heard about this morning." He searched desperately for the right words to say. "My parents are frantic. Are you okay? Just look at me."

Zari did not look at him. Her eyes were threatening to brim over at his kindness, his concern. She spoke, in as steady a voice as she could manage, that she had not meant to scare anyone, but after her panic attack at the clinic, she'd needed to be alone.

"How did you know I was here?"

"I guessed." Billy sat down beside her. "I'm going to kill Fahad. I'd never let you down like he did. I wish . . . I wish . . ."

Zari turned away from him sharply and stared at the lake. She did not want him to see the tears she could not control. It was early afternoon and the sunshine fluttering through the oak trees dappled the lake into a medley of ever-changing spots. It was a tableau that had always cheered her, but today, the unpredictability and the inconstancy left her bereft.

"I'm going to accept the proposal Khala sent to me." Zari had not known she was going to say this, let alone share it with him, but now that she had blurted the words out, she felt better. If nothing else, it was a plan, a way to leave the house, these people, and go elsewhere.

Billy frowned. "You can't marry the Frog! You don't love—"

"He's offering me a home."

"Four walls and a ceiling," Billy scoffed, quoting from some poem the title of which he couldn't remember, "do not mean home."

"That's what people who have homes can afford to say. But Khala is right. Marriage is the solution and a husband, he is security."

She was crying in earnest now. A woman jogging by glanced at Zari. Then she looked at Billy and shook her head. It's not me! Billy wanted to shout, his heart lurching, it's them.

But wasn't he a part of this 'them'? What exactly had he done so far to help Zari heal? That's why she'd come here, to America, to their house, wasn't it, to heal? But how was that to happen? By babysitting Miraage? By going for Salsabil's exercise classes? By writing in that rainbow journal his mother had handed her?

Billy felt helpless. He had come here to tell Zari that all men were not the same, that they weren't all like Fahad, that *he* wasn't like that jerk. And that he, Billy Nabi, loved her. He loved her. Billy swallowed. Yes, it *was* true. He *did* love her. But here she was, telling him that she was going to marry some frog because she needed security. Anger overtook Billy, anger at his mother, his father, at Fahad, at Zari's Khala, at the Frog, at the whole world.

"Let's get married."

"What?" Zari stilled.

"I said let's get married."

"What do you mean?"

"Will you marry me?"

"You don't know what you're saying."

"I love you. I've been in love with you since before Fahad came into the picture and, you know what, I'm glad Fahad's out."

Zari winced.

"Zari," Billy continued tenderly, "do you remember the night I saw you in the corridor, crying? I will never forget it. You looked so brave, so determined to survive everything. I know you like Fahad because he pursued you, but his interest was fickle." Billy's voice softened. "*I love you.* You're sweet and kind and pure and—"

"I'm *not* pure."

"Yes you *are.*"

"I'm damaged goods."

"You're not a dented can of soup."

A small smile tugged at the corner of Zari's lips despite herself. "Everyone else thinks so."

"I don't care what *everyone else* thinks. You're brave. You're an inspiration. You're a survivor, Zari. You're a heroine for surviving what you have, for surviving *everything.*"

"Don't be ridiculous!" Zari's mouth shook a little now. "I'm a joke."

"I'm not laughing, am I? Look Zari, we'll get married, okay, and—"

"Stop it!" She cut him short. "Your parents will never agree."

"Who cares?"

"Who cares!"

Billy nodded. "We're over eighteen. We don't need their permission. We simply won't tell them until—"

"You are going to deceive your family! And you're asking me to deceive them as well!"

"It's not deceit. We'll just keep it a secret till—"

"Keep it a secret? A dirty little secret, that's what life has turned me into." Distress clouded Zari's face. "I can't betray your parents." She shook her head emphatically. "They took me in. They've been trying to help me. What will they think of me?"

"So you'd rather marry a man you can't bear looking at? Listen, just think about it, okay? I'll get the license today, it takes two days for it to go into effect. All you have to do is think about it."

Zari thought about it as she handed Billy her birth

certificate, he required it, he said, for getting the marriage license issued. She thought about it as she looked at the license he returned with later that same day. She thought about it as she explained to Shehla the trigger that was the fuchsia nail paint on Dr Sarah's toenails. She thought about it even as she apologised for running away and worrying the Nabis. Shehla and Amman, tight smiles on their faces, worry in their eyes, said they understood. That she was not to apologise. That she should take her time. That they were not going to abandon her.

And, unknown to them, their son was asking her to repay their kindness by marrying him on the sly.

For two days Zari did not leave the prayer mat. For two days everything was a blur alternating between frightening confusion and vague certainty. A fog seethed within her, blanking everything. Nothing made sense. Only Billy's voice rang in her ears. Trust me, he had said. Trust me. I'll get a campus job. Acquire campus housing. Something will work out. I will make something work out. I am going to take care of you. Together we will make a home. My parents will be in an uproar no matter who I marry at this point in my life, so it's not you. I am sorry your family is gone. I can't bring them back. But we can miss them together. Mourn them together.

Marry me, he said, marry me. I love you.

His tone so sincere, his manner so earnest that all she could think was what's wrong with this boy for wanting to marry someone like her? Say yes, her Khala would have pled, say yes, you silly girl, to whoever is willing to marry you.

Zaar, he had said, *I'll be your home.*

Four days after Billy had found her in the park, Zari found herself outside the Fredericksburg County Courthouse, guilt gnawing at her as she sat on a sun-warmed bench, holding the lone long-stemmed rose Billy had given her. She toed a weed growing from a crack in the sidewalk. This was her wedding. No henna, no platters of dry fruits, no giggling friends, no joyful yet weepy mother, no sombre yet happy father greeting guests at the front door, no Baz dashing around demanding attention, no sister beaming with delight, no shower of gold coins, no wanawun of older women swaying as they sang their blessing, no garlands to greet the bridegroom, no jewellery, no bridal finery, no ecstasy on the day that was supposed to be the pinnacle of her life.

"Listen, Billal," Zari took a deep breath and looked up from the rose, "Listen."

"What it is?" Billy squatted before her.

"Are you . . . are you sure you want to do this? Marriage is not some game that—"

"It's not a game." Billy sat beside her and looked into her eyes.

"I mean . . ." Zari broke off and glanced away. She was afraid. Not only was she going to marry Billy behind his parents' back, thereby deceiving her benefactors in the process, but she was also *not* getting married in a mosque. And when she had said as much to Billal, he had pointed out that a mosque would mean that his parents would find out about their marriage, thanks to the grapevine, even before they returned home. A Muslim ceremony, therefore, was out of question for now.

"Billal," she spoke again, "marriage is forever and you have to be sure you want someone like me."

Billy sighed and stood up. Seated on the bench under the canopy of trees, Zari looked like a painting come to life, but he wished she didn't look so grave. He would change that. He would return to her life all the love and joy and hope and security there was. He would do it even if it killed him.

Eager to get things underway, Billy scouted the parking lot for Dan and Ameer. Over eighteen years of age, he and Zari didn't require parental permission to marry, but they did require two witnesses, therefore, Billy had asked his friends, Dan and Ameer, to step in. When Billy had broken the news to them, Ameer had congratulated him, saying it would be his pleasure to witness a love story, but Dan had been horrified: "Dude, you can't just up and marry someone like that." Billy hadn't asked if the 'like that' referred to the person or the time frame. He hadn't wanted to know.

∞∞

An hour later, they were standing before the Justice of Peace in a small room with a lectern, a beige carpet, and two chairs separated by a vase of artificial carnations.

"I do," Billy said.

"And do you, Zarina Zoon, take this man . . ."

∞∞

After the ceremony, Billy beamed at Zari. He had a surprise for her—reservations at a Kashmiri restaurant for lunch. For a moment, pure delight engulfed her, but the next instant she clouded over. She couldn't, she mumbled. She just couldn't bear to eat Kashmiri food.

"Anywhere else," she said, stroking the petals of her lone rose. "Anywhere else is fine."

They walked to the Mexican restaurant round the corner. Dan and Ameer tried to make conversation, but it was stilted and stiff at best. Billy tried to put himself in their position. Though Zari's story would have unnerved him too, he would, nevertheless, have tried to find something to talk to her about, something about movies or music or books, or even just the weather. He would certainly not have sat there smiling ineptly, fingering his dreadlocks like Ameer or tracing some pattern in the plain green table cloth like Dan. And he would have definitely not gone on and on about how he'd always been the Patron Saint of Lost Causes and how he'd always gotten involved in every club—chess, fencing, drama—only to lose interest half way through. Getting increasingly irritated, Billy looked at Zari sitting next to him and picking her enchiladas apart. She looked dazed. Were his *friends* demented? Why were Dan and Ameer regaling her with stories of his failures? Billy couldn't wait for the meal to end.

Later, after the boys had left telling Zari how nice it had been to have met her, Billy and Zari drove home in an uncomfortable silence with the *Best Mix of Yesterday and Today* serenading them over the radio. Billy glanced at Zari, wishing she would say something, anything to end the silence. He could've started a conversation, but he was scared of saying the wrong thing. It was done: they were married. And there, in the dashboard, lay the proof: his marriage certificate.

He loved Zari. That was the truth. He loved her and he was going to take care of her, his wife. *Wife*. Mrs Billal Nabi.

He was responsible for her livelihood, her safety, her healing, for her very happiness; it was his *duty*.

Billy wanted to caress Zari's cheek, but he was too shy to even hold her hand. As for asking her what she was thinking, he was terrified of what she might reply. Was she regretting it? Was she even thinking about him, them, Fahad? Marriage was forever, she'd said. Marriage was forever and she was thinking of them. She was staring out the window. It could not have been a more beautiful day outside—clusters of sapphire chicory and orange lilies abounded in the median and the dazzling sky held silver clouds in its palm. Thank God he'd at least gotten her the rose, even though she was stroking it to death, and he wished he'd had the presence of mind to have gotten the car cleaned, but ever since his proposal in the park, he'd operated under a focused blur.

Billy cleared his throat. "Zaar."

Zari turned and looked at him as if for the first time.

"I have another gift for you. It's nothing big, just something very precious to me. It's in the dashboard."

Zari opened the dashboard and found a miniature squirrel carved from wood. Billy told Zari about Mauj jee's factotum, Shafi, carver of wooden animals and rescuer from impromptu demonstrations. How this wooden animal was Shafi's departure gift when they had—Billy swallowed bitterly—run away from danger even as others remained because they had no choice.

Zari looked at Billy as if he was a human hieroglyphic which she was, suddenly, for a moment, able to decipher. She told him that this memory of his that she was holding in the palm of her hand, was fashioned from walnut wood, the dark kind from the roots, she said, the good kind. The squirrel was unpolished and Zari believed she could smell the earth the tree had grown on, feel the saw that had felled the tree, taste the grain as it split apart, this piece of wood chiselled into being by Shafi, a Kashmiri boy she would never know, and yet, whose creation meant so much to her husband that it was the first keepsake he was giving to his wife. Zari closed her palm around the squirrel and imbibed its warmth.

"Billal," she turned to him as if the wood's pulse had prompted her to life, "there's a place I'd like to visit."

They drove to the graveyard in silence. In silence they walked to Baber's resting place, his child's grave ludicrously tiny under their lengthening shadows. An adult's grave was distressing, Zari thought, but a child's was macabre. Like Baz's grave must be, she imagined. She stood before Baber's grave and cupped her hands, her lips moving in prayer, for Baber, and for her own dead. She brushed leaves off the little headstone, her fingers tracing over his engraved name, birth date, death date; these three details all that remained for the world to witness.

"Billal," Zari held the rose he'd given her, "do you mind if I use this?"

Before he could even respond, she scattered the petals on the tomb, and when she was done, she turned to him with a sad smile and she took his hand, the hand that had brushed clean the tombstone, and they walked back to the car, hand in hand.

In the parking lot, their hands parted, and in the car

Billy clutched the steering wheel and Zari kept her hands clasped in her lap. With every passing moment, their former intimacy seemed an aberration brought on by grief and regret at lives having been cut short, an aberration that caused even strangers, in times of need, to join the lifelines on their palms.

∞∞∞

Billy let Zari off at the park from where she would walk home alone. See you, he said, as if he was dropping off an acquaintance. She nodded, small, quick, already twisting away like a fish escaping a net. He recalled how she'd leaned into him at Baber's grave, allowing him to support her and, swallowing the lump in his throat, he turned off the radio and drove back to campus with his worries for company. From the moment he'd proposed, he'd been floating. He'd entered some other being, a being somewhat in control of what he was doing; that being had left the car with her. He recalled the way her face had lit up when he'd promised to have something figured out within a month. He sucked in his breath. The ludicrous time frame of a month had randomly popped out of his mouth and now he was scared. What could possibly be accomplished in a month?

Billy considered telling Salsabil, but he was afraid she would expose the secret marriage during an argument with their parents. Logistics—he needed to concentrate on logistics. Immediately check out couple's housing on campus. What if his parents refused to continue paying tuition once they found out? Perhaps it was wiser to just tell them. They would be upset, but once the shock wore off, they'd also be ecstatic that he'd married a desi girl, and his Dad would surely be ecstatic that he'd married a Kashmiri, and his mother that Zari was Muslim and religious. No. He was a married man now and did not want to hear his mother's views on the matter. He would deal with it. He would deal with everything.

10

Mummy, he calls me Zaar. You would have started to call me Zaar too.

I married him, Mummy. We got married today.

Rest in peace, Mummy . . . for I am married. Today. For you.

Your Zari—Zaar—is married.

The words stared up at her from the page, the blue ink cold against the stripes of the rainbow, and yet, for all the treachery involved in getting married behind the Nabis' backs, seeing the reality of her marriage inscribed in ink was marvellous. Marvellous, but unbelievable and surreal and of seemingly no consequence until Khala called later in the day, pressing her yet again with the widower's proposal, and Zari, hesitant, but feeling empowered, had refused it once and for all. And even though she could not disclose the reason for her refusal, the power to refuse was a gift, a splash of water upon parched land, a gift given to her by Billal.

But as the day drew to a close, Zari's elation deflated. Billy had married her, and she was beyond grateful to him, but now what? What was he expecting once he returned home?

Zari reopened the journal.

I am scared. I cannot do that.

Billy drove around in circles for an hour, increasingly reluctant to go home, to see Zari, scared of what he thought she was expecting he was expecting. Sex was on his mind, this was true, but it was the concern of how to assure her that he expected nothing. He just wanted to be in her presence, them, together, because he needed to ease himself into the role of a *husband*. He couldn't wait to see Zari, his *wife*, but he couldn't forget how she'd fled from the car in the afternoon or how, when the Justice of Peace had said he could kiss the bride and he had bent down to kiss her, she had shied away, or how, despite holding hands at the graveyard, his closeness had otherwise made her flinch. Finally he just drove home, climbed the stairs, stood outside her door, knocked gently, and upon her faint come in, went in.

Zari stood in the centre of the room, freshly showered, her hair dripping onto her pale yellow shirt. Billy could not look away and so he soldiered on.

"Hello," he said shyly.

Zari blinked.

He handed her a gift bag he'd put together at a drug store on the way home. Inside were bath crystals in a heart-shaped sachet, a cinnamon scented votive, and a brownie.

Zari took the bag from him and without a word, put the brownie on the table and took the bag into the bathroom. Billy followed her into the steamy bathroom and watched as Zari put the sachet and the votive in a basket on the rim of the tub. He stumbled on a discarded towel lying on the floor and bumped into her. His eyes met hers, and she shrank as if she feared the enclosed space, feared *him*.

"You know what," Billy said, "I have to be up early tomorrow morning so I'm going to bed. To sleep. I mean sleep. Alone. You know." He left before he could embarrass himself any further.

∞∞∞

Zari sat on the rim of the bathtub, staring at the sachet and the candle in the basket. She felt as if a handful of embers had been placed in her cold, sore, unsafe spots and she prayed: Thank you God for who he is even if he is disdainful of you, even if I don't know why he has saved me, even if I am a secret for now, even if I cannot consummate the marriage. She could not consummate the marriage, the ghosts agreed, but, and her mother's voice rose like a gale, there were other wifely duties she could, and she must, perform. And so, the next morning, when the house was empty, Zari slipped into Billy's bedroom. It was her first time alone in a man's room. But he wasn't just any man, she reminded herself, he was her *husband*.

Her husband's room, she saw now, was even messier than his car. She picked up chewing gum wrappers and cola cans that had fallen just short of the trash can. She made his bed and folded the clothes littering the floor. She looked under his bed and threw out a can substituting as an ashtray. She stacked the heap of CDs into the CD shelf and arranged the bookshelf, a mix of history and philosophy and politics and fiction. Touching and organising his belongings was imbuing her with an intimacy far greater than what she had ever known or felt, an intimacy that suggested she belonged here, in Billal's bedroom, that she was safe, that there was hope, and though memory pricked and prodded, the ghosts in her heart, for once, were calm and quiet.

That night, Billy cut his last class to come home early. He returned to a bedroom that, while still being his, had clearly been taken over by another. Later that night, he knocked on Zari's door.

"Did you clean it?"

She nodded.

"You don't have to."

"I wanted to," she said, and then, her face burning, "I found cigarette butts. You shouldn't smoke, it's bad for you."

"I seldom do."

"Promise me," she looked at him quickly, "you never will."

"I promise."

He handed her another bag. She shook the contents out into her lap: a vanilla bath sachet, a vanilla votive, and a macadamia toffee bar. She broke the toffee bar into two and handed him half.

Sharing a sweet, while the house slept, became a nightly ritual after that. Strained silences gradually filled up with the patter of conversation about favourite things, and awkwardness made way for the creation of comfortable spaces. Zari's black shawl with its glimmering silver trimmings slid off her shoulder one night as they sat talking. It pooled onto the floor by her feet and just lay there, a gathering of fabric, neither guardian nor gateway. One night, they stepped out of Zari's room into the hallway lit with a dim nightlight and Zari peered at walls covered with framed photographs.

"Is that Gulmarg?" she asked, recognising the scenic

resort two hours away from Srinagar in a photograph where Shehla sat astride a horse in a meadow. Billy nodded. Look, he said, pointing to a picture in which Shehla stood preening next to a movie star she had met there.

"Halcyon days . . ." Zari sighed and crossed her arms. She was clutching the ends of her long sleeves in her palms and Billy was overwhelmed with the desire to kiss her fingertips, her wrists, the inside of her elbows.

"Is that Dan?" Zari pointed to the boy splashing in an inflatable pool with Billy.

"Yup." Billy noticed that she'd avoided the photo next to it of him and Fahad. Walking ahead, he pointed to another picture. "This is my mother's brother, Uncle Buraaq, and his wife, Aunt Barbara. Baber was their son."

Zari looked at the droopy-eyed man standing behind a chubby woman, flaxen tendrils escaping her striped hijab, the black and white lines enhancing the pale blue of her eyes.

"And this is Baber."

A stocky toddler munched on his fist. Zari stared at the boy for a moment before turning abruptly to another photograph and asked, all too brightly, "And what's this?"

Billy looked at the picture in which Salsabil was pinching him and he was wailing with his mouth wide open.

"My sister always had it in for me," Billy said playfully.

"I wonder what you did to provoke her right before the camera clicked."

A quiet thrill ran through Billy at her instinctive understanding that the present was not an isolated incident but a continuation of the past. She was his soul mate. He

172

had no doubt.

"I love you, Zaar, I really do."

She smiled and came to stand in front of the black and white photographs, a time when people approached the probing lens of a camera warily and with quiet dignity.

"Actually," Billy said, glad for their need to whisper, a need that allowed him to stand close to Zari, "photographs make me sad. Passed down from family member to family member until they're just meaningless pieces of wallpaper." He pointed to an oval copper frame housing a man in a rattan chair on a verandah. The man was looking off in the distance, as if waiting for an elusive thought to canter out from around the bend. A ledger lay open in his lap. He held a fountain pen. If one looked close enough, it was easy to note the three fingers truncated at the knuckles: pointer, middle, ring finger. Billy had asked his father about the stump-fingers. An accident, his father had replied curtly. Your grandfather's hand got caught in a door jamb.

"If I hadn't been told that this was my Dada, I wouldn't have ever known it." Billy's whisper became quieter. "You know who the loneliest creatures in the world are? Those people in family photographs for sale. Those scribbles on them, 'love you . . .,' 'love always . . .,' 'forever . . .'" Billy clicked his tongue. "Private sentiments adrift in time and exposed to uncaring gazes." He turned back to the copper frame. "My Dada, he was a freedom fighter in Kashmir . . . maybe," Billy tried to keep his tone casual, "maybe you've heard of him? Abdullah Nabi?"

Zari shook her head.

"Oh well." Billy shrugged. He had gotten quite used to

hiding his disappointment because no one he'd ever asked seemed to have heard of his grandfather. "He looks like a journalist in this picture, which is what I'm told he did afterwards, but imagine being him for even a day. A *freedom fighter*."

Zari blinked.

"And here is Mauj jee." Billy pointed to a fat woman in a pheran, a dupatta wrapped like a bandana over her hair and forehead. "She was the one who basically blew my world wide open. I want to show you something." Billy took his wallet out and extracted Mauj jee's letter. "This is my most prized possession." He unfolded the letter. "I've memorised the translation but I can't read the Kashmiri. Will you . . . will you read it for me please?"

Zari's voice unfurled like a silken ribbon into the quiet of the night.

My Dear, Darling, Beloved Billal

I trust you are well, my one and only. Ever since you left, I give thanks daily to God that you were not injured in the demonstration that unfortunate day, that you all departed in a timely fashion for matters here are disintegrating day-by-day.

Thanks be to God that you all visited when you did and I saw all of you—I can now die in peace. Billal, remember to study hard and well. Make your parents proud, make me proud, but most of all make your Dada proud. How proud he would be of you, you are not capable of imagining.

My love, my darling, take care of yourself, and if Allah wills, we will meet once again.

My love to your bright sister and salaam to you parents

Your beloved Mauj jee.

"She said she'd written me more letters." Billy tucked the aerogramme back into his wallet. "But my Dad says she was too senile to distinguish truth from fiction. But honestly, Zaar, does this letter sound senile to you?" Billy squinted. "Mauj jee told me that someone had murdered my grandfather, who and how I don't know." He frowned. "My mother doesn't like talking about this stuff and that means Dad won't either. I wish photographs could talk. They're supposed to be a diving board for memories and all that, but it's like a lie in a way, you know, everyone in them always seems to be on their best behaviour."

"My albums," Zari wrapped her arms around herself, "are incomplete because everyone's smiling in them. My mother, for instance . . . she looked the sweetest when she was in a bad mood."

"What was your mother like?"

"She—" Zari choked up. "I can't."

After a moment's hesitation, Billy took her hand and brought it up to his cheek. She looked away from him, her breathing just a little ragged, but left her hand in his.

"It's difficult to talk about them."

"You know," Billy said, "my father says the same about his life, but, Zaar, what if our kids want to know? Will you tell them?"

Zari's voice was dull when she finally replied. "I don't want to have children. Not in a world like this, but . . . if I were to have them, of course I'd tell them. It would be their right to know and that would make it my duty."

"Yeah," Billy's jaw tightened. "Your duty. Their legacy."

11

Zari settled on the arm of the sofa closest to the living room door. On the television screen, men were dancing to music blaring from cars standing in traffic-jammed streets. She assumed it was somewhere in India, but then she saw the green and white of the Pakistani flag fluttering on bicycle handles and rear-view mirrors of motorcycles. Someone had even wrapped flags around the horns of a couple of goats. Everyone was yelling: Hum kisi say kum nahi!, we are less than no one. The ticker at the bottom of the screen was running the headline: *May 1998: India, Pakistan, Israel— three countries assumed to have nuclear capability, yet to join the 1970 nuclear non-proliferation treaty signed by 185 countries.*

"What happened?" Zari asked Billy and Shehla even as she dreaded the answer. Fifteen days ago, India had conducted the Pokhran tests, declaring itself a full-fledged nuclear state and jubilation had erupted on the streets.

"Pakistan has tested nukes in response to India's tests," Shehla said.

Years rolled by on the screen as black and white footage of Jinnah, Nehru, Mountbatten, and Gandhi changed into the Technicolor faces of young Indian and Pakistan politicians, both male and female, although they all miraculously seemed to be spouting the same lines. The screen turned a plush green. *Flashpoint Kashmir*, the anchors called it, and the camera turned to a panoramic view of the valley, lingering on the picturesque lakes and forests and faces of dignified elderly and curious children, only to zoom in on soldiers and sandbag bunkers and miles of razor wire.

The American voiceover: Since the 1947 partition of India and Pakistan, the two countries have fought three wars over the disputed state of Jammu and Kashmir, territory roughly the size of Alabama, and have nearly come to blows numerous other times. Both countries are on high alert and are beefing up their borders.

Zari rose, abruptly. Billy followed her into the foyer.

"Zaar," he whispered, "remember that meeting group, Trouble Spots, I told you I go to? Tonight, they're having an impromptu meeting on this latest development. Will you come? The guy who hosts the group will be thrilled if you spoke on what this means for Kashmir."

"It will mean even more of a crackdown," she said. "It will mean more surveillance and more shootings and more families destroyed." She did not want to speak. She did not want to go. She had a headache, and she was going to lie down.

Zari trudged up to her room, her heart splintering at the thought that sometimes, sometimes this man she'd married, this man with whom she'd been sharing desserts in the dark of the night for the past month, this man whose *wife*, whose *secret* wife she was, did not fathom at all the full extent of her loss.

Once in her room, Zari sat on the prayer mat, her palms pressed against her eyes as if that would erase the images from the TV. Kashmir had not even been an itch in the throat of the world and now, after the nuclear tests, everyone was choking on it. Though, it seemed to Zari, the current problems in Kashmir had been pushed aside in lieu of the root cause, the 1947 partition of India and Pakistan, and what effect a nuclear showdown in that particular region could have on the rest of the world. What, the American anchors demanded to know, does this mean for us?

Nothing, she wanted to assure them. This furore too will find itself filed away, like all else, into archives that would never see the light of day. As she herself should have been filed by this family, into their memory banks, nothing more than an isolated incident of a person, here today, gone tomorrow, except that Billy's decision had made her a permanent face in their albums.

Zari rose from the bed and went into the bathroom and took out her razor. She eyed the bath sachets and votives Billal had given her. She had yet to use a single one. She saw Imran's eyes reflected in the porcelain of the bathtub floor. They would have been in Australia right now, she wrapping up high school, he his MBA. She glimpsed him strumming his guitar, humming new lyrics to a new melody, the vibrating strings thrumming against his fingertips.

Whenever Billal asked about her family, she'd been overwhelmed by the realisation that her family would now only be able to speak for itself through the memories of others. She could say anything, give any spin she chose—her portraits could dilute history here, embellish it there, play with truth, tryst with falsehood, select, erase, exaggerate, downplay, snip, cut, stitch, simply recreate and change the very essence of who someone had been and in doing so change history itself, and who would be the wiser of such a betrayal, except for herself?

Tears pitted Zari's face as she struggled against judging God. She had to keep faith that eventually everything would make sense and that, if it never made sense to her, she would have to find peace in the belief that her life had to, at least, be making sense to God.

Billy drove to the suburban townhouse where the meetings took place. A winding stone walkway ended at a small patio with a porch swing and a tricycle. He stood before the sliding glass doors tidying his reflection—red windbreaker, white t-shirt, jeans, ridiculously overpriced sneakers—before entering. Extra sheets had been laid out on the living room carpet to accommodate the unexpectedly high attendance. There were the usual faces, but also quite a few Billy did not recognise. He greeted Indus, the moderator, at the door and both of them agreed that so much interest in Kashmir was excellent. Once everyone was settled, Indus began the meeting.

"Now," he said, "if Pakistan and India had the advantage of distance that the US had from Japan . . . well, then things would be different, but since that is not the case, Pakistan and India nuking one another would inevitably mean self annihilation. Brothers and sisters," Indus nodded at the few women present, "even as we speak, both countries are deploying soldiers at their borders."

"But doesn't that imply," a first-timer piped up, "that neither one is planning to use their nuclear arms? Otherwise why would they need to beef up manpower at the border?"

"Yes, thank you," Indus said. "Valid point. Welcome to our group. Does anyone know what the Kashmiris in Kashmir feel about this development?"

"That this," Billy stared straight ahead as everyone turned to look at him, "will just make each country strengthen their grip on their regions of Kashmir and try to control it further."

"I think," a voice from the back called out, "this show of force will actually prevent them from ever taking any drastic action. Look at the US and Russia."

"The cold war," a wiry guy said, "did not have the hot spot of Kashmir to broil over."

"Perhaps," spoke up a man in a skullcap, "India was sending a signal to China and not Pakistan."

"The Indian tests are an open threat to Pakistan," the wiry guy retorted, "and we Pakistanis should be proud that we have matched brick for brick."

The skull-capped guy curled his lip. "I'm from India, you Pakistani twit."

"Then you are a Muslim suffering from severe inferiority complex to continue living under Hindu fundamentalists who are hell-bent on murdering the lot of you."

"Maulana Pakistan mein barha bhai-bhai hai nah Shia-Sunni kay beech? As if priestly Pakistan is the fount of brotherhood with Sunnis and Shias at each others' throats."

"You would rather die at Hindu hands, is that it? When they had no qualms about assassinating Gandhi, what makes you think the Hindus will spare your hairy Muslim ass, huh, you bloody fool?"

"All that is history. Things have changed. Cricket, government, the film industry, it's all full of Muslims. In all sectors, you work hard, and opportunities will open up for you. What opportunities are there for Hindus or Christians or even poor Muslims in Pakistan, huh?"

"Please," Indus glared at them, "let me remind you all that our aim is to communicate, not alienate. So kindly keep all participation civil."

"The sad thing is," a woman said, glaring at the two men, "that both countries would be better off had they spent the nuclear budget on improving the lot of their people."

"I have never," said the wiry one looking at skullcap, "witnessed the extent of poverty in Pakistan that I have in India—people eating out of trash cans! Terrible."

"I'll tell you what's terrible," skullcap sat up, "the Bihari-Pakistanis languishing in refugee camps in Bangladesh since 1971. Instead of lusting after Kashmir, you moron, why doesn't Pakistan bother bringing them back home?"

"If Hindustan is so perfect then why are the Nagas," the wiry guy began counting on his fingers, "the Tamils, the Gorkhas, the Sikhs, the Assamese all agitating for secession? You can fool the West with your Mr Yogis and Ms Worlds, but the rest of us know the truth about your insides."

"Please!" Indus clapped his hands. "If this small group cannot communicate civilly, what hope do we have for large administrations and the uncountable masses?"

"Right you are," said the wiry one even as he gave the finger to skullcap.

Skullcap rose. "Bahar mil, meet me outside, bathatha

hoon tujhe. I'll beat the crap out of you. What else but brute force is to be expected from you Pakistani goons after years of dictators and coups?"

"Fuck you!" said the wiry one. "Kashmir is ours."

"Kashmir is ours!" said skullcap. "Fuck you."

Billy looked from one to the other in disbelief. For all the friendliness between hordes of Indians and Pakistanis, it was not the first time some were descending into a fuck you festival, but it angered him as it never had before that these jerks were indulging in their petty quarrelling no matter the threats posed by nuclear armament or the losses of people like Zari.

"Enough," Indus pointed to the door. "We are not in India or Pakistan, we are in the West, in USA, and here we are a united front. Both of you—out."

Bullshit meeting, skullcap stated loudly as he got up.

Maha bullshit, seconded the wiry one, staring at Indus.

Billy watched the men walk out of the room. Did they realise they were agreeing on something? Or did they know each other and this animosity was just a ploy to sow dissent? He wished there was something he could say to reclaim Kashmir from the likes of these two.

"Hey!" He scrambled up. "Both Pakistan and India need to leave Kashmir completely alone. The Kashmiris want Kashmir to themselves and the likes of you two had better get that into your thick heads."

Both the skullcap guy and the wiry guy stopped short and stared at Billy. Billy held his ground, ready to outstare them.

"Our man Billal here," a regular called out, "sees nothing beyond complete independence, he can't help it, his grandfather was a freedom fighter."

"So was mine," a girl called out. "In fact, he marched with Gandhi ji." She turned to Billal with great expectations. "And yours?"

⌘

When Billy stepped into his house an hour later, he was still feeling ill at the thought of having had to bluster his way through a whole web of lies about his grandfather marching with Gandhi. It was not fair. His parents had to tell him more. And, with that thought, he marched forward in order to find his father, only to halt when he found Miraage crouching behind a planter in the living room.

"Maju," he squatted in front of her. "Baby, why are you hiding?"

Billy gathered his little sister into his arms as she muddled through a tale of playing with their mother's jewellery box and dropping it.

"How many times has everyone told you to not touch Mom's stuff?" He kissed her forehead. "Is it broken?"

"I don't know." Big tears swam in Miraage's eyes.

"Where's Dad?

"Study."

"Mom?"

"Out."

"Salsabil?"

183

"Out."

"Come then." Billy picked her up and piggy-backed her to their parent's bedroom. "Let's go fix Mom's jewellery box."

∞⌒∞

The red velvet box lay toppled on the dark wood floor amidst a sparkle of jewellery and trinkets. Billy righted the box and, as he lifted the top case, glimpsed, under a mess of necklaces, the telltale border of navy and red stripes on pale blue paper. Aerogrammes addressed—*To: Master Billal Nabi.* Five letters. Letters he'd thought were lost in the mail. Letters he'd been told had never been sent. Letters from Mauj jee.

Billy unfolded the aerogrammes with shaky fingers, smoothing out the deep wrinkles on the aged paper, unfolding each to a geography of language he could not decipher. The letters were in Kashmiri. He needed them translated. He kissed Miraage, sat her in front of a Tom and Jerry show on the TV, and went to find Zari.

∞⌒∞

Birds the words were, birds trapped in cages of fading ink, released, one by one, as Zari read the letters out loud.

My dear, darling, beloved Billal, each letter began. *I trust you are well, my one and only. My love, I have terrible news.*

Each letter turned darker as Mauj jee told more and more tales of unrest, of disappearances, of untimely deaths.

Again struggle has come, the struggle your Dada sacrificed his life for, the struggle that he believed in above all: to bring freedom to our homeland. Freedom was in your Dada's blood, for he was a true Nabi, and you too, my Billal, my love, are a true Nabi.

Each successive letter stressed on the glory of being a freedom fighter, a saviour of the land. In the last she said, *I have given my blessing to Shafi to go fight for Kashmir's independence, and I would gladly bequeath my blessing upon you too, my beloved Billal*—Zari's voice faltered—*should you wish to do the same.*

"She said that?" Billy chewed on his lower lip. He felt warm, as if Mauj jee had leapt to life and taken him in her arms.

"Yes." Zari folded the letters stiffly. "She did. No wonder your parents kept these letters from you."

"Huh?" Billy frowned. "My parents had no right to do that."

"But can't you see? They kept these letters from you because they love you. How would these have benefited you in any way?" Zari's voice hardened. "Had my father loved us more, he would have left Kashmir, and," she licked her suddenly parched lips, "had he left, then my family would've been alive today and I wouldn't have been here. Instead, thanks to his misguided loyalty . . ." Zari broke off. "Just like your Mauj jee's sentiments here! Did she even know what is involved in a freedom struggle?"

"Of course she knew," Billy shot back. "My Dada, her brother, was *murdered* because of his beliefs."

"And yet she gave her blessings to other people's brothers and sons to follow the same path?"

"You have no right to talk about Mauj jee in that tone." Billy took the letters from her, cradling them as if they were brittle creatures that needed protection in order to be nurtured to strength.

"She's romanticising everything."

"She is not."

"Maybe your parents are right. Maybe she was suffering from demen—"

"Don't."

"Billal, those intruders who broke into my house asking for shelter, they called themselves, no they *were* freedom fighters. But I don't know whose freedom they were fighting for. They trapped us! They threatened and coerced us into helping them!"

"There are always good people and bad people. My Dada—"

"Your Dada!" Zari's voice rose. "Kashmir is more than just a place your Dada came from. It is my home. Home! You understand, 'home'?"

Billy took a step back.

"Tell me, Billal, if your Dada hadn't been Kashmiri, would you have been able to even point Kashmir out on a map?"

"That's unfair. That's like the chicken and egg."

"What chicken and egg?" Zari yelped. "You people are confused about who you are. Kashmir is just another history in the book of histories for you but, for me, it's my reality."

Billy stared at the letters. It was the first time he felt a separation between their histories, between the twists and turns that had formed their sensibilities and given story to their lives, between the connections he'd always believed linked all lives like echoes of one another. But, while he was an immigrant collage of all the collective histories that lived in this one country, Zari was a split between the shared histories of two countries. The upside and downside of August 14th and August 15th was not part of the classroom lesson plans here in America, and, though he might have learned of Pakistan and India's respective Independence days at the knees of his parents, since he did not come from a talking family, that was that—TV and books and other sources of information had to inform him and, as much as they were able, grow him up.

"My Dada is important to me," Billy said after a long moment, speaking slowly, as if he was figuring this out for himself too, "and it is true that it is through him that Kashmir has become dear to me. I can neither change the order of that nor will I apologise for it or for growing up in a place away from my origins. This is my reality and whose is more authentic, yours or mine, the inside player's or the outside observer's, is something I don't want to debate. The different trajectories of our lives are dependent on nothing more than where and to whom we happened to be born."

Zari sank into her armchair. "So basically," her voice quavered, "that's all there is to what happened to my family? Time and place? But I can't accept that. I *refuse* to accept that! God must have some plan!" She moaned. "A great plan!"

Billy squatted before her.

"I know you are hurting," he said gently, "and you're right, I have not lived through what you have, and so I would never dare appropriate your emotions for mine, but believe me when I say that I can imagine how painful, how difficult all this," he gestured to the guest room, "must be for you."

"Your mother keeps telling me to try to forget about it and move on."

"Zari, people like my mother will not be able to breathe if they cannot compartmentalise their lives and throw away the key to memories they wish were not theirs to begin with." Billy took Zari's hands in his. "But people like you and me, Zaar, we're grand halls with windows upon windows open to any and every memory."

"Am I like that . . ."

"We both are." Billy wiped her tears, his fingertips drinking them in.

"Please," Zari said, "please tell your parents about us. I cannot stand it anymore."

"I will. I will, okay. Trust me. Just be a little more patient. For my sake."

"What about my sake?" Zari turned away from him. "Do you ever think of anyone except yourself?"

"That's not fair." Billy cringed. He'd been thinking about Zari day in and day out. Even when he dreamt, it was about her, about them, about what was to become.

"Life is unfair," Zari said.

"Just let me save some money, please . . ."

"I don't care about money."

"Neither do I, but we have to be practical."

"I don't want to be practical."

"Trust me, Zaar, please. I love you more than anyone

in the whole world, you know that. Please trust me. Please don't cry."

Billy took Zari into his arms and Zari, in spite of everything, pressed her face against his chest. She had to trust him, and God. God was neither cruel nor petty— Billal routinely questioned God and God had stricken down neither him nor his family. The street lights had yet to come on, and Zari turned her face to the gloaming outside the window. The dark suckled memories out of her. She missed the breakfasts the most, she whispered into Billy's shirt, the way her mother swirled the porcelain cup to cool her noona chai, the way her father alternated bites of the bakirkhanis while throwing scraps to the squirrels. She told him about her family's burials, their bodies wrapped in white shrouds, and Sonea's funeral pyre, human bones crackling in the bright warmth. I can smell it, often, she said, the scent of death.

"Sorry," Billy whispered the whole time she spoke, *sorry-sorry-sorry*, because, though the most impotent of words, sorry was still the only sentiment that seemed to fit at all.

12

Amman sat in his study, on a cracked leather sofa, one foot under him, a slice of chocolate cheesecake balanced on the sofa's arm, a dessert fork sticking out of it like a flag. A mountain of newspapers, both English and Urdu, were stacked beside him and he was lapping them up slowly, relishing this time to himself, an elusive commodity in his busy life. He jumped, therefore, when Billy barrelled in, but his reprimand died on his lips when Billy thrust a bunch of aerogrammes in his face.

"Dad, do you know about these?"

A quiet dread settled over Amman. He'd known this day was going to come. He had known. "Where did you find them?"

"You did know!" Billy wanted to wail at his father's treachery. "But you led me to believe that Mauj jee was senile, that she didn't know the difference between fact and fiction." Billy spluttered like a trapped animal. "You made me doubt her."

"Your mother—"

"Stop hiding behind Mom! You've had years to tell me about these letters."

"We were only protecting you."

"Protecting me from what?" Billy said. Zari had made the same claim. "Look at me, Dad. I'm *not* eight years old anymore."

Amman shrank in his seat as Billy came towards him, his shadow hulking over the giant world map pinned to the wall behind him. Amman had discovered that map in a box of National Geographics at a hospital white elephant sale, and he remembered bringing it home, and Billy unfolding it and unfolding it and then lying in the centre, pretending to swim, his little boy limbs straining to reach all four corners at once.

Amman blinked.

"If I hadn't found them today, would you have ever told me?" Billy towered over his father. "You and Mom *read* them. You had no right to!" He stamped his foot like a petulant child. "You know what, Dad, I'm sorry that it makes you sad to speak of your history, but you've got to tell me right now, Dad, you tell me everything I want to know. Now."

Amman looked at the letters in his son's hand. Here was Billal, yet again demanding to be told about the past, his son who was old enough to vote, to drive, to join an army . . . surely he was old enough to be entrusted with a dark, bleak, cumbersome past despite Shehla's fears that the past would ruin him?

"Dad," Billy interrupted Amman's thoughts, "we can be here for the rest of our lives if that's what it's going to take to make you talk."

Courage, funnily enough, tasted like bad fish. Amman's mind cleared, and taking a deep breath, he gestured to Billy to sit beside him on the sofa.

"My first memory," Amman folded his arms across his

chest as if something was about to fall out, "is of my father teaching me to make a bomb."

Billy's eyes shone. "How old were you, Dad?"

"Five, six . . . maybe a little older."

At that age, Billy recalled, he hadn't even been allowed to watch movies with explosions. And if his mother had her way, he still wouldn't be allowed to.

"My mother," Amman was saying in a quiet voice, "came upon me and my father in the shed one day. She said she didn't want me to follow in the family's footsteps and die like a dog. My father sniggered and said it was a hero's death, to die for one's country." Amman drew whorls on the newspaper in his lap. "My mother thought I agreed with my father's politics because I always insisted on accompanying him to every meeting he went to, but the truth was that I liked to get away from her. My mother was extremely pessimistic while my father, well, he was always high-spirited no matter what. Drunk on self-importance, my mother used to say. I remember Mauj jee would always chide her and say she never understood my father's spirit. Mauj jee used to live with us back then. You see, my mother and Mauj jee were childhood friends. The happiest day in their lives had been when my mother married my father."

Billy leaned forward, his eyes gleaming.

"In the beginning, my mother, Mauj jee, and I would attend the rallies your Dada spoke at. He created quite an impression in these rallies and public demonstrations. His voice would be like the roar of a lion and the crowds would cheer, and I would think how no one would dare harm a man of the people." Amman raised his brows. "But one day, someone woke up to the fact that my father was seditious to a dangerous degree and sent people after him. Because he was a darling of the crowds, my father was tipped off before the men came and he hid I still don't know where. When the police finally barged in through our door to arrest my father, they didn't even bother to look for him and decided to take me instead."

Amman rubbed the bridge of his nose. The police had thought that on hearing of his son's arrest, his father would immediately turn himself in. Every moment of that evening was seared into Amman's memory. The knocks on the door, the patches of sweat darkening his mother's tunic, the aroma of the smoked trout on their kitchen table, the door swinging open, the police barging in like hungry bears, the cold of their fingers seeping in through his woollen shirt as they guided him out into the icy evening, fright freezing his heart.

"It was snowing," Amman said, his forehead crinkling. "I was tinkering with an old wristwatch I'd found in a garbage dump and my mother was blowing on roasted chestnuts to cool them."

"Where was Mauj jee?"

"Gone to the kiln to purchase bread for our dinner."

Amman clamped a hand on Billy's knee. "My mother begged them not to take me. She fell at their feet, her knees sinking into the snow . . . she hated getting wet . . ."

Amman could hear his mother's pleas—he's only eight, what does he know of his father's world?—the men's laughter, their threat to take her next.

"Dad?" Billy said.

"They kept me for three days in a room no bigger than a shower stall. Not even a pillow they gave me."

Billy clenched his jaw. He looked down and saw that his hands were balled up. He wanted to know all of this and he didn't want to know all of this, but, above all, he had to bear witness.

"They were sitting in an adjoining room, playing cards, wrapped up in their bulky sweaters and shawls and socks. The sight of them made me shiver all the more. They plied me with water, ordering me to drink" —Amman ran a shaky hand over his eyes and looked away from Billy— "and then they watched me wet myself."

Billy's stomach turned

"They questioned me about my father's activities. And I kept soiling my pants. They kept questioning. Names. Speeches. Incidents. They could have killed me . . ." Amman rubbed his eyes. "They beat me with wires."

Amman pursed his lips as Billy slumped into the couch. Perhaps Shehla was right. Of what use would it be to tell Billy that one of the men who had tortured him had lived in his neighbourhood? That when they had finally let him go, the man had just shrugged? That when he saw Amman playing marbles in the street, he would offer him a chocolate as if nothing had ever happened? Amman had understood. Everything was fair in love and war. This was his father's motto too. Amman cleared his throat. What was the use of telling Billy that they released him only after he fed them false confessions? He had never told anyone that he'd cracked under duress, not because he'd been ashamed of doing so—he was only eight years old, after all—but because

194

he'd feared that his father would admire his ability to lie so convincingly and that too at such a young age. He wanted none of his father's admiration. Or apologies. Let Billy believe, Amman decided, that evil lived in faraway places rather than in familiar faces.

"After two days, they released me and I hobbled into my house with my shredded back. My father had already escaped into Pakistani Kashmir via the mountains and was busy, so it was said, fighting lions and getting djinns to bow to him. My mother said he'd run off to save his own skin despite the police's threat to come for her next.

"She and Mauj jee dabbed warm almond oil over my wounds as they whispered frantically amongst themselves. Mauj jee was adamant that my mother and I leave the country before the police realised that I'd lied to them. The very next day, she left early in the morning for the visa office and returned with two visas in her hand—in the 1950s, the Indian government readily gave good-riddance-to-nuisance visas. My mother begged Mauj jee to come with us, but she refused. She said she would look after our house until our return and that we were not to worry about her because, thanks to my father, she was an even better shot than he had ever been and was not scared to shoot to kill." Amman stopped. "Why are you smiling?" he asked Billy.

"Imagining Mauj jee with a gun."

Amman nodded. He could still see his mother and Mauj jee hugging each other, bidding tearful farewells, promising to reunite as soon as possible. It was the last time the two women would ever see each other.

"There was no goodbye good enough," Amman said,

remembering how his mother had kissed the soil before they left, "but we said our goodbyes anyway and crossed over from Indian Kashmir into Pakistani Kashmir to reunite with my father. My mother had no idea that the journey which previously used to take a mere two to three hours, would now take three days thanks to the new borders. We took a bus and travelled from Srinagar to Jalandhar to the Wagah border and then to Lahore to Rawalpindi and finally from there to Muzaffarabad. Three days my mother held me tight enough to squeeze the breath out of me and I let her. She'd never before set foot out of Srinagar, and there she was, thrust into travelling through unknown land to live somewhere with no hope of ever returning to the only home she'd ever known . . .

"It might have been better for her if she'd at least liked Muzaffarabad, but she was like a city dweller who'd been exiled to a remote rural area. It was the topography that caused her sleepless nights. Hathay, dudwan hee dudwan, as dry as a husk, she kept wringing her hands, dudwan hee dudwan, and compared to Srinagar's verdure, Muzaffarabad did seem brownish-green.

"And the people, though they were Muslim, had more in common with the Punjabi culture than ours. In fact, my mother kept muttering that we were more like the Kashmiri Hindus and Sikhs we'd left behind. My father, of course, acted as if we were in Shangri-la.

"As for myself, I have to admit that I fell in love with Muzaffarabad quite soon. The knolls one could roll down, the boulders perfect for hiding behind, the pristine air that poured down one's throat like cold sherbet. Everything."

"Dad," Billy spoke softly, "what did Dada say when he saw your back?"

"He was," Amman looked away from Billy, "utterly devastated."

All is fair in love and war, eh, Amman, his father had said, and we are at war because of our love of Kashmir. You are no longer a boy, my son, now you are a man who has shed blood. Yes, his mother had snapped, he was no longer a little boy because of the welts on his back.

"But there was one good news my father had for us," Amman continued. "There would be no refugee camps for us. As resourceful as he was, my father had already procured a house for us.

"My mother's spirits, however, refused to lift even after she saw the abandoned house, a hump of three rooms situated at the foot of a hill. But I loved it instantly. It was a world away from the interrogators." Amman half smiled. "And I continued to love it even after our friendly neighbours informed my mother that its previous Hindu owners who'd fled to India, had cursed it and that we were the first family brave enough to move in permanently."

"Weren't you scared?" Billy asked.

"A little, but my mother had taken to sleeping with me . . ." His father was not superstitious and, in this case, neither was his mother. In fact, she'd told the neighbours she was used to being accursed since she was married to a curse.

"Why are you smiling, Dad?"

"Just, looking back . . . those years turned out to be good ones. When the faces of boys my age popped over the low boundary wall a few days after we'd moved in, it seemed as if my life was going to turn out all right despite the fact that I missed my old friends and that my mother was depressed.

I remember following those boys down the hillside, skipping along as much as my back would allow, all the way down to a bazaar, then to a red brick fort, and then to a military hospital. That first day I went exploring the town, I thought I'd never be able to find my way back, but of course, before I knew it, I had memorised every artery—it was a small town then . . . and so safe no one bothered to shut their front doors.

"Once I started school, Muzaffarabad became home. In the early morning, I would walk from house to house picking up friend after friend and we'd walk together to school. There were two routes, one through the bazaar and the other through meadows. We would always choose the meadows where, depending on the season, we would pluck plums, apples, peaches. We'd gobble up as many as we could and throw away the rest—what was the need to hoard when there was such abundance?

"In the one-room schoolhouse, we piled our shoes by the door, sat on jute mats, wrote on individual slates with chalk, and after school, played either cricket or football or kabadi all afternoon. It was a different time—no toy stores of the sort you are used to, no TV, no video games, nothing but the occasional children's programme on the transistor radio.

"We would often take walks alongside the Neelam River, waiting to pounce on the first one who absentmindedly referred to it by its pre-Partition name, Kishan-Ganga, and shove him in . . . the water would always be so icy we could hardly stand it." Amman smiled.

"Afterwards, the sun would warm us back to life as we strolled towards the Domeil bridge—Domeil meaning a 'meeting of two', because the bridge stood over the merging point of the Jhelum, flowing in from India, and the Neelam River from Pakistan—and hold ripple contests by tossing stones into the water. I used to be so excited that I'd completely forget about my back for hours at end. But my mother was always there to remind me.

"I would often catch her walking like a zombie to the Talkies, the only cinema hall in the town. She was addicted to films. Pakistan hadn't banned Indian films from playing in its cinemas yet, and, in the darkness of the theatre, with Dilip Kumar and Saira Banu or Raj Kapoor and Nargis on the screen, she said could imagine herself back in Srinagar with Mauj jee.

"In those days, she comforted herself by writing letters to Mauj jee. Forever the two were reminding each other of all the boat rides they'd taken on the moonlit lake and how, once they got together again, the first thing they would do was picnic in the Badamwari, the immense grove of almond trees in Srinagar which blossomed into a pink heaven before bearing fruit."

"Where are those letters?"

"Burned."

"Dad—" Billy began warily.

"I swear," Amman said. He shut his eyes at the memory of that bonfire. "A letter came from Mauj jee a couple of months after we'd left. She'd been attacked. For aiding in our escape."

"Attacked?"

Amman looked down. "She had to have an abortion. In

the letter, she told my father that he was to never force her to marry and that she wanted to spend the rest of her life on her own terms. Your Dada gave her our house and made sure that for as long as he was alive, she'd never want for anything. After him, I took over."

Billy caressed Mauj jee's letters as he paid homage to the woman who had not only loved him, but, as it turned out, had saved the lives of his family. Dada was a freedom fighter; Mauj jee was no less.

"After that letter, my mother was never the same. She blamed herself for not forcing Mauj jee to flee with us, for being naïve enough to believe that Mauj jee would be able to protect herself. She burned all the letters, scattering the ashes on the vegetable garden she'd planted in our backyard as if, in eating her grief, it would somehow become more palatable."

Amman closed his eyes, tired. He could recall vividly how his mother's tears had glistened as she'd set match to the letters, the letters turning to cinder, black ashes burying the tender green shoots.

"After that, I tried my level best to keep my mother happy in every way possible, but nostalgia became her identity. She was a lost woman. She had lost everything—home, status, family, friends, country, everything."

"Like Zari."

"Yes, like that poor girl." Amman drew his hands over his stubble. Their move to Muzaffarabad had given his mother misery, but to him it had bequeathed a new lease on life. In fact, the very border that was anathema to his mother was, to his young mind, a God ordained deterrent for keeping out those police interrogators. Simply, he could sleep at night without fear.

Amman sighed. "What is this life, huh? My mother's sole wish was to be buried in Srinagar, in the land which was her home, and when she died, my father tried to send her body back, but that proved impossible. My mother was buried in a land to which she had no ties, no affections. But I still think she was lucky. She was buried in a marked grave with a husband and a son present at the burial. So many people, so many refugees don't even get that much luck these days . . ."

"Where is Dada buried?"

"In Muzaffarabad, beside my mother. After her death, I left for a boarding school in Lahore and from there, King Edward Medical College."

"And Dada?"

"And your Dada . . ." Amman scratched at a fingernail. "Your Dada stayed in Muzaffarabad, beginning his career as a journalist."

"The photo in the hallway?"

"The photo in the hallway." Amman remembered well the afternoon that photograph had been taken.

"Dad?"

"Yes?"

"Did Dada ever march with Gandhi?"

"I really don't know."

"And he lost his fingers in a door jamb, right?"

"Right." Amman nodded emphatically. "Absolutely right."

"And he was murdered?"

"Beta, your grandfather was shot in his office. To date, the murder remains unsolved. Such a big funeral, people came from far and wide to honour the people's prince, the darling of the crowd." Amman smiled feebly.

"Did you find Dada's body?"

"No, I did not see his body. I was barely able to make it in time for the funeral. At the time of his murder I was at medical school, romancing your mother, convincing her that I had no interest in either fighting for freedom or joining the army like her father. We never wanted our kids to go through what we had." Amman gave a dry chuckle. "We are led to believe fighting for freedom is worth everything, but my family perished because of it, and for what? Kashmir is still not free. And look at the likes of poor Zari."

Billy held the letters up. "Mauj jee says it's not the winning or the losing but the act of trying that matters. It's the knowledge that you're doing something so important that history will record it, that your action might even be the tipping point capable of changing the very course of history."

"Your Mauj jee was an idealist."

Billy's face hardened. "It's not idealism. It's how things change."

"The world does not change, Billal. Nothing changes. No one remembers sacrifices, and everyone forgets heroes. Even villains fade from the memory of successive generations. Borders disintegrate, reintegrate, neighbours love each other one day, the next day they hate, governments fall, governments rise, maps are drawn, redrawn, wars are fought and lost, treaties are torn up, or worse, ignored, and while victory or defeat in a war belongs to a country, man himself is doomed only to the darkness of the soul. History is cyclical." Amman drew robust circles in the air. "Up, down, up, down. What choice do insignificant inconsequential pawns like you and me have but to play along with the rotations to which we are born?

"You talk of an independent Kashmir, but I don't think that will work. An independent Kashmir will be too busy defending itself from hostile neighbours to ever have any real chance at sustained success. It will become a bigger mess than what it already is."

"But Dad," Billy said, "everyone deserves a country even if they make a mess of it. And a mess does work itself out sooner or later."

"Does it?" Amman raised his eyebrows. "Few decisions are up to the Kashmiris any longer, if they ever were. I think it a wiser course if Kashmir aligns itself with whichever country, India or Pakistan, offers better prosperity."

"Very practical," Billy said, as if practical was a dirty word.

"When you are older, you too will see that 'practical' is the only way."

Billy took a deep breath. "*I* believe in revolution."

"So do I." Amman smiled affectionately. "But simply achieving independence is not the end all and be all. There is the day after independence and the day after that, and those days can prove to be the toughest days of all."

"So," Billy frowned, "according to you, people should

just suffer under oppressive governments? That's just not right, Dad. It's not fair."

Amman glanced at Billy. He felt a fierce, protective love for Billy, for this son who was listening to him so carefully, who was looking up to him.

"Had the US broken into two during the Civil War," Amman joined his fists then wrenched them apart, "then, one after the other, other states would have started agitating for independence. They would've all wanted to be declared as countries in their own rights. In my estimation, a government gives into one group and soon it'll find itself giving in to every separatist demand out there until there's no end to it."

"In my estimation," Billy crossed his arms, "people should have the right to do what they want."

"What if they don't know what they want? In the old world, empires drew boundaries willy-nilly. And in this new world, that very basis for boundaries is being tested anew. Europe is trying to come together and form a Bloc, let's see how long that lasts, while places like Kashmir are still stuck in the same old provincial nationalistic mindset—Kashmir for Kashmiris. And who decides who qualifies as Kashmiri and who doesn't? But, then again, how long before a collective Europe develops a mono-nationalist identity? Mesh or mess, I don't know," Amman clicked his tongue. "An excess of patriotism can be a fault, but then so can the we-are-the-world mentality.

"Nullify differences, ignore them, celebrate them, find a balance . . . this is the new trick the old dog must learn if it is not to blow itself up. I just do not believe that breaking countries up on communal or religious or ethnic lines will lead to the ultimate happiness of all those involved. I like to believe that diverse people can live together as long as law and order and justice are meted out equally. But then again," Amman said, "I live in the United States of America; I must believe in this."

"But, Dad, what if it isn't doled out equally? Look at Kashmir, look at what they did to you." Billy pointed to his father's back. "Look at what happened to Zari and her family. And to Mauj jee. One can't just shut their eyes and ears and pretend nothing is happening because what *is* happening is enough to make anyone pick up a gun and demand their own country."

"Violence does not work, Billal."

"The Holocaust might not have happened at all had people risen against the Nazis. And look at Tibet, Dad. China is massacring Tibet and tearing it apart because the Tibetans are sitting there doing nothing to defend themselves. No one cares about hunger strikes any more. If anything, I bet they hope the agitators will just starve to death. There's no such thing as independence without violence!"

"Perhaps, but—"

"People who are suffering cannot rely on a 'perhaps' Dad, and, if you ask me, they shouldn't have to." Billy shook the letters. "Mauj jee said as much in these letters you kept from me."

Amman pursed his lips. "And did Mauj jee also happen to mention what becomes of freedom fighters once the need for guns is over and peace treaties have been signed?"

Billy glared at his father.

"Let *me* tell you!" Amman sat up. "The end of insurgency

does not necessarily mean a government better than the one being resisted. It does not mean an end to the bribery and corruption that are rampant in state systems; it does not mean the institution of measures to rein in poverty, or programs to teach ex-freedom fighters a profession. Instead, these unsung 'heroes', as I am sure you'd like to call them, are left high and dry with no education and no practical skills to support themselves and their families in the new world with its changed order. Eventually, these discontented men either turn to overthrowing the very establishment they helped put into place or else, they turn to crime because crime pays better than some menial, back-breaking, reward-less job.

"Look at me Billal," Amman stared into Billy's eyes. "Freedom fighters don't get medals, they don't get any honours. My mother made sure I understood that, and I will make sure you do too before you get caught up in romancing an exaggerated idealisation of a lie."

Billy turned and glared at his sneakers. It was wrong, he knew, of his father to refuse to see Mauj jee's point of view. But Mauj jee was right, the fight for one's freedom was noble. And in a different world, under Mauj jee's full blessings, he and Shafi could have become freedom fighters together.

"Beta," Amman picked lint off Billy's shirt, "inshallah, God willing, you will live in peace and prosperity all your life and not suffer for a single day."

Billy scowled. "Yeah, that's just great, isn't it, for lucky me living here? But what about people like Zari? She says no place is safe."

"But a life can be," Amman replied gently. "And that is a precious blessing."

Billy stared at the map, the contours of the continents fusing together then drifting back apart. After a moment, he said, "Dad, you and Dada are just alike."

"How so?" Amman snapped to attention.

"He helped Mauj jee and you're helping Zari."

Amman stared at Billy. "Enough. I'm tired now. And Billal, do not tell your mother about the letters. Just put them back where you found them."

"But—"

Amman raised a finger. "Your mother wants you kids to have the carefree childhood she never did. Her wishes are not a sin. Put them back, and, all this, let it remain our secret."

∞∞

Billy left his father's study light-headed. He stood in the hallway, gathering himself, before turning towards Zari's room. He found her sitting on the armchair, reading her rosary. He sat down by her feet and lay his head in her lap.

"What is it Billal?" Zari stroked his hair.

"My father got his scars because he was tortured when he was eight years old. My father's mother, my Dadi, died of a broken heart because she could not return to Srinagar. And Mauj jee" —Billy choked on his words— "Mauj jee was raped. She had to have an abortion."

Zari's fingers stilled.

"They were all so brave. Dada, Mauj jee, Dadi, my father." Billy looked up at Zari. "You are so brave to have come here. I could have never endured what any of them did. You could never guess looking at Mauj jee that she'd borne such an ordeal. She did know what was involved in freedom fighting, Zari, she did know."

"Shhh," Zari whispered. "Shhh."

Billy shook his head and sat up—his watch snagged on Zari's sleeve. She shrieked as she tried to cover the bloody lines running from elbow to wrist.

Billy gawked. "What the—"

Even as she tried to hide her arm behind her back, he pulled it forward and squinted at the mesh of uneven parallel lines. No matter how hurt or confused or terrible or sad he'd ever felt, he'd never thought of injuring himself. The only markings he'd ever seen on flesh were tattoos and piercings, marks that caused pain in the gain of pleasure and not the other way round.

"Zaar," Billy said. "How can you do this to yourself?"

"Let go of my arm."

Billy let go. Zari's arm swung to her side, the sleeve falling over her cuts.

"How long has this been going on?" Billy said. "How long have you been mutilating yourself like this, Zaar?"

"Don't say that." Zari looked away from him.

"I'll say it as I see it. Look at me Zari! How long has this been going on?"

Zari continued staring at the floor. "It's the only thing that makes me feel better."

Only thing. Billy winced. Why had he thought that marriage would eradicate Zari's demons, that he would be able to chase them away? He looked around Zari's room. She had not put up even a single drawing that Miraage had made for her. There were no personal things on the bedside table, no clutter collecting anywhere; she was still, evidently, living out of her suitcase.

Billy embraced Zari. "Zaar, don't," he whispered. "Please do not hurt yourself."

He held her as if he would never let her go, the only sound in the room the ticking of the clock on the bedside table. After a minute, he said, "I'm getting some ointment for your arm, all right?"

In the bathroom, next to the taps, in plain sight, a blood-tinged razor. Billy stared at it. It looked like a pen knife, a sliver of a razor blade protruding from a long flamingo pink handle embossed with golden lettering: *Made in Taiwan*.

Billy hurled the blade into the trash can. But what good was throwing it away when there were inexhaustible ways of wounding oneself and plenty of means available? He opened the mirror cabinet next, looking for more razors, for anything else with which she could cut herself—a nail cutter, deodorant, dental floss—and he caught his breath. It was deflated, sad, and sorry looking, and he told himself to forget it. Forget it for now, later, later there would be time to address it.

"Zari," he stood before her a heartbeat later, "what's this?"

Zari stared at the deflated balloon bracelet in Billy's palm.

"I don't know," she said.

"It's the bracelet Fahad got for you on the cherry blossom trip." He wouldn't have cared if Zari were missing her fiancé, or if she wept for him, even said she'd never be able to love anyone else, but Fahad he could not bear. "Why do you still have it?"

She looked at him as if he was speaking a foreign language.

"Why do you still have it? Zari, do you even love me at all?"

"Yes."

"Why don't you ever say it?"

"Say what?"

She sounded tired, Billy grit his teeth. "That you love me."

"I love you."

"Give me three reasons why."

"Three reasons . . ."

He glared at her. "Have you ever loved me? Or am I just some convenient replacement?"

Zari grabbed the bracelet from him and threw it in the wastebasket in the room. "It doesn't mean anything."

"Sure," Billy said. "Sure it doesn't."

When he left the room, Zari didn't try to stop him. Not once. And that hurt even more.

❧❧❧

Billy spent a sleepless night in his dorm room, his

mind a frazzled kaleidoscope of pink balloons inflating and deflating, morphing into Mauj jee's emotional scars, his father's marked back, and Zari's bloody arm. The next morning, he struggled to stay awake in class. But of what use, he thought, was learning about supply and demand curves, credit and default, embargoes and tradeoffs, when he had greater problems on his hands?

Once class was over, Dan and Ameer steered Billy to the cafeteria for a cup of coffee. Where had he been? How was Zari? How was married life? Over sips of strong, black coffee, Billy told them about discovering Mauj jee's letters, about talking to his Dad, and his quarrel with Zari over Fahad.

"I'm such an asshole," Billy muttered. Ameer and Dan were staring at him, no doubt, Billy thought, wishing they'd never inquired after him after all. "And I can't believe," Billy said, trying to inject some levity into his voice, "my parents managed to secret the letters away for so many years."

"Well," Dan said, "you've married in secret."

"Your own dirty little secret," Ameer added, immediately turning red. "Sorry, dude. I'm really sorry. I didn't mean it. Bad joke."

"Everything is not a damn joke, and sorry fixes nothing." Billy got up and stalked away, slamming the cafeteria doors behind him. How dare they call Zari a dirty secret? Why could they not believe that he'd married her because he loved her and not because he'd just wanted to provide her with a semblance of security? And what security had he managed to provide her? She was cutting herself hoping for relief, and he, her husband, her only friend, the only person she had to take her anger out on, had not only fought with her, but had also left her alone, and all because of Fahad who meant nothing to either of them. She needed him whether she admitted it or not.

That night, on his way home, Billy stopped at a Kashmiri restaurant and ordered noona chai and, though wilted for being baked that morning, a half a dozen bakirkhanis, all to-go.

He waited outside his home until all the lights had been turned out before sneaking into his bedroom. He was about to venture to the guest room, when the door of his room opened. It was Zari. They'd never been together in his room before, and suddenly, it was his place, a first date, it might as well have been the back seat of a car.

"Zaar," he said when he'd locked the door behind them and she was seated in the chair at his desk, "I'm so sorry about the bracelet."

"I do love you," Zari said. "And three reasons: you're kind, good, and caring."

"You don't have to say that."

"I do have to say it," Zari said. "I do."

"I have a surprise for you." Billy handed her the take-out bag. "Your Kashmiri breakfast." He hovered at the edge of the bed as Zari unfolded the silver foil, raked her fingers across the flaky bakirkhanis, lifted the lid on the noona chai, a lukewarm steam rising off the salty pink tea and lathering the room with its oceanic scent. She crumbled the savoury pastry into the pink, salty tea, swallowing each lump with her tears. When she was done, she said, softly, thank you, and then, quietly and firmly, I love you.

Billy knelt before her and taking her scarred arm in his hand, he rolled up the sleeve of her kurta only to discover a different scar at her shoulder joint, a bullet scar. Zari put her palm over it, but Billy lifted her fingers one by one until the scar was naked, a puckered mouth, staring at him, daring him to probe further as if it could reveal such dirty secrets that he would die just from hearing.

"Tell me about your fiancé," Billy said. "What was he like?"

She told him. About everyone.

Afterwards, when she was bone tired, she put her head on his chest and filled herself with the sound of the drumbeat of his life.

"After the intruders were done, I must have seemed dead from the shot because they left."

"Who were the *intruders*?"

Zari's voice caught in her throat. She could see the final police report, the last line on the last page: An Isolated Incident.

"I don't know. The army. The freedom fighters. The army dressed as freedom fighters. The freedom fighters dressed as the army. Indian-backed militia. Pakistani-backed militia. God only knows. It could even have been neighbours holding a grudge, for all I know. It's all a blank. No accents, no words, no features, nothing."

"But," Billy squinted, "why would freedom fighters fighting for Kashmir's independence hurt Kashmiris?"

"Why would an army hurt those they call their countrymen? But someone did it. I wanted to . . . to kill them all, you know, that's why my Khala sent me here . . . in case I went mad plotting revenge."

"You're safe now." Billy kissed her forehead. "Here, you'll always be safe."

"*No one* can promise safety of any kind. You know what I wish? I wish I could just forget everything and everyone. I wish I had one of those diseases that erases memory."

"You don't know what you're saying."

"I do. I want to forget everything."

"Even us?"

Her silence hurt Billy. Later, when they lay on his bed, side by side, but with a vast distance between them, he continued to hurt. She had drifted to sleep, but he was still wide awake and he fingered her profile without touching her skin, indenting, instead, the sheet of moonlight with one soft arc after the other of her forehead, her nostrils, her philtrum, her lips, her chin. How to make her want to remember him forever? He couldn't even take revenge for her, whom would he take it from?

He didn't remember falling asleep, but Billy woke up to Zari thrashing and whimpering.

"Shh," Billy whispered, trying to hold her even as she cowered from him. "It's okay. You're in my bedroom, at home. It's me, Billy."

He could kill to take away the fear in her eyes. He could kill those who had put it there in the first place.

"I'm going to make it okay," he said helplessly. "I swear, believe me, okay? Trust me, I won't let you down, I'll find a way."

As the last wisps of the nightmare receded from her mind, Zari turned to face Billy. She reached across the divide, lacing her fingers through his. Billy stroked her palm, slowly, hesitantly, moving to her wrist, then, her forearm, his touch tickling her until she was laughing. Then they were both laughing, and she was tickling him, not letting him go and, emboldened, he pulled her against his chest. Zari met his lips and allowed Billy to kiss her, breathing deeply the pine needle scent of his skin. She unbuttoned her shirt. She took his hand and guided him and Billy clumsily undid the clasp of her bra, the same bra he'd held long ago when he'd done her laundry. He managed to undo the two steel hooks from the cloth loops. He slid the straps down her arms. He kissed the mole on her collar bone, the mole he hadn't been able to get out of his mind since the day he'd seen it at the birthday party as she cut the cake. His mouth roamed over her with a mind of its own, his firefly kisses lighting up her shoulders and neck and face.

An impassive face, steel, stone.

She whispered go on, go on, go on, and he went on with his heart in his mouth, terrified, witless, this fortress more impregnable than any virgin territory. This girl—five times, fifty times, five hundred times not a virgin, what exactly had happened to her, *to his wife*.

He put his hands on either side of her face, their gazes locked on each other. It'll be okay, it'll be all right, it'll be over soon. He very much wanted to say these things, if only because he needed to hear them.

A face—impassive, steel, stone.

And then she smiled, a smile that was a balm and she drew him in urgently, pouring herself into him.

Zari felt the breath of a billion ghosts on her body. She felt like a shikara colliding against a pier. There had to be a first time, so be it in a room perfumed with memories of breakfasts, with a man whose reasons for marrying her she still couldn't fathom, a man who asked her why she loved him rather than the other way round. She smiled, her smile as wide and as open as she could manage because she refused to stain this moment with anything less.

She drew him in, harder and faster and faster and harder, marvelling that there could be peace in this act after all. His pine needle scent inundated her each and every pore. She planted him in her body, allowing him to blossom. She kissed him until her kisses spun over them a blanket of intimacy and security. Afterwards, she locked her knees and ankles and fought to keep what she was inviting inside—the feel, the spirit, the break, the thing called moving on, getting out of a corner, appeasing ghosts, life.

∞

The raps on Billy's door were sharp and quick. Zari's eyes flew open at the sound of the doorknob jiggling furiously. Sunshine was pouring in through the half-open blinds. She saw her clothes tangled on the floor with Billy's and the remains of her Kashmiri meal on his desk.

"Billaloo," Shehla called from outside.

Zari jostled Billy awake.

"Billaloo? Are you still sleeping? Open the door, beta."

Billy struggled up. He glanced at Zari. She was trembling.

"What is it, Mom?" He jumped up, pulling on his pants.

"Why are you home today? I thought you had a test. Open up."

"It got cancelled, Mom. Go away. I'm sleeping."

"Get up and come down for breakfast. What do you want?"

"Nothing."

"I'm making omelette, paratha, pancakes. Hurry up. Come down. Also bring down any laundry you need done."

As Shehla's footsteps receded, Billy sank onto the bed and turned to Zari. She was crying, the quilt pulled up to her neck, riven with anguish. Guilt devoured him as she hid her face in her hands and said: When is this month going to be over?

13

Billy forced himself to sit still at the breakfast table and pile his plate with his usual quantity of omelette and pancakes. Although Zari sat opposite him, freshly bathed and dressed in a pale blue shalwar kameez, the portion of omelette on her plate untouched, all he could see were her tears as she'd asked him, half an hour ago, when the month would be over.

Billy looked around the table. His parents were arguing about the sanctions the US had imposed on India and Pakistan for their nuclear showdown; Salsabil was muttering something about the President's audacity when it came to his intern, and Miraage was playing with a bouquet of helium balloons.

"Billal, beta," Shehla turned to him, "it's good you came home last night if you weren't feeling well. Remember how much you had argued about wanting to go to an out of state college? See how convenient it is to be close to home!" She beamed. "But you look flushed. Let me take your temperature."

"Mom," Billy took a deep breath, "Mom, I'm . . . I'm getting married."

There was deadly silence for a moment, even the

balloons came to a standstill, then Salsabil shrieked and Shehla's spoon clattered onto the plate.

"Marriage!" Shehla smacked Billy on his head. "Marriage!"

"Mom! Stop it! Dad!"

Amman pushed away his paratha. "What is wrong with you, Billal?"

"Nothing is wrong with me."

Miraage began to sing. "Billy's getting marry, Billy's getting marry.

"Be quiet Miraage," Billy snapped.

Shehla ordered Salsabil to plant Miraage in front of the TV with a bowl of jellybeans, and then she turned back to Billy and glared at him.

"You are nineteen!" Shehla shook her head. "Nineteen! Who has been planting such stupid ideas in your head?"

"No one, Mom!" Billy flicked a crumb off his plate. "I do have a mind of my own, you know."

"Mind of his own! Who is this witch, huh?! Tell me at once. I will go to her house and dho joothay lagathee hoon mein usseh, I'll give her two tight slaps with my shoe. If you want to get married, pack up and leave this house right now. Move in with this girl foolish enough to marry you at this stage in your life."

"Calm down, Mom." Billal didn't dare glance at Zari. "I-I was joking."

"Joking?" Shehla looked at him, her tongue running over her lower lip in worry. "You were joking?" She turned to Amman. "Your son was joking." She turned back to Billy, and lunging across the table, smacked his arm. "You think marriage is a joke?"

Billy flushed and rubbed his arm. "No. Marriage is not a joke."

Shehla clenched her teeth. "Answering me back," she said, smacking him again.

"Billy's only two years younger than me," Salsabil said, "and you can't wait to get me married off."

"Shut up." Shehla turned on her. "It's different for girls."

Salsabil grimaced. "Whatever, Mom. I want to move out."

"The only way," Shehla said, "you are moving out of this house is when you get married to a boy your father and I approve. And don't think we are unaware of what you are up to."

"What am I up to?"

"Shehla, please." Amman shook his head at her to stop.

"She thinks," Shehla continued, "we are fools who have no idea about how she is ruining our reputation by running around with that Chinese boy."

"Just so you know," Salsabil said sweetly, "he's not Chinese, he's Korean."

"They are all the same," Shehla snapped back.

"If someone said that about Pakistanis, Indians, Bangladeshis, Sri Lankans, Afghanis, you'd be up in arms," Salsabil said.

"Salsabil's right," Billy mumbled, hoping to take the attention away from his marriage comment.

"Chup karo, Billal," Amman said. "You've caused enough commotion for one morning. And you, Salsabil, have you no shame defending such activities in front of me?"

Salsabil crossed her arms. "What am I doing that is so wrong, Dad?"

"You have to ask?!" Shehla laughed incredulously. "God knows what family he comes from! You will marry a good Muslim boy—"

"And his parents want a good Korean girl, so you should all get along very well. But *we* love—"

"Love all you want," Shehla banged her fist on the table, "but only the *right* person."

Salsabil got up, slammed her chair into the table, and left. Billy glanced at Zari. She was staring at her plate.

"Thank you very much, Billal," Shehla said. "Thank you very much."

"What did I do?" Billy scowled.

"As always, you've caused unrest in this house. You too, will get married only when I allow it, and only to a girl we approve."

∽∾

"What now?" Zari whispered. Billy had come up to her room straight after Shehla had left the breakfast table in tears and Amman had followed her.

"Look, it's only two more years, more or less, till I graduate. Can you just put up with everything till then?"

"Only two more years. More or less." Zari's voice caught in her throat. She felt the ghosts creeping up on her. "I won't be able to." She hadn't meant to shriek. Now, she didn't care that she had.

"Okay. Okay." Billy drew his hands through his hair. "Okay, all right, then just give me some time to figure things out, to get a job, and then if we have to make it on our own, we will. People all over the world juggle a job, college, family. I will do so too. I'll do what you want me to, law, engineering, computers, whatever. Just trust me, okay?"

She wanted to trust him. Last night she had felt raw . . . yet cleansed. Now all she felt was dirty and used.

"You've ruined me."

Her words cut Billy.

"I wish I'd married the frog. I wish Fahad had married me."

"Finally!" Billy laughed bitterly. "The truth comes out."

"It has nothing to do with Fahad," Zari cried. "Anyone would have been better."

"Especially Fahad, I get it." Billy ground his teeth. "But *I* love you."

Zari shook her head. "Love! You've kept me hidden away and you call that love! You have a country where everything seems nice and normal, and what do I have? No family, no country and *this*." She flung her arms around the bedroom. "I'm nothing but your charity case. Even your friends said all you do is run after 'causes.'"

"My friends are the biggest idiots on the planet."

"I am your global good deed!"

"Why do you say this? Because I freed you from marrying

someone like Fahad or the frog?"

"Freed me?" Zari's eyes filled with confusion. She sank onto the armchair. "I'm more trapped than ever. Just leave me alone. Go free a country. Go free Kashmir."

"You really want me to?" Billy knelt before her, his hands on either side of her thighs, holding her in. "Because I will, you know. I will."

Phut-phut-phut.

Billy jumped out of his skin.

Phut-phut-phut.

A trumpeting like giant knocks, cannon balls, gunshots.

Phut-phut-phut.

His fingers were wet.

Phut-phut-phut

Zari pushed him away. Get out, she said, her face ashen, please get out.

Phut-phut-phut.

They heard Salsabil's voice in the hallway, "what's going on?" and Miraage's excited "is it fireworks? Is it?"

Billy held his fingers before him. His bearings scattered like marbles.

At the explosive sounds she'd wet herself. Zari.

Please, please, please, leave.

I'm not leaving you. I'm not.

I beg you, please leave me alone.

223

She folded over, her face pressed against her shoulder.

Finally, he left.

It was Miraage's helium balloons. They'd floated into the ceiling fan in the upper lounge, and gotten caught between its rotating blades.

14

Billy checked his cell phone as he made his way towards the Campus Commons. No message from Zari. A week had passed since the incident with the balloons. He'd written her a letter and slipped it under her door before he left for the campus, but there was still no word from her. Had she even read his letter? He'd told her not to be embarrassed about the incident. It had happened. Given the circumstances, it was normal. There was no need to be embarrassed.

In his cubby was an economics quiz with an F minus— he hadn't failed a test since the seventh grade—and his term paper on 'Honour In *The Illiad*' with a single comment from the Professor, *See me.* He shoved both the test and the term paper back into the cubby. He wasn't seeing anyone. Fuck economic debt. Fuck Achilles. Fuck Homer. Fuck Honour. Fuck all of this.

He stalked to the newspaper office which he found thankfully empty since most students had already begun the end of term festivities before the summer break. Feedback for his last column littered his desk. He slit open a letter.

Mr Nabi is naïve to a dangerous degree. He needs to revisit Kashmir before he claims to know what Kashmiris want! This pithy letter was signed by one 'India Forevah.'

A second letter penned by 'Passionate Pakistani' said: *Naïve, dangerous, on what basis does Mr Nabi claim to speak for Kashmir?*

And the third: *Two weeks ago, Billy Nabi, your column reopened the case on whether Mr Bush and Co. barrelled into Kuwait to rescue the principality from Iraq or to secure its oil fields for itself. You concluded that it did not matter, that even if America's intent was to only secure the oil fields, as a happy corollary, Kuwait did not fall to Iraq. Too bad, Billy Nabi, that there is no oil in Kashmir for America to fly in on wings of freedom and democracy, manipulate a vote in favour of an independent Kashmir, and then, in order to gain American control, I mean safeguard peace, deposit American troops on the soil.*

Most international students, Billy had long gleaned, measured American presence and actions overseas by its gambits for oil. Yet the letter included a list, as long as Billy's arm, of all the countries American foreign policy had meddled with openly, or behind the scenes, for too many years.

Good to see, the letter ended, *that Americans no longer consider 'the world' comprising of Canada and itself, but unfortunate to see its youth—if you are anything thing to go by—brain-dead, conditioned sons of the soil and stooges of Imperial America. That includes you too, Billy Nabi, though you personally may not realise it as you pat yourself on the back each night because the world 'matters' . . .*

Billy crumpled the letters. Truth was he *had* patted himself on the back, just a little bit. But fuck feedback. And fuck the column. At least the entertainment critics got free goodies; all he got was angst. He was going to quit. He was sick of being disrespected and discredited. He wanted to get off campus and go home. He needed to get Zari to speak to him, whether she wanted to or not.

Zari lay in bed, buried under two quilts, her rosary laced through her fingers. The dim bulb in the bedside lamp cast a bluish glow over the bedroom. She replayed, yet again, for the hundredth time, the sound of those balloons going off like gunshots by a pond, and then, her urinating in front of Billal. It was not her fault, and yet it was shameful. Just the thought of it drenched her in a humiliation so overwhelming that she could not speak to Billal, let alone face him.

Zari had read and reread the letter Billal had slipped under her door a week ago, and each time shame had scalded her anew. He'd written that she need not be embarrassed about her 'little accident', as he put it. That his father too, had lost control, like she had, when he had been tortured as a child. That, if anything, the whole incident had made him want to protect her even more. That he loved her resilience. That he was lucky to have her because he was floundering and she was his anchor.

Her shame suddenly flared into anger. *She* had lost so much, and *he* was the one who was floundering. *He* had left her rudderless, yet she was an anchor for *him*. And she was not resilient—resilient people did not lose control of their bladders because of unexpected, loud noises.

She began to tear his letter, the paper giving way under her assault like a good life giving way to the vagaries of a cruel fate. Rising, she went to Billy's room and scattered the torn pieces on his bed like ashes of the dead.

Billy opened his bedroom door to find his letter shredded and scattered all over his bed. He stood surveying the scene before yanking the bedcover off and tossing it to the floor. He had never meant to *ruin* Zari. He had tried to tell his parents about them, hadn't he? But it hadn't worked and that was not his fault. He had not allowed her accident to repel him in any way either. He had married her, for God's sake. Could there be any greater proof of love?

How he wished he'd met Zari in another time where her country was nice and normal, where a simpler life would have been possible. And the more he thought about the what ifs, the angrier and angrier he got over what had been done to her, to Mauj jee, to his father, to his Dadi who had pined away, and his Dada who had been shot for his beliefs.

God willing, his father had said, *you will live in peace and prosperity for all time.*

That's what his parents wanted for him, what all nice and normal parents wanted for their children: a peaceful existence, a robust income, a loving family, healthy hobbies, cheerful friends, and happy holidays; a mediocre life. And, because he was born here and because his parents had prospered, this peaceful, prosperous mediocrity was his for the taking.

Billy felt terrible for his father's experience of torture, but shouldn't that suffering, that pain, and that fear have made him an advocate against tyrannies rather than an ostrich sticking his head into the sand? He did not want to be like his father. He wanted to be his Dada's heir. Even Mauj jee had given him her blessings in her letters. And Zari, she had once told him that had she been a man, she would have joined the freedom fighters herself.

She had challenged him to fight for freedom. Go free a country, she'd said, go free Kashmir. Well, Billy swallowed, why not? He could not avenge Zari's wrongs, he knew that, but he *could* go to Kashmir and join the freedom fighters. He could leave his mark after all. He could change the world. It would be a dream come true.

Billy balled up the pieces of his torn letter and tossed them into the trash. He was going to embark on the journey of his life. No more of the stupid, useless meetings he attended and discussions he participated in. No more, Billy thought with a thrill, was he going to be a champion in dreaming. He would pay his dues, and he would return with battle scars worthy of Zari's love. She would look at him differently then, and so would his parents, Salsabil, Fahad, everyone. Even he would eye himself with respect.

Billy called Indus to schedule a meeting. They met at a café where the sugar on the scones glittered like knives and the blistering coffee heated Billy's enthusiasm.

"I want to fight for Kashmir's independence," Billy said, "from India and Pakistan."

Indus whistled into his espresso.

"Look, I know," Billy said, "pro-independence freedom fighters are having a tough grind between pro-Pakistan separatists and the Indian army, but this is something I have to do."

Indus put his mug down. "I can't promise anything," he squeezed Billy's shoulder, "but let me look into it."

On a new email account Billy had set up for these particular transactions, he received directions to an interview at a buffet where he was met by two men, both look-alikes in their identical off-white buttoned shirts and black pants and severe expressions. They sat opposite him at a table by the kitchen doors, their keen eyes impaling him. Why didn't he join the army?

"Because," Billy said, "I'm not a robot willing to fight for just any war that has been thrust upon me by the government."

Billy looked at the wilted bamboo stuck in the golden pot on the table. The robot rule was the reason he'd never been too interested in his maternal grandfather, an army man, though his mother had told him that the army had been for her ambitious father, one of the few means readily available to rise to the very top in Pakistan where military coups routinely altered kismets.

When Billy had turned eighteen, he'd pondered long and hard the implications of signing the Select Service. Draft dodger, deserter, evader, coward, Dan had said, laughing even after Billy ended up signing. Going to Kashmir, Billy thought, would prove he wasn't a dodger, deserter, evader or coward when it came to the real deal. *He was a Nabi, a freedom fighter, it was in his blood.*

"I want to fight for an independent Kashmir," Billy repeated.

"Why independent?"

Billy looked the men in the eyes. Without giving any names, he told them about his father, Mauj jee, his Dada and Dadi. He wanted to set Kashmir free so people could return there, to live, to die, to be buried in their homeland amongst their own.

Over egg drop soup, the men told Billy what a noble and brave and blessed young man he was to have considered this path in life. The oppressed would thank him for it, bless him for it, and blessed were his parents as well, for having raised such a conscientious individual. They must be proud of him. Were they? Billy looked at the pale green chillies floating in his untouched soup. Yes, he said, they were.

The men lowered their voices. Indus had spoken highly of Billal. He'd assured them that Billal did not consider this some video game he could turn off and on at will. Neither was it an adventure. It was a difficult undertaking that taxed one not only physically but also morally. It was also an undertaking from which, if he emerged, he would emerge a greater man.

They could not look into his heart, the older man said. They could not truly find out his true intent, only God could do that, but looking at him, it seemed to them, that his intentions *were* good and honourable, and that these were traits that proved his dedication was one bestowed upon him by God, a dedication to restore honour and dignity and freedom to a blighted, fallen, and dishonoured land. It was beyond mere generosity of spirit and time, it was what any decent, civilised, freedom-loving human being would do. Billy's heart swelled. This was true.

"Listen my child," the older one said, leaning over his egg fried rice. "Freeing the fallen from oppressors is not a nine-to-five job, it is a calling. You must believe that without doing this, your life is meaning-less, otherwise better to stay at home. But if you do decide that this is indeed your true calling, then you will be required to undergo a month-long training before being sent for a stint at the front, a stint which usually lasts two months. And remember, there are going to be no proper barracks and no time-offs. There is only going to be belief in your cause and a fervour towards attaining victory at all costs." Smiling indulgently, he folded his napkin and placed it on the table. "Think about it, take your time, there is no hurry. If you decide this is your destiny, we are here, one email away."

Billy could still taste the oily fortune cookie in his mouth as he sat in front of his computer, staring at the email he'd composed. *You are on the path to true love*, his fortune had read. The two men had cursorily glanced at their fortunes before crumpling them up and leaving. They'd left a good tip, he had noticed.

Billy looked at Mauj jee's letters. He had not obeyed his father and returned them to his mother's jewellery box. That this was his calling, Billy was positive. And all it would take was a commitment of three months; three months combined for both training and fighting. For Kashmir's sake, what were three months out of his lifetime? He'd be back just in time for the start of the next semester. As for the taking of lives . . . to take a life, just snuff out someone's tomorrow because they were on the opposite side, it was . . . well . . . inconceivable, unless that person was a monster, meaning his harm quotient outweighed his harmony quotient, someone like Hitler. A man like Hitler he could kill. No second thoughts. But an Indian or a Pakistani he'd never so much as quarrelled with in his life, and now to be fighting to death against them . . . but nothing could be gained without fighting for it.

But he wasn't going to fight just anybody. He was going to fight against men who'd whipped his father, who'd attacked his Mauj jee, fettered his pining grandmother with unrequited longing for her homeland, and murdered his Dada. He would be fighting against men—be it Pakistani separatists or the Indian Army—who were choking Kashmir's simple desire to be completely independent. Surely he'd be able to kill them face-to-face, hand-to-hand, eye-to-eye? And, if he was imprisoned, tortured, and killed, it would all have been for freedom. And freedom was worth everything and everything was worth freedom.

Billy swallowed. Sooner or later everyone had to die. Since the beginning of humanity, humanity was coming to terms with one's own mortality and one's ability to take life. He took a deep breath. It was okay. He was just following in the footsteps of mankind.

Billy's finger hovered over the send key.

Hours later he received a reply.

He was going.

Three days later, Billy huddled in his dorm room over his backpack, ticking off a checklist—a sweater, an eight pack of underwear, woollen socks, a small flashlight, batteries, insect repellent, a compass, a sturdy water bottle, iodine pills, passport, and the ticket they'd purchased for him, he was booked on a flight to Peshawar and his flight left in a few hours.

Fingering the ticket, Billy couldn't help but feel excitement like when he was a child and was going to the concert, or a sports game, or anywhere likely to be an adventure. He forced himself to sober down. This was *not* an adventure. It was an honourable undertaking, one that would endanger his very life. Yet, as the fizzy bubbles insisted on erupting inside his stomach, he couldn't help but think that Kashmir *would* be an adventure, a place as changed as he himself was since his childhood.

He wished there was a whole group he was going with, wished there were others he could turn to and ask if they too were feeling apprehension as well as anticipation, wished there were others with whom he could share the moments when he felt like, anyone but himself, but, except for sending Indus a text message and receiving a rather cryptic 'good luck' in return, there was nothing else to do and no one else to talk to.

Billy lit a joint and cranked open his dorm room window to a night filled with the cry of a thousand crickets. Go free Kashmir, Zari had said. He took a drag. His throat burned. He could not leave. Not without Zari's consent. Not without knowing if she truly believed this was more important than her, than them. He stubbed the joint out. He had to speak to her whether she wanted to speak to him or not. He grabbed his car keys and headed for home.

Someone was calling her name.

Zari . . . Zari . . .

Zari tried to resist sleep, tried until she didn't know if she was half-asleep or half-awake. She was a fish trapped under a frozen pond, sinking under the weight of clotting blood and snow. She was a rabbit, a deer, a wolf, a bear caught in a trap, a trap in which even if she tore herself free, she left parts of herself behind, bleeding, body-less limbs which grew eyes, eyes that whispered and screamed in voices that had once sung lullabies.

Zari . . . Zari . . .

Kiran, is it you?

But her sister metamorphosed into her father, her father into her mother, her mother disintegrating, reintegrating into Billal dragging a heavy chair to barricade the door from intruders.

I am going to Kashmir, to fight for its freedom, to fight for you, that's what you want, isn't it?

Once, she'd vowed to take revenge. Right the wrongs so cruelly done to people who had not deserved such a fate. What had happened? How could she have become so complacent? Why was it so easy to become complacent here?

An evening by a bonfire next to a pond lit with diyas, the strumming of a guitar, playing antakshari, a cacophony of ducks, a terrified shriek.

everything

gone

go

She covered her face with her hair so they could not see her.

So she could not see them.

This time her eyes were dry.

Go, she said, the merry crackling of the bonfire a lustful carnage in her ears.

go, go, go.

I'm going then, he said, stepping back, melting, fading, gone.

∞∞

Billy picked up his backpack, took a final look around his bedroom, and shut the door behind him. On the landing, he caressed his parents' and sisters' bedroom doors before coming to stand in front of Zari's door. He had a small gift bag for her, but he resisted going in. He could not bear another leave taking. Go, Zari had said. She'd been sitting up, eyes wide open, a shadow of hair hanging over her face. Go, go, go, she'd said. He'd kissed her forehead, and when she shrank back, he'd left.

Now he opened the door a crack and thrust the gift bag inside onto the suitcase.

In the kitchen, he propped up a note on the island.

As dawn bit the sky with blood red teeth, he stepped out and over the cellophane-wrapped newspaper on the stoop. He stared at it for a second, lying there on the concrete step, waiting to be taken in no matter what news it contained, and he wondered if he would ever see it again, this step he'd never really even noticed before.

He looked back as he stepped out, but there was no wave, no movement in any window as he walked out of the driveway towards the bus station where he would catch a shuttle that would take him to the airport.

PART 2

SHOULD NOT HAVE TO SUFFER
1998

15

Zari sat up in bed, her vision adjusting to the morning light entering the bedroom through a slit in the curtains. Her nightmares were back, a more ferocious collage than before: faces disintegrating, reintegrating into a mishmash of familiar, unfamiliar faces until everyone seemed out to wrong, rape, murder, abandon. She rubbed her eyes and noticed that the armchair barricading the door was no longer in its place. She saw a gift bag on the suitcase. He was giving her gifts now.

Inside the bag were three hundred dollar bills. Her Khala, her Uncle, Mr Nabi, all of them asked if she needed money, none of them had thought to just give her some. Huddling in a corner of the bag, a tiny plastic duck enclosed in a bar of transparent soap. What was this duck meant to imply? Her accident, his hands, the armchair, that all could be cleaned up, left spotless, what? They couldn't go on like this. Billal was right, her silent treatment was detrimental because, with communications cut, they would get nowhere. She had to speak to him.

Zari tiptoed to the kitchen to get the cordless phone. The grey morning light lit up the blue carnations in the middle of the island and, propped up against the vase, a note:

For family

. . . I am leaving for Kashmir, to fight for its freedom.

I'm a Nabi, I can't help it, it's in my blood. Wish me

luck. Don't be mad at me. I mean, I'm sorry but it is

my life and I can live it as want . . . I love you . . .

Kashmir? Freedom? The world whirled before Zari. She sank onto a bar stool. And waited for it to regain balance. Her heart beat so fast she put her hands over it to protect it from leaping out. Her mind was a jumble. Her father had wanted Kashmir to remain with India. Her mother had favoured Pakistan. Imran and Kiran had been for complete independence. And all she'd ever wanted was a stop to the curfews and raids and other uncivil interruptions. Which freedom had Billal gone to implement?

Zari was nauseous as she returned the note to the counter. She climbed the stairs with leaden steps. In the guest room, she sat on the prayer mat and stared at the duck ensnared in the soap. She was scared for him. And she was scared for herself. A spasm shot through her, an irate imp tugging memory, jostling the borders of remembrance, demanding that she recall. She looked at the armchair pushed away from the door—a sweat broke over her—it hadn't been a dream—he *had* come into her room: I'm going to free Kashmir, he'd said, and she'd said *go*. Overcome, Zari ran to the bathroom and heaved up the contents of her stomach.

An hour later, Zari forced herself to step out of her room. She found the Nabis congregated in Billal's bedroom, the air pulsing with fear and confusion. She stood behind Salsabil, right by the door. Billal's room was a mess. Clothes strewn over the floor, and a toppled bottle of cologne leaking a dark blotch onto the dresser, causing the bedroom to reek of pine needles.

Amman stood rubbing his jaw, shock plastering his face. Billal's cell phone was in his hand. Shehla sat at the edge of Billal's bed, cradling his red windbreaker against her cheeks. Billal's note lay in her lap. The home phone rang. But it was only Buraaq, and Amman insisted that Shehla speak to her brother.

"Why would he say he's gone to fight for Kashmir's freedom?" Tears dripped off Shehla's chin, dampening the windbreaker. "He's not going to come back. I can feel it right here." She touched her chest. "Why should you and Barbara visit? I don't need moral support. I need my son back . . ." She hugged the jacket. "You're lucky. Your son died young while I have nineteen years of memories to smother me. At least you know where Baber is buried, you can visit his grave when you want . . . he's safe." Shehla shut her eyes. "I didn't mean . . ." Her tears began to fall fast. "I don't know what I'm saying, Buraaq. I can't talk." She thrust the phone at Amman. By the time Amman finished speaking and hung up, a pale Salsabil was trying to force Shehla to drink a glass of water.

"Should we call the police?" Shehla looked from Salsabil to Amman.

"And say what?" Amman flung his hands up in despair. He didn't even know who to turn to for help. The airlines would just tell him that they couldn't give out passenger information. Should he call an embassy? But which embassy to call? And amongst those of their friends and acquaintances who he knew were actively sympathetic with the Kashmir cause, which ones could he trust to help find Billal, force him back, and then forget his folly? But Shehla had told him not to mention a word to anyone. They were going to tell everyone Billal had gone sightseeing in Europe—and never again was he going to go against his wife.

"What happens in these guerrilla movements?" Salsabil asked. "Do they let you come back if you want to?"

"I don't know," Amman said. He should never have told Billal about his torture in police custody, never have showed him his scars, never have brought up his father. Billal's stubbornness was America's fault. Ten years of fighting a jihad for freedom in Afghanistan against Russian communism which had resulted in movies such as *Rambo*, had turned every fool into an idealistic idiot ready to fight for freedom anywhere on the planet, except only his child had been fool enough to get up and go.

"Why *don't* you know?" Shehla's eyes blazed. "Your father belonged to one."

"Shehla, that was a long time ago," Amman said quietly.

"These days they are not even called freedom fighters." Shehla's mouth trembled. "They are called terrorists."

"It's all relative."

"You are your father's son after all."

Amman cringed at Shehla's charge. "That is unfair."

"Unfair doesn't mean it's incorrect."

"Dad, Mom," Salsabil interrupted them. "Is it dangerous that he's an American?"

Six tourists had been kidnapped in Kashmir a few years

ago. Only the American had returned alive, but only because he'd managed to escape. A Norwegian had been decapitated. At the time, Amman had been adamant that Kashmiri freedom fighters could not have been the culprits. Tourists were Kashmir's bread and butter, he'd said, their pride. This brutality, he'd maintained, was the work of outsiders who were trying to malign the good name of all Kashmiris.

"I don't know, beta." Amman looked at Salsabil through helpless eyes. "I just don't know."

"It's my fault," Shehla said. "I should have insisted he go to Europe."

"It's my fault, Mama." Salsabil's voice was small. "I kept calling him a couch saviour."

"I told you a million times not to taunt your brother, but have you ever listened to a single thing I've said? See what's happened now? See? He's gone to be a saviour."

Salsabil turned red.

"Shehla, stop it," Amman said. "It's not her fault any more than it's yours." It's my fault, he thought. Had Billal been planning this Superman-Spiderman misadventure even as they'd been speaking? My God—the boy had even mentioned taking up arms! Why hadn't he suspected something was amiss?

"It is your fault," Shehla said.

Amman flushed—

"You brought Zari here!"

"Shehla!" Amman glanced at Zari shrunken by the door.

Shehla gazed at Zari. The girl looked scared, but this only

243

hardened Shehla's heart. She wanted to shake her, hit her even, ask her how freedom fighters were treated in Kashmir, but, just as suddenly, Shehla realised that she didn't want to know, that she would prefer to remain ignorant despite being painfully aware that the very acknowledgment of a wilful ignorance shattered any bliss. She caught her breath. She was not going to collapse like her mother had after news of her father's death in the 1965 war between India and Pakistan had reached them. That war too, had been over Kashmir. Kashmir. Kashmir. Kashmir.

"Her Khala hoisted her on us," Shehla said in a flat voice. "It's her Khala's fault. You and her Khala have sent my son to his death. You and—"

"Bas Shehla," Amman spoke sharply. "Enough."

"Selfish man, typical of you to be more worried about a stranger than your own children."

"That's not true."

"*He*'s just like you. Selfish. Always putting others before himself."

"Selfless. You mean selfless."

"Mom, Dad," Salsabil whispered. "Please. Stop it."

Shehla picked up Billy's note and thrust it at Amman. "What does he mean by 'a true Nabi'? What does he mean?"

Amman looked at Shehla and something rose within him, something cold and jagged, intent on slashing its way out, something he hadn't even know was hibernating within him until he heard himself say, "It means that I'm proud of my son for going to fight against atrocities."

అలా

Amman walked into the master bathroom, banging the double doors shut behind him. Get out, Shehla had said, just get out of my sight. Sitting on the edge of the Jacuzzi, Amman fished the cigarette pack out of his shirt and stared at it for one long minute, unsure of what to do. This was the first pack he'd bought since a fifteen-year-old Salsabil had riffled through his cigarettes, threatening that if he smoked then she would too. It took Amman many attempts to light a cigarette and after the initial inhalation, he stared at the needle of smoke spiralling unsteadily between his fingers, breaking apart, dispersing. Try as he might, he could not squelch the admission that, shocked and guilty as he'd been when he'd read Billal's note, he'd also been overcome with pride. He'd been arrested, held, whipped for no crime and with no recourse and his son had gone to make sure no one else had to ever go through something like that. But his father too would have been proud of his son and that fact was making Amman miserable.

His father had believed that everything was fair in love and war. Amman believed that even in the cause of love and war there should be limits such as not torturing little boys because of their father's deeds or a father persuading his little boy that torture was justified for a greater good. Neither age nor experience had changed Amman's mind, he believed Billal had stepped grossly out of bounds, and furthermore, there was a difference between taking a stand and going to fight, from where then had sprung pride?

He watched the cigarette burn, the soft faint cackling of the burning paper and tobacco the only sound in the bathroom. He took one last drag and flushed the butt down the toilet. As he undressed, he couldn't help but think that in betraying Shehla's trust, he'd overstepped his own boundaries, and in divulging secrets to Billal, he'd crossed over into behaving as if everything *was* fair in love and war. Stepping into the shower, Amman turned his face towards the water hurtling at him and cried.

16

Billy didn't sleep during the fourteen-hour flight to Islamabad. Or the hour-long transit stop in the small shabby domestic terminal where he looked longingly at the telephone kiosks and, as a final farewell to all vestiges of home, ordered a plate of fries and smothered them with a ketchup so virulently red and sweet it tasted like nothing he'd ever known. Or during the hour-long connecting flight to Peshawar even though he shut his eyes begging sleep to come. Instead, he looked at his fellow passengers—a woman in a full burqa, her short orange painted fingernails, peaking out of the sleeves; a middle-aged man in a shiny business suit, cracking pistachios with his mouth wide open; an elderly man clutching his seat rest as if he was terrified of falling any moment—and he wondered where they were headed.

As soon as they landed, Billy strode down the metallic steps of the small Fokker and onto the burning tarmac outside, the scorching sun making the air shimmer.

Inside the airport, grey ceiling fans whirred at full speed, their merciless blades slapping the stuffy air. Porters zeroed in on Billy, offering him their service, the screech of their trolleys rivalling the grunts of the conveyor belt. Billy waved them away and hurried on, stepping out of the airport doors and into a mélange of dusty, sweaty humanity. Men yelled

out taxi fares, hotel rates, hawked wares on pushcarts—
plastic visors and fake designer sunglasses and wristwatches.

Billy looked all around, fiddling with the two long red
pencils in the breast pocket of his tee-shirt, a signal for his
contact, until they met their twins in the breast pocket of
a stocky man in a chalk-blue kurta shalwar. The man was
leaning against a post, poking his teeth with a matchstick.
When he saw Billy's pencils, he tossed the matchstick and
came bounding over like an overgrown puppy.

"Billawal Sahib," he said, using Billy's code name,
"Welcome, welcome, most welcome. I, Shahbaz." His
eyes were olive green chips in a golden-bearded face, and
he pumped Billy's hand in jubilant paws. "Car is that way."
Shahbaz pointed in the general direction of the parking lot.
"Billalwal Sahib, I carry bag for you."

Grabbing the backpack, Shahbaz took hold of Billy's
hand and steered him through the crowd. Billy tried not to
gag on the body odour and diesel fumes. Anything Billawal
required? Shahbaz asked in rudimentary Urdu with a Pushto
accent. Cigarettes? Food? Toilet? Because they were not
stopping once they set off for camp—a two-three hour
journey depending on the traffic at the Pakistan-Afghanistan
border.

"I'm good," Billy said as they stepped off a sidewalk
lined with droopy trees and into a dusty parking lot crammed
with bicycles, scooters, small cars, and giant SUVs. They
crossed the length of the parking lot before Shahbaz slapped
the bonnet of an unmarked four wheel drive, the paint faded
into patchy clouds. A young teen squatted by the fender
like a cat sunning itself, the cloying heat and dust of no
consequence. His red rubber sandals glowed like embers. He

jumped up when he saw Billy, and jiggling an embroidered skullcap sunk in masses of black hair, he offered a smart salute and his name, Mohsin.

Billy sat upright in the passenger seat as Shahbaz, the camp's driver as well as a member of the kitchen staff, wove the car through a market street, bumping over potholes, one hand continuously on the horn as he swore and cursed every jaywalker and every stray dog that crossed his way. Mohsin, also kitchen staff, was sitting in the back seat, squashed between sacks of flour, lentils, potatoes, onions, and other camp rations, and humming a tune Billy could not recognise.

Billy's window was stuck half way down and the hot breeze blowing on his face smelt of fruits and spices and a hundred other things he couldn't identify. It came to him gradually, a strange sensation like looking at a box of crayons and discovering the absence of primary colours, that there was not a single woman to be seen, and that it was the men, dressed in pastel shalwar kurtas—powder pinks, lime greens, chalk blues—who brightened the weathered canvas like splashes of paint. The market itself ran along both sides of the road, with shops and shopkeepers spilling right out onto the street. Songs blared out of music shops with glass doors adorned with posters of Indian movie stars. Butcher stalls hung flayed goats while restaurants grilled meats on outdoor spits. A barber had set up shop under a tree and was giving a man a shave. Next to him, a cardboard sign showed a giant decayed tooth with a hammer over it. Apparently, the barber was also a dentist.

Billy felt dizzy. Rudyard Kipling had described this frontier town in his 1901 novel *Kim* as the insalubrious city of Peshawar and Billy wondered what he might have called it now, almost a century later when Peshawar remained a frontier city, but, with the advent of technology, a thousand times more congested, dirtier, and frenetic. As a mammoth truck lumbered past, Billy covered his nose and mouth against the woollen exhaust swirling up and beyond traffic lights, through the tangle of electricity cables, over muscular crows as grand as any European gargoyles, before settling on the pearly grey sky, just another layer of pollution

As they reached the outskirts of Peshawar, he stared at the Afghan refugee camps that began appearing along the road, the cardboard and corrugated iron shacks heaped like piles of grimy pennies. Kids scampered beside the car, their palms outstretched, yelling, smiling, and Billy wished he had something to give them. He thought of the girl with the blue-green eyes whose face was a National Geographic cover. He waved at the kids. The kids waved back. One boy stuck his tongue out at him and then burst into laughter. Soon all were out of sight.

A little later, they drove under a giant archway of stone. Billy craned his neck to read the sign: Gateway to the Khyber. Never had he imagined he'd traverse the same ground as Alexander the Great, and certainly never under these circumstances travel a route which had, for centuries, shuttled travellers, traders, and invaders on foot and horseback and in camel drawn caravans stooped with cargo. Billy was overcome, as if these people, these stories, these homes had once upon a time been the landscape of his life. He stuck his head out of the window and looked at the fettuccine road they were driving on, a road which meandered through low hills, valleys, and plains. As they turned a bend, Billy glimpsed an ancient, gnarled man lugging a television on his bent back. Smuggled, Shahbaz informed him, pointing towards the television. Apparently, a thriving black market had taken root amidst the tattered glories and splendour of past civilisations: a Sikh fort here, a Buddhist stupa there, the remnants of a Hindu temple, the dome of a mosque, British insignia carved into rock, and this very road itself a grand commission of the British, built with local sweat and blood, as was the railway track higher up, a railway track that now was a tourist attraction but, back then, Billy had read, had been crucial in transporting men and munitions to the frontiers in order to defend the British Empires' way of life. And here they were, the three of them, hurtling through the mountains in a rackety jeep, yet again towards battle.

The unexpected connection to the vast ebb and flow of history rendered Billy miniscule, an insignificant speck. He picked a ragged thread on his stone-washed jeans. He was not just any old speck. He'd shown his parents, especially his mother, that they couldn't dictate the terms of his life, that they couldn't impose their will on him. Salsabil would never again call him a couch saviour. And Zari, she would be proud of him. She had to be proud of him. Billy lay his head against the back rest and shut his eyes, willing into his mind an image of Zari feeding the ducks without a care in the world.

Billy woke up, his shoulder jostled by Mohsin. Mohsin was holding Shahbaz's rifle between his legs, his chin resting on the muzzle, his large cantaloupe face poking through the front seat headrests. He was sucking rocky candy, his lips glistening.

"Wants?" Mohsin asked in broken English as he offered rock candy from his palm. Billy looked at the grubby fingernails, the splayed palm, the life line caked with dirt, and in the centre, clumps of cloudy rock sugar rising like jagged, white cliffs. He heard his mother's voice whisper in his ear: Billaloo, never eat anything that looks dirty.

"Thanks," Billy said, taking a piece. Pure sugar drowned his mouth. Miraage would have devoured this and he smiled at the thought of his little sister, her sweet tooth, and the way she scrunched her face while Zari coaxed curls out of her tangles.

"Most welcome, most welcome." Mohsin grinned as he popped the remaining candies into his mouth and crunched loudly.

Billy sat up in his seat, his sleep all gone. They were higher up in the mountains now, the heat growing dull as they drove through Michni Post from where Billy could see the border between Pakistan and Afghanistan. He peered out of the window in order to read a commemorative tablet.

On January 13th 1842, Surgeon Bryden of the British
Expedientary Forces staggered into the post
as the lone survivor to tell the poignant tale
of the ill-fated soldiers holding the Kabul residency.

Billy had a vision of a man dazed by the unbelievable spectre of being the lone survivor; of a tall girl rocking her dead nephew in her arms and discovering that being the lone survivor was not a boon; of all the lone survivors of all the battles in the world cursing their luck at dodging death. For the next half an hour or so, until they arrived at the border town of Torkham, Billy tried to erase from his mind the haunting of lone survivors.

At the Torkham border town—a smuggler's market where chattering men with guns huddled around open air tea stalls—a man in a pink shalwar kurta, a loaded bandolier across his chest, stood on the roadside painting the panorama. A large canvas on the wooden easel depicted Pakistan's grizzled khaki green hills petering into the grizzled khaki green Afghan plain, the sort of art work, Billy recognised, that decorated desi restaurants back home. At the Torkham checkpoint, Shahbaz took a permit out of the dashboard and presented it to the Pakistani sentry. A cursory glance, and the sentry waved them off to a stream of cargo trucks crawling through the gates into Afghanistan.

It took ten minutes, Billy noted, ten minutes on his watch, to get from the Pakistani checkpoint to the Afghan checkpoint—a small mud hut behind a jute cot. Seated on the jute cot, a black-turbaned official rocked back and forth before an open Quran, apparently unconcerned by the long line of trucks awaiting his inspection. Driving around the trucks, Shahbaz honked and the official acknowledged the gesture with a curt wave, and then they were off on the smoothly paved linear road that stretched all the way, Shahbaz informed Billy, to Kabul.

Had there been no gates, no checkpoints, no demarcation of any kind, Billy would never have known, save for the variations in topography, that one country had ended and another begun, where the subcontinent became Central Asia or was it the other way round. He recalled a family trip where they'd driven from the US to Canada and how, there too, other than the checkpoints, nothing had distinguished one country from the other. Billy turned to look back at Pakistan, the land, the sky, the horizon. For a moment, the world was Pangaea still intact, with nomads on camels lumbering, grazing, plodding from one great tract to another; barbed wire fences, passports, visas, ink for stamps, all inventions still undreamt, the inventors still waiting to be born.

Borders were internal once: thirst, hunger, a need to rest, to settle for the night—perhaps just where the jeep's wheels rolled over right now—recoup, and come dawn, move on. The person who had decided not to move on, that person was the grandmaster of a world-altering vision: the foundation of a permanent home, an address, a map, the seed of a civilisation, an empire, a universe which each inhabitant believed everlasting until betrayal came as a meteor, or a river turning course, or drought, or famine, or the steps of kings, conquerors, armies, and more recently, bombs, missiles, warheads, drones.

"Shuravi," Shahbaz said, pointing to a Soviet tank sitting along the road. A relic, like modern art, Billy thought. Excellent for playing hide and seek and finding treasure, Mohsin added. Once, in one tank, he grinned, he'd found a ballpoint pen with the picture of a fully-dressed lady on it, but when he held it upside down, the lady became naked. Shhh, Shahbaz said, his nostrils curling even as Billy laughed.

They began bombarding him with questions, their voices laced with excitement: How old was he? Where had he come from? Were all Americans like Rambo and John Wayne and James Bond? Had he seen Terminator? What was his life like in America? What did he eat there? What did he do there?

"On a break from college."

After that there was silence in the car again, except for Mohsin coughing up phlegm and spitting it out the window. They passed fields of dust, some bordered with rocks painted white if the landmines were cleared and, if not, then rocks painted red. They passed pickup vans, honking wildly, rushing past them in clouds of dust. They passed goat herds, the herders walking behind their nimble charges. They passed hills stubbled with low lying shrubs and dwarfed by the faraway mountain range. They passed a thin man astride a thinner camel. They passed fat cargo trucks. They passed a mileage marker rising from the road like a pillar of salt, the numbers long faded. But no matter who or what they passed, it seemed there was nothing for miles save sun and sky, a forlorn grandeur, a wilful loneliness.

It was late afternoon when Shahbaz turned off the main road onto a dirt track. A little while later, he came to a halt outside an adobe compound, its main wall cut like a series of steps. A sentry on the top step raised his rifle and waved it like a beacon from a lighthouse.

"There's weapons training and maintenance. We've got Kalashnikov, automatic guns, RPK light machine-guns, ZU anti-aircraft cannon, 82 mm and 120 mm mortars, and rockets. There's hijacking a vehicle and an aircraft. Hostage taking and treatment. Assassination."

Billy stood before Commander Salman, a moose of a man in a well fitting uniform and crew cut, the hair on his ear lobes curling like antlers. Shahbaz had walked him across a courtyard full of men and into a makeshift office, one of the adobe rooms lining the compound wall and deposited Billy, as well as a grocery receipt, with the Commander who remained seated in a metal chair behind a wooden desk balanced by a brick under one of its legs.

Billy stood before the desk, dazed by the onslaught of

information. He was alarmed at the thought of assassination, hijacking, and hostage taking. He tried not to look at the scrappy poster above the Commander—a severed hand and foot surrounded by a light green pineapple, a medium-sized green ball, and a bright green butterfly all stamped with thick scarlet Xs. His toes curled in his sneakers. The Commander followed Billy's gaze.

"Land around camp is cleared of mines, but one can never be too careful." He smiled ruefully. "The Soviets did a thorough job laying death traps all across the land and in that way are still very much with us." The setting sun dripped in through a square cut in a wall and onto three tin trunks lined against another wall and the Commander knelt before one of the trunks and took out two sets of a fawn uniform—a pair of baggy pants and a loose shirt along with a bandolier and a rifle.

"Pre-owned but complimentary."

Billy tucked the uniforms and bandolier into his backpack. The rifle, an AK47, was lighter than it looked and his mind flooded with information he'd read: how the A stood for automatic, K for its inventor, and 47 for the year the design was conceived. How it had been mass-produced world over and was, therefore, cheap and affordable for every revolutionary group from the Tamil Tigers to the IRA. Here in Afghanistan, it was also often one's sole possession, fired in offense, in defence, to celebrate weddings and births, to mourn deaths; it awed Billy, the sheer might of this man-made creation, of what it could mean and accomplish. Was this the sort of weapon his grandfather had used? Or—his heart plummeted—was it a rifle like this which had shot Zari?

Dusk was settling in and one by one, lights were coming on all around the camp. A single bulb lit up outside the Commander's office, the light flickering in through the coarse wool kilim curtain, illuminating the green and brown diamond pattern.

Billy wanted to ask exactly what sort of training he would have to undergo and what skills he would have to master.

"Exactly how long," he began, his voice miraculously steady, "will my training last?"

"Two months of training here, maybe more, depending on your prowess."

Two months. Billy licked his parched lips. His interviewers had said training lasted for only a month. He swallowed. He was here now—what were another two months out of a lifetime? Two months at the training camp plus three months at the front equalled five months. He would train tirelessly. Make sure the two months did not extend.

Walking up to the doorway, the Commander called out for an Abid.

Abid was a swarthy, bald-headed, thick-bearded, middle-aged man with a nose which had clearly been broken at least once. He shook Billy's hand and greeted him in a British accent. He was, Abid informed Billy, basically a Kashmiri bloke who happened to have been born and brought up in England. Billy instantly felt at ease—England, America, same difference; they were both outsiders wanting in.

"Abid," the Commander was saying, "is the Kashmir group's leader. He will answer any questions you have, but any problems, Billawal," the Commander gazed at Abid, "and you come directly to me."

"No problems," Abid said, his boot tapping the earthen floor like a small, frantic animal. "No problems at all."

The call for evening prayers sounded from outside. The Commander rose.

"Start Billawal on a basic weapons training regimen, and, Billawal, like I said, any problems, you come to me. I should be here for the duration of your stay. Physical training and religious instruction are mandatory for all. One is for the body, the other for the soul. Also, strictly no alcohol, no drugs, no smoking," and, glancing at Abid, the Commander left the hut.

∞∞

Mullah Khaled, the camp cleric, his white beard hennaed a rooster red, raised his hands to his ears: Allah-o-Akbar, God is great. And the prayers began. Moonlight tapered between the dim bulbs in the compound and wove shadows onto the red tin gate, the mule, and the two goats tethered to an acacia tree, as well as a line of jute cots where the instructors, Billy would learn, always sat, though now they were standing the same as everyone, alert for prayer on the spliced octagonal patterned carpets—ample space for the hundred or so men gathered at any one time—and laid out in the courtyard under the open sky.

Billy, for whom water had always been available to perform ablutions, had followed Abid as he sped through the dry bodily purification, copying his arid motions of washing hands, arms, face, neck, mouth, head, feet, before they joined the congregation. But he felt grimy and dirty, unclean and impure, still wearing his scruffy sneakers where, before, he had always prayed barefoot in a room, on an immaculate surface. And yet out here, under the star-lit sky, breathing the open air, the solemnity of prayers seemed not impeded by unnecessary contingencies.

It was quiet, ranks rising, bending, bowing, the rustle of clothes, the murmur of Quranic verses softening the cool night air. In the US, Zari would perform this prayer too, Billy thought as he pressed his forehead to the carpet, ignoring the dust tickling his nose and the smell of sunburned fibres, the sour milk body odour surrounding him, the stench of animal, and pressing his forehead harder he prayed, sincerely, for fortitude in the quest for freedom. His head turned to the angel on his right shoulder recording his good deeds for judgment in the hereafter and then to the angel on his left shoulder recording his misdeeds. On both sides he saw rifles lying fallow by their owners' sides.

Amen.

The congregation broke noisily and Billy was surrounded by a gaggle of young men led by Mohsin. They were jostling each other to get closer to him, shake his hand, introduce themselves. In America, did all the women bare shoulders, arms, legs? On the streets? What then must they do at home? Billy half smiled at the stereotype: the all-naked Western woman versus the all-veiled Eastern one. He tried to place accents and names in the sunburned faces, all a blur with identically long, unruly beards, required by the present government of all men in Afghanistan. Billy's own was getting there.

The men were all identically dressed in crumpled, faded uniforms, their ammunition belts slashing their chests. Billy too had changed into his uniform, clean, though the rough texture chaffed his skin and smelled of mildew, and he wondered what had become of its previous owner. The only discerning feature of the men around him was their headgear and footwear. Fawn berets, camouflage baseball hats, white skull caps, combat boots, leather strapped sandals, tennis shoes. Some, like Billy, were bareheaded and sneakered.

What did the women do at home, why they—

Abid stood with an annoyed expression. Same thing happened to me, mate, he muttered. Novelty of being a Westerner dies a natural death, sooner or later. But Billy didn't mind being the centre of attention. Not at all. And he understood being stereotyped. Whenever he saw a German, all he wanted to ask was how they felt about Hitler.

Billy eventually found himself surrounded by a small group of men speaking Kashmiri. He worked hard to decipher their rapid speech and respond as best as he could in a combination of Kashmiri-Urdu-English, the mash-up and his accent, no doubt, the reason for their smiles.

"Nazeer," Abid said, pointing to a skinny man with unruly curls and beer-coloured eyes and then proceeded to introduce the others just as perfunctorily. After the first few names, which Billy presumed were codenames, he just smiled back without trying to remember their names, these men with whom he would train, besides whom he would fight, whose backs he would be expected to watch and who would, no doubt, watch his back, these men, his comrades in arm, his cohorts.

Abid's cursory introduction over, the group drifted away until only Nazeer remained, his mop of curls toppling over his bony face as he smiled deeply and reached out to clasp Billy's hand. A moment later, Abid dug his fingers into Billy's arm and spun him towards a row of flint-eyed instructors reclining on jute cots and Billy saw Nazeer shrug and walk away.

"Billawal," Abid was saying, "is from the US of A."

The instructors nodded as they gazed at him in the light of the bulbs strung over their heads, silent, nary a question about scantily clad women or movies or music. Mullah Khaled's fingers paused on his rosary beads and he nodded at Billy to come closer and Billy lowered his head until he was jowl to jowl with the cleric and he could smell insect repellent from the white hair crawling from out of the cleric's collar.

"Jihad," Mullah Khaled said, "grows from the heart and spreads through the body like a set of veins. You are prepared for that?"

Billy nodded even as a blade of ice slashed down his spine. Jihad—undertaking a just struggle, for a just cause, for a just resolution against the evil in one's heart and the evil in the world.

"Speak," Mullah Khaled said gently. "Always speak."

Billy cleared his throat. "I'm prepared."

"My son, death on this route is yet another one of Allah's ordinances for his children. You should be at peace with this. To become shaheed, martyred, to die for one's principles, is itself a blessing."

∞∞

Billy was still digesting the Mullah's words as he followed Abid into a rocky passageway between the camp's perimeter wall and the backs of the huts. They stopped in an alcove so dark, the stars above seemed to have been punched out of the sky. The stars, the moon, the very constellations looked different from the night sky back home; everything was alien. Billy wondered, this time with a guilty stab, how his family was faring.

"Why did the cleric say that to me?" Billy placed his rifle next to Abid's against the mud wall. A lizard zigzagged up a crack and crept inside.

"He says it to everyone."

Billy eyed the filter-less cigarette Abid lit with a plastic lighter.

"Report me, will you?" Abid broke into a skewed smile. "Don't worry. Only alcohol gets them truly riled. And even that can be forgiven if you're important enough. Smoke?"

Billy considered for a second if he was being tested and shaking his head, he couldn't help but yawn.

"Jet lag?"

He nodded. "I've been up since I can't even remember. Ravenous too. I hope the food's good here."

"I'm sure you'll find it so, befriending as you have the kitchen boys, mercenaries every one of them." Abid spat on the ground. "Unlike the rest of us, they're here only for the sake of salaries. No ideals, no principles, nothing but material greed. There's nothing worse than a mercenary."

"Agreed." Billy did agree wholeheartedly although, in the case of cooking and driving, he supposed, a job was a job.

"As would any decent, God-fearing man."

Don't know about God-fearing, but Billy kept the sentiment to himself even as he returned Abid's high five. There was a yell from within the compound followed by a round of clapping and more yells.

"What's going on?" Billy said as the clapping began again.

"Some clown wrestling another clown," Abid said a couple of moments later. "First time in a camp, is it?"

Billy nodded and suppressed another yawn. "And you?"

"Fought the Soviets on *this* very soil." Abid fashioned his arms into a gun, pointed his muzzle finger at the sky and let out a volley of imaginary blasts. "Stingers. Thank you very much USA. Your country is a user and abuser of the first degree—training us when they needed us to fight their battle against the Russians, and once we won the battle for them, giving us the heave-ho."

Billy gave a quick, tight smile and squatting, picked a stone, and began to gouge out a hole in the ground. The stone was coarse and roughed up his palm more than it seemed to be doing any damage to the earth.

"Why Kashmir?" Abid's question emerged in a cauliflower of smoke.

Billy wished he could mention his grandfather by name—maybe Abid had heard of him?—but that would mean giving up his identity, and he didn't trust Abid, not yet, so he simply told him about his lion of a grandfather, a real pioneer, who'd been murdered for his beliefs.

"They're all pioneers," Abid said. "Take my father for example, a pioneer who leaves Kashmir for Britain. Once there, he finds himself like-minded people and together they inject new resolve into the cause. Now, they're all one big happy party all the time." Abid's gaze bore into him, his tiny eyes scurrying like ants until Billy felt he was nothing but blood and bone. "What's your dream, soldier? Migrating to Kashmir once, inshallah, it stands on its feet?"

"Sure," Billy mumbled. "That's the plan."

"That's everyone's plan." Abid laughed. "And I'm a good son of the soil doing what my Papa ji wants. Marching towards independence. Left. Right. Wrong. Right."

Billy felt as if he was in a dark alley in an unsafe part of town. He put the stone down and brushed his palms clean. He was just jet lagged and hungry and disoriented. Once he slept, everything would seem normal. In his backpack— deposited in a communal hut where he was going to be sleeping—lay Mauj jee's letter, which, suddenly, Billy felt like a dolt for having brought along. What was he? A child going to summer camp for the first time?

This camp was certainly not Camp Shenandoah with marshmallows, sing-alongs, and anti-bacterial soap. Billy had had to pinch his nostrils shut before using the toilet, an open tract between two boulders. And the AK47 which had been thrust into his hands upon his arrival and the acquisition of which alone had apparently made a man out of him was certainly not a Shenandoah-issued Flexi-Plexi Musket for re-enacting the Civil War. The bullets here would be real and, with each shot, it was kill or be killed before calling it a day. *Martyred*. Billy reeled.

"You okay there, mate?" An amused smirk broke Abid's hard gaze.

"Yes, yes, of course." Billy crossed his arms.

"But of course! And what are *they*," Abid inclined his head sideways, "saying about the nuclear showdown?"

It took a moment for Billy to realise that Abid was referring to India and Pakistan's nuclear tests and that *they* was the USA.

"That they shouldn't have conducted the tests at all."

"Bastards! They just want the goods for themselves." Abid began bouncing on his feet as if dodging an invisible opponent in a boxing ring. "What do you think about the showdown?"

"A necessary deterrent to aggression, especially given India and Pakistan's histories and geographical proximity. Weapons for peace, so to speak."

"Weapons for peace." The tip of Abid's cigarette danced dangerously close to Billy's face. "And how did you arrive at this illustrious conclusion, my friend?"

"Professors. Books. Documentaries."

Abid suckled the last of the cigarette and tossed it onto the ground.

"Billawal." He spoke the name as if it was something to be taste-tested before purchase. "Billawal. You in the habit of believing everything you're told in a classroom, or read in a book, or see on TV?"

"Excuse me?" Billy stood up. This time he couldn't ignore his jitters.

"Original thought." Abid knocked on his own head. "You've got to rely on original thought. You stick by me and you'll be fine. You'll see." He flung an arm round Billy's shoulders. "You and I, here we're on the same side."

At the sound of footsteps, Abid's grip tightened. It was Nazeer. Dinner, he said, glancing at Abid's arm round Billy. Abid nodded curtly and proceeded to lope out of the alcove dragging Billy along.

∞◦∞

Back in the communal area, Billy settled next to Abid on the carpets-turned-eating-area even as he glanced with longing at the Kashmiri group, huddled by the foot of the farthest carpet, seemingly snug in the warmth of their camaraderie as they waited for dinner to be ladled out into the plastic plates laid out before them in a neat line. Dinner, Billy saw, was being doled out by Shahbaz, Mohsin, and an elderly man, and an adolescent boy. Even from where he sat, Billy could smell the fresh bread Shahbaz was handing out from a basket and the spicy stew in the bucket Mohsin and the adolescent boy carried between them. This feast, Abid told Billy, was on account of a victory, otherwise the food in the camp consisted of meagre meals which left one hungry, but, Abid's eyes glittered as he leaned into Billy, this hunger was practical because hunger during missions was a given and hunger, therefore, had to be tamed.

"This is good omen for you, Billawal," said Jamal from Saudi Arabia, a taut-muscled ram with impala eyes.

"Sure, good omen," Billy agreed. As the food came closer, he glanced again at the Kashmiris. If Nazeer, or any of the other Kashmiris looked his way, he'd brave the ocean of men to join them. As it was, he should have been sitting with them; instead he'd been paired with Abid apparently because they were both fluent in English and hailed from the West. But then again, shouldn't Abid have been sitting with the Kashmiris?

Billy looked sideways at Abid. Asshole. Making him feel incompetent. What was worse, let alone a smart repartee, Billy still couldn't think up an answer other than professors, books and documentaries. He should have at least asked him on what sources he based his original thoughts. Abid and Jamal were engaged in what appeared to be a fired conversation in a language Billy could only guess at. Jamal turned to Billy and so did Abid, a sly grin on his face.

"Explain please," Jamal said, "why America is not angry that Clinton has cheated on his wife—is it not worse to have lied and caused heartbreak to the mother of your child—but instead America is angry because he lied to America for trying to save face?"

"I don't know," Billy snapped. He was immediately sorry. He had not meant to be rude to Jamal. All he wanted was to punch the smirking Abid on his pimply bald head.

"You think you're a Cowboy?" Jamal taunted him. "Americans are all Cowboy. Never cow men. Always boy."

Billy had not expected great love for his country—was there any country outside of America that unconditionally even liked America?—but he certainly hadn't been expecting such vehemence, at least not in a Kashmiri training camp. And it came to him then, a dagger stabbing through his fatigue that this was not solely a Kashmiri camp for Kashmiri freedom fighters, but that this was a training camp for all those willing to fight for freedom anywhere, everywhere, somewhere; learn your business, go your way, good luck.

Billy went cold. Had Indus known he would be sent to a place like this? Why hadn't he warned him? He would have to be on his guard at all times. He might have allies here in Kashmir's independence struggle but he had no friends.

Billy shifted uneasily. He wished he hadn't left his backpack in a hut where anyone could go through it. He would pocket his money, his passport, and Mauj jee's letter right after dinner was over. He looked up as Shahbaz handed him a warm naan as thick and wide as a large chopping board. On account of this being victory victuals, Shahbaz said, as well as Billawal's first meal here, would he like another serving of bread?

Billy nodded.

"Cowboy likes to eat," Jamal remarked to everyone within earshot.

Billy ignored him and held up his plate for Mohsin to ladle out the lentil and chicken stew from the large bucket he was carrying with the boy.

"This my friend-brother," Mohsin said, nodding at the boy.

"Salaam," said the boy, looking Billy full in the face, one eye wide open and the other closed, and even as Billy smiled at him, the boy raised a stump of an elbow and rubbed open his shut eye, the eyelid lifting to expose a quivering wall of pink flesh where an eyeball should have been.

It took Billy a moment to realise that the socket was empty. His stomach turned. Mohsin and the One-Eyed-One-Handed boy began to giggle as if it was a splendid joke they'd played on the new recruit.

"Move it!" someone down the line shouted.

"Wait your turn!!" Mohsin retorted, his saucy giggle ending when the elderly man behind him smacked him on the head.

"Tch, Ahmed Baba," Abid shook his head like an exasperated parent. "How many times must I tell you not to strike your son on the head? You want to make him even stupider than he is?"

Sticking his tongue out at his father and Abid, Mohsin and the One-Eyed-One-Handed boy grabbed the handles of the bucket and scuttled away, erupting into laughter as soon as they were a safe distance. Ahmed Baba frowned indulgently as he nodded at Billy and dumped a spoonful of yogurt into his bowl.

The goat's milk yogurt was deliciously sour, the bread creamy, the watery stew surprisingly rich in flavour, yet Billy was queasy. Grease from the stew yellowed the yogurt into a massive wound. The bread came away, strand by strand, like muscles, tendons, fingers, a hand. The canned cubes of chicken bobbled in the plate like discoloured eyeballs. He forced himself to chew and swallow and, despite it all, he found the food rejuvenating. In fact, despite Abid, despite the maimed boy, despite wondering what was going on at home, despite everything, Billy was sure tonight he'd sleep the sleep of champions: deep, sound, and impenetrable.

As everyone finished their meal, the kitchen staff carried out a wooden crate and a TV-cum-VCR. Hovering behind them, Commander Salman called out "careful, careful." Billy, sucking his fingers clean like everyone else was doing, looked up with interest at the thought of entertainment. Abid was gazing at him with a bemused smile, as if he was about to make a fool of himself. A great noise erupted as if fifty lawn mowers had been turned on at once. Billy yelped. The men next to him laughed and shook their heads.

"Generator, mate," Abid said, a disparaging delight peppering his face as he patted Billy's shoulder. "It's just a generator. For electricity. Look," Abid leaned in, "here's the most important rule you'll ever learn and I'm only telling you because, me and you, we're of the same ilk: Relax. No matter what, no matter when. The way you are right now, all jumpy, all nerves, you'll get yourself killed on a mission, and everyone else too."

"Silence, please!" Mullah Khaled bellowed as he inserted a cassette in the VCR and turned on the TV. The screen was fuzzy for a moment before clearing into a sequence of images. A crimson ribbon twisting round a black braid that, in a close-up, was a stream of blood. Heads hanging upside down with rags stuffed into their mouths. Baton-bruised backs of knees. Cigarettes stubbed out on skin in elaborate patterns. Mass graves and more mass graves, no, not graves, graves were peaceful abodes, these were execution sites. Human rubble against crumbling stone. Lives deadened in the blink of an eye that cannot be brought back for all the stares in the world.

The bodies got smaller and smaller and smaller until there was no denying these were children and children and children, feeding hospital beds their meagre flesh, drips attached to thread thin arms, gazes starved of hope. They got younger and younger and younger, babies with bloated bellies and sunken fontanels. Adult eyes in the faces of infants, child's eyes in the faces of adults. We don't know what to do, our babies are dying, we are dying, no one cares, but we don't know how to stop caring for ourselves.

God keeps time, but so does Man. Tick-tock, tick-tock, tick-tock, the soothing sound of civilisation. An American journalist, concern on her face, asking, about Iraq, "We have heard half a million children have died ... that's more children than died in Hiroshima ... is the price worth it?" And the American Secretary of State, her ears and neck shimmering with jewels, replying, "We think the price is worth it."

The video ended abruptly. The tape ejected itself like a rude tongue. The generator was turned off and the silence that followed was thunderous. Mullah Khaled stood up, his words igniting the gathering. "Children are dying because of their unholy, ungodly sanctions and they say the price is worth it. Only Satan would say such a thing. The Prophet Muhammed, peace be upon him, said, 'If you kill one person, you kill all of humanity,' but they kill humanity daily and so we have to rise in self-defence. We have to bring Islam to the world. It is the best religion, with the best laws, the most humane laws. To Islam anyone can convert, and this is our holy purpose, to spread the holy word, to bring back the world to Islam. And it is to that end that we have to sacrifice our lives for our oppressed people, for our sacrifices are revered on both earth and in heaven, for here we are heroes and there we are martyrs."

Billy sat absolutely still. If he moved, he would fall. If he looked at anyone's face, he would crack. If he allowed himself to crack, he would die. Everyone rose for the last prayers of the day and Billy rose too, stumbling through the prayers, through the words, the motions. Nothing virulent had ever been shown at any meeting back home and even the

271

media made sure that death and destruction were cleansed of guts and gore. A fence lined with teddy bears and ribbons and flowers represented a hit and run. Shocked neighbours represented the body of a murder victim. A camera panning the outside of a house represented the lair of a serial killer. War, too, was sanitised. Soldiers returned in flag-draped coffins, while battlefields were marked with cenotaphs and bereft relatives looking away from the camera into sombre skies. Nothing like this continuous footage of carnage Billy had just been force fed.

The first time Billy had watched even mildly disturbing images on TV was during the Gulf War. He was eleven years old and on vacation in Pakistan, defying his parents' orders and watching the news coverage. They'd predicted it would keep him awake at nights, and it had, all those tanks crawling over sand dunes like giant crabs, all those oil fields burning like evil eyes, all reminders of the tire burning in Kashmir as he and Shafi ran through the streets.

Billy would wriggle between his parents and stare into the dark, this darkness a lesser evil than the darkness behind shut eyes. Fears of the future his parents were able to assuage, but atrocities of the past were a plague of another kind, a plague in which children were unsafe no matter what their parents' actions. That road on which his cousin was hit by the car, his Aunt and Uncle had not been on that road to save him, but where had God been? What sort of a God let children die?

There had been no guts or gore aired on TV during the Gulf War. No guts or gore when the New York World Trade Centre was bombed in 1993. No guts or gore on TV when the Federal Building in Oklahoma City was blown up in 1995. Only toys to represent and commemorate the nineteen toddler deaths. And Billy, perturbed at his parent's relief when the bomber turned out to be a white man, had called them racist. They told him he didn't understand.

"Gulf war veteran," Dan's father said about the bomber, "awarded a Bronze Star with the designation of valour, and the jerk comes home to do this and throws our military rhetoric back at us, collateral fucking damage."

When the 1996 Olympic Games held in the US were bombed by another white man protesting abortion and homosexuality, Dan's father was apoplectic with rage. Religious fanatics, he and Mr Nabi agreed, would be the death of them all. They should postpone the games, Mr Nabi said. No way, Dan's father said, we cannot allow ourselves to be frightened by madmen.

One afternoon, at age fifteen, Billy and Dan bumbled into the Holocaust Museum because they confused Holocaust with hologram. As soon as they entered, a black and white gargantuan photograph assaulted them. Dan shielded his eyes, but Billy stepped forward, and in a heartbeat, realised it was bodies piled one on top of the other, dead bodies thrown away, discarded, a pyre of people stacked in no particular order.

"Let's leave," Dan whispered, but Billy stumbled on from an empty wooden cattle car, once upon a time choked with people on their way to a death camp, through a display of prisoners arriving at a gas chamber, miniature figurines climbing teeny steps, waiting under thimble-sized showers for salvation or gas, to a striped uniform with a yellow star, once worn but now laundered and ironed and scentless, over a bridge with shoes cluttered on either side, also once worn, also now scentless, into a stark room with recorded voices: name, occupation, strategy of survival.

He survived the museum. He walked out with a triangular sticker red, purple, blue, black, brown, green, pink triangles fitting into each other and the superimposed yellow words: 'Never Again,' the conscientious person's oxymoron for being able to sleep at night, the little ant with the littler fist raised at the giant shoe about to stamp.

Stars cluttered the night sky as the prayers ended. Throughout the camp there were yawns, calls of good night, sleep well. Billy felt he would never sleep again. Abid's voice nipped at his ear: take care.

17

Zari waved goodbye to Miraage as the Montessori van left the bus stop, and turned around to walk back to the Nabis' house. She inhaled the cool crispness of the rosy blue day; a day of which she'd deprived Billal. A month had passed since his departure and she wondered, every day, where he was and what fate she'd inadvertently sent him to. Through the hedge bordering the park near the house, Zari saw people taking pictures of a sprawling tulip-poplar tree, the Liberty Tree. Many were standing around it with wreaths in their hands. Billal loved that tree. A breathing symbol of the American Revolution, he'd told her, for all those centuries ago, the revolutionaries had congregated under thirteen such trees and planned seditious acts in the name of American freedom from British colonialism. We could be standing in their very footsteps, he'd said, looking down at the grass. Just imagine.

A buzz-saw stuttered through the stillness of the morning. The Liberty Tree was scheduled to be sawn down. It had survived being hit by lightning and a prank involving gunpowder, only to rot from the inside. It had upset Billy tremendously, Zari recalled, that the tree which had stood witness to so much of the past would have no future.

Back at the Nabis' home, Zari cleared the kitchen table

of Miraage's cereal bowl and busied herself in preparing Mr and Mrs Nabi's breakfasts. That first morning she had taken tea and toast for them, she'd been gutted with guilt. It was her fault Billal was gone. Had she spoken to him when he'd come into her room the night he'd left her the gift bag, had she woken from her dreamlike state, had she spoken to him at all, he could very well still be here. She'd vowed, therefore, that though she'd been unable to save her own family, this family she would help preserve in whichever way possible. That much she believed she owed Billal.

Zari entered Shehla's darkened bedroom. The damask curtains were drawn shut and the room reeked of stale food. Next to a mug of stale, cold tea on the bedside table, the plate of daal and rice Zari had made for dinner the night before lay untouched, the fried cumin in the yellow lentils shrivelled and ominous. Shehla was curled up in bed, hugging Billal's windbreaker. All the phones in the house were piled by her side of the bed, as if quantity alone would increase the likelihood of Billal calling. Or coming home. She smelled, Zari thought, a smell she recognised all too well—the nasty combination of hopelessness and helplessness.

Zari placed the cup of tea and a buttered toast on the dresser and began picking up crumpled tissues off the floor. Amman emerged from the bathroom, dressed for work, the dark circles under his eyes and the pinched look on his face deepening with each passing day.

"Shehla, I'm leaving for the hospital." His voice was tender.

Shehla curled her lip and looked away. She had stopped going to work since the first day of Billy's disappearance. She would go mad, she'd declared, if she acted as if nothing had happened, and, Amman's confession of pride being bad enough, she'd been distraught when he'd also continued to go to work despite his claim that if he spent his entire day in bed waiting for Billal, he would go mad.

"Zari beta," Amman said, "please tell your Aunty I will return home late tonight."

"Zari, tell your Uncle I do not care when he comes home. If he comes home."

Zari stared at her bare feet, embarrassed to bear witness to such a moment. Amman shrugged apologetically and left and Shehla lay back in bed, her face buried in Billy's jacket. After Zari was done clearing up, she laid out the paraphernalia for the daily Quran recital, a ritual Shehla had begun the day of Billal's departure in order to pray for his safe return home. Zari spread a clean sheet over the carpet by the window and placed a cup of rice holding a bunch of incense sticks in the centre. As the soft scent of sandalwood ate up the mustiness in the room, she upended a bag of unshelled almonds in front of her, the counting device as they recited Quranic verses—the Quls, or Surah Yasin, or the Durood-Shareef.

Shehla rose and sat on the floor, leaning against a wall, going through the almonds at super speed with Zari almost keeping up with her, the clicks of almonds shells hitting almonds shells the only sound as one heap diminished and the other rose right next to it. They were halfway through the reading when Salsabil slunk in. She was wearing a baggy track suit, a crackling new purchase, and had thrown a scarf over her hair to join the reading. Her recitation was painstakingly slow and she had barely gotten through a handful of almonds before she glanced at her watch and got up.

"Mom," she whispered, "I'm leaving for work. Can I bring any groceries on my way back home?"

Shehla glanced at her. An inch of ash from an incense stick toppled onto the sheet.

"We're nearly out of milk," Zari said hesitantly, as if she was an intruder who had found herself welcome.

Salsabil turned grateful eyes on to Zari. "Anything else? Can you email me a list?"

Zari nodded even as tears rolled down Shehla's cheeks.

"How," Shehla said, her voice rising, "can you think of milk?"

"Mom," Salsabil said helplessly, "Miraage needs it."

Shehla swallowed and squeezed her eyes shut. She was not going to wail like her mother or tear her hair out and expect her daughter to do nothing but take care of her. She was going to remain in control of herself, of her family even if her son had gone to play Samson in an ungrateful world.

"Mom," Salsabil caressed her mother's hand. "Please, please don't wail like tha—"

Shehla wrenched away her hand and, Billal's windbreaker pressed to her mouth, she ran into the bathroom where she started to sob. Salsabil caught Zari's eye and the two girls just stared at each other.

A little later, after Shehla had calmed down and climbed back into bed, and Salsabil had left for work, Zari gathered the recital supplies and went to the den to put them away. She lingered in the hallway to look at Billal's grandfather's picture, the one in which he looked like a journalist, but it was just a mute picture of a man with a book. Billal was right—photographs were a poor bandage in the real world. She had yet to take her family albums out of her suitcase.

In the den, Zari emailed Salsabil the grocery list and then stared at the monitor, until, finally, holding her breath, she typed *rape*.

Rape fantasies: male/female, female/female, male/male, gang bang, anal, incest, wartime, other

For one stunned moment, she couldn't grasp what she was seeing, and then, she switched the monitor off.

By the time Zari went to the bus stop to pick up Miraage after school, she was still trying to banish, as best as she could, all thoughts about what she'd seen on the computer in the morning. As she walked past the park, the buzz-saw no longer sounded. The Liberty Tree was felled. Zari wished Billy had not missed the tree's end. From gaps in the hedges she saw a group of teenage girls playing dodge ball. They were radiant, piping hot with life. Even the ball looked happy, as if, between being kicked around, it had been fashioned with loving hands, was stored in a warm, dry, safe place, and looked forward to each wonderful day when it would fulfil its purpose.

fantasies

gangbang

wartime

Zari shivered. She could not distract herself. Who were these men and women who'd turned rape into a dream scenario? Into a fantasy? How could rape be a fetish? But why was she so shocked when her own culture fantasised about it no less? She recalled Kiran being barely able to sit through a Bollywood film in which a court order punished a rapist into marrying the woman he'd raped. The rapist had readily agreed that marriage would indeed cure him of his appetite for rape, as well as return honour to the dishonoured girl. By the end of the movie, the two had fallen madly in love. Kiran had been livid. What would the judge have done in the case of a gang rape? she'd fumed. Order the woman to marry all the men? Or, if only one rapist out of the many was to be so punished, on whom would the onus fall, the lead rapist or the rapist who followed obediently?

—the shrieks of a dying family sounding like people on a roller coaster having a good time—

Zari's mind baulked. A blankness enveloped her. She could dredge up *that* evening, *her* rape, but she could go no deeper than that.

She. Would. Not.

She concentrated, instead, on Miraage climbing down the school van's metallic steps and the bus driver wishing them a good Fourth of July weekend. She waved back. She smiled. She walked Miraage back home. She settled Miraage in front of the TV with a sandwich and a glass of milk. And then, as if she could not help it, Zari found herself approaching the computer. For Kiran's sake, she told herself as she sat down. For Sonea's sake, as she typed the words: *war survivor rape*. For her mother's sake, as she scanned, with great trepidation, the list of results for fantasy or pornography links. This time there were none. Instead:

In 1993, the act of rape was finally acknowledged as a crime against humanity. It is, according to the

United Nations, the least frowned upon of all war crimes . . .

In the US:

36% women who are injured during a rape require medical attention.

25 - 45% of rape survivors suffer from non-genital trauma.

19 - 22% suffer from genital trauma.

Up to 40% get sexually transmitted diseases.

1-5% become pregnant.

80% of rape victims suffer from chronic physical or psychological conditions over time.

National Violence Against Women Survey

1998 survey

Most of the data for the psychological effects of rape come from studies of adult Western women in peacetime who have suffered a single episode of rape . . . To understand the effects of rape in wartime, one must consider the additional trauma that women may have experienced: death of loved ones, loss of home and community, dislocation, untreated illness, and war related injury . . .

Journal of the American Medical Association

She read as much as she could stomach. Then she stopped.

Billy had promised Miraage a trip to Washington DC to see the Fourth of July fireworks. Nothing else would do, Miraage insisted, and Shehla agreed. Fireworks on the Mall was the very last promise her son might ever make to his little sister, and so, it was to be fulfilled and Salsabil would now take Miraage. Would Zari like to go? It would, Shehla sighed, be a good change for her.

Zari heard the invitation through tired ears. Lately, she was lethargic all the time, as if she'd eaten too much even though she couldn't keep a thing down. Instead, she'd lie in bed suffering a fitful sleep, the usual nightmares stapled with the fate Billy was faring in Kashmir as well as a growing dread of all the things she was learning could have added to her rape: pregnancy, sexually transmitted disease, bladder incontinence. That in calamity, as in all else, there was a hierarchy of luck and that, in spite of it *all*, she was one of the luckier ones, wrung her out. An outing, Zari acknowledged silently, would be a very good change.

The Fourth of July arrived sunny and sparkling. As she, Salsabil, and Miraage drove out of the neighbourhood, Zari gazed wide-eyed at the cornucopia of flags planted in front yards and over door stoops. Miraage asked about the fireworks on the fourth in Kashmir and Zari caressed Miraage's cheek as she informed her that this was an American holiday not celebrated around the world. In fact, winter being the harsher season in Kashmir, schools shut during the icy freeze while remaining open during the mild summers and, therefore, for the past school going years of her life, July fourth was just an ordinary school day for her. Miraage blinked in confusion, then insisted Zari read to her, yet again, the picture book she'd checked out from school.

In the United States, Zari read as she pointed to a picture of a cannon on top of a verdant hill, the Fourth of July is a national holiday in commemoration of the day in 1776 when George Washington formally declared the United States of America no longer a British colony even though they had yet to drive the British out.

When the book was done, and Miraage asked for it to be read again, and both Zari and Salsabil groaned and said no, Zari felt a small blossom of happiness sprouting within herself at the unexpected normalcy of the situation and for a moment she forgot about Billy, forgot about the rape website she was reading, forgot that happiness was elusive.

At the metro station, Salsabil sheepishly told Zari that she was waiting for Ohwi, a friend, a guy friend, to join them. Zari was instantly uncomfortable and the blossom, only just beginning to take root, withered as rapidly as it had bloomed. Salsabil should have told her a boy was going to be joining them, a boy Salsabil was already smiling and waving at, a slim boy in jeans and a T-shirt advertising Master Lee's Tae Kwon Do classes. Could this be Salsabil's boyfriend? The boyfriend whose existence had come up when Billal had tried to tell his parents about their clandestine marriage? Zari flushed as Salsabil hugged the boy, the embrace a little too intimate and lasting a moment too long. Salsabil introduced them and as Zari's eyes met Ohwi's and he nodded a smile, she turned red. Salsabil should have told her, Zari thought, turning her face, and thereby given her the option of remaining at home.

In the crowded train, Zari stood hunched into herself, trying to ignore the polite press of bodies around her even as Miraage, Salsabil, and Ohwi stood around a pole right next to her. Ohwi was stroking Salsabil's belly ring as if it were a delicate wing. The impropriety of the gesture unnerved Zari even as its intimacy riveted her. Wasn't Salsabil afraid that someone might see her and tell her parents?

The truth was, the more Zari learned about the Nabis, the more they bewildered her. Were they intentionally reinventing themselves or unintentionally forgetting who they were? She'd expected them to be like any other Kashmiri family, a family who would have confiscated Salsabil's cell phone and grounded her the minute they discovered that she was dating.

Dating. In Zari's world, even the word would have caused uproar, but here, here Shehla seemed more upset about who Salsabil was dating rather than the act itself. Had the Nabis remained true to tradition, had they stressed the importance of family over the idea of 'it's-my-life' as Billal had written in his note, then perhaps Billal would not have absconded, and neither would Salsabil be misbehaving like this.

Then again, had the Nabis *not* brought their children up to *be themselves*, Billal would never have married her at all. In fact, like Fahad, Billal too would have put his family's reputation and wishes before his own. Instead, the Nabis had inadvertently designed their own misery. And what of my behaviour? Zari thought. Is my standing here quietly while Salsabil does what she wants, a reinventing of myself or a forgetting of who I am?

She swallowed down her nausea and pretended to be captivated by the colourful metro map on the wall opposite her even as she took peeks at Salsabil and Ohwi's reflection in the carriage window—their interlocked fingers bridging gaps, their hips tangoing like old partners to the rhythm of the train, their mouths positioned for more than friendship.

When they did kiss, Salsabil's gaze caught Zari's, and both girls blushed.

∞ ∞

There was more of a crowd at the Smithsonian Mall—a huge area relegated to museums and other cultural attractions—than Zari had anticipated, a jolly crowd sunbathing, chattering, snacking. In the growing dusk, the Washington Monument loomed like a spire of a lofty mosque and Zari gripped Miraage's hand as they began making their way through the crowd, and past a billboard with blood red crosses within circles specifying what could not be brought to the Mall: alcohol, contraband, weapons, big tents, and personal fireworks. Ohwi left to stand in a long line to buy fries for them—though Zari felt ill at the thought of food—and the girls continued on between the throng of blankets and beanbags and canvas folding chairs, all the while keeping a lookout for space on the grass. Zari looked away from a man with a flag tattooed on his bare torso and bumped into another man—she gasped.

"Tch!" Salsabil halted. "'Of all the paths in all the towns in all the worlds.' What are you doing here?"

"What are *you* doing here?" Fahad retorted.

Zari's heart started to beat faster.

"Obviously," Salsabil said, "we're here doing exactly what you're doing here." She scrutinised the girl next to Fahad, a shapely girl with too much lip gloss, in tight white capris, a green halter top, and obese diamond studs in her ears. "And who's this? New prospect?"

Fahad turned the crimson of his baseball cap. Mimi was

285

the daughter of a family friend visiting from Pakistan. He was just showing her around town.

"How incredibly gracious of you, Fahad," Salsabil cooed as she nodded at Mimi.

"Fahad is such a good host," Mimi piped up as she ran manicured fingers through straightened, brown hair with frosty blonde highlights. "I tell you, he's taking such good care of me, I feel like a super star."

Salsabil smiled sweetly even as she put an arm around Zari and propelled her away with the whispered command to not dare look back.

ᎧᎧᎧ

She was all right, Zari assured Salsabil for the umpteenth time as they spread out their blanket by the Reflecting Pool next to a woman with a buzz cut rubbing sunscreen onto another woman's broad shoulders. Yet she'd hardly settled her heart when Fahad squatted next to her, by himself, his floral cologne overpowering every other scent.

"What do you want?" Salsabil glared at him. "Or has Ms Superstar Me-Me found out that it is actually all about You-You and so dumped you already?"

"Shut up, Salsabil. Zari, can I talk to you?"

"What could you possibly want to talk to her about?" Salsabil asked.

"Stay out of this, Salsabil. Zari, please, just for a minute."

Despite herself, Zari rose. She just wanted to hear what Fahad had to say, that was all. She was not betraying Billal. She would have heard Fahad out even if Billal were right here glowering at her. They walked off the grass onto the shade-less sidewalk. Zari waited for him to say something as they passed an overflowing trash can, passed a nursing mother, passed a man strumming a guitar, the guitar case propped open, dollars and cents strewn like dark stains on the pale satin lining, a cardboard sign in the front saying, Gulf War Vet, Please Help. Finally she stopped and stood facing him, her arms crossed in front of her chest. Fahad cleared his throat.

"Would you like ice-cream?" He pointed to the refrigerator-on-wheels surrounded by hot-cheeked children. Zari looked at him for a second; he looked away.

"That girl I'm with, she's noth—" he began.

"As they say here, it's your life."

"I'm really sorry about what happened."

To her horror, her eyes filled with tears. His jilting her, her visit to the psychiatrist, her collapse, Billy's proposal, her acceptance, Miraage's balloons—everything seemed as if it had happened just yesterday.

"I should have—" Fahad took off his baseball cap and began thumbing the rim. "I should have told you myself . . . called . . . I can't tell you how it's been eating at me, how I've kicked myself a million times for being such a coward. I am so sorry."

"Sorry is the most impotent word in the world."

"There's none stronger, Zari, none stronger." He grinned sheepishly. "It allows people a second chance."

Zari turned abruptly and ran, the flounces on her ankle-length skirt causing havoc in her wake, but she was deaf to the indignant cries that followed. In a moment, Fahad caught up with her. She shook her head as he told her he was a jackass and that he'd apologise till the end of the world and could she possibly forgive him and could he possibly call her? She shook her head thinking I'm married. And a marriage was a marriage. And that was that. Even if this was a marriage in which she'd sent her husband to his death. And again she ran.

☙❧

I swear I'm all right, Zari told Salsabil when she returned to where they were sitting. Ohwi offered his help at keeping Fahad at bay, and, for the first time, Zari looked straight at him even as she declined his gallant offer, "Thank you, but I'm really okay."

Yet, as she lay beside Miraage on the blanket, watching the sky darken, Zari felt anything but okay. She had not meant for her heart to jump the way it had when she saw Fahad. She should have never agreed to listen to his *excuses*. For what could he possibly have said that could undo her heartbreak at the fact that he'd abandoned her because— her eyes stung with fresh tears—she'd been raped? It was Fahad's fault that she'd married Billal. Fahad's fault Billal had run off to Kashmir. It was all Fahad's fault.

☙❧

When the sky had turned a dark inky black, the fireworks lit it up: crackling spirals and silver tails fizzing up the ladder of the night only to explode into a drizzle of tinsel raining back to earth; pin wheels sweeping across the smoky sky flush with the dust of gunpowder, a glittering canopy of peacock tails filling the firmament, a bouquet of rainbows bedazzling the night sky. The collective intake of breathe at the wonder, the brilliance, the spectacle of it all even as it threatened to smother the spectators below in an avalanche of colour and warmth.

Zari forced her ears and eyes open to the thunder and lightning, both a commemoration of cannon fire in battles of yore. How frightened those folks must have been at the time, she thought, at these portents of death. She thought of a bonfire, a small bonfire in a backyard that must now be overgrown with weeds, of the light it had given off, and how its warm orange flickering remained constant no matter whether the people surrounding it were singing or screaming. Her heart hurt so much her breasts ached. She turned abruptly, the sky a shower of flames above her, and pressed her mouth against the sweet, prickly grass, her tears a libation from which the earth seemed not to tire.

18

Billy ran lifting each foot as if that would provide relief to the blisters on his soles. The passport, money, and Mauj jee's letter he'd transferred to his pocket his very first night here banged against an already gaunter hipbone. A week and his body ached at the daily routine: Fajr prayer-training-breakfast-training-Zohr prayer-lunch-training-Asr prayer-classroom instruction-Maghrib prayer-dinner-footage-lecture-Isha prayer-sleep. But stamina was a virtue they had to master.

After Fajr prayer, they underwent a bout of strenuous exercise before the scorching sun rose in pink fingers and squeezed out the coolness of pre-dawn. Then sweating, stinking, drying inside out from thirst they would jog-run-sprint-jog-run-sprint—a drill Billy spent terrified of stepping on a landmine that may have escaped removal—into a scanty breakfast of bread, raw onions, and green tea. He smiled at Mohsin and One-Eyed-One-Handed and held out his plate for the food. Grinning they served him and moved on down the line as if they were at some spiritual retreat instead of where they were.

Billy picked up the onion and concentrated on chewing through its leathery layers, trying to override the fear of being where he was and the fear of never seeing his home again. He chewed faster. The rising sun was drying his sweat-soaked collar into a barbed wire which chafed his skin and he fidgeted and scratched at the rash beneath and reminded himself that coming here had been his choice—his alone.

Halfway through the bread, Billy felt eyes upon him and he turned to see Abid watching him, as usual, with a restless penetration. Abid nodded and Billy nodded back, and though it was too early for Abid's ritual onslaught of inquiries regarding American foreign policy, Billy's stomach knotted. Breakfast lost its flavour. For the rest of the morning, Billy was on tenterhooks, but, as had become customary, Abid's question came during lunch. The US already possesses enough arsenals to take out the world, so why is it accumulating still more weapons? Was it because it depended on warring people to line its pockets like a doctor depended on disease?

"Can you counter this, Billawal?" Abid asked scornfully.

Billy longed to reply that each country watched out for its best interest to the best of its abilities and that his country was no different, but he didn't dare. Instead, he stared at the clouds lassoing the sky and feigned deep thought even as he heard Abid and Jamal mutter about cowboys and losers. Billy chewed on the tough chicken they'd been served for lunch, trying to drown them out even as he began his inner mantra: I am here for Kashmir and Kashmir alone.

After lunch and Zohr prayers, another chunk of training began. Billy wormed across a stony expanse right behind the Kashmiri group, their shoes kicking up a fine dust straight into his and Abid's faces. The undercurrent of hostility between Abid and the Kashmiris was impossible to ignore, but everyone, instructors included, either didn't care about the bad blood or managed to ignore it very well. Billy would've ignored it too, except that the Kashmiri group had transplanted their feelings for Abid onto him.

How do you convince people that you are not of the tribe they have relegated you to? How do you effectively win them over when their distrust of you springs simply and blindly by an extension of association? And it wasn't as if he hadn't tried. Billy had tried to assimilate himself. He'd jumped into their midst and they'd been amiable. When he had mentioned his grandfather, they had all beamed and a few of them had even slapped him on his back. But when he began asking them about their lives, their friendliness had receded and their answers became increasingly vague until all the men had become utterly unfriendly. Nazeer had remarked sarcastically that if Abid wanted to know anything in particular, he should ask them himself. I don't understand, Billy had said, but Nazeer had only given him a searching glance and turned away. And that was that for Billy's attempt at assimilation. He'd felt worse than a foreigner; he felt like an alien. Subdued and perturbed, he'd returned to Abid's side only to be further subdued and perturbed by Abid's glare, a glare Abid did not deign to explain.

That had been yesterday. Abid was still cantankerous. Good, Billy thought. Let him stew, whatever the reason. Billy flinched as a stone dug into his elbow and his rifle slipped out of his grasp. Abid caught it, clicked his tongue, and thrust it back at him. Cowboy is clumsy, Jamal said, loud enough for the instructor jogging alongside to hear. Billy grit his teeth and wriggled faster. He'd be damned if he was going to allow Jamal and Abid to get his training time extended.

By the time Asr prayers were over and classroom

instruction began, Billy had added sore elbows to a long list of physical woes. The class sat in the courtyard, the midday heat raining upon them. Both the goats were anointing the ground with pellets. The instructor was scratching a diagram onto a chipped blackboard. He put the chalk down and held up a Molotov. The glass receptacle of the crude bomb glinted, and in another lifetime, Billy could see it living as a cola bottle, perhaps served in a crystal goblet with chips of ice or refrigerated and drunk straight from the bottle in one gulp. Enough of these, the instructor said holding it up, and you can overturn a tank. Enough of these, the instructor said, circling the Molotov like a trophy, and you have the means to a revolution.

Later, after Maghrib prayers, and shooting practice, and dinner, the footage began. Billy concentrated on the far off mountain range melting into the evening. The footage was either the compilation he'd seen the first evening or another one equally virulent. The sound of children weeping had become the eeriest sound in the universe. The footage was followed by a lecture. Each lecture had begun to sound the same with different place names inserted. Kashmir, for instance. Kashmir is being ransacked. Islam is in danger, grave danger. Muslims are being killed. Wives, mothers, sisters looted. Openly. It is our call to help. Our duty. It is up to us to retaliate, protect, bring on freedom and begin the revolution. Muslims, Muslims, Muslims, until it seemed they were an endangered species on the verge of extinction as were once Catholics and Jews.

Billy opened his eyes and turned on the uneven floor trying to find a more comfortable spot. There were no

293

pillows, no mattresses, no blankets here. Hardiness too, was a virtue they had to master. Snores hammered the dark hut he shared with others. You couldn't judge a man by the way he snored. Swarthy warriors gurgled like polite ladies. Skinny philosophers trumpeted as if elephants rushing to mate. Abid cooed as if he was hovering over a baby. And Nazeer whimpered and mumbled though he slept soundly enough. Everyone slept soundly, everyone except for him.

Billy flinched at a particularly raucous snore. How had these people gotten used to the massacre footage, for those images of dead, mutilated bodies, they were responsible for his lack of sleep. Back home, brutality on the screen was cushioned by happy, shiny advertisements, but here there was only prayer and prayer did not comfort him. Billy pressed the light switch on his watch which he'd left on US time. What was everyone doing back home? Was Zari still taking Miraage to the park every day? Sitting on the same bench under the elms by the duck pond? Was she proud that he was going to amount to something? But the whole idea of 'amounting to something' was not as clear here as it had seemed back home. Now that he was here, 'amounting to something' increasingly appeared to simply mean keeping sane and getting out alive.

Billy traced Zari's face in the pitch darkness of the hut, indenting it as he once had in the moonlight back home— her forehead, her nostrils, her philtrum, her lips, her chin, the curve of her long neck. He bolted up. Fresh air. He needed to get some fresh air.

A full moon buried the courtyard in a pale light. Billy

made his way past the instructors sleeping on jute cots and the men on the carpets towards the light glimmering from behind the brown kilim of the kitchen hut. The sentry dozing atop the perimeter wall stirred when he crossed him. Billy raised his hand and the man nodded in recognition before settling back.

Billy pushed aside the kilim and peeped in. The kitchen hut was small and warm and smoky. Indigo flames gushed from the dragon mouths of the four primus stoves that stood directly under the window overlooking the passageway and the compound wall. Mohsin looked up from the mountain of dough he was kneading for breakfast.

"Cowboy!" He grinned. Billy smiled uneasily, forcing himself to remember that there was no spite in Mohsin's 'Cowboy'. One-Eyed-One-Handed looked up too. He was squatting by the stoves, flat bread baking on three of them and, on the fourth, green tea bubbling in a cauldron. Shahbaz was fast asleep on the floor by one side of the room, a torn sheet pulled over his head, a hand curled round his AK47, the chunky moonstone rings on his fingers shining like orbs on guard.

Ahmed Baba sat with his legs stretched before him, peeling onions, his lap a forest of onion skins. He beckoned Billy to sit beside him.

"No sleep?" he asked. Billy shook his head as he settled down. Mohsin placed a glass of steaming green tea in front of him, and glancing at the door then winking at Ahmed Baba, he slipped Billy a hot naan.

The aroma of the bread wrapped Billy in its warm embrace. He took a bite, and beaming, sipped the tea, savouring the delicious silences between the soothing *thup-thup-thup* of dough being pummelled, the *saah-saah-saah* of a wooden spoon swirling the tea, the *rss-rss-rss* of onion skin yielding to the sharp blade. The hot liquid warmed him from the inside out and the unexpected bread from the outside in.

"Ahmed Baba," Billy said as he inhaled the steam, "if you don't mind, may I ask you a question?"

Ahmed Baba nodded without looking up from the onion he was slicing.

"Why did you choose to work here?"

"Excellent salary," Ahmed Baba replied promptly. Looking up, he stared at Billy for a long moment, as if making a decision, and then he began to speak. Until a few years ago, he used to work for a couple at the American embassy in Islamabad. They had no children and perhaps, therefore, doted on the then toddler Mohsin, treating him like one of the kittens or puppies they were forever adopting, nursing to health, twittering over. One day, after Mohsin answered Rachel Memsaheb in English, she decided to educate Mohsin and, mashallah, soon the boy was able to recite full ABC! Such a grand future Ahmed Baba had begun to envision for his smart boy!

"Even the heavens could not have offered such a job." Ahmed Baba sighed. "But then my mother died of cancer. Rachel Memsaheb, may Allah grant her every happiness, had borne all the costs and had sent my mother to the best of doctors in Islamabad in her own car, but Allah's will was different.

"A few months after my mother passed, my sister passed away from the same disease, and then my niece fell sick, and I could no longer ignore my father's admonitions. How many more lives was I waiting to strike down before I quit working for the Americans and served my own?

"And so here I am. My father arranged this job and negotiated the excellent salary." Ahmed Baba shrugged. "My two younger children are with my wife in Islamabad. And, ever since I left the embassy job, no one else in my family has died."

"When I grow up," Mohsin declared, "I return to embassy."

Ahmed Baba smiled at his son before turning back to Billy. "If Mohsin's English is good, perhaps he can find employment that will earn him a good life on earth or," he glanced towards the courtyard, "maybe he joins them for a good life in heaven."

"Earth." Billy said, "join earth—"

"But you join heaven." Ahmed Baba squinted.

Because I want to leave my mark on earth . . . But it was the wrong thing to say here. A foolish ambition. And so Billy remained quiet.

"Cowboy," Mohsin piped up, "where is your rifle?"

"In the hut."

"You left it behind!" Mohsin frowned. "I will always carry mine by my side like a third arm."

"As should you, Billawal." Shahbaz's sleepy voice emerged from beneath the sack he was using for a sheet.

"It'll survive without me." Billy laughed.

"No doubt." Shahbaz poked his face out. "But will *you* survive without it?"

Billy's laugh faded. He watched enviously as Shahbaz snuggled back under the sack and fell back to sleep. The kitchen staff, Billy knew, watched the footage and heard the lectures just like everyone else, and yet they were able to sleep. In fact, everyone was able to sleep except him.

"Ahmed Baba," Billy picked a crumb off his shirt and squelched it, "what do you make of all this . . . this . . . footage?"

"Billawal Sahib," Ahmed Baba spoke slowly, his nose curling over a rotting onion, "Allah looks down at the world and protects us, but Satan, Satan roams amongst us. Some people good, some people bad. We follow our hearts, but we do not know whom our hearts follow. Is it Allah's decree or Satan's will? That we will discover on the Day of Judgment. During this life, health, respect, food, clothing, shelter; that is all the likes of me pray for. "

We follow our hearts but we do not know whom our hearts follow. Is it Allah's decree or Satan's will? Billy stared into the remains of his tea. He could very well be nothing more than an automaton obeying some celestial will. Had the balloons not caught in the fan, had Zari not come to live with them, had his parents not fallen in love, had his father not been a Kashmiri, had his Dada not been a freedom fighter, had Kashmir been allowed to choose its fate in 1947 fair and square, had India and Pakistan never been partitioned, had the British continued to rule, had the British, the Dutch, the Portuguese never landed on the subcontinent soil, had there never been any trade and commerce between peoples, no taste for spices, no taste buds at all—how far did the chain of circumstance stretch, this cause and effect, where the present was merely a riddle of the past and a toy for the future to play with, and where history was nothing more than a jigsaw puzzle God, the changeling, got to arrange and rearrange at will?

Billy gazed out the door at the horizon. Could he truly be nothing more than an oxygen-breathing speck on one of the pieces of this seemingly vast jigsaw puzzle?

From the courtyard came the pre-dawn clamour of stretching, stirring, coughing, gargling as men rose and readied themselves for the Fajr prayer. Billy jumped up when the kilim was suddenly whipped aside and Abid peered in. The kitchen staff sprang into their chores as Abid threw them a dirty look before turning his glare at Billy.

"What are you doing here?!" He tossed Billy his AK47. "A soldier doesn't leave his shadow behind. Ever." The rifle crashed into the tea cup Billy was holding, smashing it to shards and cutting Billy's palm. The call to prayer began as blood dripped from Billy's palm.

∞∞∞

As they all gathered in the courtyard for Fajr prayers, Billy strode purposefully to Nazeer's side and when Abid grabbed hold of his lapel and asked him what he was doing, Billy jerked him off and looked the other way, ignoring both Abid's glower and Nazeer's alarm. You'll survive, Abid had said in the kitchen with a shrug that might have been an apology, might have been apathy, you'll survive.

When they began their morning exercise routine—jog-run-sprint-jog-run-sprint—Billy stayed close to Nazeer's side, so close that Nazeer's perpetual shadow, a man with overcrowded teeth and acne scars on a catfish face, Mohamedoo, was forced to make space. Even so, Billy felt

Abid's footsteps closing the distance between them, felt his breath on his nape, felt his hands reaching out for him.

Halfway through the morning practise session, the turmeric poultice Ahmed Baba had hastily prepared and applied around his palm began to come undone and blood darkened the muslin. The instructor told Billy to go take care of it and told Nazeer to go with him.

"What happened?" Nazeer asked as they walked side by side. Billy told him, adding a nasty swear in Kashmiri, something about Abid's body being plagued by holes.

Nazeer's gave a grim laugh. "Listen, do not get on Abid's wrong side."

"What do you mean?"

Nazeer quickened his pace.

"What do you mean?" Billy caught hold of his hand.

Nazeer shrugged him off gently. "Just don't."

Commander Salman was poking a dismantled radio with a crowbar when they entered his office. A battery-operated fan buzzed over his sunburned face, ruffling his side-parting. After a long moment he looked up and raised his brows. Billy told him that he'd hurt himself when a cup accidentally broke in his hand and he, therefore, needed the medicine box. Commander Salman squinted. Finally he rose. In the real world, he said, injuries would just have to be accepted because amenities—he extracted a first aid kit from one of the trunks and handed it to Nazeer—would seldom be available. Next time there was a paltry accident, Commander Salman said, dismissively waving them out, he was not to be bothered.

Billy and Nazeer sat on a jute cot in the courtyard. One-Eyed-One-Handed had taken the mule to fetch water as well as deposit the camp's laundry at his village nearby where his mother and other family took care of it. Mohsin was the only one around, milking the goats in one corner, all the while talking to them as if they could actually understand him. They could hear the men jogging-running-sprinting outside the compound wall. Billy unwound his bandage as Nazeer rummaged through the tin container, crammed with more junk than medical supplies, until he managed to fish out a bottle of iodine, a flimsy roll of gauze, and what looked like duct tape. Billy wiped his hand with the iodine tincture. He grimaced. He could feel the glass splinter even though he couldn't see it. It took Nazeer's eagle eyes a moment to locate it and he squeezed Billy's flesh with gentle thumbs until the glass splinter burrowed through the bloody flesh.

"Thank you."

"Welcome."

Billy wrapped the gauze round his palm and Nazeer sealed it with a strip of tape. After they were done, Nazeer rose to return the tin container, but Billy gripped his arm.

"You have to tell me," he pleaded. "You have to tell me what you meant about Abid."

"The wise need but a hint. I have provided that hint. You are wise."

"If I was that wise," Billy said morosely, "I wouldn't be here, would I?"

Nazeer sighed, his beer-coloured eyes clouding over. "What does it matter, really? Fat cats have already charted our fates—"

"What the hell do you mean by that?"

Nazeer shook his head, shrugged, and walked away.

That night, sleep eluded Billy yet again. He stared into the dark as he thought about the day he'd left home, about how adventurous, how exciting, how heroic he'd thought it was all going to be, how he was going to change the world, or Kashmir at the very least, because freedom was worth everything. When he could bear his thoughts no longer, Billy shook Nazeer awake.

"Please," Billy whispered as Nazeer rubbed his eyes, "you have got to tell me," and then, bleakly, he added, "Hu kus bu kus theliwan su kus."

Nazeer gave a quiet laugh at Billy's rendition of a Kashmiri children's rhyme: Who is that, who am I, then tell me who are you? He rose, and picking up his rifle, beckoned Billy to follow him. Together they tread through the sleeping courtyard and past a snoring sentry to an alcove, a grove stinking of cigarette butts.

Nazeer squatted against a wall, his rifle beside him. Billy sat on the edge of a small rock and sucked on his wounded palm. He'd taken the bandage off earlier and except for a slight swelling, there was nothing to indicate that he had cut his palm.

"Tell me, Billawal," Nazeer began, his bloodshot eyes skimming over Billy, "what is your story? Why you are here, Cowboy?"

And keeping the sanctity of their names to himself, Billy told Nazeer about everything that had led him to the rock he was sitting on. He spoke about his first trip to Kashmir, about Mauj jee and her letters, about Dada, about his father, and about Zari, and—he inhaled sharply—the footage that was eating him alive.

"I don't believe I'll ever be able to sleep again."

"You will," Nazeer replied. "If I can, anyone can."

A pack of wild dogs began to howl right outside the camp. They'd been hovering around the compound ever since a few men, reprimanded since then, had thrown food to them. The goats bleated, having heard the wild dogs on the other side of the wall. Nazeer shifted closer to Billy, their shadows merging into a hulking form in the moonlight, and began to speak.

Once upon a time, he'd lived in Srinagar with father, mother, and brother. After completing his tenth grade, he had joined his father in running their photography business. They were well-off. Nazeer's thick wrists protruded from his too short sweater as he rubbed his fingers to signal money. Like other boys his age, he dreamt of being a cricket player and romancing beautiful film stars, but his elder brother, Mansoor, was besotted with joining the Indian navy. But he was rejected. Weak eyesight, they said.

"Mansoor's eyesight was better than mine." Nazeer's voice was gruff. "But he was a Kashmiri Muslim, and one unconnected to any Hindu or Sikh high up in the ranks."

After his rejection from the navy, Mansoor decided to show everyone just how weak his eyesight was. He joined a local newspaper vowing to expose the truth by photographing the injustices happening all across the valley, no matter that his newspaper, like all others, was funded by the government and was therefore expected to blame every atrocity on the militants and present the army as saviours in fatigues.

Mansoor started by chronicling their family's conversion from Hinduism to Islam centuries ago via photographs of temples and mosques that both faiths used to frequent before the insurgency took hold of the valley. He traced the family back to a Suda Butte who came from a family of Hindu Brahmins so wealthy that the statues in the family temples were made of solid gold. Suda used to frequent the court of the Muslim Sultan, Zain-ul-Abideen, renowned as Bud Shah, the Great King, for the peace he brought to his kingdom through his policy of religious tolerance. One day, Suda dreamt of his conversion to Islam and upon waking up, he promptly went and told the king that he wished to turn dream into reality.

Suda had three conditions. One, he wanted to retain his high caste Brahmin identity, in name alone of course, and so change his family name to Pandit. Two, the King should provide his family with eternal funds since he came from wealth and his conversion was a jewel in the king's crown. And three, his family remain forever united.

Suda's brothers disowned him the moment he converted to Islam. When the king died, the funding died with him. And when only daughters were born to a subsequent generation and they married and their children took different surnames, the Pandit surname perished too. All that remained of Suda's legacy was his conversion to Islam.

What became of Suda's two brothers and their families, no one knows, but, in photographing 'Conversion', Mansoor invited thraht, woe to the family's door. During the day, soldiers stopped him. The press pass was all but a sorry little joke. Why was he chronicling conversions? Whose payroll was he on? Tell us the truth, or else . . . And, in the cover of night, the freedom fighters would knock on the door: Why are you chronicling conversions? Whose side are you on?? Tell us the truth, or else . . .

Mansoor disliked taking sides. The scissor of history sharpens with age, but my brother, Nazir sighed, saw parallel histories that scissors could cut—Hindus, Muslims, Sikhs, and Buddhists, all living side by side for centuries on end, sometimes happily, sometimes unhappily, but always side by side. Of course, in 1947, Kashmiri Hindus would have voted for complete independence, and had it been a question of either Pakistan or India, their vote would certainly have gone with India. It was the poorer Muslim community that continued to feel economically marginalised and therefore, it was but a matter of time before this poor and illiterate section of Kashmiri society began to be swayed by the rhetoric that Islam would bring equality, and thereby, a better standard of living.

Growing up, Nazeer said, his voice steady, I remember sporadic communal tensions, but no one lost control. Then, in 1989, the freedom movement was injected with foreign blood. Kashmiri Hindus were killed, their homes burned down, and communal tensions flared like maggots on dead bodies. The Kashmiri Hindu leaders decided to fan these flames. They told their community that Pakistan was about to take over Kashmir and massacre the Hindus. The Hindus fled, leaving the Muslims—they felt—open targets for the army. In any case, we all failed each other.

Plain fact is more depends in this life on where one is born than any other variable, and about that there is little that can be done. The rich Hindus and Muslims fled abroad, the middle classes shifted to Delhi, while the poor Hindus and Muslims eventually relocated themselves to refugee camps in Jammu and in Pakistan respectively, promised by the army, in both cases, that, once things were restored to normal, they could return to their homes. That has yet to happen. They continue to languish in temporary homes, at the mercy of others, those poor Kashmiri Hindus fearing persecution by militants and the Muslims fearing persecution by the army. Mansoor chronicled this story of loss and relocation through photographs of uninhabited, hauntingly empty houses in 'Abandoned Homes'.

After 'Abandoned Homes', Mansoor turned to photographing 'Occupied Houseboats', trying to take pictures of well-fed soldiers leisurely smoking on the decks of houseboats and enjoying the scenery with their rifles for companions. Free, Free, Free, my brother's captions said, for the army occupied the houseboats without paying the houseboat owners. Instead they said the promise of safety is payment enough. All the houseboat owners were financially ruined, but not a single one agreed to be photographed for fear of retaliation by the army.

Mansoor, however, seemed to have transcended fear. One day, he photographed a baton charge against women demonstrating the disappearance of their men folk. The very next day, soldiers raided the neighbourhood looking for militants and possible suspects.

My father, my brother, and I stood in line with all the other men of our neighbourhood. Soon enough a 'surrendered' militant, his face concealed, stood before us. His task was to identify 'comrades' who, in turn, would become government designated special police officers, just like him. It took this man a moment to 'identify' Mansoor. Nazeer laughed bitterly. "The last time we saw my brother, he was smiling and saluting bravely at us even as the police bundled him into their jeep and drove him away.

"Mansoor's editor informed us, days later, that his body had been found in the gutter behind the newspaper office with his articles scattered over his body. My parents and I agreed that we must flee Kashmir and shift to Pakistan, for all of India seemed unsafe to us now. My father managed to bribe a getaway from Srinagar to Muzaffarabad in Pakistan and so we went, and with every step, we left my brother far behind even as we remembered him all the more.

"Once in Pakistan, we proceeded to the refugee camps in Azad Kashmir, Free Kashmir. Such fantasies I used to have about Pakistan. In a matter of days I realised that even the mere mention of an independent Kashmir could be ruinous in Azad Kashmir where the official line was 'Kashmir banay gaa Pakistan', Kashmir will be Pakistan. And there were spies amongst the refugees, all too willing to inform the military personnel stationed there to make sure that no one strayed from officialdom.

"One day, those of us who had strayed were rounded up by men in plainclothes. They told us they were sympathetic to our independence agenda and that we would be trained and sent across the border back into India, and though anything was better than languishing in Muzaffarabad, the one man amongst us who did not want to participate, disappeared and we never saw him again.

"And so here we are." Nazeer glanced towards the compound. "My poor, hapless parents had one advice for me only—to do nothing that would shame my martyred brother or them, and to that end I try to live my days. Then one day, Abid appeared as did you, Billawal, except Abid took full control, ordering us around, treating us like lackeys. When we complained, we were told to obey him. It will be Abid who will do us in." Nazeer clutched Billy's arm. "Abid who will send us the way of the Indian army or betray us in some other way. We have not a doubt, not a single doubt, that Abid is ISI, or RAW, or MI5, or CIA."

"Is there any concrete proof?" Billy asked. He did not bother to mask the fear in his voice. He did not know how to. Nazeer gave a sad smile.

"Does experience in life count for nothing? I do not know what Abid wants with you, but have no doubt: all our fates have been decided—we are condemned to die, ya aar ya paar, on this side of the border or that side. There is no going back for any of us. We are homeless, so we may as well go out with a bang, may as well go out putting our wasted lives to some use.

"Billawal, if your soul burns for an independent Kashmir, then you will do this for us—you will infiltrate Abid's heart and discover what he has in store for us so that we do not unwittingly aid either the cause of Pakistan or India."

∞⚭∞

Over the next few days, as Billy constructed Molotovs, blew them up, studied the rudiments of intercepting a wireless radio and neutralising electrified fencing, ran forwards round the compound and then backwards, slept to the footage and awoke to nightmares and developed other sores, his job to befriend Abid filled him with a renewed sense of purpose. He was here for Kashmir and Kashmir only, and now he could do something worthwhile to that end even if it meant tolerating Abid's incessant lecturing on American imperialism until Billy doubted that Abid, no matter what else he was, was certainly not CIA.

Although, Billy thought as he practiced shooting rags on a pole, wasn't the oldest trick in the book to deride your side? Billy's heart faltered yet again, but again he was able to buoy it up with the conviction that he was finally doing something towards Kashmiri independence, no matter how shoddy his espionage skills.

That evening, Billy squeezed himself between Abid and Jamal during class as if they were a close knit triumvirate. The instructor was telling them which signs to look for if a hostage was considering making a run for it—shifty eyes or steady gaze, tapping feet or an absolute calm. Nazeer and Abid were both listening intently to the instructor, as if their lives depended on this lesson. Billy's head began to pound as he looked from one to the other. Who was lying? Who was not? Whom to trust? Whom to mistrust?

After the class ended, Abid put a hand on his shoulder. "Be careful," he said, casting a glance towards Nazeer and the rest of the Kashmiri contingent. "If their need is great enough, you'd be a valuable bargaining chip given your nationality."

Billy's blood froze.

"Or let's suppose," Abid continued, "your mission was to volunteer yourself as such a chip in order to draw international attention to our cause, would you?"

∞∞

Would he? The next morning, after a restless night, Billy was still rattled by Abid's question. He'd told his father in their last conversation before he left home that freedom was worth any price, but if he truly believed that, then weren't human bargaining chips just another means to that end? Billy shook his head. He was going insane.

After prayers, instead of ordering the recruits into their exercise regimes, all the instructors collected around a radio, their ears pressed to it. The American embassies in Nairobi, Kenya, and Dar es Salaam, Tanzania had been bombed.

Mullah Khaled pronounced that death had come to those whose time it was to die and that God would take care of the rest. Billy felt he'd swallowed a scorpion. He wanted to go home where everyone had access to a TV, even if they chose not to turn it on, instead of a group of men listening to a radio and choosing when to offer reticent updates. He wanted to speed down the freeway with Dan and Ameer and ponder the plight of mankind. Instead, American embassies had been attacked and here he was in the midst of jubilation. After breakfast, he cornered Nazeer near the toilet.

"Are we responsible in any way for what has happened there?"

"Ask Abid," Nazeer whispered, "and see if you can use this as a ruse to draw out the information we require."

"We!" Abid snorted as they began their daily jog-run-sprint. "Has it occurred to no one that more local Muslim civilians have been killed and injured in the bombings than Americans?"

Billy flushed. Didn't it occur to the asshole that Americans could be Muslims too or was there no such combination in his world?

"Maybe," Abid continued, smiling slyly, "the US itself is responsible. It's a popularly used decoy to plant fear in the hearts and minds of people in order to get a green light for one's actual goals."

Mullah Khaled, in his lecture after dinner, blamed the US for all the casualties, for if they had not infiltrated the countries with their ambitions and set up embassies on their soil, there would have been no embassies to attack in the first place. Billy looked at Abid and Jamal beside him, nodding in agreement. For a moment, he pretended to be busy cleaning his overgrown, filthy nails, then he could stand it no longer.

"The US," Billy said to them, "played a major role in ending the violence against Muslims in Bosnia."

"Pah!" Jamal dismissed him. As far as he was concerned, the US always had an ulterior motive when it intervened in the politics of countries, *targeted* countries, because, sooner or later, propping up or toppling dictators and demagogues, or interference of even a beneficent nature ultimately benefited only the US.

"Democracy!" Jamal spat. "Democracy is nothing but a delusionary word the public has been brainwashed to accept as the best system of governance when in reality, democracy is nothing more than majority rule over minority. If spreading democracy was truly dear to the US, then would it not have democratised its best friend and my esteemed country, the Kingdom of Saudi Arabia?"

First, Billy imagined retorting, you get the law to permit women to drive in your country and then you worry about the best systems of governance and who is and is not putting a plug to it. Immediately Billy felt petty, but when a moment later Jamal flung a derisive 'Cowboy' at him, he was glad for the pettiness because pettiness was all the dignity he had here. Here, they could shoot the Cowboy dead and no one would be the wiser. A letter would be sent to his college PO Box—Billawal died in honourable combat, a veritable hero, here are your complimentary tickets to Hajj. Enjoy.

That night Billy sat up amidst all the sleeping, snoring men. He was here for Kashmir and that was it. But it was not *it* and would not be no matter how much he tried to convince himself. Footage swarmed before his eyes—the gruesome way people were killed—was Nazeer right? Was this to be their fate too? And for what? Bringing into existence yet another country that would, sooner or later, plunge into a mess? *Just like his father had said.*

That night, after everyone had slept, Billy shambled to the alcove behind the huts and took out Mauj jee's letter from his pocket. He stared at the black scrawl bridging the red and navy borders. *This* was why he was here. He had abandoned his home, but he was not homeless.

Billy held on to the letter night after day after night after day: jog-run-sprint-jog-run-sprint-jog-run-sprint, the crunch and crisp underfoot, the sun burning a halo into his head, sweat stinging his flaking skin, his being in a constant panic—each moment he believed he couldn't go on for a moment longer—then he did.

19

Ever since the Fourth of July weekend two weeks ago, Zari had been going to the old folks home across the park to donate the roses Fahad was getting delivered to her daily. Entering the cosy lobby, she handed the bright red but scentless bouquet across the reception counter to the cooing administrator, a sweet lady who always, in turn, urged her to enjoy a cookie from the complimentary assortment kept on the counter. Thanking her, Zari selected a ladybug cookie with its red and black icing for Miraage. A minute later, when she stepped out into the heat and humidity of the sunny day, she was overcome, yet again, with nausea. The cause, she told herself as she steadied herself, was Fahad's impending visit this afternoon.

Despite Zari's snubs since the Fourth of July, or perhaps *because* of them, Fahad had called Shehla this morning and told her that he was bringing his family to their house this afternoon to 'formally' meet Zari and Zari had been startled to find a flustered Shehla in the guest room, for such was the occasion even Shehla had risen from bed. Shehla had squeezed Zari's hands and advised her to forgive and forget. Life, she told Zari, was giving her yet another chance, and it was Zari's duty to grab that chance.

Each time Shehla had mentioned Fahad's name, Zari

had meant to come out with the truth, but Shehla had spoken so gently, so tenderly, talking about her future like a parent might, fussing over her, insisting that she *would* be a fine wife for Fahad, for anyone for that matter, that Zari hadn't had the heart to confess to the truth and be turned into an instant pariah.

Zari was shocked that Fahad had managed to convince his family to visit her, but she had to admit to herself, she was also flattered. Fahad did seem truly repentant and not about to abandon her, but it was too late. It was too late and to this end she was going to be rude to Fahad's family and let them know that *this time* it was she spurning Fahad. Zari sighed. Justice. Revenge. Was there nothing else left in her heart? No wonder she'd inadvertently managed to send Billal off to Kashmir.

She stopped by a hedge as she turned a corner, certain that she was going to throw-up. When she didn't, she continued standing there, thinking, dreading. These bouts of sickness, she admitted to herself, had nothing to do with Fahad's renewed attentions or his family's impending visit in the afternoon. Zari forced herself to walk to a strip of outdoor shops surrounding a gas station nearby and to the pharmacy. As she stood at the counter, avoiding the eyes of the chirpy cashier, she thanked God that Billal had left her some money and then, clutching the shopping bag to her chest, she made her way to the restroom at the back.

A little later, Zari sat on the curb outside the shop, the plastic bag dangling from her hands. Cars whizzed past her, their metallic bodies glinting in the sunlight. A grassy wind razed her face and ruffled the bag containing the test results.

The heaviness in her breasts, the morning sickness that often lasted all day, her missed periods—her periods after the rape had till now always been heavy, but on time—her suspicions were correct. Zari wiped her cheeks with the back of her hand. People came and people went, busy in their own lives, not even sparing her tears a glance. No one stopped to inquire if she needed help. Once upon a time, this very indifference in this land had made her feel safe, anonymous, better even. Now the indifference seemed strange, callous, dangerous even. In Kashmir, a crowd would have gathered, some for entertainment, but many out of sheer alarm and concern—Adsah koorie, kyaza chuk wadaan? Why are you crying, girl? But here, passersby were neither bothered nor concerned.

Zari felt utterly and miserably alone. The plus signs in the two pregnancy tests she'd taken blazed before her eyes. In another time, in another world, she would have called her mother and they would have wept with joy at the good news. There would have been loud, excited fanfare. She would have been fussed and cooed over. And now there was perhaps even more occasion for it to be so, because, after having lost so many, should she not celebrate this miracle of having someone to call her own?

Even if this child had been conceived of the rape, Zari knew she would never have considered an abortion. And here she was, sitting on the curb, all alone, and married. Marriage, marriage, marriage. It was Khala's fault she was in this mess to begin with, and now, having gotten wind of Fahad's renewed attention, Khala was adamant she reciprocate. But she *had* a husband already and let alone the protection and security Khala had said a husband would automatically confer, her marriage had landed her in a worse

315

situation: not in her wildest dreams could she have conjured up the possibility of being a single mother.

She could not legally work here. She had no income. She had no home. She could not drive. She could do nothing. The task of taking care of oneself, let alone an accidental child, *was* a Herculean task and she was so ill equipped just the thought of it filled her with infinite despair. She had to tell the Nabis. She could hardly return to her Khala or to her Uncle with a child in her womb, and neither could she endure a pregnancy by herself. Furthermore, the Nabis deserved to know she was carrying Billal's child. No matter what they felt about her, they would hardly kick out their grandchild, would they?

An SUV barrelled down the road, a squirrel, scampering mid-road, turned and dashed back to where it had come from. This time when the nausea came, Zari didn't even bother trying to contain her dry heaves. Finally, she stood up and headed towards the Nabis' home. The bedazzling afternoon heat hammered down on the world and the heat made her stomach churn. She had two choices: she could either break her 'good news' as soon as she returned to the Nabis' home, or she could wait until after Fahad's family's visit, a visit where store bought delicacies would be devoured and weak tea would be drunk and where there would be civilised banter—how are you, very well, and yourself—while behind civil lines lay the uncivilised lies: she was married and she was pregnant.

Shehla wheeled the trolley into the drawing room and signalled to Salsabil to pour the chai for their guests. Giving her a dour look, Salsabil got up and began handing out the tea cups. Stupid girl, Shehla thought, wishing, yet again, that the Maliks were here to ask for Salsabil's hand rather than Zari's. Instead, there was that Korean. Pursing her lips, Shehla settled next to Farah, Fahad's mother, on the chaise longue in the drawing room. Farah had bought gifts for Zari. A measly box of chocolates and an insipid beige organza shalwar suit, enough of a hint regarding her feelings. Stupid woman, Shehla thought. If only she could tell her to be grateful Fahad just wanted to marry and not run off, risking his life, to save the world.

Truth be told, Shehla knew she would never have found the strength for this mid-afternoon rendezvous were it not for the fact that she believed she owed Zari. As much she blamed the girl and her Khala for Billal's rash heroism, the fact was that following Billal's departure, Zari's presence in their household had been a godsend. In taking over Miraage and all the other household cares, Zari had literally allowed Shehla the luxury to stay locked in her room, wallowing in her grief, miserable yet comfortable. It was her duty, nay, her very debt of gratitude, therefore, to steer the poor girl towards what was best for her. And, perhaps, if she was good to this girl from Kashmir, would karma not make sure that someone in Kashmir would be good to her son?

To that end, Shehla had also tried to allay Farah's fears. Farah was fearful of what the gossip mongers would do when the news leaked out. She was terrified Zari's r-a-p-e would become the talk of the town, and that Zari may have fertility issues. It wasn't as if it was just one man, Farah had whispered over the phone, it was g-a-n-g-r-a-p-e and surely that multiplied, God only knew how many times, the

317

physical and emotional damage. She was also convinced, stupid woman, that Zari practiced black magic and had thus bewitched Fahad. Furthermore, much to Farah's chagrin, instead of Fahad's Dadi jee backing her concerns, the aged matriarch had proclaimed it a sin if they failed to welcome the girl into the family. As if we are some charity hospital, Farah had fumed.

Shehla turned to Dadi jee. Dadi jee was a carefully wilted apple, a bundle of baby bones and baby fat, prickly heat powder caking in her wrinkles and creases. Her elongated ear lobes drooped with the weight of gold hoops thicker than the silver-grey braid meandering over one shrunken shoulder. She'd brought her two life lines along: her walker and her paandaan, a pure silver filigreed container snug in her lap like a tiny dog.

Every few minutes, she would lift the lid to the various compartments underneath and extract a heart-shaped leaf from between damp muslin, smear it with lime and catechu paste, add perfumed tobacco, and then, breaking a betel nut with a nut cracker, add a few slivers to the mixture on the leaf and finally roll it all into a cone and pop the concoction into her mouth, the paan, an original mouth freshener long before toothpaste and breath mints came into existence.

"Shehla," she spoke now, chewing a paan, "you look quite unwell, my dear. Everything all right?"

"Couldn't be better," Shehla replied, smiling. She wished she'd made the effort to wear some makeup. She looked as if she was attending a funeral. Zari too, for that matter. Her eyes were all puffy and swollen and had she not bothered to iron her shalwar kurta? Had she even bathed? Even her hair was greasy. She looked dazed, perhaps rightly so at this sudden turn of events, but really, did she have to look so grim and dejected? And why had Zari given away *all* of Fahad's costly flower arrangements? Thank God Farah was too perturbed to notice that none of her son's floral gifts were to be seen anywhere in the house.

"I've just had a bit of a cold," Shehla told Dadi jee.

"It's all this dieting-shieting you girls do these days, thoba thoba." Dadi jee touched her earlobes with incredulity. "In my day, my mother-in-law was after my life to fatten up, but, these days, ulta he hisab hai, complete opposite." Dadi jee turned her sepia gaze on Zari. "Idar ao larki. Come sit by my side." She patted the space next to her on the sofa, the scent of tea rose billowing from her starched white kurta-gharara. "Come, come. I don't bite, my dear, ask Farah here."

Farah gave a practiced smile. When Zari was settled beside her, Dadi jee took her slender wrist in her hand and put a finger on her pulse. After a moment she said, "Handsome, and resilient."

And then, inclining her head ever so slightly, she added softly, "your family"—and she took Zari's slim hands between hers and held on—"so sorry, so terribly sorry. I have lived through the wars of 1947 and 1971. I understand all too well, my dear, your pain. No matter what *they* say, you are far from damaged goods."

Farah looked ready to collapse. She began mumbling about Fahad's sister being out of town with her husband, in Switzerland, for the summer, they owned a chalet there. Shehla looked at Zari to see if she was suitably impressed by the chalet as other girls always were. But Zari was gazing at Dadi jee like a devotee. Shehla wondered, suddenly, why it had never occurred to her to inquire after Zari's family. Why had she never thought to show such simple forthright compassion? After all, it would do her good in these difficult times to have Zari gawk at her with gratitude and devotion— then she might not feel like such a maternal failure.

Shehla looked at Zari as Dadi jee raised her hands to her papery lips and kissed them before turning to Fahad and blinking at him. Over the years, Shehla had learnt to gauge this particular blink—as if wooden beads hanging off the old woman's snow-white lashes were slowly weighing them down. It was a blink of approval. Farah, also witnessing the blink, looked ready to faint.

The afternoon came to a close. Dadi jee rose, but, before Fahad could reach her walker, Zari helped Dadi jee to it.

"Jeethi raho, bless you," Dadi jee said, kissing her on the forehead, making her approval even more evident. Fahad looked as if he'd won the lottery. Farah didn't say much of a goodbye to anyone, and finally Shehla shut the front door.

"Congratulations," she said to Zari. "Next step, wedding date."

"Yeah," Salsabil said, "congratulations are certainly due, if this is what you want."

In the guest room, Zari prostrated on the prayer mat. It was too late. No matter what she wanted, Fahad was too late. She had meant to spurn Fahad in front of his relatives, but Dadi jee had taken her unawares. For the first time since it had all begun, Zari had met someone who'd understood her greatest loss and gone straight to the heart of it. Her family.

And then: *You are far from damaged goods.* Billal had also said as much, and so had Salsabil, but it was something else to hear this affirmation from the lips of a Grande Dame.

Zari had hidden the pregnancy tests in her suitcase and now she took them out and held them to her chest, wishing they would impart some strength, some wisdom, some guidance. She wanted to tell the Nabis the truth, but she also wanted to meet Dadi jee at least one more time. After that, she promised herself, she would come out.

She stashed the tests back into the suitcase, and zipping it up, rested her burning cheek on the cool leather exterior. But, for the first time since she had left home, the soft weathered scent gave her little solace. She imagined Dadi jee's kind face crumpling once she learned the extent of her deception. Imagined Dadi jee never bothering to extend her kindness to anyone again for fear of betrayal. Imagined Dadi jee thinking ill of *her.*

By the time Zari decided *right now* was as auspicious a time as any to confess to the Nabis, she'd unpacked the ghosts from her suitcase and arranged them on the wire racks in the closet. Out in the open, their calls seemed a little less strident and she ran her fingers over her mother's double-sided game board, over her sister's shawls, her father's winter hat, through all the photo albums, over Baz's paint box, and the pregnancy tests rolled into his clothes, until finally she turned to her suitcase, her gentle beast of a suitcase, now nothing more than a giant, empty carcass, home, yet not the only home in her world.

The family room downstairs blazed with lights. As Zari

neared, she heard Mrs and Mr Nabi talking. They sounded calm. She relaxed. They had reached a détente; it would be easier to tell them. She stopped in the doorway at the sight of Dan and Ameer. She hadn't seen Billal's friends since the day of the wedding. Salsabil beckoned her to sit on sofa beside her. Settling down, Zari gazed out of the windows to a porch light laced with gnats. She caught Dan and Ameer's reflections looking at her. She wished one of them would disclose the marriage, wished they'd just blurt it out.

"It's my fault," Ameer was saying. "I've been so busy with term papers. I feel terrible."

"I feel guilty." Dan's knees bobbed manically. "If only I'd read Billy's emails in time, maybe I could have talked some sense into the mumbo-jumbo about it being in his blood."

"Where did he get this idea from . . ." Shehla brought her fist to her mouth and shook her head.

"I suppose it was your conversation with him, Mr Nabi," Ameer said, "and Mauj jee's letters."

Dan kicked Ameer's foot.

"Amman," Shehla's voice came out with great difficulty. "What is he saying?"

Salsabil stared at her father. "Mauj jee's *letters*?"

Amman cleared his throat and inched closer to Shehla. "He found them, Shehla. He read them."

"What did they say?" Salsabil said, her face stricken.

"She was endorsing freedom fighting!" Shehla stood up, her hands trembling. "What else could she possibly say? That mad senile old woman!" She whipped around to Amman.

"Did you tell him she'd lost her mind? Did you tell him the truth?" Shehla slapped her forehead. "No. You said you were proud of him. You wanted him to go. You wanted him to be like your father. How could you? How. Could. You."

All of a sudden, Zari felt sorry for Billal. In some countries, in some families, his mere intent would have designated him a hero, but here, Shehla believed Billal a fool and Amman's pride criminal. And she too, Zari admitted to herself, was guilty of thinking of Billal's act only in relation to herself. Billal might have acted rashly, but it was a brave act nonetheless, an honourable act, an act which would make many a wife hold her head up in pride and many a parent proud. For the first time, Zari caught a glimmer of Billal's feelings for Mauj jee and his Dada and it scared her. She wrapped her hands around her waist with the guilty realisation that she was relieved it was no longer an auspicious time to confess and that someone else and not she was battling the fallout of exposure.

"You should have told me he found the letters." Shehla was shouting. "You should have told me about it immediately, but you didn't. You didn't even give me a chance to make a difference. You didn't even give me a chance."

"Shehla, please sit down." Amman's hands were joined together in plea as he stood contrite before his wife. "Please, just listen to me."

Shehla walked out, her expression as heartbroken as the one on Amman's face.

◈

Amman lit a new cigarette with the smouldering end of the old one. His eyes watered from the haze his non-stop smoking had created in the study. He couldn't get Shehla's damaged expression out of his mind just as he couldn't help but remember her defiance in medical school, her eyes bright, her mouth bold, the only female student to challenge the professors over everything. And yet how distraught she had been the first time she'd seen the scars on his back. She had warmed a bowl of almond oil and run her fingertips along the ridges of the wounds, her soft touch soothing the constant prickle he'd taught himself to ignore. The last person to have looked upon his scars with such pain, to have caressed them with such tenderness had been his mother, and she had been long dead by then.

Amman had promised himself then and there to do so well in life that Shehla never lacked for anything. He had resolved to love and honour her in every way possible. And he had. Until Zari's Khala's request for help had awakened within him a dormant affiliation for his birth place. The world map on the study wall mocked Amman with its demarcations and delineations. Land did not grow fences itself, the fences were planted and war was the planter, a planter always present in either one of its avatars—country against country, state against state, body against mind, man against himself, brother against brother, child against parent, husband against wife.

He should have told Shehla about Billal finding the letters. He should have told her about their conversation the very day it occurred. But he'd been terrified of yet again facing her assertion that he was no longer a Kashmiri. He remembered the first time Shehla had said so. He had been devastated. He had family in Kashmir, he spoke the language fluently, he thought in it, he dreamt in it in, he swore in it, his favourite food was Kashmiri. How could she say he was not Kashmiri? You could take the man out of the country but not the country out of the man. Was no part of her even a little Pakistani any longer? And they certainly weren't all-American, so where did that leave them? Who were they? What were they? A child, he'd said to her once, leaving its parent's house for its own does not mean that relations between the two are severed. You of all people, she'd replied, should not confuse the ties between parent and child to that between country and citizen.

Amman could picture Shehla, leaning against a brick wall in the lush grounds of the medical college, his head resting on her shoulder as he told her how, if he ever had children, he would do everything he could to remain alive so that they would never have to miss a father while they were growing up; how they would be more important to him than anything and any country in the world. He'd been crying when he said he would keep the children far away from race, from creed, from nationality, and from the wounds in his heart and the scars on his back.

"Shh," she'd whispered. "The son should not suffer for the memories of the father."

He'd fallen in love with her all over again in that moment and he'd known then that he would follow her anywhere. They would go to America, she said, because her brother Buraaq, already settled there, said it afforded plenty of opportunities for qualified doctors. In America, she said, there would be no past to weigh them down, only a future in which to plant the flags of their dreams. Amman was still trying to understand what exactly she'd meant by those words and how he'd allowed himself to believe that a future existed without a past. But he needed Shehla now to forgive him if he was to forgive himself. He needed her to reassure him again that the burdens of the father were not the burdens of the son.

Amman looked up eagerly at the knock on the study door. But it was Zari, come to ask if he wanted a cup of tea. It was long after that cup was served and drunk that he realised he'd answered her in Kashmiri because she'd spoken to him in Kashmiri.

20

Billy awoke to thunder. His ears were ringing. Men leapt up around him, their hair mussed, wild-eyed, snatching grim glances as they grabbed their guns, their shouts drowned out by the thunder coming closer, closer, closer, the very ground a furious tremor, *boom boom boom,* the kilim jumped out of its threads, a mighty orange-red roar engulfing the world, shattering walls into confetti, splitting confetti into bits.

Billy remembered a story his mother had told him of elephants ordered to trample the Kaaba at Mecca and Allah sending a troop of birds to stone them into retreat. They were being stoned now. Modern-day stones which erupted into heat and light. He crouched under the sheet, hearing the feeble retort of rifles, ants shaking their puny fists at feet stamping from up above.

A foot stepped on his face, then another, then one on his head, someone fell over him, swore, got up. But Billy lay there, blank, blood crashing in his ears, flooding him out. *I'm going to die. This is it. All alone in Afghanistan. Without my family. Never see them again.*

Up up up

It was Abid. He gripped Billy's one arm. Mohmedoo

gripped the other. Together they dragged him over the kilim burning atop a shattered brick.

The courtyard was an inferno. A sea of flames sucked the air, shimmering and convulsing like liquid glass. Jets of smoke hissed and writhed into the throbbing stinking night. Waves of heat splashed the choking, coughing, cursing faces. Tawny shadows limped past the mule who was tugging and braying at its tether trapped under the rubble of the broken entrance. Both goats lay belly up. Not a hut stood intact. Dying men twitched, their skin slick, shiny, as if they were wet empty bottles the tide had washed in. Jamal lay beached, his mouth agape. The kitchen was gutted. Shahbaz, still, a dead lump under his blanket pinned down with rubble, his hand bloated with moonstone rings. Mohsin, a pair of maroon rubber sandals emerging from under Ahmed Baba's bulk; father must have thrown himself between his son and the world.

And there lay Nazeer. His thin, grey wrists convulsing in his too short sweater as he pressed fingers to an oozing hole. He was dying; a slow, painful, pathetic death.

Abid aimed. One shot.

Nazeer's body jerked, then sagged.

Mohmedoo squeezed Billy's arm so hard he yelped. His knees buckled.

"Billawal." Abid snapped his fingers. "Come on, mate, walk. Baby steps, baby steps. The first time's always the hardest. But look at it this way: They are shaheed, martyrs, they died for their principles, they are the lucky ones heaven-bound while we're still stuck on earth."

☙❧

He found himself repeating the prayer for the dead he'd been religiously taught for Baber's funeral:

In allah hi wa inna allah hi rajaoon.

To you God we belong and to you we return.

To you God we belong and to you we return.

To you God we belong and to you we return.

It was a small group with whom he stumbled away from the compound, the mule with them.

There was no shape shifting of the land they tread upon, no closing his eyes to the secret it gave up in the crackling blaze they left behind: that it was a path to put one foot in front of the other, a road and what was a road anyway but a fancy term for any stretch of land that took you towards something or away from it. He counted his steps, one to hundred, again, again, again, until they stopped to rest for the night, squatting on stony ground, heads lowered on bruised, burnt forearms.

Billy tasted the blood in his mouth from the gash he'd gnawed in his cheek. Felt now the pain in his right calf, the flesh scraped hard, sticky blood pooling and congealing into his shoe and sock. Of the previously calm men, some were now crying, some whimpering. They were all, for the moment at least, just men who were scared, no matter how many times they'd lived through, or dreamt of doing, what man could do to man.

Mullah Khaled, his rooster red beard no less diminished in colour than the first time Billy had set eyes on it, was praying for the souls of the departed, was speaking of evil times making martyrs out of husbands and fathers and sons and brothers, times so evil that the only promise life held was of death, death which transported to heaven, heaven that river of milk, that union with Allah, home of the hoories, those promised female companions.

Billy wished he could believe. How much easier it would be if one believed there was more to life than surviving on earth. But he did not. At least not without a doubt. And so here he was. But was he willing to die not having achieved any goal? Was he willing to die for principles alone? What were his principles? Why was he so mortified of death when it was the one inevitability?

Abid had saved his life.

That could have been him Abid shot. An act somehow worse than that of bombing faceless, nameless people. Or was it the other way round? Had Abid's act been a mercy killing? Bits and pieces of colour flashed before him. Maroon sandals. Moonstone eyes. The hide of a goat. Billy stuck his icy fingers in his pockets, touched passport and money and Mauj jee's letter in one and, in the other, rock candy. He snatched his fingers out. His eyes burned with tears.

Mohsin-dead.

Ahmed Baba-dead.

Shahbaz-dead.

Nazeer-dead: murder or mercy?

From here the compound seemed like the rim of hell, as if some devilish God was lolling under the open skies, leg upon leg, smoking a cigar, and the compound just the ember glowing at the tip. Billy curled up on the ground, squeezed his eyes shut, and tried desperately to still the shivering of his bones and the trembling of his soul.

21

Zari found Shehla kneeling by the mailbox in the driveway, sorting through the mail spread out on the grass. The ends of her grimy bathrobe trailed over the flower beds, the morning dew beginning to stain its lace trimmings. Her hair, unwashed and matted, hung around her face which, without her sparse eyebrows filled in, looked naked. Ever since Dan and Ameer's visit, Shehla's sole excursion out of bed was to check the mail, and that she got up at all was, Zari thought, less a miracle and more an accusation that she trusted no one to tell her the truth anymore.

"Nothing," Shehla said, glancing up at Zari as she began to riffle, yet again, through the pile of coupons and bills and brochures. Miraage skipped up to them, the arc of her jump rope flying behind her. Coming to a stop next to Zari, she pulled at her mother's robe, demanding to know what was planned for International Heritage Day at the Montessori.

"I don't want to sing chanda mama duur kay yet again! Or bring store bought samosas. Or wear a shalwar kameez."

"Miraage," Shehla said, "I cannot do this right now. Please, just let Salsabil repeat last year's stuff."

"But Gretchen's mother is bringing homemade strudel, and Mei's mother animal-shaped dumplings, and Asa's mother is going to teach everyone to wear hair-wraps like they wore in Nigeria. I want to do something new too!"

"Miraage, please," Shehla said, "please stop it."

Miraage burst into tears and Shehla, looking at her as if she did not know what to do, mumbled that she needed to pray and hurried back indoors. Zari gathered Miraage in her arms and held her until her sobs subsided. Then, picking up the mail scattered on the grass, she carried Miraage inside, seated her in front of the TV with a plate of baby carrots smothered in dressing, and made her way up to Shehla's room to pray with her.

As Zari settled next to Shehla, she wondered if this might not be the best time for her disclosure. Surely with the Quran between them, Shehla would be more tolerant. She peeped at Shehla who caught her glance and managed a woebegone smile. Mentally bracing herself for the moment of confession, Zari jumped as the phone rang next to Shehla who, checking the caller ID, passed it to her.

"Hey, what's up?" Fahad's voice, bright and confident, always unnerved Zari. Since his family's visit two weeks ago, he called numerous times a day, probably to hear his own voice since she barely spoke and she would not have entertained his calls at all had it not been for the fact that she longed to meet his grandmother again. But each time she broached the subject of meeting Dadi jee, Fahad said she was unwell.

"The sky," Zari replied.

"Ha ha," Fahad said. "What you doing?"

"Praying."

"For anyone in particular?"

"Let me call you back when I'm done."

"I'll call you."

Zari hung up, uncertain whether she found his persistence annoying or impressive. Her Khala and Shehla insisted it was proof of true love, but according to Salsabil, Fahad was a stalker.

"Look how rosy your cheeks are looking," Shehla said, smiling a little as she hurriedly took back the phone in case Billal was trying to call home. "Fahad is good for you, and you will make a fine wife for anyone. His grandmother adores you and it is just a matter of time before Farah warms up to you too."

"Would you, if it was Billal?"

Would you, if it was Billal?

The naked ferocity on Shehla's face shocked Zari, the startled protectiveness of it, as if, just by association with her, Billal was damned. At least Fahad's mother's disapproval dangled from her face. Shehla was a liar—*fine wife for anyone*—and a hypocrite, one standard for her son and another for her friend's son.

"My poor son," Shehla whispered a moment later, sniffling. "When he returns from this trial, I will find him a princess."

Zari bit her inner cheek to keep her angry tears at bay. She was Shehla's charity case and nothing more, merely someone to pity and help out. She had accused Billal of the same, but he'd gone to Kashmir, he'd put his life on the line for her, there was substance there; for Shehla, she was merely someone to wash her hands off by getting her married off to Fahad

For a moment, Zari was glad Billal had gone away to Kashmir and that Shehla was hurting. The moment passed. Why should she wish ill for her husband because his mother was selfish? Billal was not selfish like his mother, thoughtless perhaps, but not selfish and never had he been mean-spirited. But was not she herself mean and selfish, more upset over Billal's going because of the lurch in which it had left her rather than at the mess he'd gone to join and the risks he would face?

But she missed him. She missed him.

She and Shehla both.

Zari was about to leave the room when loud shrieks erupted from the upper lounge. The next instant, the bedroom door flew open as Miraage burst in with a man and a woman.

It was Buraaq, Shehla's brother, and his wife, Barbara. They had flown in from Florida for a surprise visit. After the tears and the hugging, Barbara drew all the curtains wide apart and threw open the windows, sunlight rushing in, the open air expelling the dankness from the room, while Shehla stood in her brother's tight embrace, chiding him for surprising them. When she finally took note of Zari standing on the threshold, unsure of whether to stay or leave, Shehla smiled.

"Buraaq, this is our blessing in disguise, our angel, Zari."

Zari flinched. Angel yes, but not princess.

Buraaq let go of his sister, and walking over to her, he

334

patted her head. Barbara embraced her and the crook of her neck, warm and soft, smelt of roasted chestnuts like an oven in Kashmir in the deep of winter. Zari caught her breath, muttered something about having to put the prayer paraphernalia away, and she hurriedly left the room.

As the day progressed, Zari noticed that both Buraaq and Barbara talked non-stop, as if a hush might let something horrible in. They bantered the entire morning away, began anew when Amman returned from the hospital mid-afternoon, and continued through an early dinner where Shehla and Amman sat at the same table after a long time. No topic was off limits for the couple and even Billal was brought up, as if he was only vacationing in Europe and not lost somewhere in Kashmir.

Zari wondered if Buraaq and Barbara pretended that their son was on a holiday too. But, after dinner, accompanied by the Nabis, the couple went to Baber's grave. Zari longed to ask them if moving to a different part of the country and away from their son's grave had helped them in any way. She presumed they'd be subdued when they returned, but Barbara walked in with popsicles for everyone and Buraaq and Amman went directly down to the basement from where they returned, a little while later, reeking of smoke and carrying a basket of board games.

They played Monopoly well into the night. Zari kept peeking at Barbara and Buraaq sitting side by side, playing tokens in hand, cheating indiscriminately, laughing when they were caught. They didn't look like a couple utterly devastated by the death of a child. Certainly not devastated enough to never dare such a loss again, and looking at them, it seemed to Zari that life after death was possible. But would a dead child want his parents to play board games and laugh the whole time no matter how much time had passed? Why not? How much more, then, would a living child expect?

That night, as Zari lay in bed, caressing her belly, trying to quell the need to walk through the night—after all, babies needed their mothers to rest—she glimpsed Baz's face in the medallion crown moulding on the ceiling. Baz had just begun to crawl and was on all fours, his chubby hands and feet splayed, rocking back and forth, going neither forwards nor backwards. Yet he chuckled, his mouth open, delighted with sheer movement for as far as he was concerned, without going anywhere at all, he was conquering the world.

Would *it* be a boy or a girl? Zari drew a sharp breath, shocked at the sheer nerve of her mind and heart to make her think and feel things her soul did not want. She couldn't stop. If the child resembled her mother, or her father, or her nephew, would the resemblance make her love the child more? And what would she possibly tell the child? The truth? How would she say the words? *They were killed, and I survived. I was raped, by so many.* How would the child react? If it was a girl, would she be scared of being a girl? And if it was a boy, would he be ashamed of being a boy? Or would he be scared too?

She would never tell the child about her past. But, what if the child found out from somewhere, like Billal had? What if it came up to her and asked why didn't you tell me yourself? She owed it to her child. Hadn't she said as much to Billal? That it was her duty to tell her child about its history? But what if she was asked: Why did you tell me about all this?

But what if the child never got to ask the question? She had conceived the child. She would carry it, deliver it, nurture it, and yet, it could die. Like her nephew, like Buraaq and Barbara's son, like all those children on the news: an adolescent shot to death, a toddler who'd drowned in a swimming pool, an entire classroom dead of an earthquake. What if her child died?

Zari had thought there would be nothing left in her to shatter, that she might never be able to love anyone so much that even the thought of its death would find something in her to splinter further, but here it was, this child. *Her* child.

She ran to the bathroom, grabbed the razor. She had barely rolled up her sleeve, when she caught a glimpse of her belly in the mirror. There was nothing to see, yet, but that did not mean that there was nothing there. Shehla had protected Billal—didn't this child deserve a *mother's* protection too, *its* own mother's protection?

Zari hurled the razor into the trash can and splashed cold water onto her face. The duck soap sat on the sink in a boat of suds. The beak was beginning to emerge, a tiny red scimitar, a miniature mouth, asking her how she was going to survive alone with a child. She was driving herself crazy. She needed a glass of water.

In the family room downstairs, Zari saw Barbara sitting on an inflatable mattress in front of a muted TV and working on her laptop, and she tiptoed to the kitchen, not wanting to talk to anyone, and also shy about what she might say. From the kitchen window, she caught a glimpse of Buraaq and Shehla sitting on the swing in the deck, Amman standing before them, his face pale.

Zari drank the water as quickly and quietly as possible, but Barbara caught her on her way back.

"Hi sweetheart." Barbara smiled. "You're up awfully late?"

"I can't sleep," Zari stammered. She wanted to ask Barbara how she could laugh! How she could laugh so much!

"Well, come join me then." Barbara removed the bowl of ice-cream beside her and Zari settled next to her on the mattress, hugging her legs to herself. Barbara's thick, muscular legs in pyjama leggings were crossed at the ankles and, above one ankle bone, a tattoo of a cobalt blue kangaroo with the bottle green ears of a joey peeking out of its pouch. Her hijab had loosened and Zari saw a delicate gold chain pressed into the plump of her soft neck. Wife and husband wore identical lockets with Baber's picture inside, Salsabil had told Zari earlier that evening.

Salsabil, Zari had noted, had not left the house even for a moment since their arrival. Neither had she stolen away to whisper on her phone. She was fast asleep now, sprawled under a blanket by Barbara's feet—Barbara's toenails, painted a bright scarlet-pink.

Zari looked away. When she caught her breath, she turned to Barbara and, very simply, said, "I'm so sorry about your son."

"Thank you, sweetheart, so am I." Barbara reached over and squeezed Zari's hand. "Amman and Shehla keep telling us what an angel you are."

"I'm not such an angel." Zari spoke so softly Barbara had to lean in to hear her. "I . . ." Zari's voice broke but she forced herself to speak, the kindness in Barbara's eyes compelling her to try. "Do you ever feel jealous . . . Miraage . . . I mean . . . looking at other children?"

"All the time, sweetheart." Barbara stroked Zari's hair away from her face and tucked it behind her ear. "At one point in time, both Buraaq and I could not see straight with envy."

The truth was, Barbara continued, after Baber's death, she'd been crazed with jealousy. So often she'd looked at Billal and cried for her son . . . on Billal's birthdays, when his voice first broke, when she saw the beginning of his moustache, his school graduations. She cried for her son, and she cried also for the woman she was becoming, a woman who coveted other children's milestones.

"But I . . . we never begrudged Shehla and Amman a single milestone . . . Buraaq and I, we never wished ill . . . We mourned what we had lost, not anyone else's gains."

Zari nodded. Neither did she. And though she kept silent, she agreed with Barbara that the two ways of coping were bitterness or betterness and who really knew what made one person go one way and another the other way, something within them or something without, a combination of both, or neither one . . .

"We love Billy . . . you understand," Barbara said. "Billy was Baber's idol. We could not see Billy without seeing Baber."

"Is that why you moved away?" Zari asked with a sudden insight.

"Yes. At first the move was supposed to be temporary, but then we realised that our son was more than just a grave, in fact moving away allowed us to celebrate the little bit of life God allowed him rather than fixate on his death."

"How much," Zari asked, "does faith help you?"

Barbara fingered her necklace, the thin chain gliding over her nail. "Children whose parents die are called orphans, but there is no such word for parents who have lost their children. Omissions like that used to frighten me. As if the world was Godless just because my language was incomplete." Barbara smiled wistfully. "When I was a child, my mother used to say 'pray to God, sailor, but row to the shore' and, after Baber's death, Buraaq kept praying and praying and praying while I just rowed and rowed and rowed. And the shore, it came and went and came and went . . . I went to the mosque daily, trying to find solace in the faith I'd converted to. I went to the church I'd grown up in. I was willing to go everywhere, anywhere. I didn't care which God answered me—whose faith gave me a moment of solace. They all did. They all did not. God is time and time is God." Barbara gave a short laugh. "Zari, people kept saying in those days right after Baber's death, that time was a healer, and it is a healer, no doubt, but credit should go to the heart that allows time to stretch it out, the heart that stretches and stretches itself to contain all the loss and gain of a lifetime and keep them tethered in the same place." Barbara looked into Zari's eyes. "Sweetheart, there's no going back, that's for sure, there's no road leading back to the way it was, only roads leading to how you can now choose to live—bitterness or betterness—and there is always choice. God is choice and Choice is God."

Zari pulled the blanket over her knees and snuggled down as Barbara continued talking, her voice a mellifluous lullaby.

When Zari awoke, the sun had risen and engulfed the family room in golden gauze. Barbara and Salsabil were curled up together. And, at some point during the night,

Miraage had crawled in and joined them, snuggling into Zari, her arms around her belly as if she was protecting what was there. As Zari stroked the little girl's hair, she knew what she had to do.

∞∞∞

By the time Miraage woke up, Zari's list for a presentation on Kashmir for Miraage's International Day at school was complete. When Shehla read it, she once again proclaimed to everyone that Zari was an angel of an addition to their household. It did not escape Zari that Shehla used the word 'household' instead of 'family'. She was doing this for Miraage, Zari reminded herself as she gave a short stiff smile. Only Miraage. From across the room, Barbara gave her warm smile; a smile Zari returned with warmth.

Since Miraage did not own a pheran, Zari decided that she would simply have to cut and sew to size one of her own. Turning to Salsabil she asked if she could get her a sewing machine from somewhere as soon as possible.

"You can sew?" Salsabil stared at Zari as if she'd just announced that she'd been to the moon.

Zari nodded, slightly perplexed. "My mother . . . she decided that teaching me to sew would be a good way to also teach me mathematics . . ." She stopped, unsure if she could trust her voice to speak of her mother making her convert measurements from one system to the other repeatedly until she could do so effortlessly.

"Let me check with Ohwi," Salsabil whispered. "I think his mother owns a sewing machine."

Zari nodded.

"Miraage," Zari turned to the excited little girl as Salsabil got on the phone, "instead of a song, how about we teach your class a hand game?"

Miraage clapped in delight.

"Splay your fingers out like mine." Zari lay her palm on the table top and began reciting the rhyme. Hu kus bu kus, theliwan su kus, who is that, who am I, then tell me who are you. She tapped each finger 'out' at the last word and Miraage squealed when, with all her fingers tapped 'out', she won the first round.

"Okay," Salsabil said as she got off the phone, "Ohwi can get us a sewing machine. So we have clothes, and a game, now what about arts and crafts?"

Zari's mouth turned to cotton as the idea came to her. It would be a way to incorporate Baz into the day, a way to honour his memory.

"That will be beautiful," Salsabil said after Zari had told her. "Thank you."

"Okay then." Zari stared intently at the list. "Now, food. What about pakoras with a Kashmiri twist? Nedru pakoras?"

"What's nedru?" Salsabil asked.

"You don't know nedru!" Zari teased her. "What sort of a Kashmiri are you?"

"What's ned-ru?!" Miraage chimed in.

"The stem of a lotus flower," Zari replied, smiling. "We'll have to slice it thin and then microwave till soft but still crunchy, coat the slices in a batter of chickpea flour, salt and pepper, and then deep fry them. You can serve the nedru pakoras with ketchup, just like fries."

"Mines is going to be the bestest heritage ever!" Miraage said, dancing around.

"And where," Salsabil cut in, "might these lotus stems be available?"

It was Ohwi, purveyor of the sewing machine, who led them to an Asian grocery store where they found bags of sliced lotus stems in the freezer section. Back in the car, Zari caressed the sleek black sewing machine on the seat beside her. It reminded her of her mother's sewing machine, the ebony body, the curlicue gold pattern, the scuff-marked stand. She could remember her mother's fingers entwined in her own as she taught her to thread the needle's eye, her mother's warm breath on her cheek as she leaned over her shoulder and guided her into sewing straight lines.

"Whose is this?" Zari asked softly.

"My mother's." Ohwi turned around. "In fact, she and this machine are what put my father through graduate school. She keeps talking about getting a new one, but she can't get herself to part with this one. I think this is also her way of teaching me and my brothers that everything of value does not have to be bright, shiny and new."

"How many brothers do you have?"

"Four." Ohwi grinned. "My parents kept trying for a girl. For the first two years of my life, my mother dressed me in nothing but frocks made with that machine."

"Thank you." Zari looked at the sewing machine. "Thank you for lending it to me."

"You're welcome."

"I'll . . . I'll send a batch of nedru pakoras for you . . ."

"Thanks," he said warmly. "I'd appreciate that."

When they dropped Ohwi off, and were on their way back home, Zari found herself telling Salsabil that Ohwi seemed like a nice person. Salsabil just smiled. It hit Zari moments later that she had thought of the Nabis' house as 'home' and that her teasing and bantering with Salsabil had made her feel as if she was back with Kiran and Sonea.

For the next couple of days, as Zari busied herself preparing for the International Heritage Day at Miraage's school, she waited for her ghosts to assault her with furious accusations of letting them go, of forgetting them, of murdering them anew. Instead, she heard them sighing, rich heavy sighs, as if *they* were letting go of *her*. It should have panicked her, the disappearance of their voices which had, till now, been a loud and constant chorus in her head, but she was too busy concentrating on measuring Miraage, cutting and sewing her an outfit to size, slicing the lotus stems, whisking up the batter, frying batch after batch of nedru pakoras, too busy working towards the future to be sucked into the past.

22

They rose for Fajr prayers under a smoke smothered sky, the reek of scorched heat spreading for miles. Afterwards, they headed back to the camp compound to bury the dead. Outside the compound, the jeep smouldered. At a distance, stray dogs snarled at them. The mule sat still, calm, as if day light had blacked out the very terrors that had made hell out of night. Billy dug into the hard earth as they buried remains: Mohsin, Ahmed Baba, Shahbaz, Nazeer, all the dead. He tried not to think of how he could not care for Jamal's death. He tried not to think of Mohsin's red rubber sandals, of Ahmed Baba's dreams for Mohsin's future, of Shahbaz, of Nazeer—he tried not to think about anyone or anything.

After funeral prayers, the men made a cairn to mark the spot and after salvaging what they could—the dented radio, a torch, rifles, a spade, the mule—they proceeded towards the mountains to set up a temporary camp. Some of the men let out a volley of shots from their rifles as they left the camp, a fitting adieu as far as they were concerned. This was it then for this place, Billy thought as he climbed over the rubble and walked out into the land, sun-blistered, smoke-pocked, stinking of burnt flesh, this was it—you live life, there comes a change, you give up, or you move on.

Memory, Billy thought as he put one foot after another one foot after another, limping on his injured leg, memory was the crutch that either supported moving on or buried you under its weight, and he thought of Zari, of how she'd wanted to forget, and for the first time he understood his mother wanting to erase the past, understood how the only way to do that was to stop talking about it, to never bring it up, to smash it with silence.

He wondered what exactly his mother had gone through, what mortifications she'd clamped up on to make her feel this way. He thought of his father, of his ambushing him. Tell me my history. Tell me. Tell me. Tell me. Until he'd forced his father to crack open. What would he say if a child of his ever cracked down on him? What would he say if the child said 'in order to know myself, I have to know everything about you'? Was that even true? What would he tell? That people died for places and places did not even remember their names?

Billy glanced at One-Eyed-One-Handed. He'd escaped the gutting of the kitchen with copious scrapes and minor burns. His head bowed, he was walking just ahead of Billy, leading the mule behind him. What was he thinking? Billy wondered. And though he longed to ask, Billy knew he dreaded the reply even more.

The sun stung as morning bled into afternoon. Clouds of smoke from the camp dribbled overhead. Azeem Khan, a tall, wiry Afghan familiar with the terrain, led the group. Following him were Commander Salman, Mullah Khaled, the handful of other instructors, all of them listening to the radio—Sudan was one of the countries bombed in reprisal for the US embassy bombings. The other was Afghanistan.

As news travelled down until it reached Billy, trudging at the tail end of the group, his being sank in a quick sand of confusion. He had come to fight for Kashmir, but had ended up in a place bombed by *his* country; he baulked at the implications,

"Dresht." Azeem Khan's voice rang out. "Dresht."

Billy came to an abrupt halt with everyone else. Azeem Khan lobbed a stone at a half-embedded ball of swampy green in the distance. Nothing happened. He threw another and then another—all clear, no landmines. And they started walking again. Billy's knees weakened and he would have stood still for a moment, gathering himself, had Abid not started walking beside him, his face grim, yet without a glimmer of fear or uncertainty, and Billy envied him his strength and his calm.

"How's the leg?" Abid asked.

Billy shrugged. He kept his eyes averted from Abid's gun and the fingers that had delivered that one merciful shot. Or had it been a murderous shot? His own gun was somewhere in the ruins of the camp, caught under the rubble, buried until someone dug it out. The surviving Kashmiris were huddled round Mohmedoo. Was Mohmedoo also hearing, over and over and over again, the echo of Abid's lone shot that had sent Nazeer to an eternal rest—a term much nicer than the crude simplicity of 'death'?

They walked in silence, their steps crunching on the ground in unison. Abid struck a match, lit a cigarette, the tiny flame come and gone in a flash. Billy's breath quickened— flames, melted rubber sandals, mass graves.

"Drag?"

Billy took a drag of the cigarette and coughed.

"You'll be fine," Abid said. "You'll be fine."

If so, Billy thought, then was he not already fine? Walking on and on and on? Leaving the dead behind? What else was this 'being fine'? A reconciliation to the arbitrariness of loss? Never forgiving or forgetting? Or striving to forgive and forget? Did it mean that one day he would be able to use his gun as Abid had? That one day he would be able to, with a straight face, tell some shell-shocked recruit that he would be fine? Or did it mean simply the absence of public displays of grief?

For the first time, Billy wondered what it meant for Zari when people told her she'd be fine. He'd said it himself. "You'll be fine, Zaar, you'll be fine." Then he'd simply meant that life would go on and she'd go on with life—as if it was that simple.

A thicket of smoke began to cloud the air again. Billy started coughing and his eyes began to water. A few moments later, they saw sinewy black beanstalks twisting and turning out of the ground ahead. They were not the only ones hit. Of course not. Billy felt stupid for having thought so. One-Eyed-One-Handed began to run. It was his village that had been hit.

A story Billy had read as a child: two knights in gilded armour, shivering by a bonfire, frightened to death and perturbed over how to fight a dragon with gargantuan eyes and gigantic steaming nostrils and a roar to match. Turned out, the dragon was a steam engine. It was a simple ghost story, a straightforward shift of space and time, though who had intruded into whose universe, Billy had never been able to figure out. It came to him now, as they neared the ruined village, that what had occurred here was eluding him like that: a mud-walled hamlet had been annihilated by an almighty dragon from up above.

☞☜

The village had clearly been much bigger than their training camp. An earthen wall about twelve feet high and two feet thick ran all around it. Once a protective barrier, it sagged now like the weary shoulders of the elderly. Debris, that cheap junk jewellery of the land, cluttered the courtyard inside the wall. Every tree was truncated, their ropey roots burning. Craters as big as skateboard rinks engulfed the compound and were piled high with smoking rubble. Flies buzzed over gooey lumps and stumps. The air sizzled with the sickly sweet stench of burning hair and charred flesh: chickens, goats, mules, humans.

This was collateral damage.

Only five villagers had survived—two women, one in a blue burqa and the other in a brown one, two little girls, one still a toddler, and a baby boy—because they had been by the stream, just a little way outside the village, washing clothes and utensils when the bombs had hit, and they had dived into the water as soon as they had heard the bombs whistling through the air.

They all clung to One-Eyed-One-Handed now as if he was a pair of crutches and wailed: Wali! Wali! Wali! So that was One-Eyed-One-Handed's name. Billy looked at him as if his having a name must have happened in a different life. Wali was the last surviving male member, save the baby, of his kin, and the women had lifted the front flaps of their burqas off their faces, and though he knew it was rude,

349

Billy found himself unable to look away either from their furrowed lips and their crumpled cornflower blue eyes, or from the children with their dirty blonde hair.

The toddler had gotten shrapnel in her head. She was perched on Blue's hip, her distended head against Blue's chest, her eyes unfocused. A goat stood next to the girl, butting its head against her bare, mud-caked foot. It had managed to survive in a flock otherwise all dead. *Why me? Why did I survive when no one else did? Do I have a grand purpose in life? Am I the chosen one?* Billy shook his head. The goat had not been speaking. It had not. It was not suffering from survivor's guilt.

Mullah Khaled organised them into teams and they set about digging a mass grave and burying the dead for the second time in the day. Billy did not know how he managed to go around the village looking for bodies and scattered limbs and carrying them all, one by one, back to the grave. He focused on believing that this, and this, and this, was better off dead, souls awaiting judgment day and a guaranteed admittance to heaven on account of being martyred. Indeed, Mohmedoo told Billy, any Muslim killed in enemy fire was a martyr.

But martyrdom was no solace for Billy because he always dwelled on earthly futures lost rather than the heavenly futures gained. If only he were blessed with an absolute faith in God, all this loss might be bearable, but without that faith, was he simply to be consoled by the dead being faceless, nameless, anonymous? What you don't know, can't hurt you, ergo the death of those you didn't know shouldn't bother you . . . but no, it did bother him, the thought of people going about their lives one second and the next being lifeless.

Did he care about life *too* much?

Did acceptance rest on numbers—only one civilian death this time round rather than last month's thirty; tonight I'll sleep. Or was it the method that made civilian deaths easy to accept? Death was inevitable, should he accept that dying the victim of someone's bomb was just the way that person was destined to die? Would you rather the slow torturous death of a long-drawn-out disease or the instantaneous goodbye of a bullet or bomb set off for the good of mankind? The good of mankind?

His cousin had been the victim of an accident, simple as that. The Holocaust and its likes were genocide, mass-extermination resting on hatred. Death at the hands of a cause was something else altogether—it was neither the sheer randomness of an accident nor the singling out of genocide—it was bystander death: merely being at the wrong place at the wrong time or, if one subscribed to death being ordained then it was being at the right place at the right time.

Billy took Mauj jee's letter out of his pocket and, crouching by the grave, placed it in.

When they were all done with the burial, they shambled off to bathe, fully clothed, in the stream outside the village, a gurgling strip of water in the stony ground. On one side of the bank lay clothes spread out on tufts of grass and shrubs for drying, along with two saucepans and a couple of other sundry utensils. Billy shook his head. It was surreal. Turn his face to the right, and it was utter destruction. Turn his face to the left, and a scene of pastoral idyll.

Grime and grit and blood sloughed off in minutes as he waded into the water along with the others, but his clothes retained the mouldy lemon scent. This was where One-Eyed-One-Handed's—Wali's—mother, one of the camp's launderettes, used to wash his clothes and dry them. Billy felt guilty now for not having appreciated the dead woman who had scrubbed his clothes. Then again, he didn't know what exactly he was to have appreciated about this woman, these people he did not know at all, and it was this limbo which wrung him out: grief as if these people were his own flesh and blood, and yet, because they were not, the world had not fallen apart, really, because his family was safe at home where such things did not happen.

Did insects eat burnt bodies?

Thoughts bombarded him unbidden; it had been this way all day.

How long would a neck support a distended head?

Would charred skin absorb the dye of red rubber soles?

Would rubber smell of charred flesh?

As Billy went through the motions of funeral prayers, he believed he was going mad. Had Zari suffered similarly from the intrusion of such unbidden thoughts? He had never asked her. He had not known to ask.

The motley group resumed their trek towards the mountains to a temporary camp site. Smoke from the burning village accompanied them for a long while. Their sweat-soaked clothes dried in the hot sun only to soak through again. Billy lagged behind the villagers. Wali shambled alongside the women, striding tall, their faces covered again. The elder girl sat astride the mule, the baby asleep in her arms. The injured toddler, her head a bulging tuber, was being passed from Blue to Brown, from hip to hip, not because her moaning was the burden it seemed, but because both women wanted to hold her.

How complacent they were, Billy thought. How stoically they appeared to have accepted what had happened. He couldn't imagine any place back home, village or city, taking its utter destruction with such complacency, dignified or otherwise. Billy recalled asking a Cambodian friend why Cambodians were so silent about the atrocities Pol Pot had inflicted on them.

"Karma," his friend had said. "We believe what goes around comes around, so we, as a country, must have done something in our past lives to have collectively deserved such a punishment."

Billy had found the explanation cruel. Had Baber done something so terrible in a past life that he had come to deserve an early and violent death in a future one? Had Uncle Buraaq and Aunt Barbara too deserved the death of a child? And what of those parents who became bitter, mean people? Were they accruing further karmic wrath? Since then, karma had seemed to be nothing more than an extraordinary method for accepting whatever cruelty was dealt by life, destiny, God.

They reached the foot of the mountain, high and mighty, a couple of hours later and began climbing up. Billy looked at the injured toddler, Palwasha, piggybacking on Blue, her little paws clutching Blue's shoulders, her head flopped forward, her forehead swelling visibly with every passing hour. God, Billy said, if you're there and if there's a shred of humanity in you, you will heal this little girl and you will keep her safe and you will keep her happy and this ordeal will not be the defining moment of her life. Perhaps his problem was that he personified God rather than thinking of it as a noor, a bright light or some such unearthly being. Still, a light or a dark did not change what was happening.

They stopped eventually at a plateau, a wide, flat stretch of land against a cliff with a stream running in a far corner between clumpy sagebrush. Billy wheezed as he settled under a rocky lip. A little way off, Palwasha's fate was being discussed amongst men like Mullah Khaled, Commander Salman, and Abid—men who made it a point to give their input—and Wali, who would answer for his folk.

"There is no help for the girl here," Commander Salman said. Afghanistan was a mess this year already. Two earthquakes, an outbreak of malaria, drought, record unemployment, no resources to break the continued tribal infighting and now, again, the bombings, only this time, instead of the Soviets, it had been the Americans. Walking to Pakistan through the mountains was feasible, and they had to make the six hour trek to Peshawar anyway, but if it was for the girl's sake, then they needed to leave promptly.

"Wali?"

The boy squatted, his pointy chin between his knees, his good hand pulling to pieces the soft down on his upper lip. Palwasha whimpered in Blue's lap. Blue gently rocked her back and forth, all the while muttering and blowing over her, muttering and blowing. Praying over her, Billy realised. Blue glanced at Brown, a look passed between them, they turned to the men, Blue gazed at Wali, their eyes met. Wali rose.

"We go."

For the first time in his life, Billy wished he had a camera so he would never forget the faces of forbearance. Struggling up, he took some money from his pocket and walked up to Wali.

"For her," he pressed the crumpled notes into Wali's hand, "for the best medical care."

Wali stared at him before hurling the money as far away as he could. "Your country do this! How you could? You kill my family. You. You."

He leapt at Billy and caught him by his throat—*I kill you, I kill all of you.* A moment's silence, then everything burst into noise and activity. Billy was freed from Wali's grip. Abid picked up the money and pressed it into Wali's shaking fist. Wali was not to be stubborn, he said, the money was for the injured girl. He could not let his pride get in the way, the girl would need it. It was going to be useful, these American dollars. And then Wali and the women and the children, Palwasha a small flounce between the two women, flashed round the bend and were gone.

Afternoon slunk into evening. Billy sat on the ledge staring out at the land. Many a time over the last few hours, he had touched his throat exactly where Wali's fingers had struck. What did Wali know about Americans? Billy swallowed. But it was a trap to get sentimental about the goodness in one's country, in oneself, and expect it to override the rest, just as the rest could not, must not, override the goodness. But a moral middle ground was a near impossible tight rope to walk. But was not he as little to blame for the annihilation of the village as the villagers were to blame for the bombing of the US embassies? Was not Billy himself the collateral damage of Wali's emotions?

Billy saw Abid waving him over for the evening prayers. He was glad Abid had forced Wali to take the money. Perhaps there was some goodness in Abid after all. Or perhaps Abid was just practical and practicality rested on amorality. Palwasha would need the money, so what did it matter where it came from? Nazeer would have died anyway, why not make his death a little easy?

Evening slipped into night. Moonbeams chewed up the ground, turning the greens and browns of daylight into a wash of pale silver. Billy lay listening as tired, hungry men fell asleep all around him. The man on the first watch dozed a little way off, his shadow as still as the rock he was on, his rifle just another dark crag. Once the torch in the makeshift camp was turned off and a ghostly darkness blanketed the land, Billy panicked. Fuel was all, he decided. It *was* the life blood of a modern nation, for what was the modern nation if not a place able to sustain daylight and defy God's timings? He liked that God could be defied; that humans could play God, be God, out-God God at least enough to command 'let there be light'.

He was still awake when the men began to stir, no longer tired but still just as hungry as the night before and waiting for the men who'd left to return with food and supplies. When the sentry shouted the approach of a car—a dark speck scuttling like a spider, looming larger and larger— Billy realised he'd been waiting for, and dreading news of Palwasha all night long.

356

Abid sat cross-legged on the tarp spread over the ground as the new cook, a sullen fellow, dished watery lentils from the pot on the kerosene stove into paper plates and passed them down the line of hungry men. He was followed by the new driver, a half deaf old man, his age-mottled hands quivering as he distributed the naans brought from Peshawar. Had Billy arrived at the camp now, it would have been this new driver picking him up from the airport instead of Shahbaz, and instead of Ahmed Baba, this sullen new cook who would have been doling out food.

Billy tried to shake his head clear of time and fate and destiny. Commander Salman had returned with news that Palwasha had died two hours after their departure. The woman carrying her, her mother, Blue, had refused to bury her daughter on the mountain and had, instead, carried her into Pakistan. Some of Billal's money had been used to bury her under a poplar tree in a very nice refugee graveyard. As for the remaining money, Billal was to rest assured that it would go towards some good cause.

Billy nodded dully. There was no God—moral, immoral, amoral—there was no God at all. Billy's belief in this was instant, definite, infallible. Of all his prior doubts he felt instantly freed now, and, just as instantly, utterly lost for all the freedom.

He stood up, unable to stomach the food anymore, and taking a cigarette from Abid, walked away from the others wolfing down their meal. Abid joined him for a smoke a moment later, and they stood by a boulder, their backs to the camp. Billy shivered at the chill in the air at this elevation even though no wind blew over the plateau. He took a long drag of the cigarette. His bowels loosened. His head swooned.

"It didn't have to happen, mate," Abid said, "that little girl, her village, none of it had to happen. But she won't be the last, not as long as it can be gotten away with. What really pisses me off is how this won't make a difference in the lives of the people it should affect the most—Muslims like my brother. I used to be just like him. My life revolved round work and sports and food and women."

Smoke swirled out of Abid's mouth. "My brother thinks the persecution of the Palestinians, the Chechen, the Kashmiris is bad and he is sad, he will pray for them he says, but ultimately it's not his problem. Apartheid in South Africa was his problem, anti-Semitism is his problem, but not his brethren being slain." Abid's temples twitched. "Justice is up to the likes of you and me, Billawal, we who've lived in two different worlds, who understand that a melting pot breeds only a nation of confused mongrels . . . You know why armies rape?"

The word knocked the wind out of Billy. He leaned against the boulder, the rough edges digging into his spine.

"The more babies born of rape, of violent copulations, the more confused conflicted identities and the more hatred all around . . ." Abid exhaled a smoke ring. "Only fools think this mixed-race multi-culti bunkum is a boon. If we were all meant to be the same, wouldn't God have made us so? We're separate but equal. Look at the Jews, they depended on law and order and equality and fairness and look at what happened to them. The Holocaust was nasty business, but it got the Jews a space and, most important of all, solidarity amongst their ranks. Solidarity, that's the key.

"Imagine if this century's superpower persecutes the Muslim next door. Imagine if the rest of the West follows suit. Muslims like my brother will leap for cover and that would mean they will come straight to us, to fellow Muslims. They will realise no matter how assimilated they thought they were, no matter how international was played up and nationalism played down, ultimately you aren't what you believe yourself to be, but what others perceive you to be.

"Wali called you an American, you identify with Kashmiris, but remember this," Abid blew smoke in Billy's face, "you're neither American nor Kashmiri. The only identity you have is of a Muslim no matter where you go, what clothes you wear, or which language you consider your mother tongue. Creed trumps colour and cultures.

"What, Billawal? You say history is cyclical. The Islamic Empire has seen its heyday, you say? But why you are content with that? Ask yourself what other contentment-conditioning professors, documentaries, books have instilled in you? They mock us, Billalwal. We appropriate the names they call us, but tell me, how am I powerful by referring to myself as a cockroach? Do you feel at home when they say our cooking stinks, our values stink, *we* stink? In Britain perhaps, but not in America, you say?" Abid patted Billy's cheek.

"How naïve you are, how brainwashed and blind, to think the two are not in bed together, one learning from the other the art to divide and rule. To that end, my humble goal: united we must find a way to garner solidarity." Abid edged closer. "How can a Muslim hurt America so bad she'll go mad? Bring out all the skinheads, even the ones who blow-dry their heads full of hair, to take revenge on Muslims top, bottom, right, left, and centre? Yellow crescent markers? Fingerprints? Ghettos? Deportation? Gas chambers?" Abid lit a fresh cigarette. "Believe you me, a Muslim Holocaust that will lead to pan Muslim solidarity, that's the final solution to this mess that allows villages to be wiped off the face of this earth without a hue and cry. For the sake of that little girl who died in vain. For the sake of the children."

☙❧

Billy stumbled to the area behind a boulder designated the toilet. He trembled as he loosened the drawstring on his pants and squatted under the boulder's shadow. A Muslim Holocaust was what was needed, Abid had said and Billy had muttered 'the International community will never allow it' and Abid had laughed: what *international community?* Billy shut his eyes. A Muslim Holocaust. As if the world would tolerate something like that. As if it would permit it. A melting pot was its strength. Billy was its strength, his muscles those puny hyphens that attached all the lands he'd come from. Kashmiri-Pakistani-American. That hyphen, that squiggle on paper, it was a bridge and Abid was banking on that bridge collapsing in the long run, both in a court of law and in people's hearts.

Will you help us, Billawal? Abid had said. Will you play a role?

In a world which had been dubbed a global village, Abid had visions of challenging the global villager's prime meridian. The circumstance of births and the choice of residences were going to be pitched against each other. Could he ever be thrown out of America just because he was a naturalised citizen and not a natural born one? Would the words 'born here' even matter?

We have a plan, Billawal. Abid had said. We need you.

Billy jumped as a shadow fell over him. It was Mohmedoo,

looking like a catfish with a hook caught in its mouth. Billy stood up and hastily tied his drawstrings even as Mohmedoo spoke. They were leaving for Kashmir tomorrow morning—Billy's knees turned to jelly—no doubt his buddy, Abid, had already informed him? Billy shook his head. Mohmedoo shrugged. What he wanted to know was whether Billawal had discovered his buddy's intentions for them?

"No."

Mohmedoo's eyes hardened.

"Nazeer was wrong about you. So wrong. Whose payroll you are on? ISI? RAW? MI5? CIA? Are you nothing but a filthy mercenary? Money your God and morality immaterial. Thoo."

Billy stared at the blob of doughy spittle as Mohemedoo strode away. Kashmir. Tomorrow. His knees trembled. Forget Kashmir, Abid had said. What is Kashmir when you can turn the tide of the world? For the likes of you and me, for us, more important fates await. Consider my offer, Billalwal to help us bring in a new world order. Though sometimes, Abid had ground out his cigarette, decisions of this magnitude need not be left to one because often, one does not know what is best for oneself, don't you agree?

The menace in Abid's voice had chilled Billy. He was not going to make it to Kashmir because Abid was not going to let him. And, if he resisted, what was there to keep Abid from shooting him dead too? And, even if he made it to Kashmir, the minute he was alone with Mohmedoo and the rest, what would keep them from killing him, the man they thought the lowest of the low, a mercenary, the man they thought had betrayed their beloved Nazeer?

I was here, Billy spelled out with his urine. The earth absorbed it, sucked it down as if it were a libation. He had to escape, leave Abid and all of this behind. Billy glanced quickly, furtively towards the camp. The new cook and the half deaf driver were hunched over a primus stove. To their left, a group of men sat cleaning their guns. Some were doing sit-ups and push-ups, and some were playing chess with rocks for pieces. Here in Afghanistan, chess was forbidden under Taliban decree. Apparently chess bred competition, led to gambling, and wastage of time. Time that could be spent praying. But, these days, no one was paying much attention to the rules.

Billy's heartbeat raced along his every nerve. This was his chance, his chance to skulk away. He began to walk, to leave the camp behind, walking forward feverishly as he tried to gauge the direction the men had taken for Peshawar. Upstream, yes. Towards the crag that resembled a ragged fin. And beyond that . . . beyond Peshawar something would work out. Something had to.

And yet, had he come all this way to simply run away again? Didn't he owe something to Dada, to Mauj jee, to Zari? Didn't he owe them going to Kashmir? To run away now would be to dodge his duty, wouldn't it? It was Abid who was scaring him off—Abid and his psychotic, nefarious plans to unify Muslims into an 'us versus them'. He had to resist Abid's intimidation. He'd come this far and he couldn't let Abid prevent him from reaching Kashmir now. To that end he would kill Abid if he had to. *I don't believe in you God*—a cold sweat bathed Billy—*but help me.*

Billy stopped before a circle of jagged stones encircling a glinting plastic green butterfly. His mouth in ashes, he bade a silent thanks to whoever had encircled this hazard. In Afghanistan, fifty types of mines bided time hidden in grass and buried in sand and in potholes. Some could blow up tanks. Some exploded in a short burst and neatly severed a hand or a foot. Some burrowed out of the ground to detonate at the level of an adult's stomach or a child's head. Some shot out pieces of metal, like a firecracker. This plastic 'butterfly's' wing before him was filled with liquid explosives waiting for a child to be lured in; it had been on the poster in the Commander's office back at the camp.

Billy jumped at the frantic shouts behind him. He stiffened at the grip on his shoulder. He turned. Abid, shouting, waving at the stones. *Leave me alone,* Billy hissed as he shoved Abid away. Abid teetered. Skid over loose pebbles. His fingers clawed the air, his hands stretched out towards Billy. He tumbled towards the stones, careening into the craggy circle headfirst.

Billy watched the ground lift up like a heaving pregnant belly and shoot forth a series of explosions.

They found Billy covered in dirt, bleeding from small cuts, staring at Abid's decimated body. Commander Salman squatted next to Billy. What the hell, he asked, had Billy and Abid been doing so close to a landmine zone? Billawal may not have known anything, but Abid most certainly had known that a mine encircled with stones warned of a landmine zone.

Billy's sphincter loosened. Fear dribbled out of him. Abid's shouts, his hand on his shoulder—he had been trying to warn him of the landmines. And now, Abid was dead.

Billy tried to erase the image of Abid helping him out of the bombed training camp, erase the image of Abid's hands reaching out to him before his fall, erase the fact of his momentary hesitation before he'd extended a helping hand a moment too late.

He had not meant to send Abid to his death. It had been an accident. And yet, though he had not meant to carry out vigilante justice, wasn't it better for the world to be rid of such a man? Billy stared at Commander Salman, then he lowered his head in his hands. He could not tell anyone what had happened; there was no one who could tell him whether he'd committed an act of murder or mercy.

Later, after Abid had been buried, prayers offered, and Billy had vomited behind a rock, Mohemdoo squeezed Billy's arm in solidarity: Billawal had avenged Nazeer's death, no further proof was required of his allegiance. He was one of them.

If he was one of them, then why did he not feel that they were a part of him? If he was one of them, then why did he feel utterly alone? If he was one of them, then why, even as he stood between them, was he so sickeningly lonely?

23

───⟨∞⟩───

Zari stared out of the car window as Fahad droned on about how grand their wedding was going to be and how their honeymoon would be even grander. That she was stuck in traffic with him was courtesy of Salsabil who had agreed to a dinner with a 'suitable boy' in order to make Shehla feel better, and Shehla had, in turn, requested Zari and Fahad to play chaperone.

Fahad was talking about the Cayman Islands. Apparently it was quite a place to see, and moreover, the place to be seen in. Zari sighed. At least he was no longer mocking Buraaq and Barbara. Mrs and Mr Don't Worry Be Happy, he'd called them.

"The only tolerable aspect of this traffic is being stuck in it with you." Fahad flicked the radio from station to station. "When is Christopher Columbus headed back from the Old World anyway? It's his job to chaperone his sister, not ours."

"Don't call Billal that."

"What should I call him? Alice in Wonderland? Why do you always take everything against them so personally?"

"They've been very good to me."

"Yeah, they've been absolute saints. But *we'll* be even better." He nodded towards the cell phone he'd give her. He claimed it was a lifeline, but Zari had a sinking feeling that it had been given to her in order to keep an eye on her. Fahad had been distressed at being unable to reach her when she'd been at Miraage's Montessori for the International Heritage Day.

"My sister," Fahad was saying, "is so excited to meet you, she's thinking of cutting her Europe holiday short. By the way, she's the one recommending Cayman Islands. I'm personally veering towards Polynesia."

"How's your grandmother?"

"Fine."

"I'd like to meet her again."

"She's not feeling too well these days."

"Whenever I ask about her you say she's not well." When Fahad remained quiet, Zari added, "I hope it's nothing serious."

"Nope," Fahad said brusquely, "nothing serious."

"Then when can I meet her? I'm sure I won't disturb her."

"Look," Fahad twisted towards her. "I need to apologise to you . . . that day when we came to see you, my Dadi jee was most inappropriate. She should not have brought up your" —he addressed a spot somewhere above Zari's head— ". . . thing, it was inappropriate of her and I'm sorry if it made you feel sad."

"No it—"

"But," Fahad licked his lips, "since we can't reprimand Dadi jee, you have to promise to discourage her from even mentioning such things. Matters like these really upset my mother, but one can hardly blame her, can one? Such matters are hardly appropriate for dinner table conversation, let alone pleasant or even acceptable."

A lash of hatred flicked Zari. She pressed her suddenly burning forehead against the cool car window. Billal might never have wooed her as Fahad did, but Billal had never belittled her family's plight. And he had definitely never treated it as insignificant or shameful. It must have been awkward and difficult for him to talk to her and listen to her, and yet, not once could she remember him giving her any reason to suspect so. Never had he shut her up or told her to shut up. In fact, Billal had always encouraged her to speak out, to seek support, to do anything but put herself away like so much dust under a rug.

With a person like Fahad, she would never be able to share the experience she'd had standing in front of Miraage's class on International Heritage Day. Billal would not only have understood her need to do what she had, but he would also have coaxed her to relive it. For her own good, Billal would have said she needed to share how she'd served the nedru pakoras and been asked for seconds. How she'd played 'hu kus bu kus' with the kids. How she'd finally stood before the class, ready for the art activity, all those small, pudgy thumbs and pinkies dipped into circles of paint awaiting instructions to finger-paint birds flying over the Dal, their eager little faces completely unaware that Zari was seeing splashes of Baz's sweet little face, hearing his sweet little squeals, watching his short sweet little life play out in the palette of colours spread before her.

Zari had pulled herself together and managed to

somehow smile as she pressed her thumb and pinkie into the paint and pressed onto the paper a thumb of a body and her pinkie for wings. The classroom had come alive with finger-painted birds. And then it was over and the teacher was thanking her, parents were shaking her hand, and the children were all clustering around her like petals on a flower, tugging at her clothes, looking up at her, wanting to know when she was going to come back while Miraage proudly looked on. Soon, Zari had said, soon, and she'd gathered Baz's memories in her arms and whispered, *you are irreplaceable.* And from somewhere deep within she heard him answer that he knew, that he'd always known.

During the drive to the airport, Buraaq and Barbara advised Shehla to resume speaking to Amman. Why couldn't Shehla see, Buraaq said, that Amman cared about Billal as much as she did? As for Billal, he was an adult and perfectly capable of taking care of himself.

Shehla gripped the steering wheel of Billal's car which she'd taken to driving in order to feel that he was still with her.

"Please Buraaq," she said, glancing at her brother in the passenger seat. "Don't call me childish just because I expect my husband to tell me the truth and nothing but the truth. And just because some law says Billal is an adult doesn't mean that he is," she grit her teeth, "anymore than I was when our mother expected me to act like an adult when I was just as much of a child as you were."

"When are you going to stop living in the past?" Buraaq combed his beard with long, patient fingers.

"I don't live in the past just because I happen to be stating fact." Shehla slapped the steering wheel.

"Shehla, relax," Barbara said, shifting uncomfortably in the back seat.

"It's easy for him to advise forgetting the past," Shehla said, meeting Barbara's eyes in the rear-view mirror. "After Papa died, Buraaq remained the son-shine whose life and studies should not be disrupted by our mother's widowhood."

"I know, honey," Barbara said. "But you've got to move on."

"Moving on doesn't mean pretending it never happened. You," Shehla jabbed her brother's arm, "were allowed to mourn Papa like a child, with your own fears and tantrums and demands. *I* was the one who had to become a father figure to our mother. I had to manage everything, including her emotions. And now no one's taking care of mine. Instead, you're sympathetic towards Amman and I'm the one who has to be an adult all over again."

Buraaq sighed. "Just listen to yourself! Our immature mother is still governing your every day. How long are you going to let what happened back then dictate your present as well as your future? That's not only unfair on everyone else, but it's also unfair on you."

"No one dictates anything to me; I know what's best for me and my children."

"Do you really?" Buraaq said quietly.

"Are you trying to imply that I had something to do with Billal going?"

No one answered and they drove to the airport in silence.

On her way back home, Shehla could no longer contain her tears. At first, they were angry tears at Buraaq and Barbara for being judgmental, especially at a time when she wanted sympathy, then came the pitiful tears for the fact that she wanted sympathy, and then came the tears of despair. Even Zari's attitude towards her seemed to have changed right after their last prayer session just before Buraaq and Barbara's arrival. God knew how much Zari's question had taken her unawares—*would you, if it was Billal?*—not to mention the way Zari had taken Billal's name, as if she'd known him for years on end. The intimacy had upset her even if it was one, Shehla believed, engendered through praying for him daily. Her reaction had brought to head that while she admired Zari's resilience, in her heart of hearts she considered Zari irrevocably damaged. Yet, it was an assumption proven baseless when it was she lying in bed and Zari rising to the occasion.

Shehla turned on a CD and tried to hum along to Abida Parveen's guttural voice. But it was no use. She stopped humming and decided to have a good sob without a care if people in other cars saw her. This lack of propriety made her sob all the more. She didn't know what was happening to her or how to stop it from happening. If only Billal would contact them, then she would never ask God for anything again. For God's sake she had no idea what condition her darling beautiful boy was in, if he was even alive, and it was Amman's fault, and how was she to forgive him?

It took Shehla a few moments to realise the police sirens and flashing lights were for her.

"Ma'am," the officer said, knocking on her window, "license and registration please."

Shehla handed him her license. Apparently she'd been speeding. She opened the glove compartment and, reaching for the car registration document in the mess of papers and CDs, she extracted an official-looking document and unfolded it. How she managed to subsequently find the registration paper and speak to the police straight-faced, Shehla would never know. All she knew was that when she re-entered the freeway, she was trembling so badly she had to take the first exit out and park in the first spot she found. There she sat, turned to stone, staring at the document in her lap: Billal and Zari's marriage certificate.

∞∞

Virgin strawberry daiquiri.

Zari's was the last order the waitress took before disappearing down a dark wood-panelled aisle. Everything was dark wood: the slatted ceiling strung with fairy lights, the lacquered tables and bar stools, the bar stocked with bottles—amethyst and sapphire, topaz and amber, crystalline onyx and smoky white—glinting glass gems to flower this urban forest.

"I love the coconut-battered bass," Salsabil said over the music to Mohammed, call me Mo, the matrimonial candidate she was here to meet. Mo was a beanpole with a sandy goatee and an assured voice. He was Farah's friend's friend's friend's son and came with the highest of recommendations. He'd graduated with top marks from a top business school and his parents were wealthy and well pedigreed. Back home, in Pakistan, the family owned many businesses and it was a given that when Mo became fed up with the US, he would return to take over what was his. In the meantime, Mo was a banker, but his real passion was radio and as such he did a stint on a local show.

As they waited for the drinks to arrive, Fahad and Mo got into a conversation about the value of various companies and Salsabil began to follow a baseball game on one of the mounted TVs above the bar. Another mounted TV, in Zari's line of sight, was switched on to a news channel. A few weeks ago, the American embassies in Kenya and Tanzania had been bombed by guerrillas. The civilian causalities consisted predominantly of the locals. Zari stared at the television, mesmerised as the screen went from shots of hospitals in Nairobi and Dar es Salaam filled with relatives searching for missing ones, their fingers running down lists of survivors posted outside hospitals and lists of dead posted outside morgues, to close-ups of victims lying burned, limbless, shell-shocked. The footage ended with a clip of a wooden coffin strapped to the top of a car driving away and the voiceover saying 'family members looking for miracles.'

Today, the subtitles said, in retaliation for the embassy bombings, the US has bombed strategic targets in Afghanistan and Sudan, both supposed havens for terrorists. So far, said the anchor, there has been absolutely no report of collateral damage—

"Excuse me," Fahad called out to a waitress, "excuse me! Can you please change the TV channel? This sort of news is hardly conducive to a pleasant meal."

"Hear, hear," seconded other diners.

Zari watched as the footage of the carnage was replaced by celebrity infotainment. Every hour, every minute, every second, things happened which no one could be cognizant of twenty-four hours a day, yet, she suddenly felt as if she'd betrayed someone, something, somehow. Her family had been on the news for a total of three days. Day One: headline news. Day Two: item number two. And Day Three: a blip before completely disappearing. As for American coverage of the India-Pakistan nuclear showdown, that event was already a thing of the past and Kashmir had disappeared from the public radar. How long before Afghanistan and Sudan too, disappeared into a once-upon-a-time-something-happened-somewhere?

"Reality TV!" Fahad was saying, "Which moron would agree to have cameras follow him day in and day out?"

"A moron with nothing to hide," Mo said.

"Are you guys in grade school?" Salsabil said. "Stop saying 'moron.'"

Zari looked at Salsabil, Fahad, Mo.

"My family," she took a deep breath, "my family was on TV."

"No kidding?" Mo's eyebrows shot up.

Fahad kicked Zari under the table and Zari's insides, already burning, began to smoulder. She fell silent and didn't say anything during the entrees, or the desserts or Salsabil and Mo's cappuccinos, but, as they walked back to the cars, their footsteps echoing on the concrete of the parking lot, she said, "They were on TV because they were murdered. And I-I-I was raped . . ."

☙❦❧

Shehla walked unsteadily to Zari's room. Though she

held the marriage certificate in her hand, she could still hardly believe it. She found what she was looking for in the bedside drawer. The rainbow journal.

Mummy I am married now. Rest in peace.

I am married now Mummy, but I cannot do that.

He has married me and I am turned into a secret.

Baby. My baby. Billal's baby. Ours.

Shehla stumbled her way to Amman's study without even realising what she was doing; all she knew was that she needed him. He wasn't home. On the wall in front of her was Amman's map of the world, a gigantic cartographer-approved jungle of colour, the variegated blues of oceans swirling between humps of browns and reds and greens. A thick black marker had staked out the routes Billal could have taken. All the places he could possibly be were circled in jagged lines. But where were the maps laying out moral terrains? Where were the zigzags signalling the emotional routes taken by those left behind? And what of journeys travelled between yeses and nos, between cost and benefit, good and bad, heroism and villainy, between making your mother proud of you and making your mother cry?

On the bookshelf lay photos of their family. Billal, the dimple-kneed baby. And she and Amman, in college, on their honeymoon, in front of their various residences—rentals, a condo, a townhouse, the house which they now called home. How handsome Amman had been. Still was. How adamantly opposed to marrying him her family had been. Good looks were immaterial, her family had raged. Amman was a penniless Kashmiri, a refugee, a man with no future, from a disputed land, who *claimed* to come from the best stock but had nothing to show for it, no wealth, no property, no title. Why would she want to marry someone like him instead of an army officer with a great future?

Because an army officer's great future depended on devotion greater than that a man could nurture for his family—a devotion to his country, Shehla had argued. And Amman didn't have a country, not really, therefore instead of patriotism, their life together would be his greatest love affair.

She'd listened to no one.

It's my life, she'd insisted, my life and I can live it as I want.

Just like Billal had written in his letter:

I'm sorry but it is my life and I can live it as I want.

Zari sat on the curb under a street light, pressing her hands against her stomach. Mo had long left. Salsabil was sitting beside her on the curb, patting her back, telling her it was all right, everything was all right. Fahad was pacing up and down the road before them. Zari concentrated on the dirty pink gum stuck to the sole of Fahad's loafer. Up down, up down, up down. She could not believe she'd come out the way she had. He came to a stop in front of them, towering over them, sweating indignation, fuming.

"I'm going to ask you one more time," he spoke through clenched teeth, "why did you tell him?"

Zari touched her arm. She had never shown Fahad her razor cuts or her bullet scar. She wondered if he'd cut her arm off. A clean, clinical sever. Pretend there was no

375

bleeding. Pretend there never was an arm.

"She'll tell whoever she wants, whatever she wants, whenever she wants, wherever she wants," Salsabil said without missing a pat on Zari's back.

"How many times do I have to tell you to not interfere?"

"Or what?"

"Even American girls don't do what she has."

"American?" Salsabil flicked her blue lock away.

"White. White girls."

"Anglo-Saxon White? Italian White? Or Irish White?"

"What?" Fahad's eyes bulged. "White girls who know better than to advertise unpleasant pasts."

"So," Salsabil said, "are we to assume that if white, sorry *American* girls did go around advertising their unpleasant pasts, then you would deem such advertisement okay?"

"Oh shut up!" Fahad said. "You put her up to this, didn't you?"

"I can think for myself," Zari said quietly.

"What's the use if you can't think right?" Fahad looked baffled. "A complete stranger comes to meet a prospective spouse, and you tell him this, why?"

Zari gave the same answer she'd given half an hour ago. "He asked me why they were on TV."

"*You* told him they were on TV to begin with. Why did you tell him *that*?"

Zari could not stop her tears; she did not try.

"Oh this is great! Just great! Start crying, why don't you!" Fahad gave a theatrical sigh. "For God's sake control yourself, Zari, before someone sees you."

"*You* control yourself." Salsabil put an arm around Zari. "Do you have any compassion?"

"I was marrying her, wasn't I? But don't think I can marry her now." Fahad ran his fingers through his hair. "My mother—shit, Zari, *I* don't want you dredging up this sort of a past. I don't understand . . . why, why would you deliberately make people uncomfortable? Did you see Mo's expression?"

Salsabil flashed her eyes at him. "It was fine until *you* started yelling like a madman."

Fahad sucked his cheeks in. "Zari," he said, "unless you swear to never do this again, unless you swear to control yourself like a normal person, I'm going to have to rethink this whole marriage business."

"Fahad," Zari stood up on glass legs, "when have I ever agreed to marry you?" Her heart was hammering so loudly Zari feared her ears would burst. "You are the last person I would ever marry."

"Huh?" Fahad blinked.

"I thank you, Fahad, for considering me your soulmate, but you are not mine. You could never be mine."

"You're joking." Fahad took a step towards her. "You don't know what you're saying."

"I do."

"I fought for you. I told my mother, I told her 'who cares if Zari may not be able to have kids, if she was raped!'"

For a moment, the world swirled before Zari's eyes.

"Let's go," she said to Salsabil.

"I yelled at my mother for you!" Fahad slapped a fist into a palm. "My Dadi jee likes you. You can't do this to me. If you walk away from me then I swear that's it, then it's really over."

Zari began to walk towards Salsabil's car.

"Zari!" Fahad called out.

"I'm sorry."

"Sorry?!" He ran after her and grabbed her arm. "I thought you said sorry was the most impotent word in the whole damned world."

"Let go of me," Zari said. "And never dare to touch me again."

Instantly Fahad released her. He opened his mouth and closed it. Then he snatched the cell phone from her hand, told her to tell *them* to buy her one, got into his car, and screeched out of the parking lot.

Shehla sat by the window in her bedroom. The curtains were wide open, the half-moon aglow between the bare branches of the tree right outside the window. Every so often, a car turned into their street, its head-beams lighting up the cardboard box she'd left on the ottoman, her box of affection, where she had stored all the cards the children had ever given her—birthday cards, Mother's day cards, no special occasion cards except that they wanted her to know she was beloved. It was ages since Billal or Salsabil had added anything to the box. And there would come a day Miraage would stop too. Another car, another illumination, another drifting into dark. Moving on doesn't mean pretending it never happened, she'd said to Buraaq and Barbara in the car. How easy it was to invoke platitudes to others and ignore them oneself.

"Shehla?" Amman opened the bedroom door. "Shehla, did you go into my study? What's happened? Why are you looking at me like that? Did you hear something? Is he—"

She held out the certificate.

Amman peered at it.

"My God." He sank onto the bed. "Where—"

"In his car. Glove compartment."

"My God. But Fahad—"

"Her Khala . . . even I encouraged her . . . I think . . . with Billal gone she's covering her bases, I think, covering her bases in case . . . in case he doesn't come back." Shehla laughed feebly. "She's pregnant." She handed him the journal. "She's carrying Billal's child."

"I cannot believe, when, how . . ." Amman shrank into himself. "By God, you didn't want her to come, but I insisted."

Shehla shook her head slowly. "No, I'm not going to blame you for his actions. It's his life, that's what he says." Shehla picked up Billal's note from her lap. "Look," she tapped at the sentence. "*It is my life and I can live it as I want.* That's what my son writes." She tossed it next to the red windbreaker on the bed. "But Amman, isn't that what I did too? I decided we would disconnect ourselves from our pasts because this was our life and we could start all over again by choosing what to remember and what to forget. I remember you said 'a man can cut his fingers off, but phantom pain remains.' And I laughed. I laughed and gave you a lecture on the control of mind over matter and memory.

"How naïve that was of me. How arrogant. You know, Buraaq accused me again of living in the past when I was driving them to the airport. I denied it, as usual and, as usual, tried to block out what he was saying, but then it occurred to me that what has happened with Billal is like phantom pain. I amputated your father, your scars, Kashmir . . . I tried my very best to truncate it all . . . but Billal had the circuitry to feel all that." Shehla rested her head on Amman's shoulder. "I'm feeling so tired, so drained. And I'm sorry I shut you out. If I do so in the future, remind me that in the past I've apologised for this very behaviour."

Amman smiled ruefully. Everything was fair in love and war. He switched the light off and held her. He held her for a long time and, afterwards, when he'd fallen asleep, Shehla tucked the quilt under his chin and kissed him on his forehead, because their memories, good or bad, bound them together whether they were at peace or war. They were each other's history; they had no choice but to agree to a cease fire. Yet she was engulfed with sadness. Tonight she and Amman would sleep in the centre of the same bed, but tomorrow? And her children—she could hold them in and still be out of touch. Salsabil had gone to meet someone she didn't want to for her sake alone, and Billal had married someone she would never have wanted him to. A familiar anger, the old disease, swept through; she stifled it. What was the use—it did not work. Husband-wife, parent-child, needs-wants, love-hate. She had no choice but to accept that between actions-intentions, approval-acceptance, expectations-reality, that between everything lay the distance of a hyphen, separating-connecting; a bridge, unbreakable.

A baby. There was a baby.

They drove back from the restaurant, Zari tethered to earth with a gossamer thread, floating this way and that, sure one second, unsure the next. Had she really said what she'd said? Done what she'd done? Begun what she'd begun? All along Zari had been accusing others of making the loss of her honour paramount over the loss of her family, yet all this time, was she not guilty of the same? Her mother would have considered Fahad and his family a perfect match, in any case, a better match than Billal and his family. But it was Billal's family she wanted to be a part of, a family trying to find new ways to walk on old paths. Geographically, the Nabis were here, culturally they were everywhere, and politically between somewhere and nowhere. There was freedom in that, a freedom to reinvent, to make her place within their space, to write anywhere and in any way she wanted: *I was here.*

And, if they didn't want her, she would still be all right. She would learn to navigate on her own. To her shock, the other day, a woman, an event coordinator for the public library system, had telephoned for her. She had been one of the parents at Miraage's Heritage Day and she wanted to know if Zari would be available to give a talk on Kashmir's history and heritage. How much would Zari charge? Zari had nearly fallen over at that. Also, lately, she'd been thinking of selling the residence in Kashmir—it would always be home, but it was no longer the home it had once been—and put the money aside for college, and the baby. And why not? Why couldn't she look after herself as well as her child? She could at least try.

Salsabil stopped the car by the side of the road and held Zari's hair back as she heaved again. She was letting out a lifetime, Zari told her, in preparation for a new one, a new one where she would not allow others to make her feel ashamed for a wrong done to her, make her feel as if shame and silence were the good and decent choices, the only choices, she would not be ashamed and guilty, and neither would she remain silent because silence imposed by one upon oneself was a living suicide. She thought back to the magazine article Salsabil had given her a lifetime ago, the one in which four American girls, all survivors of rape, had smiled out from their photographs—no longer did those girls, or Salsabil for that matter, seem so alien after all.

She turned back to Salsabil and asked if her parents would be home and would it be all right to wake them. She had something to tell them. Salsabil nodded. As the car roared to life again, she prayed Billal knew, even if she herself had not known then, that, of all the things she'd wanted to forget, he was not one of them. She loved him. She'd loved him for a long time. She'd only realised it now. *You are not damaged goods*, he'd said . . . he'd said, *Zaar, I'll be your home.*

∞∞

Shehla snuggled under a blanket on the deck swing as she waited for the girls. The neighbour's tabby was stretched out beside her. Night noises filled the silence around her, shadows within shadows, the scurry of feet, a hoot, a short frantic digging, an abundance of nocturnal life in her backyard. When the garage door cranked opened, the cat shot up and disappeared into the garden. A few minutes later, she heard the girls come in, quiet footsteps on the kitchen floor, the silhouette of two women, heads close together as if they were whispering secrets, sharing a quiet laugh, helping each other along, then the figures straightened and parted. She called out to them just then and they turned, Zari's hand resting protectively on her belly.

Zari knew as soon as she stepped into the deck—Shehla holding the marriage certificate and pointing to her belly—she knew it was all out, every single secret. Relief left her weak-kneed and she leaned against a railing, strapping her arms around her waist. Two pairs of eyes, mother's and sister's, took her in, and she felt it bubbling deep within her, rising yet again, this thing called resilience, determination, temerity, the sheer will to go on, to survive, this thing which had sustained her through everything so far and would go on doing so—a faith in herself to get up and keep moving on because, always, the only choice had been survival.

"You could have told me," Salsabil said. "Billy could have told me . . ."

Shehla had a single question, that was all, one question only. "Did you have anything to do with Billal leaving?"

PART 3

———∞∞———

FOR THE MEMORIES
1998

24

Billy awoke to Commander Salman looming over him. Any rest he'd gained during the night drained out at the Commander's terse expression. Despite Abid's untimely demise, Commander Salman said, they were sticking to the plan: the Kashmiri contingent was leaving.

They drove away from the camp after morning prayers. The car, a badly dented Toyota, reeked of sour milk. Commander Salman sat up front, next to the half-deaf driver, while the rest of them squeezed into the back. The car raced passed the rusted Soviet battle tank, past the Afghan border where a sleepy-eyed, black-turbaned guard waved them through, and past the Pakistani border where a guard in khaki uniform peered at the laminated permit before waving them through too.

As they roared onto the Khyber Pass, Billy forced his mind blank against the muddle of Abid shooting Nazeer and Abid's outstretched hands; he could not. When they entered the outskirts of Peshawar, the car came to stop in a tiny alley strewn with garbage. They got out. The stench was unbearable, wafting up even as they climbed a narrow wooden staircase and into a room with an armoire. They were to wash up, the Commander said, pointing to a mildewed basin and unlocking the armoire, he took out scissors and a duffel bag stuffed with assorted clothes.

Billy washed up and, as best as he could, trimmed his beard and brows. Tossing his discarded clothes into a corner, he pulled on a plain beige shirt and left it hanging over his jeans to cover the bulge of the passport and wad of cash he'd transferred from his old clothes. How little it took to be comforted, to look civilised, to conjure up a transformation, and to believe one was a new man.

When everyone was washed and dressed, and Commander Salman had inspected them as if they were machines and not human, they filed back into the car, sitting in the same spots as before, as if they'd been assigned the seats. For you, Dada, and you, Mauj jee, and you, Zari, Billy said. He kept up the mantra as the sun rose in hateful heat and signs to the airport began to crop up along the road. He wished Commander Salman would cough up some information. At the airport, a man was waiting in the parking lot with plane tickets. Commander Salman ordered Billy alone to step out.

"And them?" Billy's voice warbled as he pointed to the Kashmiri group in the car.

"Not to worry," Commander Salman said.

"But—"

"I said, in fact, I advise you, to worry about no one except yourself."

Before entering the airport, Billy glanced back at the car. Mohmedoo's forehead was pressed against the window where Billy had nursed his own worries until a few minutes ago. Mohmedoo was expressionless. On an impulse, Billy waved. Mohmedoo did not wave back. And just like that,

Billal assumed he'd been expelled from the fold: he was not one of them, he'd never been, so why did he feel so bereft?

It was a short, bumpy flight on the small plane from Peshawar to Islamabad. The woman in a chador next to him kept humming along to whatever song was playing on her Walkman. Commander Salman was seated across the aisle one row behind him, and each time Billy glanced back at him, the Commander's eyes bore into his.

The plane landed expertly. Billy followed the Commander onto the runway and into a bus that drove the passengers to the arrival terminal. Weary and dazed, Billy stood inside the pristine hall overwhelmed by the odour of disinfectant. His arrival had coincided with the arrival of an international flight and, as if in a dream, he heard European, American, Australian accents gathered round the conveyor belts. He felt he was floating, while somewhere down below, his feet walked through the customs checkpoint and out into a terribly humid day with the Commander close at his heels.

Marriot. Intercontinental. Holiday Inn. Serena. Billy snapped back to earth as a gaggle of men holding up placards with hotel names loomed up in front of him. Around him, saluting peons whisked foreigners into embassy transportations while other drivers, anxious for rides, cried out: AC bus. Non-AC bus. Minibus. Wagon. Van. AC coach. Non-AC coach.

"Sir." A bulldog of a man with two ballpoint pens in his breast pocket called out to them and tipped his head to the Commander. This man, Commander Salman told Billy, was going to drive him into Muzaffarabad—Billy simultaneously felt both relief and angst, he was headed to Kashmir after all—where he would be taken to a wait-house where he would await further instructions. Commander Salman gave him an envelope which he was to give to the man at the wait-house.

"With Abid gone . . ." Commander Salman squeezed Billy's shoulder. "You are our hope. God go with you."

"I don't believe in God," Billy said through his fear.

"Is that so?" Commander Salman removed his hand from Billy's shoulder. "No matter. God goes with you whether you like it or not."

The bulldog of a driver led Billy to a minivan. Billy climbed in the passenger seat and the bulldog took the wheel. At the turn of the key, the tape player sprang to life with folk songs.

Billy opened the envelope Commander Salman had given him and extracted a letter from inside. He wished fervently he could read it, but the script resembled tiny ants scrambling madly across the paper and he put it back and turned his attention to the road. Once out of the city, the car began an ascent through a barrier-less, median-less, cliff-hugging road carved through mountains and valleys carpeted with pine trees and the occasional village. Oncoming vehicles barrelled towards them with neither driver bothering to avoid a head-on collision until the very last moment. Each time Billy would jump and clutch the door handle as if it would save his life, Bulldog would slap his beefy thighs in mirth.

Hours later, it was with immense relief that Billy spotted the sign planted on a stone crusted bank of the Neelam River—*Welcome to Muzaffarbad: The Beautiful City that is Gateway to the Kashmir Valley*. The river itself bubbled like blue champagne in a sunshine flute. Bulldog, as if he too was suddenly lulled by the picturesque landscape, eased slowly onto the Domeil bridge. This is the bridge, Billy thought, looking at the wooden and steel girders passing by, whose railings my father and his friends leaned over to play games. Once upon a time this bridge had been nothing but lengths of rope strung from one end to the other, and before that, a passage made possible only by boat, and even before that, a walk on water only for swimmers brave enough to risk drowning.

This valley they were entering was surrounded by mountains and split in half by the river. This was the city where his grandfather had been shot dead and laid to rest next to his grandmother, but Billy knew not where or how to find their graves without exposing his identity. So near and yet so far from being able to pay his respects . . . the realisation filled Billy with panic, and rolling down the window, he swallowed deeply the cold mountain air.

Muzaffarabad, with its wide paved roads housing the Secretariat, the Supreme Court, the High Court, banks, and other official structures, their whitewashed walls gleaming through majestic cypresses and red brick planters, was more developed than his father had made it sound, but then, decades had passed since his father had raced around the city, committing to memory paths long gone or added to. They left the posh locale behind and turned towards a downtown ceilinged with electric wires, like black snakes twisting and coiling and looping, and banners advertising fast-food restaurants. Billy took in the men lounging in dhabas, sipping tea and talking. No one carried guns, nor did they seem particularly troubled by the accumulation of forces on the Line of Control a paltry thirty miles away. There were no sand-bunkers of the type Zari had described across the border in Indian Kashmir, no checkpoints, no expressions discernibly distressed by military occupation. Nothing. The only indication that this might be territory under dispute was the spray-painted graffiti on the stone walls.

'Kashmir is Pakistan!!!!' The exclamation marks elongated alternately into crescent moons and swords.

'Kashmir Pakistan kee Shah Ruhg hai'—Kashmir is Pakistan's jugular vein.

'Ambreeka Hai Hai'—America Down Down.

However, nothing seemed reason for instant alarm as customers haggled with vendors in the afternoon sunshine, and women, weighed down with plastic shopping bags, dragged along bright, ruddy-cheeked kids, and men on bicycles whizzed through bumper to bumper vehicles. Billy was mesmerised by the yellow license plates inscribed with 'Azad Jammu Kashmir.'

He was here all right. He was here.

Soon the minivan eased into a residential area, the sea of flat rooftops dotted with satellite dishes, and stopped outside a small black metal gate flanked by skinny, decrepit cement pillars on both sides. A plaque on one of the pillars read: *Ahmed Villa. Residence of Mr Ahmed Butt/Chacha Palmistry, Numerology, Astrology. Appointment best, Walk-ins Welcome, Rates upon inquiry.*

Bulldog wiggled his brows, gesturing towards Ahmed Villa, and told Billy he would wait for him to enter the house before he drove away. Billy got out. Four strides across the cement driveway and he crossed the tiny but well-kept garden with a tarp-covered motorcycle standing in one corner, to stand before two wooden doors at right angles to each other.

On one door, a nailed sign said *Chacha Palmistry*. From behind the other door, Billy heard film music. He rapped on it. A half a second later, an adolescent girl stood in front of him, a remote control in her hand. On the TV screen behind her, dancers waltzed to the song *Papa Kehtay Hain Barah Naam*.

"Yes?" the girl looked him up and down.

"I'm looking for Butt Sahib?"

She pointed to the other door and slammed her door shut. Billy knocked on the other door. Waak in, Waak in, a deep voice said. Waak-ins most welcome. And he walked into the handshake of a middle-aged man who introduced himself as Chacha Palmistry. Chacha Palmistry looked like a giraffe—legs longer than his torso, ropey neck, face dappled with acne scars. He pumped Billy's hand with a firm grip and pointed to a wicker chair in front of an office desk. Billy sat down. Chacha's beam deepened: job forecast, marriage calculation, love resolution—what did young man want?

Without a word, Billy handed him the envelope as instructed by Commander Salman and within seconds, Chacha Palmistry's good cheer was replaced by a grim mien. After he was done reading the Commander's letter, he mumbled, wait, and disappeared through a door covered by a curtain of beads. Billy crossed his legs and looked around the room. Chacha's desk held an appointment book, a fountain pen, and an ink pot. Next to a black rotary phone stood a plastic frame with the photo of an overweight young man squatting before a rustic shack: *World's First Pizza Hut, established 1958 Wichita, Kansas*. Behind Chacha's desk was a cheap glass cabinet full of shabby hardbacks. On Chacha's walls hung a super-sized poster of the constellations mapping out the zodiac signs, a large portrait of Jinnah in an elegant suit, and Chacha posing with, apparently, various puffed-up dignitaries and over-dressed celebrities. And lastly, a framed photocopy of a page from a newspaper.

The Dawn

Founder: Mr M A Jinnah

Under the Supervision of NAWABZADA LIAQUAT ALI KHAN, Hony. Secy. All India Muslim League

DELHI, SUNDAY, FEBRUARY 8, 1942

Vol 1	*Price*
No. 6	*2 Annas*

The Pakistan Manifesto

ISSUED BY

Muslim Youth Study Circle

<u>PAKISTAN</u>

IS OUR

DELIVERANCE: DEFENCE: DESTINY

WE DENY

THAT WE ARE ONE NATION WITH THE HINDUS AND THE REST

Nothing unites us save arbitrary geographical boundary and temporary shackles of slavery.

Nationality based on either of these must, in its very nature, be unnatural. It cannot, it will not last.

THAT WE HAVE ANY IDEA OF EXPLOITING OR DOMINATING OTHERS

We are a self-respecting people, We respect others rights as we respect our own, We want to live

And let live, None need fear PAKISTAN !

WE DECLARE

That we are a NATION not a "minority"

A NATION of a hundred million greater than Germans in Greater Germany/and what is more, we are a NATION with our own distinctive culture and civilization, language and literature, art and architecture, names and nomenclature, sense of value and proportion, legal laws and moral codes, customs, and Outlook on life and of life. By all cannons of and nomenclature, sense of value and proportion, legal laws and moral codes, customs, and Outlook on life and of life. By all cannons of International Law we are a NATION.

That no amount of threats or intimidations will ever deter us from the chosen path.

Hints about "a long civil war" we brush aside with contempt. On our part we do not want a civil war but in the event of others making it inevitable, a hundred million souls shall look forward to it with the calm confidence of a people who know their intrinsic value.

WE DEMAND

Only the right of self determination. The absolute right to regulate our affairs in our own lands ourselves according to the genius of our own people, without in any way being ordered

About either by the British or the Hindus.

PAKISTAN IS OUR ONLY DEMAND!

* History justifies it,

* Numbers confirm it,

* Justice claims it,
* Destiny demands it,
* Posterity awaits it,
AND
BY GOD, WE WILL HAVE IT!
Muslims unite! You have a whole world to gain.
You have nothing to lose but chains!! *-Reproduced from the Spirit of Youth, Lucknow*

Billy's hands curled into fists. Why had he been sent to this house whose walls bespoke a pro-Pakistan bent? Did Chacha know Billy supported independence for Kashmir? Who was Chacha really? Was Commander Salman going to materialise any second? Claim him for the ends Abid had spoken of?

Billy jumped at the banging of pots and pans somewhere inside the house and a woman shrieking. After a moment, an abrupt silence, and then, Chacha returned. He sank into his chair, dropped the envelope into a drawer, and slapped it shut.

"Billawal, is that your name?"

Billy nodded.

"Very good." Chacha scratched his scarred cheeks. "I have informed the driver that I have taken you into my care. My wife thanks you for bringing the vitamins our son" —Chacha glanced at the photograph of the fat boy in Kansas— "sends her from the US"

"I didn't bring any . . . Oh." Billy caught on. But why the need for a guise within one's own walls?

"She says you are welcome to stay with us until . . . it is time . . . for your return."

Billy blinked. Chacha looked as distressed as he felt.

"Excuse me?" Billy said, realising Chacha had been speaking.

"You cannot understand Kashmiri?"

"No." Billy lied, not knowing why he did so.

"Urdu?"

Billy half shrugged.

"Yeeh gasuh Kusheerah haaq dilawan," Chacha mumbled. Billy managed a dead pan face to Chacha's derisive—this is the class of dolt off to free Kashmir these days.

"Well then," Chacha put his hands on his knees to help himself up, "let me show you to your sleeping quarter. Inshallah, God willing, they will come for you very soon."

Billy followed Chacha through the curtain of beads into a small corridor that opened to a joint dining and family room where the girl was still watching the film. The next room down the corridor was the kitchen. A man in his early twenties—Abdul-Haye, the kitchen help—was slicing ginger root, and a stout woman stood over a stove, stirring whatever was cooking and mopping her forehead with the cotton duppatta draped loosely over her hair. When they passed, she called out to Chacha and handed him a bath towel which Chacha turned around and handed to Billy.

Billy followed Chacha up a flight of stairs covered in a rough periwinkle carpet. They came to a small landing and stopped before a door. My son's room, Chacha said, where you will be sleeping. The prayer mat is in the wardrobe, and this—he swung open the adjacent door to chip tiles and white porcelain fixtures—is the bathroom. Chacha glanced at his wristwatch. We eat dinner in an hour's time. Let me know if you require any toiletries.

Shampoo, soap, toothpaste, toothbrush, deodorant; in fact, everything please.

Billy stood under the shower a little later, luxuriating in the hot water. His injured leg, a mess of scabs and bruises, was healing nicely. He squirted toothpaste directly into his mouth and chewed, savouring the spread of spearmint on his tongue. He picked up the silky bar of yellow soap and wondered if the duck had emerged yet in the soap he'd given to Zari. He rubbed the soap on his beard, his chest, his groin, lathering himself with great vigour. Billy's tension flowed down the drain along with the soap suds and the dust and grime of the road. Was it just this morning he'd woken up on a mountain, believing that one way or another he was doomed? Was it just moments ago when he had been fraught with worry over Chacha's political bent and Commander Salman's transferring Abid's plans onto him? Was a long hot shower all he'd needed to believe that every challenge was conquerable?

Stepping out of the shower, Billy wiped the mirror above the sink free of steam. It was the first time he was seeing himself bearded. He couldn't recognise himself. Chacha had provided a razor blade, but Billy had been instructed to keep the beard and so he tossed the blade onto the sink ledge.

He tried to see if Wali's grip on his neck had left any marks. He found none. After dousing himself with the spray musk deodorant, Billy headed down.

The cane seating in the family room was fitted with maroon velvet cushions. A rectangular 'Home Sweet Home', woven in black cross stitches, hung framed on the wall opposite the TV. Other than that, Mrs Chacha's idea of home décor amounted to cluttering every available inch of surface with her son and daughter's faces in mismatched frames.

Chacha, Mrs Chacha, their daughter, and Billy gathered around a plastic tablecloth spread over the carpet—the dining table was a modern necessity reserved only for formal occasions—upon which Abdul-Haye, the factotum, set steaming dishes of cilantro garnished chicken korma, bay leaf scented white rice, and a red hot tomato chilli curry. They ate the food in the traditional fashion, their fingers spooning neat morsels into their mouths, the traditional style Zari had said she was too uncomfortable to employ at the Nabis' with all their gleaming stainless steel spoons and forks. Billy tried to eat with his fingers, until Mrs Chacha called to Abdul-Haye in the kitchen to bring a spoon. Billy accepted the spoon with heartfelt thanks.

Once dinner was over, Mrs Chacha and the daughter disappeared into the kitchen, and Billy, declining Chacha's half-hearted offer of a cup of tea, bade him goodnight and went up. In the bedroom, Billy slid into Chacha's son's bed, and though the mattress was hard, the pillow thin and the blanket scratchy, for the first time in three months, Billy felt like a man. After a while, he turned to face the bedside table where an empty jar of honey housed a steel compass and a pencil. Opening the bedside drawer, he found empty cassette covers for Vital Signs, Beatles, and U2 tapes atop a TOEFFL practice test. He took out the test. At the back was a wishlist Billy presumed written by the son:

Get accepted into A-1engineering masters program in US.

Get A-1 financial package

Excel at studies

Get A-1 job

Get green card/citizenship, inshallah

Sponsor family

Inshallah all in good time

Billy returned the practice test to the drawer and turned towards the wall. Then to the ceiling. Then back again. He tried to banish from his ears and eyes the memory of Abid's frantic breathing as he fell, and the shot that had killed Nazeer, and Ahmed Baba lying over Mohsin, and Palwasha's bloated skull. He tried to concentrate instead, on his grandfather's apparent serenity in the photograph in the hallway back home, the one where he was sitting with the ledger in his lap. He thought of Zari throwing breadcrumbs to the ducks in the park. Billy hoped that tonight he would be spared dreams of burials, mass burials, masses of burials, that footage tattooed into his mind.

Billy must have drifted off to sleep because he was awoken by the muezzin's call for Fajr prayers in the still dark morning. A little later, Abdul-Haye knocked on his door: breakfast was ready.

Downstairs, the family room was empty of all photographs, and Mrs Chacha and the daughter were gone.

"To stay with relatives," Chacha informed Billy, "in order to distribute the multivitamins you so kindly delivered."

Billy sat down on the floor beside Chacha to a breakfast of onion omelette and parathas. Had he inadvertently done something the night before that had scared them off? Or, in cases like this, was it routine for women and children to evacuate the residence?

"When will they be back?" he asked timidly.

"Inshallah as soon as you get lost," Chacha muttered in the Kashmiri he believed Billy could not understand. Keeping quiet, Billy stared at the TV where a man in a green track suit was giving yoga lessons and blew into the sizzling mug of dark tea Abdul-Haye had placed before him. After breakfast, Chacha put his hands on his knees and helped himself off the floor.

"Well then, I am off," he said, wiping crumbs off his mouth.

"Off?"

"In the morning I teach mathematics at a refugee camp. After my return in the afternoon, my clients come. When my clients come, kindly keep to the bedroom. The fewer people who see you, the fewer I will have to answer. Abdul-Haye will leave for errands soon. Please do not answer the telephone or open the door to anyone."

"But what if they come for me?"

"They can wait outside till I come home so I can personally hand you over."

"When do you think they'll come?"

Chacha's face clouded over. "Today. Tomorrow. A

month. Six months. God knows."

"Six months!" Billy blurted out. He made a pact with himself. If, fate forbid, he was still at Chacha's after two weeks, he would send home, at the very least, a postcard.

"Young man," Chacha frowned, "are you aware that talks between PM Sharif and PM Vajpayee have broken down? Are you aware that soldiers are firing at each other at the border? That seventy villagers in Azad Kashmir have died in the crossfire? That one hundred and thirty are injured, and fifty thousand displaced? Or are you just concerned with when is the right time for you to cross over?"

Billy flushed. "I wasn't aware," he said, and then added in a small voice. "So you think it will be a while?"

"I am not a magician." Chacha looked at Billy sharply. "Who exactly has sent you, where exactly you've come from, what exactly you are up to, when you are to be up to what you are up to—I know nothing."

"The letter—"

"The letter ordered me to keep you safe and sound and within my sight and that is all."

After Chacha left, Billy glared at the TV. The few channels available were showing either Quran recitations or morning chat shows for women with home decorating and cooking segments. He switched back to the yoga show. Chacha, Billy figured glumly, did not get cable. As for the stack of videos he'd seen with Chacha's daughter, not only were they too gone, but the tape slot in the video player was also empty.

"Sir, I am leaving."

Billy jumped as Abdul-Haye entered the room with his limping gait. A canvas bag for groceries dangled off his forearm.

"Okay," Billy said.

The yoga program segued into a children's puppet show. Billy switched the channel. He watched a jet-black bearded man in a golden embroidered cape recite the Quran for a while before switching to another channel where a bride-to-be was being taught how to pluck her brows. Restless, he picked up a magazine from the coffee table next to him. *Akbar-e-Jehan* it said in English on the front cover, but the rest was in Urdu. He vaguely recalled seeing an issue or two of the same magazine on his mother's bedside table. The girl on the cover of the one in his hand looked like Zari. He turned to an earmarked page—a recipe for coal-stewed chicken—at least it looked that way in the photograph. Billy returned the magazine to the table. He began to pace the room. Then did some sit-ups and push-ups. Then prayed the summons came today, this minute, right now, before he forgot everything he'd learned at camp, and most of all, because he did not want to be alone with his thoughts.

∞৩৯

Two mornings later, Billy leapt up like an eager pup when Chacha rose to leave.

"Please," Billy said, "may I accompany you to the camp? I could help out, I would love to."

Chacha shook his head.

"I'll go crazy waiting by myself."

Chacha squinted. The boy did look a bit wild-eyed.

"Why not take a few books from my office—"

Billy shook his head. "Please. Please. Can't you say I'm your son's friend—"

"You are *not* a friend of my son's."

To Billy's horror, his eyes filled with tears. Chacha sighed and motioned for Billy to follow.

∞∞

A morning drizzle had brightened the shrubs that bordered the houses along the road and Billy took welcome sips of the rich, damp soil-scented breeze. He marched down roads, Chacha always a few steps ahead, and passed a graveyard with a vendor selling loose rose petals by the entrance, past a corner shop stacked with a billion brands of cigarettes, and a small mosque with a green awning. As Chacha began a nimble descent down a meandering path of rocks and pebbles, Billy stepped carefully from one rock to another, resisting the vision of Abid's outstretched hand, until they stopped at a circle of shacks with tin roofs.

A meaty man hunched over a canvas chair was fanning his face with a baseball hat and he jumped to attention when he saw Chacha. He was still waiting, he said, for supplies from the Pakistani government—books, pencils, uniforms—he'd been waiting since early this morning and so were the students. Chacha pulled a list from his wallet of the children who had been disappointed the last time round because supplies had been short; this time the line was to begin with them. The man nodded as he took the list and peered curiously at Billy. Chacha glared at the man and hurried to one of the shacks.

In the shack, adolescent boys hovered around—Billy strained to see—an overturned cockroach flailing on the dhurrie covering the dust floor. Their excitement volleyed between stomping the roach to death or carrying it out and letting it go, but none of them dared to touch the roach. They sprang back at Chacha's approach and watched, spellbound, as he pinched up the roach and tossed it outside. They burst out clapping and cheering. Chacha smiled, stern, bemused, signalling for them to settle down, and once they were all sitting cross-legged, he began the lesson.

Billy stood in a corner of the fan-less, windowless room, gazing at each inquisitive face as the class progressed. Three kids at a time were sharing a book, a book that was all but coming apart and which was being held as delicately as if it were treasure. And their enthusiasm for reciting multiplication tables was so infectious that Billy found himself relaxing, for a moment, against all the slingshots in the world. What a dolt he was, he thought, as he gazed at the industrious boys, and again he wondered what the hell he was doing here? It might be naïve to think that education was all, that the promise of gainful employment guaranteed a good life, but surely it held more promise than simply killing or being killed. The trick was to make life on earth worth living over any heavenly pleasures.

A rotund man ducked his head into the classroom, and from the way the children scrambled to stand, Billy gathered it was the headmaster.

"Khwaja Sahib. Salaam-ai-laikum." The headmaster shook Chacha's hand. "All is well? Someone saw Mrs and beti at the bus stop this morning. This is correct report?"

Chacha glanced at Billy. "Cheeku sent his mother

multivitamins and minerals from US. She went to Quetta to share with her sister."

"Good, good. I am informed a young man is accompanying you today?" The headmaster turned shrewd eyes to Billy.

"From Cheeku's university," Chacha said, signalling to Billy to step forward. "He conveyed the vitamins."

"Very good deed on your part, young man." The headmaster slapped Billy on his back. "He is well, our Cheeku? He is still," the headmaster puffed his cheeks out in imitation of a fat person, "or he has lost weight since he is not eating home-cooked food?"

"He's the same." Billy reddened.

"Good good. This is your first visit to Kashmir?"

"Yes."

"And how long you are here for?"

"And, sir, how are your haemorrhoids?" Chacha interrupted. "I heard you might have to operate?"

"Sadly, it seems that way." The headmaster turned his hands up in resignation. After a few more pleasantries which included a cursory dinner invitation to young man, the headmaster left.

"Tch." Chacha stared at the headmaster's retreating back. "He is a regular radio, a big gossip, and the last thing I need is you receiving undue attention. Billawal, please, you return to my house and stay there."

"But—"

"Please." Chacha said. "Please. Do as I say."

Chacha's directions memorised, Billy walked away from the makeshift classroom, retracing his steps past the mosque, the corner store, and the graveyard. He stopped at the graveyard and peered over the low boundary wall at the tombstones. It occurred to him that this might be where his grandparents lay and so he entered. A little while later, however, as he wound his way down dirt paths between the graves, staring at resting places of earthen mounds, at marble and calligraphy, staring at epitaphs scripted in Urdu letters, he realised it was useless. Unless his grandparents' epitaphs were in English, he would not be able to read them. He trudged out of the graveyard, wishing he'd learnt this language despite his parents' disinterest in his doing so and telling him that English was the only language in his life that could ever matter.

Back at the house, Billy met Abdul-Haye coming out of the gate.

"Salaam-a-laikum," Billy said dolefully. And then, on an impulse, he asked, "Where's the local library?" Because, it had just occurred to him that surely the library would contain material in English and surely, Muzaffarabad was the best place to look for information on his Dada.

"Sir, where is Chacha?"

"Camp school."

Abdul-Haye eyed Billy suspiciously. "Chacha said you are to go to liebree? I am to take you?"

"Yes." Billy dug into his pocket and extracted some money.

"Sir, no, sir."

"Please," Billy gazed into Abdul-Haye's charcoal eyes. "It's for the excellent meals you've been serving. Look," he forced the twenty dollars into Abdul-Haye's palm, "why don't you stay outside the library while I'm there?"

∞∞∞

It took them a little less than an hour to walk from the congested downtown to the wide, cypress-lined roads where the public library was located along with other government buildings, the towers and arches and domes of officialdom set in spacious, manicured lawns. Abdul-Haye's limp was becoming more pronounced by the second. He finally stopped in front of the Prime Minister House to rub his thigh.

"Have you hurt yourself?" Billy said.

Abdul-Haye raised his right shalwar cuff to expose a prosthetic leg. "Sir, landmine."

A shiver ran up Billy as he thought of his own close call. "Afghanistan?"

"Sir, no, sir." Abdul-Haye shook his head. "On the ceasefire line in my village."

"Of course," Billy murmured even as he felt stupid for his assumption. During the 1965 and 1971 wars, hundreds of anti-personnel and anti-tank landmines had been planted on both sides of the Indo-Pak border. Abdul Haye was seven when his leg was blown off. He'd been out gathering firewood. Luckily, Chacha had been in their village that day, compiling notes on the local school. He'd rushed Abdul Haye to the Civil Military Hospital, paid his medical expenses, and saved his life.

Billy digested this information as they began to climb a grassy knoll towards the library. Chacha, he thought, was a hero and a saviour. You couldn't tell by looking at him, and there were no medals announcing as much.

∞◦∞

The Muzaffarabad library was a single-storey rectangular building with trees towering over its flat roof like protective arms. Abdul-Haye squatted against the front wall under a wooden meter box.

"Sir," he said, "I will wait here."

Billy entered the quiet library and followed a librarian thrilled to lead him to the basement where tube lights lit up the space crammed entirely with bookshelves. He was looking for material on the freedom fighters of Kashmir, Billy had said and the librarian had nodded proudly. He'd come to the perfect place. There was nothing he wouldn't be able to find in their Kashmir Collection. It was simply the most extensive archive in the world pertaining to everything about Jammu and Kashmir's history and the liberation movement—3,500 books and then there were manuscripts, journals, microfilm, and in the audio-visual section documentaries, and songs, and speeches, everything totalling to over 40,000 sources.

Billy began at the audio-visual section. There just had to be at least one recording of his grandfather's speeches where he'd roared into the microphone like a lion. He sat at a table next to a square window, the short curtain pulled back, and sorted through the material before him. It would take him days to go through everything available in English, and after that there was material in languages he would need help with.

After a fruitless few hours, Billy contemplated asking the librarian if there was ready information on Abdullah Nabi. But no, before taking such a gamble, he had to give the search his very best. When he finally emerged in the late afternoon, he was exhausted and disappointed, but he promised himself with wry fortitude that tomorrow was another day.

They found Chacha pacing the driveway, clutching his chest, when they returned.

"Where were you?" he shouted at Abdul-Haye. "Where did you take him?"

Abdul-Haye burst into tears even as he rushed in only to rush back out with Chacha's blood pressure medicine and a glass of water.

The evening meal was eaten in a terrible quiet despite the drone of the TV. At one point, Chacha slapped down the twenty dollar note by Billy's plate.

"Keep your bribes to yourself," he said. "Abdul-Haye's loyalty is not for sale."

After dinner, Abdul-Haye was sent off to the cinema to calm his nerves.

Billy went upstairs where he indulged in a cold shower to soothe his own nerves. When he came out of the shower, he could hear Chacha talking in a somber voice. Billy squatted at the top of the stairs and cupped his ears. Chacha was on the phone.

"I know I promised they'd never send anyone else again, but, try to understand, it is out of my hands! Of course our house is not a hotel. But I am helpless! What to do? Once you get involved in these things, you can never get out no matter how much you want. *I* am not saying this, this is what *they* say. Of course I want to get out once and for all. Of course. But it is out of my control! All I desire is to be left alone to live my life. You know that. You know that. Don't breathe a word to Cheeku. I don't want his studies disrupted over this. Inshallah, God will help us through this trial.

"No I have not figured out if his American accent is real or fake. I have only to figure out who exactly has sent him and for what reason. Of course my project is top secret. No one knows. I said no one! Kashmir is an integral part of Pakistan—I have been endorsing this view for years now. Not too worry. I will make it clear to the boy that I am pro-Pakistani. Why should he suspect otherwise?

"He wanted to go to the refugee camps today. Then he tricked Abdul-Haye into taking him to the library! Why library? Abdul-Haye said no one suspicious entered the library, but . . . the boy, he is good actor . . . acting perturbed and disturbed at being left alone . . . Even if it is not acting, it is none of my concern. The letter instructed me to keep him safe and sound, otherwise I will be held accountable. It did not instruct me to entertain the young man."

After the conversation was over, Billy took a deep breath, and went downstairs. Chacha was sitting before the TV, his head in his hands.

"Chacha?"

Chacha jumped. "What is it? What do you want? Why are you not asleep yet?"

"I'm pro-independence. I trained in Afghanistan with a

motley group. I don't know why they sent me to your house. I've been scared out of my mind . . . I thought you were pro-Pakistan."

"I am pro-Pakistan, of this rest assured."

"But you said . . . over the phone—"

"But you said . . . cannot understand Kashmiri!" Chacha smacked his forehead. "I am a rusty wheel. Out of touch. I should never have taken your word for it. I should have tried to trip you up and even then played safe."

"I swear, I swear I have not been sent here to spy on you or do you any harm. I don't even know who you are . . . please, trust me."

"Trust *you*?!"

"How was I supposed to trust *you*?" Billy bit his lip. "Even now, how *am* I to trust that your phone conversation is not a ruse to trap me in some way?"

"And what if, by referring to this fear, you are not, in turn, entrapping me?" Chacha shot back. He motioned for Billy to sit down. "Divide and rule. It remains the golden strategy. Tell me, why did you go to the library?"

Billy blinked. "I'm looking for information on an ancestor of mine."

"Who?"

"I can't tell you."

"You can't tell me or choose not to?"

Billy shook his head helplessly. "Look, I'm really sorry about displacing your family like this. I swear I didn't mean to."

"Did you ask to be sent to my house?"

"No!"

"Then why are you apologising for something that is no more your fault than it is mine?" Chacha clasped Billy's shoulder. "Tell me truthfully, your accent is real? This is not a veiled threat they are sending against my son?"

"Absolutely not. Please believe me. My family is Kashmiri, and I'm here for its independence."

"Bit too late for that, young man." Chacha gave a short bark of laughter. "Bit too late for that. Just months back they forcefully closed down a pro-independence camp . . . cracking down on militancy, they said, but pro-Pakistani camps were not touched. Still, I suppose a bit of a farce suits them by having the likes of you around."

"Chacha, how come you are in this position?"

"What to tell you?" Chacha tipped his head sadly. "I belong originally to a small village outside of Srinagar. My father was a stove mechanic who liked nothing more in life than to drink and make merry."

Chacha's father died of burn wounds the year Chacha was born. With six appetites to sate, Chacha's illiterate mother marketed her sole skill and, as luck would have it, the village mosque retained her for cleaning. Instead of a salary, she was given free housing—one room with a pit latrine—and a patch of garden to do with as she pleased. Following in his brothers' footsteps, Chacha should have learned some trade, instead, news travelled far and wide that he could correctly calculate in his head the sums that the shopkeepers in the village miscalculated despite pen and paper in their hands. No one disputed that Chacha must go further than the government funded primary schooling, but it was, in the end, his brothers who scrimped to further his education.

Off he went to Srinagar, where he attended school in the morning and upon his return in the afternoon was factotum to the family with whom he'd been placed.

"They did not overwork me," Chacha said. "And I learned very early on that one can tolerate anything as long as one believes it is his fair share."

Chacha studied diligently through high school and won a scholarship to Srinagar University. Politics entered his door through friends who began to whisper that something had to be done to make India accept that Kashmir was a disputed state. It's only fair, Chacha reiterated, as he found himself, one mist-addled morning, at the Line of Control, detonating a crude bomb by an army encampment after which, Indian soldiers catapulted into action from all directions. The getaway car was shot at, which scared witless the boy driving it.

When the car crashed, all Chacha knew to do was get out and run. It was only later that he realised he'd run across the khooni lakheer, the bloody border, from Indian Kashmir into Pakistani Kashmir and that he was badly hurt with shards of glass from the car's shattered windshield embedded in his face.

"People assume these are the remnants of acne or chicken pox." Chacha stroked his face. "It is just as well."

Chacha found himself in a refugee camp at the outskirts of Muzaffarabad. He wrote to his mother, begging to be forgiven, hoping to return, but return was a sweet dream, for the Indian government would never issue him a visa back to

Kashmir. And suppose he did manage to re-cross the border illegally without being shot, sooner or later he would be arrested and accused of being a Pakistani agent.

Pakistan, in turn, accused him of being an Indian agent. If he wasn't an Indian agent, they said, then why was he not signing a chit affirming that Kashmir belonged to Pakistan?

Truth was, Chacha said, when the insurgency first broke out against India's proxy rule over Kashmir, Pakistan had extended help to the original freedom fighters, but, once it built its own insurgent network, aid was diverted to pro-Pakistan guerrillas while pro-independence guerrillas were incarcerated on petty charges and the leaders shunned while their offices and training camps were shut down. In Pakistan, men who had fought in the Afghan war, men who believed in the Saudi creed of Islamising the world, men who believed that Kashmir belonged to Pakistan, these men were the hallowed men.

"To remind them that Muslim brotherhood is not a guaranteed fact," Chacha said, "that the creation of Bangladesh out of Pakistan is proof of that, would have been tantamount to death, so we, the original freedom fighters, kept quiet."

Chacha's unruly brows knitted together as he peered at Billy. Living through these situations had strengthened his faith that there was only one system, the system of self-rule even if self-rule was a mess.

"Because," Billy said, "messes sort themselves out sooner or later." Then, feeling suddenly miserable, he added, "Or not."

"Or not," Chacha echoed, "but at least it will be *our* mess."

Chacha had seen his future Mrs at a traffic light. It was love at first sight for him. When he'd become financially stable enough to propose, thanks be to Allah, his proposal had been accepted. By that time he was teaching mathematics at a girl's school and doing decently well.

It was Mrs Chacha who made the initial observation, and soon Chacha had agreed with her that the girls he taught mathematics to, were riveted by numerology, palmistry, and Linda Goodman's astrological matchmaking guide *Love Signs*. In matters superstitious, Pakistanis as a whole were still very much a pagan lot, no matter the Quran forbidding such beliefs, so why not, Chacha mused in the staff room one day, leave teaching, which was at the end of the day an underpaid and thankless headache anyway, and invest instead in the esoteric? Three months of heavy reading on numbers, stars, palms, and janter-manter, abracadabra, Chacha opened his shop which, to this day, by the generous blessings of Allah, was doing very well.

In fact, life would be excellent if only *they* would leave him alone. As for India, his visa applications were consistently rejected. His mother had died a few years ago without ever seeing him again or his children. Five hours distance, but his siblings may as well be a separate race altogether. In their partition speeches, Jinnah spoke of the 'beginning of a new and noble era,' while Nehru spoke of 'light and freedom.'

"I suppose," Chacha sighed, "they could spout such nonsense since they would never have to face visa issues. As for me, naa aaar naa paar, I belong neither here nor there . . ."

For a long time now, Chacha had been trying to immigrate abroad, but his application was denied every single time. In fact, Chacha was still shocked that his son's academic visa for the US had been granted at all.

On the TV, two white men in suits and ties appeared. Chacha turned the volume up. Headline news: "US Senators on a visit to Islamabad for three days are going to talk to the Pakistani PM to hammer out a swift and fair solution to the current border crisis with India. The Azad Kashmir PM is planning a trip abroad in the coming weeks. In sports news . . ."

"Looks like" —Chacha turned the volume back down— "our esteemed AJK PM has finally received a green signal from Islamabad to travel. Puppet rule in India and puppet rule in Pakistan, but one maintains that it is a part and the other that it is apart . . . it is the water. The origins of the water are in Kashmir, and whoever controls the water supply, controls, ultimately, all. Bah!" Chacha pursed his lips. "Young man, you look like you are from a good family, did you not know the situation here?"

Billy mumbled this was his calling, something he had to do. Chacha looked at the boy.

"Adal-badal," he said, "replacement." His son had gone to the US to study while Billawal had journeyed here to fight. But then, as far as Chacha was concerned, this exchange was written in the stars long before the two were even born.

"Young man," he said, "give me your right hand."

He smoothed Billy's palm and began to squeeze it gently, plumping up the lines, deepening the cervices.

"You are a sensitive fellow. You have a close relationship with your mother . . ."

Billy made a face.

"You are at odds with her?"

Billy nodded.

"This is why I said *close* . . . the very act of antagonism demands closeness." Chacha flipped Billy's hand and studied the ridge alongside the little finger. "Hmm . . . you will have . . . have had . . . many marriages . . . remember a marriage is taken not literally but as any meeting of the hearts . . . I see love, true love . . ."

"Will I return safely from the mission?"

Chacha turned Billy's hand back up. "What do you mean safely?"

"Alive?"

Chacha had decided long ago to tell the truth of what he saw—infertility, infidelity, insanity—his honesty was the secret to his success. He drew the line on death, but in the young man's case, he was on a path where he need not be sheltered from such a fate.

"Alive?" Chacha repeated. "No."

Billy snatched his hand away and hid his face in his forearm.

"Inshallah," Chacha said gently. "Allah will help you."

"Allah can't." Billy's voice was muffled. "I don't believe in God."

"And yet you believe in what I see in your palm . . ."

Billy looked up, dazed.

"The time of your death is foreordained," Chacha

418

quoted the poet Ghalib, "why then sleep eludes you?"

Billy swallowed. If he was to die, so be it. But, if it was the last thing he did for himself, he was going to find and listen to at least one of his grandfather's speeches.

"I need to go to the library tomorrow."

Chacha shook his head. "I have been instructed to keep you safe until you are sent for, and if I fail in my task, I will jeopardise my family's life. Please try to understand."

"I do understand," Billy said, genuinely distressed, "and I mean no disrespect and I wish to cause you no trouble, but I have to go. Only to the library and back, this I can promise."

Chacha looked at the boy, his arms folded over his chest, the armour of the stubborn. He'd seen the same posture and the same expression plenty of times—they were the stances of youth and of fools—once he'd been both himself and for what he was about to do, he was still very much a fool. But it seemed necessary to let this young man know that there were men like him who were recording their dead, wounded, missing, and captured amongst the pro-independence freedom fighters for the memorials that would be built once independence finally came.

"I have a task," Chacha said, "and it should serve your purpose for the time being, as well as mine to keep you occupied and inside, and after that," Chacha smiled apologetically, "we will see."

෴

The small room Chacha unlocked was lit with a high voltage naked bulb hanging from the ceiling. Piled against the walls were stacks of papers and files. Some held photos, Chacha said, accompanied by notes. These were the stories of the men who'd sacrificed their lives for the cause of independence. There were also interviews with their families, as well as Chacha's own impressions. What he wanted Billawal to do was transcribe the notes onto the computer in proper English for, God willing, one day, Chacha eventually hoped to publish everything.

Billy opened a file in which a passport-size photograph of a young man was stapled onto notes about him. Billy took out another file marked *Minors-India*. In one photograph, a woman held a child while two other children pressed up against her. Billy turned the picture around.

'My little child was held as a hostage. I was threatened that my son would die if I cried.'

In other photographs, children lay bloodied, and in some cases dead.

'This child was bayoneted while his mother was gang-raped.'

'This kid was beaten to death during a cordon and search operation.'

'Soldiers crushed my child under their boots, while I was gang-raped by their officers—'

He stared at a little child, a toddler almost, sitting in his mother's lap while she pointed out the scars on the child's back.

In another photo, a man with a walking stick stood next to two women. They looked away from the camera with haunted expressions on their faces. 'I am a tanga driver,' it said at the back, 'the rifle was aimed at my chest, and my beloved wife and daughter were gang-raped in my presence.'

Another photograph. Lost expressions staring at lost homes, it read, *'Abandoned Homes: houses destroyed by arson and explosives. The occupants left high and dry under the sky.'* Billy turned the photo. In a corner was scribbled *Photo credit: Mansoor Pandit.*

Billy stared at the name. His knees grew weak. This photo in his hand, this photo was taken by Nazeer's brother. Nazeer's brother had taken this photo. Nazeer's brother, Mansoor, who'd vowed to be witness to atrocities in his backyard, he had taken a photo which had survived long after his own bones turned to ash, these photos, a testament to a small world, yet the largess of individual lives. Mansoor's had not been a wasted life. While Nazeer's . . .

Billy shut his eyes for a moment. When he was himself again, he opened a photo-less file. On the first page were notes:

Human cost of proliferation of small arms enormous. Destroys cultures and lives, exacerbates and intensifies conflicts. Small arms kill & injure/Human benefit of proliferation of small arms enormous. It keeps safe cultures and lives, contains the means to contain conflicts. Small arms defend and protect—

in Kashmir both POV applicable.

Billy placed the folder on the table next to the monitor. He began pulling out folder after folder, setting them in different piles. Pictures. Essays. Statistics. It was a fairly easy project, one that would have him finally doing something for the pro-independence movement, and one worthwhile enough to devote a little time away from searching for his grandfather, and as soon as he was done, he would return to his quest and proceed to the library whether Chacha liked it or not.

Billy was half way through a large stack when he opened a folder and inhaled sharply. He held up the photograph of his Dada squatting by the side of a road with three other men. His Dada dangled a baton between his knees. All ten of his fingers were intact. A cigarette balanced between his lips at a rakish angle. He was smiling into the camera.

No notes accompanied the photograph, and neither was there anything written at the back.

Folder clasped to his chest, Billy raced down.

"Everything okay, young man?" Chacha said.

"There aren't any notes for this set." Billy handed Chacha the folder. "And they're the only photos I've found so far with anyone smiling."

"Smiling!" Chacha's nose curled up as if the folder stank. "Sneering, more like it. Ek soond khasith ek, each out doing the other. If one was a sadist, the other was a masochist. There are three types of men—idealists, brainwashed, and mercenaries—these three here are the third type and of that type a particularly nasty bunch. Petty thugs of the worst kind. Contract killers and rapists. Name the right price and they will murder, torture, rape, and no one is exempt . . . elderly, infirm, handicapped, children." Chacha's shook his head. "Some of these rogues were family men themselves . . . buying toys for their children from their nefarious earnings. Ghulam Shah, Azam Srandah, Abdullah Nabi—inhumane, the lot of them, morally bankrupt.

"This man here," Chacha tapped on a face, "was like a Hitler. And this one," he flicked Abdullah Nabi's face, "it was said he specialised in torturing children."

Chacha shut the folder. "The two-fingered wretch lived in Muzaffarabad a long while back. The man who shot him to death," Chacha gave a wan smile, "he was feted."

His grandfather was a hired gun.

His grandfather was known for torturing children.

Mauj jee was either delusional or a bona fide liar.

His father had lied to him.

He was a Nabi, it was in his blood.

His father had tried to protect him from the legacy of bad blood.

Back in the computer room, Billy sank into the plastic chair. He placed the folder on the keyboard. He put his hands on his knees to stop them from shaking. He shook his head as if clearing water from his ears. After a couple of minutes, he opened the folder again, and, snatching a glance, gently closed it. He felt such a piercing pain, he doubled over. This was the time to cry. He found he couldn't.

Billy jumped off the chair. He balanced from one foot to the other trying to find some middle ground. He picked up the folder again, and the pictures slipped to the floor. He stared at the man staring back up at him, the cocky cigarette in his mouth a forked tongue. Money his God. Morality immaterial. Always Billy had accepted that his father's silence was a deprivation. Never had he supposed that his father's silence might be a gift.

He could give his father a gift. He could—Billy sank onto the floor—revise history, rewrite it, regenerate it into palatable fare. He could take Dada's photos from this pile and drop them into another folder. He could add Dada's name to the right list, write him up a new legacy, come up with captions for the photos, furnish history. *Abdullah Nabi marched with Gandhi.* It would be there in the books, from which would be filmed the documentaries, from which professors would teach classes and so on and so forth until Billy's captions would lead unto indelible fact, make Abdullah Nabi an angel, a good guy, the man he'd spent his life looking up to, the man for whom he'd come here, the man, *the legacy* he couldn't let down. And he and his father, they would be able to hold their heads high and say 'an honourable freedom fighter, Abdullah Nabi, a humane individual amongst all that inhumanity.'

Billy's portrait could dilute history here, embellish it there, play with truth, tryst with falsehood, select, erase, exaggerate, downplay, simply recreate and change the very essence of who someone had been and in doing so change history itself; who, except for himself, would be the wiser of such a betrayal? In wilfully creating a life of lies, would he be able to live with himself or did lies become one's own truth too?

By the time Billy would be done with the books, by the time Chacha, or anyone for that matter, suspected anything, it would be too late, the die would be cast, and, at the very least, there would be a debate about the reality of one Abdullah Nabi.

He was a Nabi, it was in his blood.

He gathered the photos off the floor—

. . . it was a long night.

ळ✇ळ

The next morning, after Chacha left for the refugee camp and Abdul-Haye left on his errands, Billy shaved off his beard. When he looked into the bathroom mirror, he was no longer the person who'd left the US, nor was he the person who had left the training camp. That Billal was gone.

After placing a note by the computer, Billy slipped out of the house. At the graveyard, the florist was setting up his stall and Billy asked him directions to the bus station.

At the station, he purchased a ticket for the first bus to Islamabad. A half-hour later, it was a half full bus that meandered its way along that modern hieroglyph, a ribbon of concrete civilisation, a grey tarmac road, twisting and winding its way alongside mountains on one side, and on the other, a steep drop. Billy looked out of the window and through his reflection with its oval outline and bloodshot eyes onto the dreary land. Forgive me Chacha, he muttered, forgive me for running away, for endangering your life. He prayed the letter he'd left for Chacha to give to *them*, saying that he'd run away, would absolve Chacha of any blame.

The quiet within him was rendered hypnotically quieter by the monsoon rains, the inch long liquid chisels carving and fashioning the earth as they pleased. Half-dressed children stamped in and out of puddles by the roadside and waved at the bus while soaked adults, their wet clothes plastered to their thin limbs, held open plastic bags and collected a rainfall which stopped as abruptly as it had begun. Billy wondered if Chacha had discovered his note yet.

Soon enough, the mountain road gave way to flat land

and turned into a dual carriageway leading to Islamabad/ Rawalpindi—the blue sign was in English. Billy blinked and turned to look back at it. Any moment now, Abid's ghost would appear, or Commander Salman's long reach, or Chacha's troubled face. Billy glanced at the Pakistani Rangers seated around him, at the badges on their camouflage fatigues and berets. On leave, perhaps, or returning home. He'd always thought there was no difference between freedom fighters and soldiers, and that if there was any, then it was the former who were far superior to the latter on account of choosing their cause. But here was the difference: freedom fighters absconded, if they were so lucky, while soldiers were honourably discharged. His Dada would not have run away. His Dada would have gone along with Abid's plans—or anyone's—as long as the price was right. He did not want to think about his fallen Dada. He wanted to stand on his own two feet. He wanted his own face. He had questioned losing his morality, but he was not going to lose his life in memory of a man who had been the lowest of the low—a mercenary.

But Kashmir was more than his grandfather.

If your grandfather wasn't Kashmiri, would you have even been able to point Kashmir out on a map? This is what Zari had said. How confidently he'd answered her once upon a time. *Chicken and egg,* he'd said. *chicken. and. egg.*

It would make no difference to Kashmir, to the world, to anybody, whether he lived or died for it, and he wanted to live, he wanted to live the safe and secure life he'd left behind. Zari was right. He did not care enough about Kashmir to become a casualty, a mere statistic. No. He did care, but he did not want to lose his life for a country that, after independence, might go on to disintegrate into a mess.

But Nazeer had been wrong about him being stuck here. He had a country. A country that took care of its own and he was one of its own, no matter what doubts the likes of Abid tried to sow. Of this he had to have faith. Or he was once and for all truly lost. He wanted to live a life where the world did not matter, if you so chose, beyond your front door, and his country could give him that. A life revisited without his grandfather. A life where he would have the good sense to question even his beloved Mauj jee.

Shame flooded Billy again. Hot, thick, disgraceful spurts. He was embarrassed for all the hours he'd spent in front of the TV daydreaming about his grandfather saving the world, the hours he'd spent fantasising about his own place in history, his noble mark, scratching *I was here* on the face of time, the hours he'd spent fantasising about following in his grandfather's footsteps.

The last time his legs had tingled with the need to move on, to get going as far and as fast as he could was on account of Zari. Zari, the girl he'd married in a fit of 'rescuing', not for her sake—Billy's guts clenched—but rather for his own. Zari, the wife he'd abandoned when all she had expected from him was to be a husband, to tell his parents that they were married, to get his life in order, to get *their* life in order. He'd left her to fend for herself, left her with a note, a bar of soap, and the assurance that Salsabil was there. He'd simply dodged his responsibility.

No. He'd run away from it. He'd been running from responsibility his entire life. He was never going to amount to anything. All he wanted to do was return home to his cocoon of a life where the only badge of honour was making plenty of money and the only palpable contribution one made to good was being a conscientious neighbour, if even that. Salsabil was right. He was a couch saviour. A deserter, an evader, a loser, a coward. There: he'd admitted it. He was a coward, the ultimate survivor. Or was it the brave who survived? A soldier caught his eye and nodded. Billy nodded then looked away.

Eventually the bus arrived at the station. Billy stepped into the wet, chaotic traffic and into the first rickshaw he saw. Where did Sahib want to go?

"Any hotel."

Billy's rain-soaked shoes squelched on the tiled lobby, empty except for a fake palm tree behind a threadbare sofa. A man in a sallow shirt looked away from the Bollywood dance playing on a small wall-mounted TV. He frowned at Billy. No room, he waved a knobby hand, no room. Only after Billy flashed his dollar bills did a room miraculously appear, as did the gushing, fawning courtesy. After checking over the phone, the man assured Billy that there was a flight to the US the next day, although he would have to be on standby at such a short notice, that a taxi could be arranged to take him to the airport, that he could make international calls from the privacy of his room, and that *anything* he required could be gotten for him for the night for the right, the man bowed his head, price.

Billy sat in the window seat of the plane, the blanket pulled up to his chin, wishing he could sleep a sleep that was not a restless one, a sleep devoid of dreams caught between the past and the future, between imagining how Chacha must have taken his departure and how his family would greet his arrival. He'd spoken to his parents over the phone. "We know about Zari," they had said, "and nothing matters except that you are safe and sound and coming home."

The mass of clouds they were flying above seemed to him a patch of a pillow imprinted with Zari's hair. He looked away, at the empty seat next to him, but she was there too, her shape rising out of the curlicues in the upholstery. And there was her bullet scar in the grainy pattern of the plastic food tray. She had not come to the phone herself, and he'd felt shy asking them to put her on the phone. And what would he have said to her? He had not avenged her. He had done nothing. Would she hate him for that? Would she hate him for wanting to return home and start all over again in a nice life where he could just bury his head in the sand and not think about anything? After all, the freedom to fence oneself in was a freedom too.

Billy's flight landed early in the morning, the mists parting over roads lined with matchbox vehicles, the tops of grey-green trees, the runway. He walked down the ramp as if in a trance. His parents and Salsabil and Miraage hovered by the entrance. Miraage waved a green crayoned sign 'Welcome Billy'. And before Billy knew it, he'd stepped into his definitely thinner father's tight embrace. Salsabil punched Billy's arm and then hugged him. His mother simply clasped his hand and didn't let go until they reached the car. He couldn't look them in the eyes.

Amman drove and Salsabil sat upfront because Shehla wanted to sit with Billy at the back. Miraage sat on Billy's other side, her head bobbing to the nursery rhymes playing softly. Shehla touched Billy's two faces—a sun hardened forehead above and below, a pale, soft-skinned jaw.

"I had a beard this long." He waved his hand under his chin.

"You did not!" Salsabil turned around. Her unnatural cheeriness matched all their tones, as if, as long as they maintained jollity, no one would ask questions to which answers might bring despair. Instead inanity: flight? food? in-flight films? all good?

Good, good, and good.

Oh good.

It seemed all was to be forgotten and forgiven after all. He found he preferred this convenient lack of accountability, preferred this pact with silence, these invisible walls, memories strung around his tongue, clinging, clasping, holding on without having to let go; if he remained quiet all could be as it had been before, before all of this, as if his going had been nothing more than an aberration, an isolated incident, like breaking an arm or a leg or wearing a sling or being in traction for a couple of months.

Yet, he wanted to tell them everything.

In return, he needed to know the absolute truth about his grandfather.

He wanted to ask where was Zari, how had they found out, what had they said to her, she to them, why hadn't she come to bring him home.

"Billal," Shehla said, "Zari is pregnant."

Billy's breath nearly stopped. Did he deserve such a happy ending?

Did he deserve?

❦

No one slept the night Billal's telephone call came—he was fine, he was coming home, he needed money for the ticket. Zari loitered in the shadows, too shy to ask to speak to him. The Nabis were saying, "we know about Zari, and nothing matters except that you are safe and sound and coming home."

After the phone call, Zari stood in the kitchen, washing mugs of tea. She could see the family in the living room. Salsabil was chewing on her fingernails. Amman was breathing loudly, as if he'd just surfaced from being underwater after a painfully long time. Shehla sat with the red windbreaker pressed to her mouth, as if to contain every ounce of delight. Intermittently, they would comment: sensitive boy, humanitarian . . . idealism . . . hardly a crime, should be proud of him . . . thinking of others . . .

Shehla's voice was measured, as if she was searching for a space within herself, stretching herself to accommodate, but doing so very gently, little by little so that she would not break. Zari dried the mugs she'd rinsed, her cloth-wrapped fingers circling the insides bit by bit. It was the same measured voice with which Shehla had inquired, the night Zari had returned from dinner, if Zari had anything to do with Billy's leaving, the same voice with which she'd responded to Zari's confession that yes, Zari believed she did have something to do with Billal's leaving for Kashmir, and though she was very sorry for it, she didn't know if the responsibility was solely hers—he was not a child and she had not put a gun to his head. No, Shehla had said, Zari had certainly not put a gun to his head, no one had. The next day, Zari had sat in the guest room waiting to be exiled, instead Shehla had told her to move into Billal's room.

Afterwards, Zari kept accidentally stepping into the guest room, kept having to remind herself that it was no longer hers, this space to house guests, and that, in bundling her belongings from shelves in one room and rearranging them on shelves in another room, she'd gone from guest to family within the space of four walls . . . four walls containing the scent of pine needles and underneath that, of pink tea, a room in which she had memories, good memories.

After washing the tea mugs, Zari went to Billal's room—*their* room, she corrected herself. With each passing moment, her heart beat faster. She'd been planning a life in which Billal never returned, in which he was but another loss, and here he was, coming back home. To her. And her equilibrium was adrift at the unexpected gain. He was returning in God only knew what state. Would he hate her for having inadvertently sent him away from them all? Blame her for whatever had befallen him? Would he agree that no matter who was to blame, in the end one could only mend oneself?

When she'd moved in, she'd cleared his room up a little each day, gathering coins, folding clothes, straightening books. Now she began to set things back the way they had been—slanting books, planting clothes, depositing coins all over the place. He would like, she was sure, a return to something familiar even if just a deliberate mess. After the room looked itself again, Zari drew a bath in Billal's bathroom—*their* bathroom. She lit the votives he'd given her, a temple of bodies, a cornucopia of colours, the flames flickering in the mirror like a million souls.

Zari entered the bath and poured the heart-shaped

sachets he'd given her into the warm water. She swirled her fingers through the dissolving pink crystals, and though it didn't seem the bath could temper her burning skin, she lay submerged in the blushing water, the water a playful creature, cavorting over her rounding belly, and allowed herself to daydream. She imagined herself opening like a fan, fluttering over the world, delivering her own kindnesses.

Zari was still brushing her hair when she heard the garage door grating open. They were back from the airport. By the time Billy knocked, she was half-sitting, half-standing, half-flitting, uncertain about what to say, what to do, it was why she hadn't gone to the airport. She stood with her back to the window, her yellow butterfly clip clutched to her chest.

Come in.

He came in and shut the door behind him ever so quietly. He had scratches on his arms. His hair was longer. He was taking out of his pocket a cookie, a cookie, he stammered, from the plane. He held it to her, his fingernails clipped so close to the cuticle, pillows of flesh swelled from beneath. He placed one hand on her belly, with the other he held out the cookie: Share?

PART 4

OF THE FATHER
1998

25

Dark lifted gradually over the park, the tepid moonlight yet to fade completely into the pearl grey of morning. Billy finished his first run around the jogging path and began his second. He ran slowly, so slowly it seemed he might never get to the end, and that was all right, he was in no hurry, there was nowhere to go, and he liked it that way, and the end, it would come. He was flushed. His earlobes tingled. He unzipped his windbreaker to a cool dawn breeze which found a path down his tee shirt; it found a new path daily, it seemed, since his return three months ago.

He liked this coming out. Preferred it to those first weeks he'd spent in his bed—*our* bed—curled up, staring at Zari's half of the room, believing he would not make it after all. Chacha had been right: he had not returned alive—physically yes, but emotionally dead. He'd held all of Mauj jee's letters close to his heart for one last time before putting them away; it did not matter whether she had been senile or sane—she had loved him. That was all. His decisions had been his alone.

His father had finally told him the truth about Dada. After being tortured, Amman had asked his mother if the things those men had accused his father of were true—that he tortured children for money, children younger than himself, babies even? Her silence had been answer enough, but Amman had not acknowledged it. And he didn't until Mauj jee's letter with news of her attack and abortion had reached them. His father had said he was glad Amman's mother had not been able to say that Mauj jee's abortion was, like everything else, his fault—it had been Mauj jee's decision, after all, to abort. It *is* your fault, Amman had replied. It is the aftermath of your actions, everything is your fault and don't you ever try to exonerate yourself. Everything is fair in love and war to you, even the torture of your son.

Without a word, Abdullah Nabi had placed his fingers in a door jamb and banged the door until his fingers broke.

"This pain," Abdullah Nabi had said, "is nothing compared to how much I love you." But his father's actions were not, for Amman, a proof of love. Rather, his father's broken fingers, not his mother's silence, brought home the truth about his father, for if the man, on an impulse, could break his own flesh and bone, God only knew what torture he was capable of inflicting upon a stranger.

"A right-handed man," Amman said, "he broke the fingers of his left hand. He didn't play fair in war, and he didn't play fair in love."

Amman had smiled feebly as he told Billy that, later, three fingers had become gangrened and had to be amputated. After his father died, Amman had resolved to never speak of his father again, but he had soon realised that he could just as well recreate the memory of his father into one that was palatable.

"The grand meetings, Dad? The speeches where he roared into a microphone like a lion? The funeral so overcrowded people had to stand?"

Amman looked away from Billy.

"The photo in the hallway?"

His father and his cohorts were horsing around, pretending to be the very men they mocked—men who believed the pen is mightier than the fist, and honour the greatest commodity, men who believed in something other than themselves. Out of all the photographs of his father he could have kept, that was the one Amman chose, perhaps out of a subconscious desire to have been the son of an upright man. But in this new world, unlike the one he'd grown up in, the sins of the father were not automatically the sins of the son; in this new world his children could live taint free, and he was grateful to this new world for this opportunity— it was why he'd migrated, so he, his children, his son, you, Billal, could be yourself, make your own reputation free of the past.

"Beta, had you known the truth all long, would you have gone?"

"No. I don't know."

"Forgive me . . ."

"Dad," Billy's eyes pricked with tears. "I could have changed it . . . I could have rewritten who Dada was. I could have made him an honourable freedom fighter. But I didn't. I couldn't."

And Billy told him of the folder and the hours he spent deciding whether to stick to the facts or weave fiction until finally he left the file untouched. Amman kissed him on the forehead and then they'd sat in silence, a good silence which spoke volumes to both of them.

On his first day back, Billy had switched on the TV. On the History Channel the lone footage of Anne Frank caught on tape as she leaned over a balcony to watch a parade, on a news channel the government of Sudan claimed the US had bombed a pharmaceutical plant and not a terrorist site, on another channel a documentary special on the Hutu and Tutsi civil war in Rwanda and its British legacy. A despairing déjà vu encompassed him. He switched the TV off. Sat in utter despair until he realised he did have a choice no matter how choice-less he felt: he had the choice to live half-dead or live half-alive. He kept thinking of the Kashmiri contingent, of humans everywhere without homes to seek refuge in, to escape to, and that it was his safety net of a country that had allowed him his escape. His safety net of a country which had rendered life precarious for so many others. Something had changed within him. His heart had either hardened towards the world, or else it had softened towards himself.

Billy jabbed away tears. But what exactly had changed? Everything, nothing, something, anything? Cry baby. Be a man. God, fate, luck, chance, something in the world had decided that Billy Nabi was going to be one of the privileged, a survivor; he'd just have to learn to accept this particular entitlement. And do something with it. *Something*.

That first night he and Zari sat side by side on the bed in the dark, she'd traced paths between the calluses on his palms, she'd said tell me.

So he told her.

The greatest deception is reaching into history to crack the code of life, believing there are lessons to be learned, that they shall be applied, that our lives, lived in our own little times, will make a difference, always good of course, for the rest of time. Listen closely, there is no message, no saving grace, no balm that will outweigh a final blow: a smile is no different from a scream in the galaxy of indifference that is time.

Billal, Zari squeezed his hands, granted the human race is neither fair nor nice, but often people surprise us and we are able to surprise people in turn; unexpected smiles, surprising generosity, small kindnesses, the good wishes of strangers, unknown leaps through great divides: this is how life survives.

Billy hung his head. He'd set out to be someone great and he'd become someone miniscule, diminished—his was a failed state.

Zari held him and rocked him. She did not tell him that there was no future in those memories. She told him, instead, that he was brave and noble to have realised that his convictions had changed, that he was braver and nobler still to have acted on that change instead of clinging to the familiar, to the same because there was security in the same. Self-acceptance was a small heroism perhaps, but it was heroism nevertheless.

I am no hero.

He confessed his shame. He told her about Abid, how he had inadvertently caused his death. He told her that by escaping he had advertently endangered Chacha and his family. Billy felt he would never be able to forgive himself, yet, forgiveness is cheap when it comes to forgiving oneself, and being cognizant of the potential for self-reprieve made him all the more ashamed. He told her about Wali, about the little Afghani girl, Palwasha, about Mohsin, Ahmed Baba, Nazeer.

"I buried them. I ran away. It was not Kashmir after all, but my own selfish desire."

"The first time you laugh," Zari stroked his face, "the laughter will be a vomit that *will* make you sick, but it's a purge, that laughter . . . a purge that empties out some grief so you can replace it with some little bit of joy. You know there will be an empty part in your life but that life itself won't always have to be empty."

One morning, Billy was sitting in the kitchen, his gaze fixed on the backyard. His mother was whisking jalapenos into eggs for his favourite omelette and his father was trying to coax Miraage away from the sugary cereal and get her ready for school. Salsabil glided in with the mail, the engagement ring Ohwi's family had given her perched on her finger like a glass bird in flight. She was reading out loud from a silk scroll invitation—Fahad was getting engaged to Mimi, remember, Zari, the girl he was showing around on the Fourth of July?

"Such a lucky girl," Zari sighed as she spooned butter onto a muffin. "Guaranteed to spend at least one summer at the Swiss chalet."

Billy frowned and then a moment later, laughed, such a bellow that Zari looked up and he caught her glance, caught it and held aloft the tiny bridge between them.

That evening, Billy led Zari to the porch swing and told her that he'd been thinking, thinking of doing something, something else other than just returning to college for journalism, doing *something* or he *would* go *mad*, that he was thinking of establishing a non-profit organisation, an organisation that would help fund supplies for refugee schools, and sufferers of rape. Billy stopped the swing and looked into Zari's eyes: I want to name the organisation The Zoon Family Foundation.

Zari shut her eyes so the tears would remain inside her and water the seeds of the future the man in front of her was planting within her. Then she opened her eyes and she told him she loved him.

"I love you, Billal," she said. "I'll be your home."

A whistling gust wrinkled the pond. Billy stopped and looked for the ducks, far out, way out, plump twinkling teal in the first light of dawn. He resumed jogging and padded past the Liberty Tree, a stump in the grass with a sign next to it: the salvaged wood was going to be used to make memorabilia—guitars and pens and photo frames. He might like to get hold of a frame, but already he could see it hoarded away, a useless treasure to all but him. One day, even the map—the world map his father had marked his journey on—would come off the study wall, it had to, though for now his father was adamant it remain pinned up because, Billy supposed, journeys did not end just because you came home.

His parents' journey had not ended. Not with his coming home. They had wanted to know and they'd sat him down. Why had he gone? The why of it—Mauj jee, Dada, his father's scars, Zari, his unhappiness with monotony because he hadn't known what a blessing monotony could be. Yes, yes, yes all of this. But then he fell silent. How could he tell them that he'd wanted to get away from *them* when, all along, it was them he'd wanted to come back to? He had gotten up and, walking up to the map, begun pointing out the route he'd taken to leave and to return. He told them he'd buried Mauj jee's letter in the remains of a village they'd never see, a village that had never been on any map and was now obliterated from the world even as it was seared on his heart.

His mother had turned to look at his father, but she didn't say anything and it seemed a wilful silence of a good sort, the sort that spared rather than inflicted wounds.

Billal called Indus who apologised for unwittingly having sent him in harm's way and invited him to talk at one of their meetings. He talked about the Zoon Family Foundation. He talked about Chacha, the tin shack schools, the eager-to-learn refugee children; he talked about Palwasha buried in a refugee camp next to a poplar tree, and about the angry bereft young boy, One-Eyed-One-Handed, whose name was Wali. He talked about the training camp, about Nazeer, about men who desired good but fell into bad—men like him and like all of them—because they believed they had no other choice to do good. But there was always a choice.

There was always a choice. And one night, Billal called Chacha.

"Chacha?" he said. "Chacha, it's me, Billawal . . . actually Billal . . . Billy. Are you all right?"

He cried silently as Chacha cursed him, told him he was all right though no thanks to him, note or no note left behind, that he should have trusted him and told him that he wanted out.

"Would you have helped me?" Billy said. "Would you have really helped me leave?"

After a long moment, Chacha sighed. "Had I been in

444

your position, know that I would have done exactly the same."

Billy told him he was returning to school and going to do journalism. Maybe one day he could help people like Chacha leave behind the lives they were being forced to live. He told him about the Zoon Family Foundation, that Chacha's school was the first he and Zari were planning to fund.

"Know," Chacha said, "that already you will bring hope into the lives of people, and that spreading hope is the finest, most noble act in the world."

∞⊙∞

Billy turned into his street just as the street lamps went off. Miraage still thought it was pure magic, the lights switching on and off every morning and evening. When he was younger, he'd thought so too. He would stand under a street lamp and try to catch the whiff of a potion, the cadence of a chant, and even when he knew better, the sound of a switch being flipped off and on, but there was nothing, just dark one moment and the next illumination.

His bedroom—*their* bedroom—was still dark when he returned, save for the strip of light from the bathroom door Zari always left ajar. Her rosary lay on the bedside table next to the wooden squirrel, the un-caged plastic duck, and a framed photo of her family. She was still fast asleep. Billal got into bed and wrapped his arms around her burgeoning belly. Then he shut his eyes and slept.

EPILOGUE

Spring came over many nights, a softening up of tight spaces, cotton ball skies, the flowering of nests. Their blanket was spread by the duck pond in sunshine that was pale but warm. A breeze riffled the Zoon Family Foundation documents Billy was scanning. Zari had sold the house in Kashmir and they were using the money to set up the Foundation after having sent a little something to the cleaning woman and the family of the kitchen boy who'd perished along with Zari's family.

Zari picked up the bottle of Baz-Baber's expressed milk that she'd been using to hold open her high school diploma textbook and turned towards the little boy next to her. He was sucking on his fist in delight as Miraage bounced him on her knees. When Zari caught his eye, he lunged at her, gurgling when she grabbed him and kissed his pudgy knuckles. God was in heaven and all was right with the world, at the very least nothing was wrong except the usual fare.

As she fed her son, his soft body nestled against her own, Zari sat facing the ducks in the pond. When Baz-Baber was older, he might ask her to tell him a story. She would tell her son a love story. Once upon a time, she would begin, a girl and a boy meet, or perhaps time and time again girls and boys meet or, may be, only once in a lifetime a girl meets the right boy or the boy the right girl. Or perhaps there are no love stories, only stories in which love is a part.

She will tell her son about a girl sitting by a pond, oh very much like this one here. She will tell her son that the girl looked up by chance and by chance lifted her hand to smooth her hair and by chance a boy jogging past caught her gesture and thought the girl had waved to him.

She will tell her son that love sometimes is a matter of accident, like death, like life, like survival. The boy jogging by had looked at her and she at him, and it might never have happened. But it had. And right before she had smoothed her hair, what had that girl been thinking? Yes, correct, she'd been reliving the past, a picnic in Pahalgam.

Their mothers had arranged a picnic in Pahalgam. It was the first time Zari and Imran, prospective spouses, were to meet. It was the middle of the afternoon on a spring day. The creamy almond blossoms of spring had been the prettiest in Kashmir that year. The garden of the guesthouse they were all meeting in had been quivering with merriment and excitement—a serious game of cricket was underway

They had divided themselves into two teams, a toss of a coin had Kiran captain of one and Sonea captain of the other. Don't play or you'll get hot and scruffy, her mother said before Zari could tell her that she wasn't planning to play for that very reason. She was wearing a gold mirror-sequined kurta over a pair of jeans, her arms crammed with myriad silver bracelets, silver pins holding back her hair, and gold hoops dangling from her ears. She looked like her namesake, zari, a delicate wisp of silver-gold thread. If helping the older women set the picnic table was going to keep her looking fresh then that was what she would occupy herself with the entire day. Already Sonea, opening bowler for her team, was perspiring; already Kiran's braid had come undone.

"What are you looking at?" her mother asked, winking. Blushing, Zari looked away as Imran cracked bat against ball. Then she heard him shout chukha, sixer, and she looked up just in time to see the ball soar to the heavens like a prayer. She looked back at him and his arms were up in the air as if he was high-fiving God. Then he was looking at her, and she, at him. Then she was setting out sandwiches and he was wielding his bat. It might never have happened, their exchange of looks. But it had. And it was such a sunny day and Baz was skipping after the ducks he'd refused to leave alone at home and Zari's eyed tears up.

"What's wrong?" Her mother cupped her chin. "Puz, puz wun, be honest. You like him?"

She inhaled. She couldn't get it out. "I'm just so happy."

Her mother kissed her forehead and dabbed a dot of black kohl from her eyeliner on to Zari's cheek to save her from the evil eye.

∞∞

Zari touched her cheek where the kohl had marked her. She looked at Billal and Baz-Baber and Miraage. She thought of Shehla and Amman and their generosity, Khala and Khaloo, Uncle and Lili, of her brother-in-law, and Sonea's parents—of all these people who had prayed for her and wished her well. She smiled even as she blinked away tears.

"Zaar?" Billy glanced up from the papers.

"I'm fine," Zari said. "I'm just . . . content."

The word came out with some difficulty, as if she couldn't believe it possible. Billy nodded and caressed her cheek. Together they watched their child attempting to crawl. The baby was on all fours, his plump hands and feet splayed against the blanket, rocking back and forth, going neither forward nor backward. Yet he chuckled, his mouth open, delighted with sheer movement for as far as he was concerned, without going anywhere at all, he was conquering the world.

Soniah Kamal was born in Karachi, grew up in London-Jeddah-Lahore, and resides in the US where she has called many states her home. Currently, she lives in Georgia where Margaret Mitchell wrote *Gone with the Wind*, Flannery O'Connor kept pet peacocks, and Alice Walker set *The Color Purple*. Soniah has a BA in Philosophy from St John's College where she received the Susan B Irene Award, and is now pursuing an MFA from the Georgia State University where she is the 2014 Paul Bowles Fellow in Fiction. Soniah enjoys long strolls around koi ponds and doodling forests of curlicues. She cannot resist the drumbeat of a dhol and her talisman is a globe in any size. Her favourite activity is time-travelling through books. Soniah has shared her life with a sandy dog, a silky cat, a sweet turtle, two guinea pigs, one long haired and one short haired, frogs as big as thumbnails, and a multitude of budgies and betta fish, red, blue, green, and yellow. She believes that kindness can change the world.

An Isolated Incident is her first novel.

ACKNOWLEDGEMENTS

Like many writers, I flip first to the acknowledgements page of every book because it is the names on this page that sustain the dream, and the reality.

My parents Kamal Qureshi and Naheed Kamal: for giving me the world as best as you could, I love you more than you can ever fathom. Buraaq, Indus, Miraage: you are the heart of my soul and the soul of my heart; the best stories I will contribute to. Mansoor Wasti: my friend and husband, for still making me laugh after all these years. Sarah Kamal and Fahad Kamal: essence of my memory, for being there, for sibling solidarity. To my darling Khalas: Tahira Majeed, Haseena Parveen, and Mahira Sukhera, thank you for showing me what a Khala is and is not, and my mother, also a Khala. Shikha Malaviya, my kindred spirit, for always being there for me no matter the time difference, for saving this novel from being set in a pet store, and Anjali Enjeti, my wonderful friend and gracious mentor, for so much, including rescuing this novel from dying in a harddrive and being fifty times the length. To family: Farhana Taj Alvi for your constant generosity, and also Manaal Pandit, Huma Pandit, Sharmeen Shehdad, for all your help on Kashmir, thank you so much, any mistakes are all mine. For their help on Muzaffarabad, thank you, Naheed Kamal for sharing your precious childhood memories, Naseema Seema Jogazai especially for the map, and Tariq Naqash, and Ellora Puri.

Again, all mistakes are mine. I was twenty years old when I came upon *The Rape of Kashmiri Women* by Shabnam Qayyum—a book can change the person you are; this was one of those times. To my heroes—foreign correspondents and photojournalists everywhere, thank you for your bravery and your perseverance. To writing colleagues everywhere who teach me, guide me, and, most importantly, help laugh away the rejections. Kola Boof, your praise, your belief in my work feeds me. Khaled Hosseini, a world of thanks for your unexpected gift. Ayesha Mattu, Jessica Handler, Christal Presley, Ali Eteraz—thank you so much. Balaji Venkateswaran, for your honest critique that began a voyage, thank you. Dipika Mukherjee, for reminding me that I was more than just one book, thank you. Kristal Smith Tyler, you were the first to hear the idea of this novel, your enthusiasm truly encouraged me, thank you. Amy Robertson, for back then when writing was something both of us just talked about and for discussing the characters in this novel as if they were real people until they were, thank you. Anu Kumar, thank you for your encouragement. Thank you: Christina Poodt, Naeem Khokar, Manu Herbstein, Lisa Lau, Mehrene Shah, Reema Khan, Nazia Zaidi, Ammarah Chaudry, Erin Smyth, Rachel Trares, Samrah Chaudry, Muneeza Shamsie, Jennifer Taylor, Zainab Kakar, Laaleen Sukhera, Sabrina Rahim, Sarita Sarvate, Amulya Malladi, Moazzam Sheikh, Laura Lanford, Annie Gilson, Sabahat Zakariya, Asma Khalid. George Weinstein, Valerie Connors, Clay Ramsey, and The Atlanta Writers Club. Dream-makers: Mita Kapur, Arushi Pareek, and everyone at Siyahi, and Gayatri Goswami, Shikha Sabharwal, Sunil Kumar, and everyone at Fingerprint!—thank you.

My late grandfather asked me to write about Kashmir—I kept my promise, Abaji.

KASHMIR CALLING
a memoir

They arrived in chariots called rickshaws. In my earliest adolescent memories, the chariot always came late at night, its deep grumbling engine crumbling the dark silences. And then the sudden quiet as the engine was turned off, hands banging-clanging on our metal gate, the doorbell trilling nonstop, the coughs and footsteps of either the live-in driver or the cook passing underneath my bedroom window as he hurried down the driveway to unlock the padlock on the gate, my father rising to unlock the main entrance, my house suddenly alight with life as my mother and maternal grandparents scrambled downstairs, sleep still simmering in their eyes, and then loud shrieks in Kashmiri: "Keri chu? Vari chu? Ahnaz, Ahnaz? How are you? How's everything? Fine, fine." I would bounce out of bed and bound down the stairs and there they were, my Khalas, my mother's sisters, having arrived, unannounced, from this magic kingdom called Kashmir.

In the living room, the gas heater leapt to a blue flame-orange ember enchantment over the revellers, all talking at the same time, louder and louder, elation filling our house like excited children in a schoolyard, and yet everyone caught what everyone was saying and there was so much laughter, too much laughter.

"Stop laughing, stop laughing, for fear of the evil eye," Moji, my grandmother, cautioned, but although all three sisters were prone to superstition, at this time they would calm down only for a moment before starting up again. I watched my Khalas peel off their beige bobby socks and wiggle their winter-cold toes before the heater, and my mother, a fount of sudden serenity, sandwich herself between them, and my grandfather, Abaji, beam even as Moji handed him his heart medicine, which he put under his tongue lest this unexpected arrival of his daughters be too much to bear.

"Tea? Biscoots? Kebabs? Samosas?" The cook entered, his pale blue eyes twinkling, for he knew the arrival of my Khalas meant fat tips at the end of every good meal served and every errand run.

"Is that even something to ask?" my father asked in his forever quiet yet jovial tone. "Of course! Of course!"

I sat on the winding staircase that led from the living room to upstairs, savouring the sizzle and scent of cocktail samosas and homemade shami kebabs frying in Kashmir Banaspati Oil—because in Pakistan, adding 'Kashmir' to every venture is considered good luck—emanating from the kitchen and mingling with the tales of my Khalas' journey—a flight from Srinagar to Delhi and from there either a train ride into the Lahore Railway Station, or, from Delhi to Amritsar and from there via foot through the Attari-Wagah border-crossing which connected Amritsar and Lahore. Attari. Wagah. Amritsar. To me these places sounded like fairylands children travelled to on flying carpets. Tomorrow, my Khalas would have to report to the police station, as would all Indians visiting Pakistan, as would all Pakistanis visiting India, and though this was a mild inconvenience for them, for me a trip to the police station was always an adventure: portly policemen with pert moustaches, jotting down names and dates in obese rosters, smoke from their cigarettes clouding the sign above their heads: No Smoking.

For the duration of my Khalas' visit—never less than three months, and once even six months long—my home became a warm, fuzzy, true love spell. My mother craved her sisters. That she was the baby of the family was a strange concept, yet it was stranger still to see her transform into a little girl with them, pouting to get her way, cajoling them into making her favourite delicacies, hunching between them as if they were her shelter in the world, her voice taking on a little girl's hue, like a little sister who expected to be pampered and indulged, and was. My mother became almost *cute*.

Apart from Aunty Tahira and Aunty Haseena, elder to my mother by over a decade, there was another sister too, Aunty Mahira, who lived across the road from us. My mother dialled the phone to call her: *They have come.*

I remember all four sisters together as if they were a still life painting. Tahira, Haseena, Mahira, Naheed. The eldest, Aunty Tahira, was a hummingbird, her fragile features and delicate rosebud mouth resembling Moji's, although her ivory complexion and blue-green-grey eyes were Abaji's. Aunty Haseena had Moji's black eyes and jet-black hair, but like Abaji, she was tall and regal with a prominent, aquiline nose. In her younger days she had been compared to the film star Nutan, and the superstar actor Raj Kapoor had even offered her a film role. Aunty Mahira had her own uniquely pretty button features surrounded by masses of frizzy, curly, wild hair no one knew had come from where or how to tame. My mother was a beautiful mixture of Aunty Haseena and Abaji.

My Khalas came laden with gifts from Kashmir: pashmina shawls, beige and navy and purples and pinks with vines of embroidery climbing up the edges, unshelled almonds and walnuts plucked straight from their gardens, and fresh Kashmiri tea leaves that looked like any old tea leaves, but, when brewed, dyed the water, milk, and cream with a pink so deep and pretty it seemed a sin to drink it. During their visits, Abaji always decided it was his job to make Kashmiri pink tea—noona chai, salt tea, because instead of sugar it is flavoured with salt. The cook watched wide-eyed as Abaji, who otherwise certainly did not enter the kitchen to *cook*, stood at the stove stirring the concoction for hours. I too was riveted as Abaji boiled the tea leaves, stirred in the milk and the cream, added the salt and a pinch of bicarbonate-of-soda to coax out the pink, adding a little more of this, a little more of that, until he finally garnished the tea with ground pistachios and almonds which he'd blanched and slivered himself, for when it came to noona chai, he trusted no one.

I can still hear Abaji scoff at the sorry version of pink tea often served at Pakistani weddings—an oily, watery, beigish-pinkish tea which was seasoned with, of all horrors, sugar. When Abaji's tea was prepared, the cook served the pink delight in turquoise teacups and Abaji would watch his family sipping and crumbling savoury pastries such as bakirkhanis or qulchas into it, his face etched with deep satisfaction, as if he was back in his beloved Kashmir. He wasn't. But no matter, his daughters surrounded him, their children were healthy, their marriages were fine. Life could not get any better.

Abaji coloured every morning with a ritual no matter where we lived: England, Saudi Arabia, Pakistan—he bathed and then in his white vest and towel-lungi, he sat on the prayer mat to repeat one of God's ninety-nine names for at least an hour. His chanting sounded like he was gargling his soul and I said as much once and got into a lot of trouble for talking about religion in this way. Moji defended me. She always defended me irrespective of whether I was right or wrong.

Routines were the same, yet life changed with my Khalas' arrival. Now, when Abaji chanted the daily early morning prayer, my Khalas joined him, hot cups of tea waiting for them all once they finished. When my mother ate her breakfast of tea, sliced apple, papaya, and oatmeal, my Khalas ate with her and bid her farewell when she, an anaesthesiologist, left for the hospital, and a little later, they would do the same for my father. When my grandparents came downstairs, they'd order another round of tea and all of them would sit and read the Quran first, followed by the Urdu newspapers—religion and state, I observed early, both came in ink and lived on paper, though the contents of one were supposedly indisputable and that of the other always open to dispute. The rustle of newspapers, the *shur-shur-shur* sound their mouths made as they read under their breaths, the way they shared their reading glasses, as if their eyes were one and the same, the ticking of the small grandfather clock behind the sofa that was 'Abaji's chair', the morning sunshine pouring in from the wall of windows, bathing them in pale fronds, all came to signify for me a deep sense of 'home'.

"Baji?" The cook would come in to inquire about lunch and dinner.

That my mother had already purchased groceries for the entire week and that my Khalas had merely to tell the cook what to prepare—chicken or mutton, eggplant or cauliflower, yellow daal or black daal and always, always white rice because without white rice a meal for Kashmiris is incomplete—did not stop my Khalas from frequenting Ghalib Market, the crescent-shaped bazaar close to our house, on the pretext of buying groceries. They needed only the smallest of excuses to pull on their flat sandals, wrap shawls over their plump shoulders, cover their heads with dupattas, and set off for the bazaar. Sometimes they went several times a day to browse through the vegetable and fruit stalls, the fabric stores, or to check out the buttons, laces, and embroidery at the haberdashers.

During vacations or after school, I tagged along, a rare treat to walk that short, potholed distance rather than merely observe it from the confines of an air-conditioned car. In the winters we plodded through air a-sizzle with cart vendors roasting corn on the cob or sweet potatoes with their white flesh sprinkled with spices and orange juice, and, in the summers, we waded through a soup of humidity and dust and heat boiling with the stench of roadside garbage heaps and the buzz of mosquitoes.

Abaji often accompanied us, and all their voices boomed over the honking horns and hawkers' calls. My Khalas bargained in their Kashmiri accented Urdu, their mispronunciations, their incorrect grammar, their oddly-worded phrases in no way diminishing their celebrity status: they were from Kashmir, Indian-administered Kashmir. Every shop showered us with warmth and plied us with soft drinks and biscuits, a courtesy my Khalas returned by usually purchasing a little something. And, on the walk back, they would chuckle over their celebrity status even as they lamented over their lighter wallets.

My Khalas' arrival also meant that Kashmiri would become the lingua franca of our house, and my Urdu-speaking father, who could understand little, would sit in the midst of them all, unfazed. I could understand it fairly fluently and Kashmiri often struck my childhood ears as funny, the strange, guttural sounds of words like 'gagur', meaning rat, and 'cockur', meaning chicken, doubling me over with mirth. But Kashmiri was also a complex language in which a single word had several meanings depending on the inflections. So for instance, 'soont' could mean either apple or fart with just a slight variation of the way the 'soo' was pronounced. It was a language that kept me on my toes, for my mother liked to play inflection games and she would rattle off, 'tshoot, tshoot, tshoot', and my untrained ear would stretch to hear 'bread, short, garbage'. Kashmiri was simply my mother's tongue, the language in which she scolded and cursed, the language in which she hummed melodies such as the love song "kaathu chook noondabanay, valo mashauk a meyanay, where are you my love, come to me . . ." the language in which she was so much at home. Kashmiri was a bridge between my mother and me, the language of games, of love, of laughter, a secret language even, the full benefit emerging when my Khalas were in town.

In the chilly months, the four sisters sat before blazing heaters, an old newspaper spread between them as they peeled chestnuts, or, in the hot months, lolled under ceiling fans and air-conditioners as they sucked on the ruby flesh of ice-cold watermelons, hendthwendths—another Kashmiri word I found so very funny—and chattered away in the safety of each other. Chatter inevitably turned into gossip. The sisters would lower their voices even though Abaji would be napping in his chair and my oblivious father would be reading his newspaper, and there I would be, tucked into a sofa or perched silent and still on the winding staircase, as good as invisible to them, the keen, hungry ears of my childhood devouring everything: scandal, adultery, fraud, embezzlement, raunchy jokes, abandonment, love affairs, runaway daughters and useless sons, and, of particular interest to me, children who had aced their exams versus those who had altogether failed to accrue any distinction and had thus broken their mother's dreams and hearts.

Little did I realise then that this language would come to give me a semblance of 'home', no matter that I could not speak it. But it was a bridge and in that vein I remember one incident during one visit to India. My mother and I were at the Kashmiri handicrafts shop in Janpath Hotel in New Delhi, the retailers advising each other, in Kashmiri, to quote "these tourists from Pakistan" an inflated price, when my mother replied to them: "Beh theh ches Kehshir, I am also Kashmiri." Suddenly, the price fell dramatically and out came complimentary samosas and soft drinks. They too had recognised 'home' and a 'bridge' in a stranger's tongue.

Bridges-to-homelands and so many evenings, other Kashmiris would visit my Khalas, eager to hear the news from what used to be their or their ancestors' homeland. I witnessed tears in Abaji's eyes during these get-togethers, for he had not been to Kashmir for a long while. I don't think when he'd left Kashmir as a young man, he'd ever thought he would be at the mercy of visa officers with borders and partitions in their minds and hearts.

The tale goes something like this: A long time ago, a time before birth certificates, birthday parties, and birthday cakes, Rabea Bazzaz and Mehraj ud din Pandit were born to their respective families. They grew up as all children in that land did: Mehraj went to school and played outdoor games and Rabea did not go to school and played indoor games. Rabea and Mehraj were betrothed at a very young age and when Rabea became a woman at around thirteen, she was married to the probably sixteen-year-old Mehraj, and so it was that the young woman left her father's home for her husband's.

While Mehraj continued to attend school and play

outdoors, Rabea navigated her way around her in-laws' house, and in her free time, cradled her dolls. Soon, Mehraj and Rabea were blessed with a daughter, a child Rabea discovered was a living doll and playmate. In all, the couple would go on to have six living children, four daughters and two sons—one of the sons, despite Rabea's wishes, would be adopted by childless relatives, as was often done in those days. While Rabea was occupied with rearing her children, Mehraj completed his education, eventually graduating, in the early 1940s, from Sri Pratap College in Srinagar with a Bachelors degree, after which he joined the family carpet business.

Life was decent to Rabea and Mehraj. Business thrived. Their children thrived. They lived in luxury and plenty. But then, despite Rabea's admonitions, Mehraj got involved in the politics of Partition. The end came before they knew it. Actively pro-Pakistan, after the 1947 partition of India and Pakistan, Mehraj became a target for the Indian government and, one night, though no one can remember the exact year, he fled to Pakistani Kashmir. For days he travelled through dense forests where he battled lions and outsmarted djinns, or so it is told, until he arrived in the city of Muzaffarabad.

Rabea and her children followed soon after, her youngest child a toddler. They had lost everything, it seemed to Rabea, and in many respects, she never did recover from the loss of her birth land, the life she'd lived there, and the fact that her two eldest daughters, who accompanied her initially, had to eventually return since they were betrothed to Kashmiris settled in Indian Kashmir. It had never occurred to Rabea and Mehraj that India and Pakistan would perpetually be at war over Kashmir and that they would permanently lose the ability to visit their homeland whenever they pleased, let alone return to live.

They lived in Muzaffarabad for a number of years. Mehraj established a carpet business while Rabea looked after home and hearth. Their son and two daughters walked to school through meadows, picking and munching on seasonal fruits, their playgrounds the sparkling, ice-cold Neelam River and the Domeil bridge above it. Then, once again, despite Rabea's contentions, Mehraj got involved with politics, and though he would go on to become Minister for Information and Commerce, when the administration lost favour, Mehraj also lost office. Weary of partisan politics, Mehraj decided to resettle in the port city of Karachi where he supplied Kashmiri goods to handicraft stores. And so, Rabea once again packed up the home she'd made for herself and travelled, for all intents and purposes, to yet another foreign place.

Slowly, Rabea began to settle down in the port city with its palm trees and hot summers tempered by the evening sea breeze. Though Mehraj and Rabea never regained their former prosperity, these were happy days for Rabea. Her children excelled in their studies while her daughters in Kashmir, their own children in tow, began to visit her. She revelled as her grandchildren praised her cooking, and relaxed when the entire family snuggled around Mehraj as he read out loud from Alexander Dumas' *The Count of Monte Cristo*, or recited Coleridge: "water, water everywhere/ not a drop to drink", or regaled them with stories of fiddlers who played on while Rome burned and obedient children who braved flames but did not run because they did not have their father's permission.

Mehraj was progressive in so far as to make sure his son and younger daughters received an equal education, but, although the youngest daughter wanted to be a journalist,

Mehraj was adamant they all become doctors. One by one the elder two left for medical college and the youngest one found herself alone and in charge of Rabea's failing health as well as being her parents' primary caregiver. It was a role she would decide to honour for the rest of their lives.

One day, the daughter received a proposal from a young chartered accountant returned from England. On a visit to an ill relative, he saw her working in the hospital and was smitten by her beauty, as were so many others, and beseeched another relative to make inquiries about who she was and where she lived. And so it was that he arrived at Mehraj's door with his Uncle, who was the Superintendent of Police, in a forbearing Police jeep, to ask for the young woman's hand. The young woman had a surfeit of proposals, but Rabea liked the young man's countenance; he was gentle, she said, and there was great kindness in his eyes, and so she and Mehraj gave their blessings, and so it was that their youngest daughter was married. A year later, a daughter was born to the newly-wed couple; six months later, job opportunities took them to England, and soon after, at their youngest daughter's behest, Rabea and Mehraj left for England too.

I was the first daughter born to my parents. My memories of England are of summer rains and winter suns. Of Abaji fashioning telephones with two paper cups and one long strand of red wool. Moji buttoning my duffel coat, the brown oval buttons fat and slippery in her powder-frail hands. Abaji building me castles of cushions and chairs. Moji's worried face at the window relaxing only when the bus from Ms Brown's Nursery arrived at our front door and I stepped down.

I would stand in Moji's coat shoes, beige with chocolate tassels, and, most important, a two inch block heel. She'd follow me, one hand on her bony hip, as I teetered and tottered in front of the budgies' cage, my arms akimbo, flapping as if I was flying.

"You're ruining her," my mother said when I broke a heel and Moji merely handed me another pair of high heels.

But it was said affectionately, for if anyone was allowed to ruin me, it was Moji. She let me slide down banisters and leap off stairs. She let me make messes of flour and water. She let me overflow the sink. She let me jump from sofa to sofa pretending I was Peter Pan. She let me be destructive and called it constructive. For I was the beloved one. I was the eldest child of her youngest child who had looked after her in sickness and in health, the child of the couple who had given her a permanent address no matter where we lived in the world—London, Jeddah, and finally, Lahore.

In Moji's eyes my family seldom did wrong; no one else got off so easily. She had nicknames for everyone—Zenga Zeet/Long Legs, Thool Kun/Egg Ears, Beeyore Utch/ Cat Eyes, Nastha Vyhut/ Fat Nose—and it upset her that people were full of themselves and duplicitous; she refused to play along. In another time she might have been a wit or a comedienne, except her time had turned her into a nervous woman who found it very hard to trust anyone, an anxious woman who reminisced a lot about the past, a lost woman who could not understand how she had become a refugee, an immigrant, a foreigner, a human who had grown up in one village but was now adrift in the big, strange world.

Adrift she may have been, but she was my anchor. In England, when I spied the bald, orange-toga-clad Hare-Rama

Hare-Krishna devotees jogging and singing on grey drizzling streets, I was terrified—the monotonous chants, the shorn heads, the orange outfits, all filled me with angst—and I crouched into Moji and she held me tight, urging me to look from beneath her wing. "Beh chus na?" she would say. "Am I not here for you?" She wiped my tears when my white best friend was not allowed to invite me to her birthday party because I was brown. She encouraged me to swim fast and fierce despite the lifeguards whispering how my brown would muddy the pristine pool. "Kanas kash," she'd instruct me. "Ignore them." When, every year, I was cast as Joseph in the Christmas Pageant—"Moji, am I Joseph again because I look like a boy?"—she assured me I was a pretty girl. She taught me to cross the road, my fingers laced in hers, looking left to right, right to left, until finally time came to let each finger go.

But there were things she could not and would not do in London, or in Jeddah, or in Lahore: switch on the TV or put a tape in the VCR, turn on the tape recorder or plug in an iron, dial a phone, rotary or digital. And as she got older, her helplessness and dependence became less endearing, and adolescent that I was, I began to question her. Why would the evil eye care if we laughed too much? Why would the devil push me over if I stood close to the balcony's edge? Even if djinns did live in trees, why would they try to enter me only if I walked under the trees at night? Though she'd always been bemused by my questioning, she was not amused at my questioning her and she would eye me sadly, as if she'd always suspected that I too would let her down. I hope she knew how much I loved her.

In the last few years of Moji's life—by then we'd long returned to Lahore—she became sicker and frailer until she was finally bedridden. The scent of sickness—sweet sweat,

Dettol, and Cuticura talcum powder—coexisted with acts of love: Abaji wiping her lips with the softest of tissues, my younger sister turning into my mother's diligent helper, my mother nursing Moji round the clock, giving her sponge baths, monitoring her medicines, spooning broth into her mouth, combing her grey hair into a whisper of a braid, and above all, keeping away bedsores.

Moji passed away in her bed in 1992. Death is a shock for those living, no matter how expected or how much of a blessing it is for the patient in pain. Abaji sat with his head in his hands, stunned, tears gushing out of his eyes. I lay with my head in his lap, his words felling me.

"But how can she be gone? She was with me my whole life. How can she be gone?"

But she was gone. And my Khalas arrived in Lahore, their presence a balm for Abaji, and for all of us. Moji was buried in the same graveyard as Aunty Mahira's six-year-old daughter Shazia—a cousin I didn't know in life, but I was four years old when she passed and her death is literally my first memory—and it seemed a consolation to me that Shazia and Moji were together. The graveyard was a walking distance from our house and for the longest time we went daily to shower their graves with red rose petals, garlands of golden marigolds, prayers, and memories. Gradually, loud mourning for Moji turned into quiet sorrow turned into measured remembrance turned into learning to live with absence turned into living again: the morning prayers, the reading of the Quran and then the newspapers, the walks to Ghalib Market, and the making and drinking of noona chai.

In the summer of 1995, Abaji and I found ourselves

alone, so to speak, in Watford, a suburb of London. He was visiting his son, my uncle, and staying at his house and I was at the nearby YWCA. We got together daily, me in my silver buckle black boots and Abaji with his walking stick, insisting we go to Watford Town Centre, sit on a bench, and watch humanity pass us by. He watched; I read.

Abaji always warned me that too much reading would further ruin my eyesight, and yet, whenever he could, he would let me browse a bookstore forever and would always buy me a book. In my memories, Abaji could take one look at a rug and tell you if it was handmade or machine-made, its thread count, its history. He would pass shawls through rings to check for claims of shahtoosh purity. When I was a child, he would connect two paper cups with a piece of string and play telephone and he would let me play drums on his balding head. He taught me mathematics throughout my school years and when, even as an eighth grader, I struggled to read a clock-face, he called me Dull Headed, a moniker which, to his consternation, brought on giggling fits instead of shame. He christened me 'Late Latif' because finishing a book trumped punctuality. He taught me to drive in our bright blue Toyota Corolla. Round and round Gaddafi stadium in Lahore we would go, he yelling at me to slow down—"but Abaji, any slower and I may as well park the car!"—his hand to his heart even if it was only a donkey cart coming our way, and every second he'd let out a *krekh*, a loud shriek, and he would, without fail, say, "Kya Goy? Pratanav chum gassan. What is wrong with you? You are scaring the daylights out of me."

He would shake his head when I giggled. And there was always reason to giggle—he called Dracula 'Dercola' and spaghetti 'fergetti', and insisted that mispronunciation was his prerogative as an *old* man. Of course when it came to wearing his hearing aid, let alone turning it up, he conveniently forgot he was *old* and insisted we were the ones with our hearing impaired and that we turn the TV's volume on full, and when we played pranks on him, turning the volume down yet insisting it was blaring, he'd always eventually laugh.

When I went away to college in the US, Abaji sent aerogramme letters written on his typewriter and complained about my standard one line response: *Miss you, Abaji.* His favourite film was *The Guns of Navarone*. His favourite meal seemed to be white rice and spicy keema with a glass of milk poured in. Perhaps the milk was to counter heartburn, but I did not think of this then, and instead, supposing it a matter of taste alone, also developed a yen for this odd combination. He told me I had a pretty face, but, "khoran kya goy? What happened to your feet?" He thought they were rather plain and he was most displeased when I said my feet were carbon copies of his. I cajoled him into disclosing his favourite heroine and he shyly admitted to the voluptuous film star Sridevi, and since I too liked Sridevi, we commemorated our mutual like by watching one of her films.

He liked my friends. He was the only one who always liked my friends. In my teenage years, I was forever in trouble at home, forever being sent to bed without supper, and there Abaji would be, late at night, knocking at my door, slipping in a full plate, food for my soul. There Abaji was that summer, always smartly dressed in his yolk yellow dress shirt and grey trousers and blazer and walking stick, making some remark or the other as we sat on that Watford Town Centre bench, nodding and smiling at people who passed us by, smiling and nodding in return.

And always my heart locks onto one image: my Abaji

peering through the glass slit in Uncle's front door as I saunter down the gravel driveway to return to the YWCA, peering as I step into the street, turn the corner, his forehead knotted with deep concern, in that land-before-cell-phones, that I might not make it back home safe and sound.

Abaji passed away five years later in the November of 1997 in Lahore. His heart gave out even though, upon hospitalisation, he was told he was going to be fine. He sat up in the hospital bed to take a sip of milk from my mother's hand and collapsed. I was in the US. I was not there. Neither were my Khalas. Perhaps Abaji had a premonition, for from the moment he'd stepped into the hospital this time, he repeatedly asked for his daughters in Kashmir. Emergency visas and they might have been able to make it. He especially wanted his eldest daughter, the child who'd been born to him and Moji so soon after they were married, but he desperately wanted to set eyes on his daughters all together one last time.

"Our father is dying," my Khalas beseeched the visa officer, "please, our father is dying."

They were not granted visas. Not in time. And finally when the visas came, diplomatic relations between India and Pakistan were so broken, there was no car, no train, no plane travelling between the countries and so, instead of a half-hour flight from Delhi to Lahore, they had to fly in via Dubai.

Abaji passed away without seeing them and when my Khalas finally crossed the border, it was in order to see a grave.

I also arrived in Pakistan too late for the funeral. My Khalas flew in days after me and I went to pick them from the airport. It was the very first time they did not arrive as late night unexpected surprises delivered to our door in chariots called rickshaws. Instead, there was the long wait at the airport because of delays, and, once they walked out of customs, a sombre reunion. The world changes; change is the world. This was the last time, to date, that I saw my Khalas. It was not the same. Nothing was the same. Moji was gone. Now Abaji was gone. *His* chair was empty.

ஓௐௐ

I will meet, after seventeen years, one of my cousins from the fairytale land. Over the phone I will tell her that my husband is half-Kashmiri, although I always tease him that he's not Kashmiri at all, that his mother's family had left Kashmir so long ago that no one in his family could understand Kashmiri, let alone speak it, while I can understand Kashmiri and speak it rudimentarily too. My cousin will chuckle at that.

"Anyone can learn a language," she will say, "but that doesn't make you Kashmiri."

Pourquoi? (I readily accept that a smattering of French does not make me French). I stopped laughing.

"How am I not Kashmiri?"

"Because you've never lived there," she will say. "You've never lived in Kashmir."

I will hang up and go about my day, conjuring up menus to dazzle her when she comes for dinner, go about my day and tell my husband how I've been renounced by one whose claim is stronger, go about my day getting ready for my night, and, as I will finally lie down to sleep, I will think, it is true, I have never lived in Kashmir, but it is also true that *my* Kashmir lives in me.